Something Remains

Something Remains

INGE BARTH-GRÖZINGER

TRANSLATED FROM THE GERMAN BY

ANTHEA BELL

HYPERION BOOKS FOR CHILDREN

NEW YORK

Published in Germany as *Etwas Bleibt*, Stuttgart 2004

Copyright © 2004 by Inge Barth-Grözinger

English translation © 2006 by Hyperion Books for Children

First U.S. Edition

1 3 5 7 9 10 8 6 4 2

Printed in the United States of America

This book is set in 12.5-Point Granjon.

Designed by Christine Kettner

Reinforced binding

Frontispiece: Foto Zirlik, used by permission of Mr. Reimer, Ellwangen, Germany

Library of Congress Cataloging-in-Publication Data

Barth-Grozinger, Inge, 1950–

  [Etwas bleibt]

Something remains/Inge Barth-Grözinger.—1st U.S. ed.

    p. cm.

Summary: In 1933, as Hitler becomes Chancellor, twelve-year-old Erich and his family, who are Jewish, find they need to make changes in their everyday lives as hatred of the Jews grows.

ISBN 0-7868-3880-9 (trade)

[1.Jews—Germany—History—1933–1945—Juvenile fiction. [1. Jews—Germany History—1933–1945—Fiction. 2. Prejudices—Fiction. 3. Friendship—Fiction.
4. Nazis—Fiction. 5. Germany—History—1933–1945—Fiction.] I. Title.

PZ7.B2678So 2006

[Fic]—dc22

2006043354

Visit www.hyperionbooksforchildren.com

* Words and phrases marked with an asterisk are defined in the glossary
at the end of the book.

For Jacob and Elena Levi,
and Nina and Daniel Grözinger:
the next generation,
with love and hope

The best thing in the world is to be at home.

Berthold Auerbach
(real name: Moses Baruch Auerbacher)
1812–1882

January 1933

T HE BOY OPENED the small window and leaned out, kneeling on the narrow sill. He drew in deep breaths of cold air. It smelled of the smoke rising thinly from the chimneys of the houses opposite. Above the dirty gray rooftops he saw dark piles of cloud, blown apart now and then by strong gusts of wind. The pale disk of the sun would show as it gradually sank below the irregular zigzag of the roofs. The boy watched the drifting clouds for a while, and when the milky gray sun had finally sunk behind the buildings he sat down, sighing and lost in thought, with his back to the sloping wall as he massaged his aching knees. He felt safe in the dark, low-ceilinged attic room, and the rage that had driven him up here died down, giving way to a vague, muted melancholy. The Sabbath was over now. The boy's thoughts went down to the Levi family's living room. His mother would just have extinguished the candles in the silver candlesticks and put them carefully back in the cupboard inherited from Grandfather Elias, while Fanny cleared away the china. And Father would be sitting in the big, brown leather armchair with a cigarillo in his hand. As a cattle dealer, Julius Levi had to work even on the Sabbath, but he didn't allow himself to read the Saturday paper until evening when the sun had set and Sabbath was over, just as he waited until then to smoke one of the cigarillos he enjoyed so much. Later they'd switch on the radio, and amidst the usual affectionate teasing, the family would argue about which program to listen to. Father preferred light entertainment and Mother liked opera, for instance the works of Richard Wagner, though the rest of the family couldn't stand his music.

So everything was the same as usual, yet there was something different about this Saturday. And he had fled from whatever that "something different" was, running up to the dusty attic because he just couldn't take it in, couldn't understand it, and because it had been hanging over his family like an invisible veil for many days now, subtly changing them. For some time his mother hadn't laughed as often as usual, and his father's mischievous face suddenly looked gaunt, with two deep lines running down from the corners of his mouth.

The boy knew that it was something to do with the newspaper reports. The same names on the front page, in big fat type, had been leaping to the eye again and again these last few days. Those names were back today, and although he had been carefully avoiding the Saturday edition that lay on the chest of drawers in the corridor, the black characters held a magical fascination for him. They said HINDENBURG, they said SCHLEICHER, and over and over again they said HITLER. The boy couldn't make much of these names. He did know that

Hindenburg was the president of Germany, whose picture hung on the wall at school and in people's offices. He looked kindly, an easygoing old grandpa with a white sea-dog's beard. Schleicher was chancellor of the German Reich, his father had told him. And he'd heard that man Hitler on the radio several times, but only briefly, because when he came on, Father was always quick to switch the set off and silence his screeching, crackling voice.

From where he sat, the boy could see only a small section of the evening sky now. The outlines of the buildings had merged into the darkness. The boy listened. He could hear the clatter of china downstairs; Fanny had begun washing the dishes. Occasional voices, distorted as the wind carried them up and through the attic window, rose from passersby, probably on their way to the Red Ox on the other side of the street for an early evening drink. Only now did the boy notice the keen cold, and he rose and made his way carefully through the attic, which was entirely dark now, to the steep stairs. Down below he heard Mother calling, "Erich!" and then again, more urgently, "Erich, where are you?"

He let a few moments pass before he answered, rather gruffly, "Coming." He wasn't really melancholy after all; he was angry. In fact, furiously angry. Angry with those men. Their names told you nothing about them, but they were the reason for the strange atmosphere these days. Most of all that Hitler. For some reason he didn't understand, his parents seemed to be afraid of Hitler. That made him angry with his parents too. What did all this fuss in Berlin have to do with their family? What did a well-respected man like his father have to fear? Everyone in town raised their hats to him. As for Mother, there was hardly another woman in Ellwangen as pretty as Melanie Levi or as elegantly dressed. Many women were envious—you could see from the way they looked at her—and the men bowed a little more deeply than usual when they met Frau Levi in the street. Erich was proud of his parents, and he simply couldn't understand what had changed them so much.

So he made a sulky face when Mother said, sounding a little reproachful, "Where have you been, Erich? I thought we agreed that you and Max were going to help Fanny this evening. You know she has the evening off when she's done the dishes, and she wants to go dancing." She gave him an affectionate tap on the nose and gently stroked his hair. "Goodness, you're cold. And just look at your trousers, all dusty! Wherever have you been? Go on, find Max and off to the kitchen with you."

Max, two years younger than Erich, was lying on his stomach on his bed in their room, reading an adventure story by Karl May. Erich tiptoed up to him, and then suddenly snatched the book away. He studied the title, *Through the Wilds of Kurdistan*, and with his left hand fended off Max, who was trying to punch him in the ribs and retrieve his book. Finally Erich gave Max a push that sent him tumbling back on the bed. "Come on, we're off to the kitchen to do the dishes!"

Max turned to face the wall. "Don't want to."

Erich opened the wardrobe, found a clothes brush, and went over his trousers with it. Fanny had once told him he was the vainest boy she knew. With a glance at Max, lying there unmoved, he set off for the kitchen himself, sighing. "Was I as idiotic as that when I was ten?"

Fanny, standing at the sink, laughed when Erich posed

the same question to her moments later. "Much worse! Do you remember how you wanted to marry me then?"

That made Erich laugh too, for the first time today. He went solemnly up to Fanny and looked her in the eye. "What do you mean, *wanted*? My heart still beats for you alone!"

Fanny's hand emerged from the soapsuds, and she ran her fingers through his hair until it stood out in all directions, wet and gleaming. "Erich Levi, I swear you're the most impossible boy in the whole world! Oh, the hearts you'll break some day with those big brown eyes of yours! Eyes like a dachshund's, they are! Don't look at me like that, you Casanova—the tea cloth's over there."

They worked in silence for a while, and then Fanny nodded toward the living room door. Father's voice could be heard on the other side of it. He had started on the newspaper, and was reading the most interesting stories aloud to Mother.

"Bad atmosphere," whispered Fanny.

Erich nodded. "I don't understand why. All because of this Hitler."

"He's going to be chancellor. The election's on Tuesday."

"So?" asked Erich dismissively.

Fanny was whispering again. "He hates your people."

By *your people*, Fanny meant Jews. Being a Jew was no big deal for Erich. He didn't even know when he'd first realized that he was Jewish, not Catholic or Evangelical like his friends. It was perfectly normal, it was a part of life, like getting up in the morning, washing, eating, drinking. So their special day was Saturday, the Sabbath, not Sunday, but all the same he and Max had to go to school and Father had to see to the cattle and deal with customers. They celebrated Pesach instead of

Easter, but Mother still hid eggs and chocolate rabbits for him and Max, and gave the neighboring children a taste of fresh matzo. At Chanukah, the Levi family had a Christmas tree like everyone else.

To Fanny, he said, "That's nonsense! I mean, sure, we were persecuted in the Middle Ages, when a lot of Jewish people dressed differently and had different customs, but it's not like that these days."

Fanny shrugged her shoulders. "I think it's ridiculous too. Still, I've heard that Hitler says the Jews want to destroy the German people."

Erich began to laugh. "Well, so now you see how idiotic it is. I mean, we're Germans ourselves!" He helped Fanny to carry the good china into the living room.

"Off you go, Fanny. I can see your feet itching to start dancing!" said Mother with a smile, and she began putting the glasses and plates away in the sideboard. Max, who had come downstairs after all, helped her.

Erich sat down at the big dining table under the round porcelain lamp that gave a bright, warm light. There was only one plate left on the table, the Sabbath plate. On Friday evenings Mother took the candlesticks and Sabbath plate out of the cupboard and arranged the loaves of challah on it. They lay there under an embroidered white cloth until after prayers, when Father solemnly broke the bread and gave everyone a piece. The Sabbath plate symbolized the festive Sabbath mood; it reminded Erich of good food, of being allowed to stay up late even though there was school the next day, Saturday, and of the warmth and security of the family meal they ate together. Erich carefully picked up the plate.

There were Hebrew letters in a circle around the rim.

After two years of studying Hebrew, Erich could decipher them easily. "And the evening and the morning were the sixth day." Beside the Hebrew inscription were small painted symbols, oddly shaped triangles. No one was sure what they meant. Suddenly, however, he remembered how he had thought of those signs when he was a little boy: eyes. The eyes of God looking at us.

*Brownshirts**

ERICH RAN UPSTAIRS two steps at a time, because even from the street he could smell the delicious aroma. Crepes! Tuesday was "Dessert Day," when Father was busy at the cattle markets and often ate lunch with his customers. The boys loved Fanny's desserts, and her crepes were best of all. She was standing by the stove, her face flushed, holding the big cast-iron pan in both hands, so that she could spread the batter evenly over it with careful circling movements. Max was sitting at the kitchen table with his mouth stuffed so full that bits of crepe filled with apple puree were spilling out of both corners.

"You eat like a pig," said Erich, holding out his plate to Fanny, who slid the gleaming crepe onto it.

After a while, when Max's mouth was emptier, he asked, although rather indistinctly, "Did a whole bunch of your teachers come to school in uniform today too? Old Bartle wore his to our class."

Erich knew Bartle by sight. He taught at the elementary school that Max attended, and he was one of the people around here whom his father described as "the Hitler gang." There weren't very many of them in town, and Erich hadn't seen them in groups very often. He thought they looked rather silly in their funny puffy-looking breeches and those ugly brown shirts.

Fanny joined in. "Are they allowed to do that? I mean, so their man Hitler is chancellor now, but all the same, in school . . . ?"

Erich had heard about it too. People at school had been talking, and his English teacher, Herr Senftleben, had been blathering on about a great moment in history. But he didn't mention that, just shrugged. "I don't expect the headmaster liked it, but if their leader got to be chancellor yesterday . . ."

Max leaned toward Erich, who suddenly saw a flicker of alarm in his brother's eyes. "Hey, listen, old Bartle was picking on me the whole time, and when I got Willi to whisper me the answer to a question, he grabbed hold of my arm and said, 'There's changes coming for you now, Levi, and don't you forget it.' What do you think he means?"

Erich clapped him on the shoulder. "Oh, never mind him! He's always boasting. He thinks he can risk shooting his big mouth off these days!" But Max didn't look convinced, and Fanny kept her head bent, fiddling with the corner of her apron. Suddenly Erich felt burning rage rise inside him. What did the man think he was doing, frightening his quiet, dreamy little brother?

"Trust me," Eric said. "Just look at old Bartle—I mean,

he's a joke, with his short, bandy legs and the weird way he sticks his belly out." He jumped up and stalked around the kitchen, knees bent and leaning back as far as he could go. "That's how Herr Bartle goes around. Like a june bug on two legs."

Max couldn't help laughing, and Fanny laughed behind her apron too. Erich was the actor of the family, and he was a really good mimic.

He clapped Max on the shoulder again. "You don't have to be afraid of someone like that, see? Now, may I have another crepe please, Fanny?" But eating was only mechanical; suddenly the crepe tasted like cardboard. After a while he asked where his mother was.

"In the living room, writing your auntie a letter. She says she isn't hungry," Fanny told him.

Erich quietly pressed the handle of the living room door down. His mother was sitting at the big desk with the heavy silver fittings that stood in front of one of the windows. The clouds had parted, and a few rays of sun made their way in and shone on the polished surface of the desk. Mother wasn't writing anymore. She was sitting there motionless, with her hands folded on her lap, and didn't react until Erich quietly came up to her and put his arm around her.

"Oh, it's you. Hello, dear. Forgive me for not coming to lunch straightaway, but I have a bit of a headache, and I wanted to finish writing Aunt Mina a letter." She gave him an affectionate hug. "Well, how was school today?"

Erich swallowed. He didn't really know whether or not to tell her about Max. And two teachers had turned up in his own school wearing those brown uniforms, but he hadn't felt like telling Max and Fanny about that just now. What's more,

Professor Wagner, his German teacher, had seemed very down-cast today. German was Erich's favorite subject, and he liked old Wagner, a distinguished-looking, white-haired man who spoke beautifully, particularly when he was reading poetry. The whole class always listened spellbound when he recited something like Goethe's "The Erl-King." Today he had read them a strange poem. Erich had memorized the first verse:

Sleeping soft on downy pillows
Germany, take your repose,
While the storm surges and billows:
For what may come, ah, no man knows.

Erich hadn't quite understood what the poem was meant to be about, but old Wagner had told them it was by someone called Georg Herwegh. He'd never heard of the poet before, but he and the rest of the class had been impressed to hear that this Herwegh had had to leave Germany in 1843 because of his political opinions. Anyway, Erich had decided to memorize that first verse and ask someone to explain it more fully some other time. No, he didn't want to tell Mother about all this just now, in case it made her headache worse.

So he laid his forehead on her dark brown hair that always smelled so pleasantly of eau de cologne, and whispered, "Oh, school was fine. And we don't have too much homework. We just have to practice the fifth declension of Latin nouns."

Mother drew him close. "Well, that's good. Now let's go and join Max and Fanny."

Long Shadows

FATHER CAME HOME in the afternoon. He looked tired as he slowly took off his thick, dark brown wool overcoat. He was usually tired after market days, when he had to keep talking and bargaining and thinking, because after all, much depended on buying and selling wisely. Business hadn't been too good for some time now. The boys had picked that up from overhearing conversations between their parents. Many people were unemployed, and so they had to scrimp and save. "There's not so much meat eaten now," Father often said. "Other things are more important these days. Meat on the table comes last, that's how it's always been."

The family welcomed him into the kitchen, where he rubbed his hands over the fire in the stove. Without waiting for questions, he told them he'd bought two calves from a farmer from Untergröningen, a couple of fine beasts. "They'll be excellent dairy cows some day, but the best of it is I sold Blaze."

Some good news at last today, thought Erich. Although he always felt a pang when one of the animals was sold. Blaze was a beautiful dairy cow. Erich often used to scratch her between her horns, and she was his favorite because she had such soulful eyes. "She looks like you," he had often told Max, who would protest and throw hay at him.

"Although," added Father, and his expression darkened, "I didn't get a particularly good price for her. In fact, it was a poor one, just three hundred reichsmarks. I wasn't going to sell her for so little at first. . . ."

Father didn't finish his sentence, and it lingered ominously in the room, because everyone knew why he had had to sell the cow.

"Who bought her?" Mother asked calmly, interrupting the oppressive silence.

"Schlosser from Gaildorf," replied Father. "He's a good sort. Blaze will be comfortably off with him." As he spoke, he gave Max a comforting pat on the head, seeing the little boy sitting sadly in his chair. "The calves will be delivered tomorrow and we'll go and see them right away; how about that, Max?"

Erich quietly disappeared upstairs to work on his Latin homework. After a while he heard two whistles in quick succession. Helmut and Kurt, his best friends, were standing down in the street. They both wore black jackets and ankle-high lace-up boots. Kurt had a scarf draped carelessly around his neck, for it wasn't particularly cold for the end of January.

"Finished your homework?" Helmut called up, and Erich shouted back, "Not really, but I'll come anyway!"

He quickly closed the window, grabbed his tweed jacket, and put his boots on. Running past the open kitchen door, he called to Fanny to say he was going down to the Jagst River with Kurt and Helmut. As he clattered downstairs he heard her call back something about being home in good time, and then he was through the front door of the building. He ran along Schmiedstrasse, where Kurt and Helmut were waiting for him, leaning against the window of the shop on the ground floor.

The Levi family lived on one floor of a large, double-gabled building consisting partly of apartments and partly of business premises; the ironmongery and china shop on the ground floor sold household goods of every kind. The whole building belonged to the Fräulein Pfisterers, two unmarried ladies who ran their business with a firm hand, and were highly respected by everyone.

"Well, great master, all clear?" asked Kurt with a grin.

"All but that fifth declension! How about you two?"

"Haven't even started on it." Kurt nudged Erich in the ribs, laughing. "Why do today what you can put off till tomorrow?"

The three boys laughed. They strolled off together to the railroad crossing, where they waited until the big black locomotive pulling a long line of cars had thundered past.

"It goes all the way to Prague," said Kurt knowledgeably when the barrier rose with a creak. "I'd like to travel there by rail some day, I'd like to travel everywhere. See the world and so on. America—that'd be great!"

"You need money for that kind of thing. A lot of money," said Erich.

"That's right." Kurt laughed. "And I'm going to be a millionaire some day. You don't need to know Latin for that."

They ran to the bridge over the Jagst, where they turned right. The Levi family's cattle sheds occupied the ground floor of a large, yellowish-brown building. The big shed doors were wide open, and Peter the cowman was leaning against one of them with a cigarette end in his left hand, staring down into the green, gurgling waters of the Jagst with a gloomy expression on his face.

"Father sold Blaze!" Erich called from some way off.

Peter muttered something that sounded like "Yup." He added, "And a poor price he got for our Blaze, too. I told the boss so myself."

Erich shrugged his shoulders. "Times are bad, Father says."

Peter began forking up hay with a pitchfork, and the familiar sounds came from the darkness of the sheds, along with the usual smell of muck and hay. For a while the boys helped Peter feed the cattle, but that soon bored them, and they went on along the river, following it upstream and throwing pebbles to skim the surface of the water. They argued about soccer. Kurt supported the Kaiserslauten team, heaven only knew why. Erich and Helmut were sure Stuttgart Football Club would win the championship next season. Then, inevitably, the talk turned to school. Scheuerle had given a silly answer in biology today, and Herr Senftleben had been in a really foul mood with his vocabulary test. Suddenly Erich could restrain himself no longer. "And what on earth did he think he looked like in that crazy uniform? Dr. Kaiser ought to forbid that sort of thing!"

Helmut kicked a stone into the sloping bank. "Oh, well, Senftleben's crazy anyway. Did you see the way he marched through the classroom?" Helmut took a few brisk steps forward, imitating the Hitler salute with his arm stiffly outstretched. "But my father says his kind are in a strong position these days."

"Mine says we'll be better off under Hitler," said Kurt, rather hesitantly. Kurt's father was a minor civil servant with the regional law court, a tall man with no sense of humor, who wore rimless glasses and was always looking disapprovingly over the top of them. How such a dismal, joyless person had come to have a lively son like Kurt was a total mystery to Erich.

"And my father says if Hitler comes to power there'll be war," Helmut added. The three boys stared at each other.

Erich suddenly felt cold. "Come on, let's go home."

Without another word they left the riverbank and turned toward town. The shadows of the buildings were very long by now, and to Erich they suddenly seemed especially black and cold.

Supper was laid out in the kitchen, as was usual on weekdays. Fanny poured tea, and Erich reached gratefully for the steaming plate of soup that Mother handed him. Father was talking about all the people he'd met at market, and suddenly added, "Schlosser agrees with me, this won't last long."

"What won't?" asked Mother, with a slight warning nod of her head in the direction of Max, as Erich noticed out of the corner of his eye.

"The government we were landed with yesterday," said Father briefly. "A few weeks at the most and then they'll stop making such a fuss."

"Suppose they don't?" Erich suddenly heard himself asking.

Mother gave him a quick look. "The Eternal One is our God," she said quietly.

The family went on with their supper in silence. Erich knew those words. They came from the "Sh'ma Israel," the

Jewish prayer that he had been learning by heart in religious instruction classes to prepare for his bar mitzvah. It was written on a small scroll of paper fixed to the entrance of their apartment. And he knew what Mother was trying to tell him by quoting it; they had talked about it for a long time in those classes. It meant you must trust in the Lord. The boy's eyes wandered to the dimly lit living room, which he could just make out through the open door. The panes of Grandfather Elias's glass-fronted cupboard shone in there, and behind them were the candlesticks and the Sabbath plate. Suddenly everything seemed to him as fragile and breakable as the platter with the eyes of God on it.

The National Community

A WAVE OF BLACK, brown, and gray jackets and coats, and caps with different colored bands for different grades, filled the square outside the mighty sandstone building of the Collegiate Church. The doors of the high school next to it were open wide and still letting out students, some of them older boys walking out soberly, some of them lively younger boys running down two steps at a time, making their way into the square outside. Erich and the rest of his class stood in the middle of the milling throng, waiting for their teacher, Professor Wagner. They were going to march to the nearby gymnasium with him. There were to be celebrations in the hall, the students had been told, and probably there'd be long speeches, as usual. The choir would sing, and someone would play the piano. But at least there wouldn't be any lessons, and it would be easy to doze off, particularly in the middle and back rows. Even so, Erich had conflicting feelings, although he wished he were looking forward to all this like his friends, who were shoving each other and joking around. They fell about laughing when fat Müller actually did topple over and landed on his well-padded behind. Two weeks ago there'd been an election, and Erich had seen his parents go to the town hall to vote, his father's face grim.

"Every vote against *them* is important," he had said. "Not that I expect it will be much use." And then he had muttered something about "undemocratic" and "intimidation"; Erich had picked up that much. But Father had walked with Mother past the line of bloodred banners that now waved from all the buildings, down Schmiedstrasse into Lange Strasse, past groups of brown uniforms, with people eyeing him suspiciously and sometimes calling out abuse.

"The Jew Levi," they had spat again and again. "Jew Levi, Jew Levi." He wasn't "Herr Levi" anymore, as he had been all these years, and he had talked to Mother about that when they came home. Over the last few weeks there had been more and more of those banners in town, and more and more of the brown-clad figures, and many shops had put ads in the newspaper offering genuine storm trooper uniforms for sale.

"Disgraceful," Father always whispered when he saw those ads, and he would throw the newspaper down. Of course the votes of Melanie and Julius Levi hadn't been any use, and now the Nazis really were the strongest political party.

"But not in Ellwangen," Erich pointed out to Max the next day. The people of the town had voted along the old Catholic lines. As usual, the Center Party* had won a clear majority, with more than two thousand citizens voting for it.

Nonetheless, there were some votes for the National Socialists too, more than eight hundred, said Father, quivering with anger. And now Erich was standing in the church square with his classmates, thinking that even being let off lessons didn't mean he felt like celebrating the fact that the Nazis had won this March election. Kurt nudged him.

"What's the matter? You seem so dismal. I was just telling Helmut he ought to take a look at some of the cute girls here." Kurt meant the few girls now attending what had traditionally been an all-boys school, a small group with their hair worn in braids, or cut short and waved in the new fashion. Among them was tall, strong-boned Marga Fels, daughter of the senior judge, who would get her high school diploma this year.

"Imagine girls being able to take that exam, maybe even study at university," whispered Kurt. "All the same, she's not my type."

"That's right, you like brunettes, don't you?" Helmut clapped his friend on the shoulder. Kurt went bright red. Everyone standing around them laughed, because it was well known that Kurt had fallen for a girl at the Catholic secondary school, and even went the long way round on his journey home just to get a glimpse of her pleated skirt. Erich automatically laughed along with the others. He thought girls were bewildering, fascinating creatures, but he'd sooner have bitten his tongue off than admit it to his friends.

The school staff suddenly appeared at the top of the steps, led by Dr. Kaiser, the headmaster, a tall man wearing pince-nez. He was popular with the students. Behind him came the other teachers, and it was noticeable that several of them were wearing brown uniforms.

"So Gumprecht's joined the Nazis now—just look at him with his big belly—and there's that eager beaver Herr Eisele. My father says he's dead keen on getting somewhere in life," Helmut whispered in Erich's ear.

With the appearance of the teachers, calm had suddenly returned. The students quickly formed double rows, lining up by class. To Erich's surprise, Senftleben made straight for them, although he wasn't their class teacher. He stationed his thin form menacingly in front of Erich, who was small for his age, so that he could only stare at the Party badge on the teacher's chest.

"Levi," came his voice from above Erich's head, "Levi, you go to the back of the class with your cousin. By 'the back,' I mean behind everyone else, even the youngest boys."

Erich sensed rather than saw Senftleben's eyes searching for his cousin Erwin, who was standing two rows behind him with his friend Rudi. Suddenly everything seemed to him very quiet, a silence palpably settling like cotton wool. From a distance, he heard Helmut's voice, cracking a bit but determined.

"Sorry, sir, but Erich and I always walk together. We're friends. We sit together too."

"Did I ask you to contribute to this discussion, Noll? Then if you would be so kind . . ."

Erich turned, and felt a burning sensation behind his eyes. He must not cry, he simply must not cry, not in front of that man. . . . His legs felt as if they had taken root, it was so difficult to take the first step, and still there was that intolerable silence.

"What's going on?" He suddenly heard his class

teacher's familiar voice behind him. Thank goodness, here came old Wagner. Everything would be all right again now. Everything would be all right.

"Erich and Erwin have been told to sit in the back of the class." Helmut's voice, high and agitated, almost cracked.

"My dear colleague, may I ask you . . ." Wagner sounded upset too.

"My dear colleague, may *I* ask *you* not to interfere? This is done in the higher interests of the country. I am sure you will agree that in the spirit of our new great aims, and for the good of our national community,* we must identify and weed out alien elements." The words came out as sharp as knives.

Say something, thought Erich desperately. Go on, good old Wagner, why doesn't he say something?

But there was only silence and then, suddenly and quietly, a very weary voice. "As you like, Herr Senftleben."

Erich turned and saw his cousin Erwin's face. Erwin was standing there, rooted to the spot, eyes wide. The cousins didn't get on particularly well. Erwin was too well behaved for Erich's liking, too much of a conformist, but at that moment they belonged together in a curious way, and one that they could easily understand.

The two of them slowly went to the very back of the line. Wide eyes stared at them, and were lowered when their glances met.

Hesitant scraps of conversation started to reach his ears again. The wall of silence that had risen around him was broken by timid whispers, and the long line of students began to move. Erwin walked beside Erich. They did not exchange a word. Erich was fighting the burning sensation behind his eyes, paying careful attention to putting one foot in front of the other. If he had stopped, he wouldn't have been able to walk on again.

"Alien elements . . . national community . . ." The words kept echoing in Erich's head during the ceremony, which, as he had expected, consisted of speeches, piano playing, recitation of poems, and more speeches. On Senftleben's orders, he and Erwin also sat apart from the others in the back row. Then Dr. Kaiser delivered his address, and Erich, who had been sitting slumped in his chair until now, straightened up expectantly. The Head was stern but fair, he knew that. He was sure Dr. Kaiser hadn't heard of the incident yet, but all the same, now he would take a stand against what was going on around him. Yet strangely enough, the Head himself was using the phrases that were now familiar to Erich. He hated them.

"National community . . . national revival . . . renewal of our nation . . ." It droned on and on, and Erich knew it was all about the Nazis. Suddenly the headmaster started to speak about the school itself and its mission, and Erich listened with his hopes reviving. Now he must surely say something about the brown uniforms and Senftleben and the others, and how it wasn't right to say "Heil Hitler" every day instead of the usual "Good morning" when school began. But the Head was talking about "the peace and quiet of our classrooms," and said the mission of the school had nothing to do with politics. Erich couldn't get the hang of it. He lets the Senftlebens do as they like, he thought bitterly, and then he claims that his school has nothing to do with politics.

At the end of the ceremony a tenth-grade boy with a determined expression on his face began to hammer out a march on the piano, and everyone rose to sing the national anthem. But to Erich's surprise, the old music master Immig conducted them to a different melody, one he'd heard the Brownshirts bawl out as they marched through town. "Raise high the flags* . . ." At first a few people sang it, hesitantly, but then they all joined in. Only Erich and Erwin and a few others kept their mouths shut. After a short pause, Erich sat down in his chair, and Erwin followed suit.

I'm never going to sing that song, not even if Senftleben kills me for it, thought Erich, his heart thudding.

In the afternoon, Erich met Helmut and Kurt by the Jagst again, at the swimming pool used by men and boys during the summer. The weather had turned colder these last few days, and there was a skin of ice over the water.

"Funny if it freezes now, when we haven't seen any snow all winter," said Helmut, staring into the water. Erich, who was sitting on a rock on the bank and doodling in the sand with a stick, was silent. Kurt was standing a little way from them, hands buried in his jacket pockets, his Norwegian cap pulled far down over his forehead. For a while none of the boys said anything.

They don't know what to say, thought Erich, and in a curious way he felt guilty. Finally he pulled himself together and suggested, "Let's go to the cave and see the bats." He rose to his feet and looked encouragingly at his friends.

"Listen, Erich," Helmut said, "what Senftleben did today was bull. Total bull. I told my father, and he thinks your father ought to complain to the Head. He had no right to do it—Senftleben, I mean. After all, you haven't done anything wrong."

Erich shrugged his shoulders and turned away so that his friend wouldn't see the tears rising to his eyes.

Helmut came up behind him. "What did *your* father say?"

Erich shrugged again.

"You did tell him, didn't you?"

Erich shook his head hard.

"Why on earth not?"

Erich gulped back his tears, and began answering several times before he managed to say, "He has other things on his mind right now."

Helmut came round in front of him. "What do you mean?"

"A lot of farmers don't buy from him anymore. For fear of the Nazis. They're saying openly that people shouldn't buy from Jews. And my father says some of the farmers feel the same way. All of a sudden they think we're all sharks. Even though they've been buying cattle from Father for years."

Helmut was silent for a while, and then said, "You have to tell him, all the same."

"And what do you think will happen then? You heard Wagner today. Wagner, of all people, always so keen on honor and honesty. The headmaster was just blowing hot air too."

"My father thinks that's because he's afraid himself. If he'd said anything against the Nazis, it would have got around town at once." Helmut was silent for some time, and then he said quietly, "They arrested twelve people in Aalen yesterday. Just for being against the Nazis. Father says they're going to be taken to a camp in Ulm within the next few days."

Erich stared at him. Helmut's father was a highly respected attorney who had been on the town council for years. He was certain to know a lot of news, and Erich had no doubt that this item was true. "So you think my father should go to the Head and complain? And maybe get arrested himself?"

Helmut bowed his head. "But if we don't defend our-selves at all . . . ?"

"Maybe you and your father can, you're respected, but we—" Suddenly Erich stopped short, realizing what he had said. And *we* were respected people too, he thought bitterly. We don't really belong anymore. Mother says a lot of people look away when she walks past them. I don't even really belong with Helmut and Kurt, only with Erwin.

Aloud, he said, "I think we'll have to be careful. My Uncle Süssel thinks it will only be as bad as this to start with, until they've worked off their grudges. But for now we just have to watch out."

Helmut said nothing. He looked uncertain.

Kurt came over to them. His face was pinched, and he seemed annoyed. "You two are always chattering on. Can't we *do* something? Come on, let's go to the cave!" And without looking to see if they were following, he stormed ahead. With his shoulders hunched and his torso thrust forward, he looked like a young bull.

"What's eating him?" Erich asked.

"Oh, he's just in a bad mood!" Helmut grabbed his sleeve. "Come on, let's see who's fastest!" And they ran up the hill, over the brown winter grass in the meadows, to the Benzenruhe, a small wooded area that was their favorite place in the summer months. Erich remembered how they used to play cops and robbers or hide-and-seek here. And once, when their old friend Lutz, showing off, had climbed an old oak tree and was too scared to come down, they had had to run off to the nearest farmhouse for help. The farmer had come with a ladder, and gave Lutz such a thrashing that he couldn't sit down for three days.

It was best in early summer, when the grass was green and lush, like a quilt spread under the trees, and you could just drop into it. Now the grass was withered, and the trees reached bare branches into a gray winter sky that seemed to Erich as bleak as a mirror reflecting his own state of mind. But he didn't want to let any of that show, and he raced with Helmut until they had almost caught up with Kurt.

After going along the path that led from the woods, they turned left and ran up the last slope to a cave, which according to an old legend had led straight to Ellwangen Castle. In the boys' imaginations, knights, pirates, and highwaymen had once lived in that cave and had met mysterious envoys here to take confidential messages up to the castle, or sallied out to rescue captive princesses or kidnapped heirs to the throne. Now, in winter, the cave was a cold and slippery hole in the ground, and the most interesting thing about it was the bats that hung motionless from the ceiling. Kurt had a flashlight with him, and they were clambering carefully over the wet pebbles farther into the cave, when suddenly the light went out.

"You idiot, Kurt," said Helmut, who was leading them. "Turn that flashlight on."

Instead, they heard a deep *"Whooooh!"* behind them. This was one of Kurt's usual tricks, and normally Helmut's fury and Kurt's ghostly wailing would have made Erich laugh. But suddenly he felt pressure in his chest, and something tightened his throat so that he could hardly breathe. He couldn't explain it. He leaned back on the wet rock and let himself slide down it. All the fears he had been holding back until now attacked him like wild animals. He saw Senftleben, and the people in their brown uniforms; next he heard Senftleben's shrill voice, saw Erwin's wide, startled eyes again, and saw Father bending wearily over his business accounts. He thought of Max and his eternal question, "What does that mean?"; Mother with her eyes red from crying; then he saw long lines of prisoners, and Father was one of them, and—

"Hey, Erich! Erich!" Suddenly he heard Helmut's shout of alarm. The flashlight was on again, its flickering light wandering along the walls of the cave until it found him.

"Hey, Erich, what's up?" Helmut was kneeling beside him, shaking him.

Kurt shone the flashlight on him. "Everything okay?"

Erich nodded with difficulty. With their help, he scrambled to his feet and whispered, "Let's get out of here. I felt sick."

Marching in Step

THE NEXT MORNING, Erich went to school feeling apprehensive. He dreaded coming face-to-face with Senftleben; he even feared meeting his classmates. He couldn't guess how they would deal with the situation. But it all turned out easier than he'd expected. Some of the others in his class greeted him in a deliberately casual way, others were noticeably friendly to him. Lutz patted him on the shoulder and whispered, "Don't let it bother you. Senftleben's a bastard."

But Erich also noticed that some of the other boys had moved away into a group. They were leaning against a window, looking at him with malice. Now and then one of them made some snide remark, and then they all laughed and looked his way. He wasn't surprised about Kampmann, a tall boy with his hair cut short. Kampmann's father had joined the Nazi Party in February, after Hitler was appointed

Reichkonzler. "He thinks it'll be good for his business," Helmut had told Erich. Kampmann's father owned a printing works, and at first Erich couldn't see what good he hoped the Nazis could do him. "Printing pamphlets and so on," Kurt had explained.

So he could understand Kampmann, but it was annoying to see that Klaus, always known as Schluffi, had joined him, and fat Müller too. Erich went over to Erwin, who was standing in a corner with Rudi. The three boys were staring at Erwin. He looked anxious and frightened, so Erich whispered to him in a carefully casual tone, "They can't hurt us. The best thing is to take no notice."

Suddenly Reger, the class spokesman, dashed into the room. "No lessons today! Wagner just told me! Stand to attention!"

The boys stood to attention to the right and left of their desks as old Wagner came in, looking wearier and more bowed than usual. He let his gaze wander briefly over the class, and for a moment it rested longer on Erich, or so it seemed to Erich, anyway. Then he said, "There will be no lessons anywhere in the country today. It's because the newly elected German Reichstag is meeting. You're all to go home and listen to the radio broadcast. And anyone who doesn't have a radio at home may go to an inn to hear it, just this once."

Yelling their delight, the boys packed their bags. Caps flew in the air, and they all raced to the exit. Erich breathed a sigh of relief. No English lesson with Senftleben!

Kurt pulled his sleeve. "Come on, let's go to the Crown Cellar. I'll try wheedling a beer out of Marie."

Erich nodded in agreement. It was all the same to him. He could have jumped for joy! He ran home, threw his satchel into the hallway, and called, racing downstairs again already, "We have the day off from school! I'll be back for lunch." At the front door of the building he met Max, who was pushing it open.

"Why are you looking like that? We have the day off school! Terrific, right?"

But Max just shook his head and ran upstairs. For a moment Erich watched him go, bewildered, and then he ran out to where his friends were waiting. The red flags with the swastika on them were flying outside the gymnasium again, as they were all over town, and a small group of Brownshirts was standing at the entrance. Kurt went boldly up to them.

"What's up? Anything going for free?"

"Sure, a walloping if you want one, my boy!" said one of the SA men, to the amusement of the others.

A man of middle height with a small mustache like Hitler's detached himself from the group and went over to the three boys. "Come on in, lads. They'll be broadcasting the führer's speech over a large loudspeaker. There'll be fizzy drinks too."

"You could persuade me in for a beer," called Kurt, keeping a safe distance from the SA men. One of them made as if to catch him, and the boys took off running, followed by the raucous laughter of the Brownshirts. Almost all the seats in the Crown Cellar were taken, even though it was so early. The strapping barmaid, Marie, had her hands full, while Gustl, the landlord, was frantically turning the buttons on the People's Radio set, which had broadcast only crackling and rushing static sounds so far. The boys sat at a free corner of the table favored by regular customers, and Kurt called in a lordly tone, "I'll have a beer, Marie!"

"You'll be lucky!" Marie laughed, but all the same she

put a large glass down in front of the three of them. Kurt had the privilege of the first sip. He drank with relish, taking great gulps, and wiped the foam from his mouth with the back of his hand. The others at the table, mostly farmers from the surrounding villages, made witty remarks, and one gave his opinion that the snot-nosed lad needed a good hiding. A tall man with a gray mustache puffed thoughtfully at his cigar and suddenly turned to Erich. "Aren't you Julius Levi's son?"

The boy felt every fiber of his body tense. Instead of answering, he just nodded.

The old man twinkled at him from behind a cloud of smoke. "Remember me to your father, will you? Regards from Albert Schremser."

What's the matter with me? Erich wondered. But he also noticed several men at the far end of the table nodding their heads his way and whispering. He drank his share of the beer in cautious little sips; he didn't like the bitter flavor. He was really drinking it only to please Kurt, and because he didn't want to be a spoilsport. But he noticed a pleasant warmth and drowsiness spreading through him. Feeling relaxed, he leaned back in his chair and realized, in surprise, that the noise, the talk, the smell of alcohol, and all the laughter seemed to be coming from far away.

Meanwhile, Gustl, who had little rivulets of sweat running over his temples and down his forehead, had given up trying to get the radio to work. Cursing, he mopped his face with his blue apron when a slender, smartly dressed young man had pity on him and took over. Erich knew him. He was a sales representative for animal feed, and had often visited the Levis' apartment, where he would flirt outrageously with Fanny. Suddenly a booming voice rang out in the room.

"Attention! Berlin calling!"

Erich jumped. All fell still. The boy heard the words "führer and reich chancellor," and there it was again, that rasping voice, calm at first, then getting faster and louder, spitting venom, tumbling over itself. Erich glanced at the faces all around. Some were looking grave and thoughtful, like the farmer who had sent Father his regards. One or two seemed more amused or even bored, like the young sales rep, who preferred chatting to Marie, but many appeared spellbound, and some even listened with their mouths open, forgetting about their lighted cigarettes.

"He certainly has plenty to say for himself," Erich heard one of the men sitting nearby whisper appreciatively, and the man's neighbor agreed. "Yes, he speaks well, that Hitler." The voice was still ringing out from the radio, rising to a hoarse screech that filled the entire room.

"*. . . in which the millions who now curse us will stand behind us, and together with us will greet the new German reich that we have created, have fought and toiled for, have won at a bitter cost—the great new German reich of honor and power, splendor and justice. Amen!*"

Suddenly Erich felt ill. He struggled convulsively for air and ran out with his hand pressed to his mouth. Behind the building he retched and threw up, and then leaned against the wall, breathing hard. All of a sudden Helmut was beside him, giving him his handkerchief in silence.

"All right now?" he whispered, and Erich nodded, exhausted. He felt so ashamed.

"Helmut," he whispered, "it wasn't just the beer."

Helmut nodded. "I thought so," he said.

* * *

That evening the family sat at the supper table in silence. Erich just drank a little tea, not quite sure of his stomach yet. The others didn't seem to have much appetite either. In the distance, faint brass band music and voices drifted toward them. There was to be a big procession, Fanny had said, and then a rally in the gymnasium hall because Hitler was reich chancellor now.

"Yes, and tomorrow they'll pass a law finally handing this country over to him," Julius Levi added. "And old Hindenburg will give it his blessing, and so will all the others, the Prussians and Conservatives and Catholics and all decent citizens."

All Erich understood was that Hitler had finally come to power, and Uncle Süssel's optimism was unfounded. He wanted to ask his father what it would mean for them, but he didn't dare. It can't get very bad here in Ellwangen, the boy consoled himself. Father always says they're staunch Catholics in this town, they'll have nothing to do with the Nazis. Well, there's Senftleben—he'll carry on making life difficult for me—and perhaps now Kampmann and his friends too. Then there's the local Nazis like that man Kolbe, the loudmouth-in chief, as Father always calls him; and a lot of people who don't mind one way or the other, or are just cowards, like the people who won't say hello to Mother anymore. But there are plenty of others too. And after all, it's not as if we'd done anything wrong.

Suddenly there were snowflakes dancing outside the dark window, now dimly lit by the streetlamp. They became a dense flurry.

"Snow!" cried Max in excitement. The snow they'd been waiting for in vain this year, the snow they'd longed for—now it was here, in the first days of spring! Of course it wouldn't stick, the ground was too warm for that. All the same, Max ran to the window, beaming with delight, and pressed his nose to the pane. Down below, the noise suddenly swelled, and Max jumped as the martial *crash-crash-boom* of the brass band rang out. The whole family went to the window. There they went, marching past below: the Brownshirts with their banners, the brass band, some boys from school who had started wearing the Hitler Youth* uniform recently, the police, the Gymnastics Club, the Veterans' Association, and many more. And they were marching in step, their feet coming down on the asphalt with a thumping noise that rose to the window where the four Levis were standing. The family linked arms and looked down in silence.

Onlookers were pushing and shoving at the roadside, gaping and whispering. Some had retreated as if in alarm and were pressing close to the buildings, but others stood well to the fore, hands raised in the Hitler salute. They all watched this almost endless procession wind its way like a snake around the streets. And the snow fell soundlessly as if to cover it all up.

Boycott

"NO, MAX, look. You have to multiply here." Erich sighed. Teaching his little brother the mysteries of mathematics was tough work. The entrance exam for the vocational high school to which Max was supposed to go would be the day after tomorrow.

"The prep school is out of the question for Max," Mother and Father had decided. "The work would be too hard for our daydreamer." Max, who preferred wandering through the desert or fighting hostile Indians in his imagination, had far more trouble with schoolwork than Erich, to whom that everything seemed to come easily. Erich knew that his father planned for Max to take over the family business some day, while he dreamed of an academic career for Erich.

"You must study, boys, study!" Julius always told them. "Remember that no one can take away what you have in your heads. We Jews know that better than anyone." His sons had smiled at this saying, and didn't really understand it. But they knew that their parents felt sure they would do their best, as if that were only to be expected of a Levi. And now Max was toiling away on a mysterious, complicated exercise that involved working out what five bread rolls cost if you knew the price of three bread rolls.

After a while he bent his head and began to cry. Erich put a comforting arm around him. "Come on, it's not that hard." He thought to himself that Max had been crying a lot recently. Something must have happened on the day when Erich and his friends were listening to Hitler's speech in the Crown Cellar. Max had told him that someone had called him "a bad name." What that bad name was, he could not be persuaded to say. They had both been lying in bed, listening to the babble of voices rising from the street. The rally was over, and people were all going home.

"Erich, why don't they like us?" Max had asked, and Erich, who knew exactly what he meant by "they," had said, sighing in the dark, "I wish I knew, Max. But listen, there are plenty of others who have nothing against us, they're even our friends."

"But it wasn't like this before," Max had persisted.

"It's because of Hitler, that's why."

"And they do everything he says?"

"Well, he's their leader. That's why they call him the führer."

"But *I* can't suddenly turn nasty to someone I know. Bartle always used to be so friendly to Papa, and he even took his hat off to Mama. And now . . ." Hesitantly, Max told Erich about other kinds of harassment. "Whenever Willi talks in class

I'm the one who gets punished. And I've been given a black mark in the register three times even though I didn't do anything at all!" And then, said Max, one of the others in his class had called him that "bad name," and Bartle just stood there smiling.

"There are always idiots around," Erich had said, "and Bartle and people like him have the upper hand now because their man Hitler is in power. Once he's gone it will be different, you just wait and see."

"But do you think he ever will go again? Fanny says there's nothing anyone can do to oppose him now."

"Oh, he'll be voted out of power some time!" Erich was trying hard to believe what he had just said. "Keep on working, and then, when you go to the high school, you'll never see Bartle again." Although you might fall into Senftleben's hands, he thought.

Now he was sitting at the table, looking at his brother's bent head and shaking shoulders. Pretending to sound casual, he tried to cheer Max up. "Come on, an Indian doesn't know the meaning of pain, so begin at the beginning again!"

At that moment Father came into the room. Julius Levi stood in the doorway for a moment, looking at his sons. "Max, you go out and play for a bit. You need to air your brain now and then! Erich, will you come with me, please? I'm going down to check up on the cattle shed. I've been worrying about one of those calves since yesterday."

Max had already shot out of the door like lightning, and Erich hurried off to fetch his jacket. He and his father walked down to the Jagst together. A pale spring sun warmed his face, and he left his jacket open as if he could absorb the mild air better that way.

Father had walked beside him in silence for a while, then said, "I'm worried about Max."

"Oh, he just has to concentrate a little harder, that's all."

"I don't mean that. He's been crying a lot, and Mother says he sometimes just sits staring into space."

"He often does that anyway."

"Yes, but he looks so sad. I'll be frank with you, Erich, Mother and I are afraid he's being bullied at school." Julius Levi gave his elder son an inquiring sideways look. Hesitating, Erich passed on what Max had confided to him. For a while Julius Levi said nothing. He had compressed his lips, and he was rather pale.

"So what about you, Erich? I heard something about . . ."

Erich was quick to interrupt his father. "That was just Senftleben. Another idiot like Bartle. You don't want to take them seriously." He realized that he was blushing, and suddenly felt that he couldn't tell his father the truth, not at any price. He wanted to spare him the shame that had surrounded him, Erich, since that day. It burned like fire inside him, a fire that he couldn't put out. It was the shame of being humiliated in front of other people. Because then I'd be shaming the name of Levi and Mother and Father too, thought the boy, and whatever happens I must not do that.

"I'm afraid we do have to take them seriously now," replied his father, with a sad smile. "You know, Erich, I've always felt I was both a German and a Jew, but they weren't mutually exclusive, far from it. We are Jews, we obey the Commandments, we keep the Sabbath and our holy days just as Christians keep theirs; but first and foremost we're Germans, we respect the laws of the state as its citizens. Uncle Ludwig fought for Germany in the last war, and our mother's cousin fell at the front, and another of your ancestors, one of the Süssel family, was on the barricades in the 1848 revolution! And now they suddenly try denying us the right to be German! But we're not letting that right go. Did you hear me, Erich? We're not letting them take our honor and dignity from us!" Julius Levi had stopped, and put his arm around his son's thin shoulders.

Erich looked at his father's familiar face. It was unusually grave now. Father's grown older these last few weeks, Erich thought again; he's really worried. Out loud, he said, "I agree with you entirely, Father."

"Good, Erich, so now I'm going to see the elementary school head, and Dr. Kaiser too. I'm not having my children bullied."

In the cattle shed, Peter was waiting for them with bad news. The calf was ill, standing in a corner of the shed with sore eyes. Erich tickled the place between its ears where little curls of hair grew.

"You want to know what I think, boss?" said Peter. "You let them palm you off with a bad bargain there."

Julius looked undecided for a little while, and then ordered, "Get it slaughtered. Take it away tomorrow."

"But, Father," said Erich, shocked, "aren't you going to call the veterinarian?"

"Not worth it now, Erich. That calf is really very sick. Yes, a bad bargain! And now of all times, when business isn't going well anyway."

Of course Father was bound to think that way, thought Erich. Sadly, he went over to the calf again and patted it. The grown-up world was so difficult: business, money, and politics—always politics.

When they came home at dusk, Mother met them in the hall, very upset. "My brother phoned just now. He's heard there's something being planned for the next few days. Some kind of move against Jewish businesses. He heard it from a friend in Berlin."

Julius put a soothing arm around her. With a slight nod to Erich, he led Mother into the living room. Erich could hear her nervous voice in there for some time yet, and then his father's quieter tone. Sighing, he went to his room. What now? At midday he'd felt much better when Father talked to him.

At supper, Father calmly announced that Uncle Ludwig had phoned. "It seems there's going to be some kind of large-scale Nazi operation in the next few days. Against Jewish businessmen. But there's nothing for us to fear. It won't affect us here in Ellwangen. The only Jewish businessmen here are Uncle Sigmund and me, and we're known as serious, good, professional men. And Uncle Ludwig thinks Hitler is showing aggression at the start to satisfy his supporters, and then it will all die down again."

On Wednesday morning, Erich glanced at the newspaper that Fanny had just put down on the kitchen table.

"What's a boycott, Father?" he asked, when he had studied the headlines. Julius came out of the bathroom, half his face covered with soap lather.

"It's a call for people not to buy from certain businesses or companies," said Father, picking up the newspaper. "Ah—so that's the way the wind is blowing. They're telling people not to buy from Jewish businesses on the first of April."

"What do the Nazis expect that to achieve?"

Julius shrugged his shoulders. "It's a special form of

harassment. And of course they want to whip up popular feeling that way. We Jews have always been accused of being bloodsuckers and exploiting other people. Which of course is nonsense. There are just as many rogues among us as there are among Christians, and just as many honest folk too. I'm sure a great many people don't even know when they've been buying from Jews."

The boycott was to be on a Saturday, and it occurred to Erich that that wouldn't be too bad for Father. Julius did business only in exceptional cases on the Sabbath anyway, and so the boycott couldn't affect him. The same was true of Uncle Sigmund, a cattle dealer like Father. Julius had consulted with him yesterday evening, after his brother-in-law Ludwig's phone call, and Uncle Sigmund thought the same.

School Reports

THEY HAD OTHER things on their mind in school. The end of term celebrations would be on Friday—when the school year came to an end—but the really important thing was that reports would be handed out and the spring vacation would begin. Erich wasn't afraid of getting his report; far from it. On the days leading up to that occasion he felt a kind of excitement, a pleasant tingle of anticipation, because he always knew he would have a good one. The only question was whether his Latin would earn him an "Excellent" again this year, and what marks he would get for math, his least favorite subject.

And then there was English! What would Senftleben say this year? In Erich's last report he had given him only a "Satisfactory," because of what he called "inadequate oral contributions in class." Erich had stood beside his desk while

Senftleben scrutinized him for a long time, tapping his pen in a staccato rhythm against that dangerous little black book of his.

"Your oral work isn't good enough. You're slow to speak up in class, you don't take an interest." And so saying, he stared fixedly at him until Erich lowered his gaze, feeling ashamed, and slipped back into his place. It wasn't true, either. He did at least as well as Helmut, who had been given a "Good" last year. And he always raised his hand to answer questions, but Senftleben never picked him. He deliberately overlooked him, indeed he hardly registered the existence of a student called Erich Levi except at certain moments. But I'm not putting up with that anymore, Erich thought. And next time I shall look back until he lowers his own eyes. After all, Father had a word with Dr. Kaiser!

And the harassment had in fact mostly stopped since the memorial ceremony. Erich put that down to a warning from the headmaster after Father, as he had promised, had gone to see him. That afternoon he had felt better, for when he came home, Father had briefly patted his head and said, "I only want to tell you that everything's all right. Dr. Kaiser himself thinks these are difficult times, but they'll soon pass. Senftleben won't be bothering you anymore."

The last day of the old school year had arrived. The students were scurrying around in colorful groups on the big square outside the Collegiate Church. You could tell what classes they were in from the colors of the bands on the boys' caps. The twelfth grade, wearing white bands, all stood together. The school was saying a solemn good-bye to them today, and they were already acting very grown-up. They took little notice of the eighth-grade boys jumping around, trying to catch each other amidst loud shouts. The group with green bands were his own classmates. He saw Helmut and Kurt waving to him. Erwin and his friend Rudi were with them too.

That's where I belong, thought Erich happily. Some day Helmut and I and the others will be standing where the boys in the top grade are now, with our high school diplomas in our pockets, and then . . . well, perhaps then I'll study at university in Tübingen or Heidelberg, along with Helmut. Or maybe I'll go even further afield some time, perhaps Leipzig or Berlin. He wanted to study law, he knew that for sure—like Helmut, who would be taking over his father's attorney's office some day. But Erich wanted to be a judge, someone who had authority and could help true justice prevail. He had often heard Helmut's father complain that an attorney couldn't pick and choose his clients. But a judge was above all that, and when he was a judge he'd never let innocent people be hounded in the courts, or imprisoned. That's what Erich was thinking as he ran to join his friends.

Helmut was excited. "Heard the latest?"

Erich shook his head. "How would I?"

"Senftleben's being transferred to Stuttgart."

"Are you sure? How do you know?"

"Kampmann was telling us just now. He heard it from his father. That bunch had a meeting yesterday, and they were saying good-bye to Party Comrade Senftleben. Seems he's going to make his career in a ministry department there."

Erich took a deep breath. So Senftleben was leaving—that was the best news he'd heard in a long time. Since the March election another two of the younger teachers had joined him and the math master Bönninger as Nazi Party members, strutting around in their new uniforms during every conceivable occasion. But Senftleben was easily the worst of them.

No more harassment, and a good mark in English next year, he thought with relief, and he entered the classroom to receive his report feeling light at heart. What did he care that there was a large, conspicuously written "Still only satisfactory" beside his English mark this time? He wouldn't let that last little act of cheap revenge spoil his pleasure in his report.

Helmut was beaming too. Only Kurt looked glum. "When my old man sees my Latin mark—yikes! Too bad about this vacation."

A group had gathered around Kampmann in the niche by the window. He had become popular recently. Lutz and a couple of other boys—boys Erich used to play with in the past— now showed up in Jungvolk* uniform on special occasions. Helmut had told Erich that the old school chaplain, Merz, was very concerned about it, because fewer and fewer young people attended Catholic Youth Club meetings now. Suddenly Kampmann left the group that had been standing around him, whispering. He was almost a head taller than Erich, and when he planted himself in front of him, Erich could see a slight mustache already sprouting on his upper lip.

"Hey, Levi, let's take a look at your report." And before Erich could react, Kampmann had snatched the booklet out of his hand. "That's just amazing—a Jew-boy getting such a good report! Well, of course your lot aren't stupid. . . ." He was going to turn to Erwin, who ducked behind Rudi's back, when Helmut barred his way.

"What's the idea, Kampmann? Leave the Levis alone! They haven't done anything to you."

Kampmann gazed at him with the superior expression of someone who is absolutely sure of himself. "What's the idea? You'll see. Then you won't have such a big head. My father says you and your sort will be in for it soon. Your fine father . . ." But he got no further.

Quick as lightning, Helmut had seized him and was holding him fast, while Kampmann tried to free himself, kicking and writhing. The others stood there paralyzed. Erich's report had dropped to the floor, but he ignored that. Kampmann and Helmut were on the floor too now, and it was soon clear that Kampmann, as the stronger, would win the fight. He was lying on top of Helmut, punching him hard in the ribs.

Erich could hardly contain himself. He wanted to go to his friend's aid—Helmut's nose was bleeding profusely—he wanted to pull the strong boy off him, but he knew he mustn't. Two against one would be unfair. The school code of honor required Helmut to fight Kampmann on his own.

Suddenly the classroom door was flung open, and there stood old Wagner. The boys scattered, allowing him a clear view of the two opponents, still lying on the floor grimly locked in a wrestling hold.

"Kampmann, Noll, stop that at once!"

The teacher came closer, and the two boys on the floor—only now becoming aware of his presence—let go of each other. With some difficulty, they rose to their feet. Helmut wiped the blood off his face with a handkerchief and brushed the dust off his clothes. On the other side of the room Kampmann was still breathing heavily, while the others patted him on the back and congratulated him.

Fat Müller came forward. "Noll began it, sir. And it was Levi's fault!"

"I don't remember asking you for information, Müller. I suggest you all go out now and get ready to go to church together." Wagner turned and walked with measured tread to the door, while the Kampmann group began whispering excitedly. Erich could pick up a few scraps of words ". . . outrageous . . . ought to be reported . . . I'll tell my father . . ."

He picked his report off the floor. It was slightly crumpled, and you could see the imprint of a boot on the bottom right-hand corner. He carefully wiped the booklet down, put it in his satchel, and then went out to the church square with Helmut and the others.

It was left up to him and Erwin to decide whether they would go to the school services at all. Sometimes they attended Mass in the Collegiate Church with their friends. Erich loved the solemn ceremony of the church services, and he always liked the interior of the church. What a difference between its splendor and the plain, bare prayer hall of the Jewish community! He particularly loved the magnificent colored ceiling paintings, with their vivid figures, telling all kinds of stories. And he admired the gorgeous vestments worn by the priests, the incense, the murmuring of the large congregation, the joyous organ music, and the sunlight that made the gilded stucco shine. But today he shook his head when Helmut, with an inquiring nod in the direction of the church, invited him to come too.

"Oh, come on, Erich, just to show them! Kampmann wouldn't dare call you names in church."

"Forget it, Helmut. I don't feel like it today."

Shrugging, his friend turned away, and Erich sat down on the steps outside the school entrance and watched his classmates as they walked, in well-ordered groups, through the wide double doors of the church. Suddenly he realized, to his surprise, that Erwin was sitting beside him. In answer to his unspoken question, his cousin whispered, "I didn't dare go in."

Erich nodded. "Yes, somehow it wouldn't be right for us to be with them today." And he couldn't explain, even to himself, why he suddenly longed for the little prayer hall, or why the mighty organ music and the voices raised in song sounded so discordant to his ears just then.

Fanny

MOTHER BEGAN preparing the Sabbath meal in the afternoon. It was to be a particularly festive Sabbath, in honor of "our two learned scholars," as Father had jokingly said. Max had passed his entrance exam for the vocational high school with excellent marks, even in math, and Erich's report filled his parents with pride. They had both given him a loving hug, and no one mentioned the bad mark for English. Nor did they discuss the crumpled paper and the boot print, still faintly visible, although his parents exchanged a glance full of meaning.

But now the fragrance of freshly baked bread hung in the air. The challah loaves were on the Sabbath plate, carefully hidden by the little embroidered cloth. Mother was just preparing her famous pigeons stuffed with white bread crumbs, mushrooms, and egg, when Fanny stumbled upstairs laden with two bags. She seemed depressed, and began unpacking the bags mechanically.

"There's Brownshirts all over town handing out leaflets."

"And what do they say?" asked Mother quietly.

Fanny shrugged. "Nothing special. Respectable citizens must be protected and people ought to shop in their home-towns. That kind of stuff." Fanny began putting away the things she had bought.

"Fanny, what's the matter? Did something happen?" asked Erich in alarm.

Fanny vigorously shook her head.

"Come on, Fanny, tell us! We know you. What's bothering you?" Melanie Levi put her arm around the maid and led her to the table. Erich was shocked to see that Fanny's eyes were red with weeping.

"Erich, fetch Fanny a glass of wine. Calm down, Fanny dear."

Erich went to the sideboard in the living room, where the bottle of red wine for the evening meal stood, already opened. Normally the first sip at the beginning of Sabbath was for Father, but that didn't matter just now.

After Fanny had taken a few cautious sips, she did calm down a little and began to tell her tale. She had been to the Heebs' bakery to fetch the tart that Mother had ordered for the Sabbath. The whole baker's shop was full. And then Frau Heeb, the master baker's wife, had said, with her nasty laugh, "Ah, so here's the Jews' girl Fanny." She had said it in a horrible, loud, sneering tone, and everyone in the shop had laughed too. Well, not quite everyone. Some of them had looked upset and said nothing, but most people laughed. Then Frau Heeb had asked if she wasn't ashamed of working for Jews, a good Christian girl like her? But she gave fat Frau Heeb as good as she got, said Fanny. "I'd ten times sooner work for the Levis than for many Christian families in this town," she'd told her. Then old Schuster from just over the road went up to Fanny and told her sternly that she'd better not say such things now or it would be the worse for her. "And no one contradicted him. It's a shame, it's a crying shame," whispered Fanny, clutching her handkerchief in her right hand.

Mother patted the girl's arm. "Poor Fanny, to think of you being dragged into it too. I'm so sorry."

Erich leaned against the table and took Fanny's other hand. Max was standing close to the kitchen cupboard. He looked as white as a sheet. For a while there was silence, broken only by Fanny's diminishing sobs.

The door opened and Father came into the kitchen. He stopped briefly in the doorway, surveying the scene before him, and then cried, "Well, here's a happy party, I must say!"

Erich realized that Father was trying to gloss over the situation, and replied in a deliberately cheerful tone, "Hey, you've come at just the right moment." He went toward his father, who was holding a small package. "What's in there?"

"A surprise! From the family in Pirmasens. But it's not to be unpacked until Pesach." He ruffled Erich's hair. "And you haven't heard the best of it yet. I had a letter from Aunt Mina and Uncle Louis today. They're planning to come and see us at Pesach."

"Hooray!" Erich clapped his hands, and Max came closer too and started eyeing the package. As if by magic, the dismal mood was suddenly swept away. Fanny blew her nose noisily and then set to work at the stove, while Frau Levi began taking the good china into the living room. Erich beamed. It really was good news. Aunt Mina was Father's eldest sister. She was several years older than Julius, and had grown-up children. Erich and Max considered her their favorite aunt, and a long visit to her and Uncle Louis was a tradition every summer vacation. For a moment all their troubles were gone, and when the family sat down at the festive Sabbath table that evening, Erich felt better again, almost as if his uncle and aunt's visit was some kind of good omen.

Perhaps the worst of it's over now, he thought. Perhaps it really is like Uncle Ludwig says. Back in January it was almost worse because you didn't know what was going to happen. But now Senftleben's off to his ministry department in Stuttgart, and Father's business will soon be doing better again. And Kampmann and Heeb and the others . . . well, there are idiots everywhere; Uncle Louis always says so. He felt it was a very solemn occasion this time when he took the bread from the plate with the eyes of God on it, and he even quietly whispered the blessing on the house along with his father as Julius, at the head of the table, spoke the prayer aloud.

> *"Praise be to you, Eternal One, our God, King of the World, who made the fruit of the vine.*
>
> *"Praise be to you, Eternal One, our God, King of the World, you who have sanctified us with your commandments, you who have chosen us, and have given us your holy Sabbath to be celebrated with love and with pleasure. . . ."*

Pesach

DURING VACATION, the days slowly flowed by. Erich missed his friends. Kurt had gone to stay with his godmother in Upper Swabia, and Helmut and his family were on vacation in Merano. Max either lay on his bed devouring adventure stories or ran down to the Jagst with Willi to try fishing with homemade rods. It was a dismal April, with frequent drizzling rain; the clouds parted only occasionally to let a weak spring sun send a few rays down to warm the earth. Erich spent a great deal of his time in the attic watching the drifting clouds through the skylight.

Mother and Fanny had begun the annual spring-cleaning that traditionally took place before Pesach, getting the apartment spick-and-span. It was uncomfortable living in a place constantly dripping with water, where you stumbled over rolled-up rugs, and couldn't find a chair to sit on because they were all stacked upside down on the tables. In addition, the family was living on what Fanny called "short rations," because all the china had to be cleaned too. Max hated the food he had to eat in the week before Pesach, so he went off to Willi's place. Mother was always saying she was sure he was eating "things we aren't allowed."

"They won't hurt him," said Erich, grinning. He didn't observe the dietary laws very strictly himself, and now and then he enjoyed a slice of salami or ham when he went to the Golden Cross inn and butcher shop to fetch the meat Mother had ordered from the Biegs. It was different at home. But Erich often thought you could live pretty well the way the Biegs did, and it was to be hoped the Almighty didn't take the dietary laws too literally either.

Erwin often dropped in to ask Erich to come and play. They hadn't necessarily grown closer, but recent events had brought the two boys together in a way that they couldn't quite explain even to themselves. They played board games lying on their stomachs on the floor of Erich and Max's room, talking about all sorts of things; for instance, their bar mitzvahs, which were to be in October, or their religious studies teacher, Herr Silbermann, who came over from Crailsheim just to give them classes. Studying with him was a strain, because old Silbermann was a real slave driver.

"The others have it easier," said Erwin. "Rudi told me you can just doze off in confirmation classes."

The others, thought Erich. There's us and then there's *the others*. He had never felt like that before, but Erwin was right. In spite of Helmut and Kurt, the others were different. But they never discussed those feelings, or the events of the last few weeks.

* * *

At last the first day of Pesach came, the day of the Seder evening. Early that morning Franziska, the apprentice who worked in the bakery in the building next door, delivered the matzo bread that Frau Levi had ordered. She was a tall, freckled girl about a year older than Erich. When Erich came into the kitchen, still rather sleepy, Franziska was there with Frau Levi, who was giving her a coin and a small present: an embroidered handkerchief. Franziska had blushed when he came in, which filled him with considerable pride. Looking confused, she picked up her basket and put the handkerchief and the coin carefully in her pocket.

"Thank you very much, Frau Levi, and a happy festival to you!" She bobbed a curtsy, and with a shy sideways look at Erich, who was spreading a slice of bread and butter and grinning, she hurried out the door.

"Do you have many more deliveries, Franzi?" Mother called after her, and Erich heard her call back as she ran downstairs. "Only to the other Levis and the Heinrichs, and then I'm through!"

"A nice girl," said Mother, sitting down with Erich. "Hard-working too. She has to lend a hand with everything."

"Well, there has to be *something* good about her," said Erich heartlessly, starting on his bread and butter. "She's ugly as sin."

"Oh, really, Erich!" Melanie Levi was indignant. "I'll pretend I didn't hear that. I like Franzi."

"And she likes you. So do lots of other people, because you're always so generous."

"As one should be," said Mother. "A girlfriend once wrote in my autograph book, 'Do as you would be done by.' Don't laugh, Erich. I hope you'll understand about that later. Now, off with you to fetch that meat."

Sighing, Erich rose from the table and walked the short distance to the Golden Cross. His father, who had fled from the upheavals at home, was in the main room of the inn talking to the landlord over a glass of wine. They had their heads close together and were deep in discussion; the room was already full of blue smoke rising from their cigars.

"Ah, Erich!" the landlord of the Cross greeted him in friendly tones. "How tall you're getting! You'll soon have a grown-up son, Julius."

Erich beamed. His short stature had always annoyed him, but he'd recently grown taller, and Mother had already let down the hems of his trouser legs, saying he'd soon be needing new clothes. Now other people were noticing it too!

"You'll have come for your mother's meat, Erich—just sit down here a minute, the shop is crammed out in front, but Lore will fetch it for you." He went to the door beside the bar and shouted, "Lore, Lore, the Levis' meat, please. Erich is waiting!"

Erich sat down with his father, who was studying the blue smoke rings from his cigar. "Like anything to eat or drink, son?"

Erich shook his head. "I have to get straight back, Mother's waiting. You know what day it is today."

Julius Levi made a face. "These feast days are all very well, but . . ." He did not finish his sentence, and the two Levis exchanged a conspiratorial wink. At that moment little Lore came in, hauling a gigantic package.

"It's bigger than you are." Erich laughed. "Hand it over. And come around to our place later. There'll be fresh matzos." Lore nodded vigorously, and Erich couldn't help smiling. Ever since he could remember, the Levi family's matzos had been a great attraction to their friends and the neighboring children. Frau Levi was always generous with them, and it had become something of a tradition to go and have some of the Levis' matzos. Even though they taste of nothing much, thought Erich, and no one wants to eat them the day after they're baked. But their Christian neighbors felt that they were special.

"Would you like some salami, Erich?' asked the landlord of the Golden Cross slyly, and Erich glanced inquiringly at his father, who laughed and nodded. Next moment he was biting with relish into the large piece of sausage that the landlord, grinning, had held out to him. For years this had been part of a game that the Levis, father and son, enjoyed at least as much as the landlord of the Golden Cross.

In the afternoon, Julius Levi took the handcart and asked Max and Erich if they would like to go to the rail station with him to meet Aunt Mina and Uncle Louis. The brothers were happy to go along. As they left, Erich cast a thoughtful look back at his mother. Melanie Levi looked depressed. Apart from little Lore, few children had come for any of her matzos today.

"People are scared, that's what it is," Julius had said briefly when she mentioned it at lunch. "Look at the newspaper and you won't be surprised." Erich would have liked to ask his father what was in the newspaper that was so special, but out of consideration for Mother and Max he didn't. He'd find a suitable moment to ask Father later.

The black steam locomotive came puffing into Ellwangen's small station, gave a long, drawn-out whistle, and then came to a halt with a squeal. Erich narrowed his eyes and searched the platform up and down. Sure enough, here came

Uncle Louis climbing out of a compartment; he recognized that dark-clad, sturdy figure from a distance, and ran toward him. His uncle helped Aunt Mina out, and then gave Erich a big hug.

"Hey, how tall you are these days!" Erich's uncle held him away by his shoulders and looked hard at him. "You'll be grown up soon!" Then Erich landed on Aunt Mina's ample bosom and was hugged again. The baggage was loaded up on the handcart, and the Levis triumphantly escorted their relations the short way back to their apartment.

Erich walked with Aunt Mina, telling her about school and his good report. In the past he used to hold her hand or link arms with her, but he was too old for that now. Max sat astride their big suitcase and had himself wheeled along by Father and Uncle Louis, who were deep in conversation. Uncle Louis was a cattle dealer like Father, and of course the two men exchanged stories whenever they were visiting.

A few days ago a large notice board in a wooden showcase had been hung on the house opposite the Levis' home. Old Schuster, who owned the building, had agreed to let the local Nazi group put it up. "Better not to look at it," Father had said.

Naturally, Max had gone off promptly the next morning to see the notice board, and Erich couldn't resist taking a peek too. "There's only some kind of a newspaper* on it," Max had told Erich, "with funny pictures too. I don't know what Father's going on about." Erich did. It's to do with us, he thought as he studied the drawings of men with oversized hooked noses.

Now Louis Straus noticed the showcase as he walked past, and indicated it with a tiny movement of his head.

Julius shrugged his shoulders. "The same with you too?"

"Could be worse. It *is* worse in the big cities. Ilse brought us bad news from Heilbronn when she came home on the first of April." Ilse was Uncle Louis and Aunt Mina's youngest daughter. She worked as a laboratory assistant in Heilbronn, in a brandy and liquor distillery. The owner of the firm was Jewish too, and Uncle Louis told Father, lowering his voice, a story of broken windows and a large Star of David painted on the door of the liquor store. Herr Löwenstein, the proprietor, had gone out among the crowd that had gathered in front of the entrance to the distillery, said Ilse, and they abused him, spat at him, even hit him. Ilse had been able to make her own way through the crowd with difficulty, and she had come home that afternoon in tears.

Erich listened intently to all of this, although he knew the conversation wasn't meant for him. He thought of Ilse with her brown curls and the twinkle in her eyes, and how when he was a little boy she was always picking him up and swinging him around until he had a funny feeling in his stomach and had to cry, breathless with laughter, "Stop it, Ilse, stop it!" He couldn't imagine his cousin in tears. He thought of Herr Löwenstein too, though he didn't know him. He imagined him trying desperately to calm the crowd. Perhaps there'd been people he knew in it, people who had respected him in the past. Erich thought how bad it must be for Herr Löwenstein to find that they were his enemies now, although he had done nothing to harm them. Not so many people say hello to us now either, thought the boy, but at least they aren't smashing our windows.

However, no one mentioned such subjects at the Seder evening. The festive table glittered and shone, and Erich felt that it was a solemn occasion. Mother and Fanny had laid the table with the old damask cloth that was very fragile where it had been folded. There was a pattern of grapes and leaves around its hem. It was brought out only on very special occasions because it was a family heirloom—more than a hundred years old—that Mother had inherited from her great-grandmother. The good china and the silver cutlery shone in the candlelight, the richly decorated kiddush goblet stood in front of Father's place, and in the middle of the table Mother placed the Sabbath plate, with the matzos on it protected by a cloth, and the small bowls of special Seder dishes.

The place beside Father was unoccupied as usual, but it was laid with a silver goblet, a plate, and cutlery. Erich knew that the place was set for the prophet Elijah, who foretold the coming of the Messiah. Once, as a little boy, Erich had genuinely believed that they were expecting another guest, and waited impatiently for him to arrive. Max was always afraid of the mysterious stranger who never put in an appearance.

Then the guests arrived: Uncle Sigmund, Aunt Lea, and Erwin, bringing Grandmother Babette with them. Holding herself very erect in her black silk dress, with her white hair neatly pinned up, she looked proudly at her family assembled around the table. The only one missing was her younger daughter Betti, who had married and gone to live in Ulm, but they would remember her in their prayers. As a small child, Erich had always marveled at the ritual of the Seder evening. It seemed like a sequence of mysterious acts with some significance which he couldn't quite grasp, although it had a magic of its own that made it all fit together. Now he knew the meaning of the ritual and of the special foods they ate, yet he could still feel that special magic. He realized, with surprise, that it was comforting to be together at the Seder table, and felt the power behind the words recited in the ritual, which had seemed just a boring necessity to him last year.

When Father began the Haggadah,* reciting the words "This year here—next year in Israel; this year servants—next year free," they suddenly had a very special meaning. And when Max, as the youngest at the table, asked the traditional question, "What makes this night different from all other nights?" they contained something of the comforting certainty of an indestructible hope held in common by all Jews.

Gremm

THE PESACH FEAST was over, spring vacation was coming to an end, and Erich's uncle and aunt had gone home. As they said good-bye, Uncle Louis had taken Erich by the shoulders and said, "See you in the summer, then! And I'll tell Ilse it's a young man coming to visit this year, not a boy who will hide her new shoes and bring mud into the house because he's been building dams down by the river. Or are you so grown-up and superior these days that you won't want to visit your old aunt and uncle during your vacation?" Erich had laughed and denied any such idea. A summer without a visit to Oedheim was unthinkable.

"And give Ilse my love. I won't tease her anymore. I guess I'll still be building dams down by the river—but I'll wipe my feet on the mat afterward."

His uncle had laughed. "Good boy. And don't look so

glum, Erich. These are bad times for us, it's true, but think of the better times to come." Erich sighed inwardly. Father must have told Uncle Louis about Senftleben and about Max, who still wouldn't say what the "bad word" was. Julius and Uncle Louis had talked a great deal in private, while Mother and Aunt Mina had generally banished him from the kitchen when they were doing the dishes or preparing meals, and they too had whispered together. Erich could imagine what they were saying. Business was worse than usual for Uncle Louis too, and he had said to Father over and over again that he didn't understand how people could fall for the Nazis like that.

"Don't buy from Jews, they say, yet I'm known to be an honest, straightforward businessman. But suddenly the farmers I know act as if I had some disease."

Father shook his head. "They're afraid, Louis, simply afraid. Now our maid Fanny is being called names too, just because she works for us, and there's talk of arrests everywhere. People are arrested on the street merely for thinking differently. Protective custody, that's the clever name they've thought up for it. No, people are plain scared, that's what it is."

The next week Fanny came back. She had been away spending Easter with her family in Neunheim. Erich thought she seemed more serious and less cheerful than usual, but she just smiled in answer to his questions and dismissed them with an airy gesture.

School ought really to have begun on Thursday, but there was a day off right away—"Just because it's that scoundrel's birthday," said Julius Levi with contempt. Erich thought that for the first time in his life he had a reason to be grateful to Hitler, whose birthday meant an extra day's vacation. The whole town was flying flags that Thursday—bloodred banners with the black swastika symbol hung from the windows—and toward evening the sound of marching in the square outside the Collegiate Church came into the Levis' apartment. Erich hated the sound of the brass band that played almost every weekend now. Mother closed all the windows, but the sound of the music still came in through the cracks, lingering in the rooms like something slimy. There was no escaping that brass band music, or the metallic voice of Kolbe, the local Nazi leader, as the loudspeaker broadcast it into the apartment. Erich had seen him from a distance a couple of times, a lean figure of medium height with jerky movements, his thin face adorned by a small mustache. Presumably a mustache like that was fashionable in Nazi circles these days. Kolbe's echoing voice always sent Erich fleeing up to the attic, where he buried his head in his hands until twilight came on, and familiar, everyday sounds rose from the street again.

He found that he was looking forward to the first day of school, and seeing Helmut and Kurt. He now proudly wore the school cap for the next grade up as he walked the few steps from home to school, carrying his satchel. His friends were waiting for him on the corner of the courthouse building: Kurt in a good mood and at least a couple of pounds heavier; Helmut tanned and full of news. There were three new teachers, he said, one fully qualified graduate teacher from Stuttgart and two probationers. The friends whispered excitedly. Young teachers were nearly always a good thing.

"So what's this new senior teacher from Stuttgart like?" Erich and Kurt looked at Helmut, who was regarded as an authority on all matters of public interest, because of his father.

"No idea. We weren't there. Krumm just told my father yesterday evening that the new teacher had come to a Veterans' Association meeting and seemed very intelligent and correct."

Intelligent and correct—what did that mean? Erich and his friends raced upstairs to their new classroom. Now that they were in the next grade, they had moved to the first floor. Kampmann and his friends were already waiting at the top of the stairs, wearing their Hitler Youth or Jungvolk uniforms in honor of the day. As they all scuffled for the school desks, Erich feared another offensive remark from that quarter, but Kampmann just looked him over in a condescending way and then moved to occupy the back rows with his friends. The boys' excited whispering suddenly stopped as the door flew open and a tall, thin man entered the classroom.

The students leaped to their feet, and at the back of the room the hands of Kampmann's group shot up in the Hitler salute. The man stood to attention like a soldier, and after a brief moment, raised his own hand, responding to the back rows with a little nod of the head. A deep sigh escaped Helmut, and Erich felt that his friend was looking sideways at him. So we've exchanged Senftleben for this man, he thought, feeling a strange sensation inside him—disappointment together with an emotion that he couldn't explain.

While the man briefly greeted them and introduced himself as their new teacher, Erich had a chance to observe him more closely. He had a thin, angular face; his smooth, dark blond hair was combed severely back, and his part could have been drawn with a knife. As if you could cut yourself on it. Erich jumped when he suddenly heard his name.

"Levi, Erich," the man repeated, going up to the boy, who stammered, "Yes," and stood there, for the new teacher was still right in front of him. Erich noticed him inspecting the other pupils, and then looking at Erwin, who was sitting behind Erich.

"Levi, Erwin," Erich heard the man say, and the grating noise told him that Erwin was jumping up too. "You two are related?" the teacher asked, and Erich replied, after clearing his throat several times, "We're cousins, sir."

"Ah, yes, and obviously of the Mosaic persuasion." A faint giggle passed through Kampmann's group. Erich stayed where he was; there wasn't a word from Erwin. He guessed that something was about to happen. The strange emotion he had felt just now had been fear, and now that fear was stirring inside him like an animal with sharp teeth.

"Levi and Levi, as you clearly belong together, you'd better sit together too. Here in the front row. And that means not just for German lessons with me but for lessons with all my colleagues, do you understand?" Every word was keenly emphasized. It all sounded so clear and final that there could be no further questions, no objections. Erich noticed Helmut beside him, opening his mouth, but only to exhale sharply. Suddenly it seemed, even to Erich himself, logical, in an absurd way, that he should have to sit alone with Erwin in the front row, as if the new teacher had finally passed a sentence that had been hanging over him for a long time.

He packed his satchel and moved forward, seeing, to his horror, that there were tears in Erwin's eyes. The Kampmann gang was watching this spectacle and smirking. But Erich also saw that some of the other boys were sitting there looking grave and upset, and when their eyes met he saw fear, and they bent their heads. Kurt was fiddling with the metal lid of his inkwell as if he might tear it off, but the new teacher didn't reprimand him. Instead, he began the lesson just as if he hadn't noticed the tense atmosphere in the classroom. Erich wasn't listening. He was trying to remember what the teacher had said his name was just now, something beginning with G, a short, harsh-sounding name—Gremm, that was it, Dr. Gremm. He kicked Erwin's foot. His cousin was giving a sigh almost like a sob now and then. Erich thought of the pale blue eyes that had looked at him so coldly, and knew this man was his enemy.

At break it seemed as if an invisible circle had been drawn around him and Erwin. Only Helmut remained with them, eating his sandwich and looking defiant. The others stood to one side, murmuring; most of the boys from Kampmann's group were openly triumphant, many pointing at them and laughing, others whispering to students from the senior grades who were watching with curiosity. As if we were exotic animals in the zoo, thought Erich, desperately trying to have something like a normal conversation with Helmut. Erwin stood with them, letting his eyes wander over the groups of boys. Erich knew he was looking for Rudi, but Rudi had gone off with Kurt.

Somehow or other, the morning passed, a difficult, slow morning. The start of almost every lesson held some new terror. How would the other teachers react? Some of them knew Erich from the younger grades; others were new to him and his classmates. Would there be more sarcastic comments, smug remarks about his and Erwin's Jewish origins as the teachers looked through the register? Would the older teachers who knew them and their friends say anything about the new seating arrangement? But nothing happened. If Erich had been hoping that one of his former teachers would at least ask him or his cousin about it, he was disappointed. They talked about the subjects to be studied, tests in class, homework; they warned or threatened the boys, sometimes they encouraged or praised them, but no one asked a question or made a remark about the two Levis, sitting at the front of the class where the weaker students usually had to sit.

After school Erich ran the short distance back home in a daze without waiting for Helmut or Erwin. He opened the front door as quietly as possible and hurried into his room without a word to Fanny. Once there he flung himself on his bed, burying his face in the pillow. He heard the familiar household sounds outside: Fanny clattering pots and pans, his mother's quiet voice, Max clumping his way upstairs, his breathless, "Hello, what's for lunch today?" A little later he heard Father's firm step, the squeal of the living room door, his parents' murmured conversation. The aroma of the freshly baked challah loaves drifted through the door.

Of course, this was the beginning of the Sabbath. It was a Friday like any other, and yet something entirely out of the ordinary had happened today. Something worse than Senftleben's bullying and Kampmann's provocative remarks, worse than seeing faces turned away when the Levis passed by, even worse than Father's anxious expression as he sat over his account books. It was much worse than any of that, and Erich couldn't say why. He knew just one thing: fear had eaten its way into him, and he couldn't shake it off anymore.

Suddenly he heard the front doorbell ring, and a surprised exclamation from his mother. "Who's visiting now, in the middle of the day?" Footsteps went to the door, and in the distance he heard Aunt Lea's voice, shrill and upset. Breathlessly, he turned over and half sat up. Aunt Lea and Uncle

Sigmund had come, undoubtedly to talk to Mother and Father about what had happened. Voices approached and were then swallowed up behind the living room door as it closed. Then came footsteps, headed toward his door. The handle was pressed down, and he heard Father's voice trying to sound calm and firm.

"Erich? Would you come into the living room, please? Aunt Lea and Uncle Sigmund are here, and we want to talk to you about something." Erich swung his legs off the bed and followed his father. Aunt Lea was sitting on the brown leather sofa. Her eyes were red with crying, she had two circular red spots on her cheeks, and she was crumpling a handkerchief in her hands. Mother was sitting beside her, and Erich saw to his horror that she was crying too. She was holding Aunt Lea's arm, and kept her head bent, but her shaking shoulders gave her away. Uncle Sigmund sat hunched up in an armchair, withdrawn into his thoughts. As Erich came in, however, he straightened up and greeted him with a kindly, "Erich, my boy, come in and sit down with us."

Erich almost imperceptibly shook his head. He had to stay on his feet now so that he could move around, and he was glad to see that Father remained standing beside him, an arm firmly placed around his shoulders.

"Erwin has told his mother and father what happened in school this morning. Why didn't you tell us about it?"

Erich swallowed. How was he to explain to his parents? How was he to tell them that besides the nameless fear, another sensation had been churning about in him for some time: a sensation rather like the shame he felt when he had done something stupid or wrong? He was ashamed of what was happening to them. Even though we can't help it, he thought, I'm ashamed for us, and in a way that's not right either. But he couldn't say these things. Instead, he shrugged his shoulders and lowered his eyes. Father quietly asked him again to tell them, but Erich shook his head. He didn't want to describe what had happened, not at any price, because he felt that talking about it would be like going through the whole thing again.

Father relaxed his grip on Erich's shoulder. "Well, as you like. The situation's clear anyway. Uncle Sigmund and I are going to see Dr. Kaiser today. We don't have to put up with injustice. I thought we had taught you that, Erich. You can go back to your room." The last words were spoken in a stern voice, and Erich realized that his father was disappointed in him.

He would have liked to say something to Mother and Father; for instance, "It's not that I don't trust you or that I'm cowardly. But I didn't know how to tell you. I don't want to worry you. And it's not a case of injustice you can protest about now; it's more than that, much more, and I don't know just what it is, but it frightens me." However, he didn't say any of that. He went back to his room and watched Max through the half-open kitchen door. His brother stared at him wide-eyed, until Fanny gently drew him into the kitchen and shut the door. Erich felt like taking refuge up in the attic, but they'd probably come looking for him any moment.

And sure enough, a little later Mother came in and sat down on the edge of his bed. She patted his cheek affectionately. "Don't take what Father said just now so hard, Erich. He didn't mean it like that. He was very angry, that's all. And then there was Aunt Lea . . . you know how she gets on his nerves."

Erich couldn't help smiling. It was a standing joke in

the family that Julius was inclined to get irritable around his sister-in-law. He blamed her for spoiling and mollycoddling her only son, whom she adored. Of course, all the Levi family thought a lot of their own offspring, and petty jealousies had rubbed off on their children now and then. But now we're tied together for better or worse, thought Erich. What a joke! Mother hugged him firmly and gave him a kiss, although she knew that Erich didn't usually like to be kissed anymore. Today, however, it felt good.

"Mama, I don't want any lunch. May I stay in my room?" he asked, and his mother looked hard at him.

"Very well, go and ask Fanny for something later. I'll make sure I keep Max off your back today." Erich gratefully pressed his mother's hand, and she went off to the kitchen. Once again Erich heard the murmur of voices and the clink of china. He drifted off into a deep, dreamless sleep and didn't wake up again until he heard footsteps in the corridor. For a moment he wasn't sure where he was. Then he rubbed his eyes and saw the slanting rays of the afternoon sun as they fell into the room. The door opened, and Father came in. For a while he stood by the window with his back turned to Erich, staring out at Schmiedstrasse.

"I've just been to see the headmaster with Uncle Sigmund. He called this Dr. Gremm in to explain, in our presence, what he called 'the measure he had taken.'"

Father turned to look Erich in the face. The boy was alarmed. Once again he saw how much his father had aged recently. The two lines at the corners of his mouth were more marked than ever, if possible, making his usually mischievous face look bitter.

"Do you know what Dr. Gremm said? It was for your

own protection, according to him. You two had to be separated from the others, as he put it, to keep you safe from attacks. There had been complaints too, he claimed. Many parents didn't want their children to be in the same class as Jews. Some of the students had complained. He also said that you and Erwin were always bothering the others, so he'd been obliged to separate you for their protection."

Erich couldn't take it in. "What did the Head say?"

"He just sat there in silence. Finally he said, 'So you see, gentlemen, there's nothing I can do for you.' I had the impression that he didn't like any of it, but he was afraid."

"Afraid? Afraid of Gremm? But he's the Head!"

Julius Levi shrugged. "Gremm is a very dangerous man, and not to be underestimated. Highly intelligent and slippery as an eel. A committed Nazi."

Erich could only stare at his father. Julius turned to leave the room, looking weary, with his shoulders hunched. In astonishment, Erich watched him go.

"But you don't seriously believe what Gremm said, do you? About us bothering the others . . . You know I'm good at schoolwork!" However, Father had gone. Horrified, Erich realized that exactly what he'd wanted to avoid at all costs had happened. . . . He had been afraid of seeing his own father look so helpless. The injustice had spread, and even a man like Julius Levi could do nothing about it. Least of all a man like Julius Levi, in fact.

Alone

THE NEW SEATING arrangement remained in force, and there was a subtle change in the behavior of the class over the next few days. Erich realized that the others were avoiding him and Erwin. It wasn't obvious, and it didn't happen all at once, but there were changes. An embarrassed silence when he went up to a group of his classmates at break, open malice from Kampmann and company, even from Kurt. That was what hurt most. Kurt, who always had new excuses now for not getting together with him after school. Kurt, who slipped away at break when he saw Erich walking his way; Kurt, who couldn't look him in the eye anymore. Only Helmut was still his staunch friend, even in the face of mockery and unconcealed threats from the Kampmann gang.

On the last Sunday in April, Erich was walking downstream along the Jagst, deep in thought, off to go fishing with his homemade rod near the men's swimming pool. Helmut had gone to visit relatives with his parents, and Max was deep in his adventure stories again. Erich had just sat down on the slope of the bank and thrown out his line, when a bicycle came jolting along the narrow footpath toward him. Shading his eyes with his hand, he saw that Lutz was riding it. He abruptly turned around again, expecting Lutz to cycle past him without a word, but the bike stopped and footsteps approached. Yes, it really was Lutz. At first he stood there undecided, and then, to Erich's surprise, he sat down on the bank too.

"Hello, Erich, are they biting?"

Erich nodded, and said vaguely, "Not yet." They sat side by side for a while in silence. Lutz pulled up blades of grass and mechanically took them apart. Erich looked sideways at him. Lutz was wearing his Jungvolk uniform: brown shirt and black trousers.

"On duty?" asked Erich at last, unable to bear the silence any longer.

"Yes," said Lutz, visibly relieved. "We're going to decorate the gymnasium hall later. The first of May celebrations are on Monday, and there'll be a big rally in the evening. And our school will be celebrating in the morning." Something else to be grateful to Hitler for, thought Erich bitterly. At least it's another day off lessons, not that I can see what the point is. "Labor Day," and they celebrate it by doing nothing?

He said out loud, "Do you like it in the Jungvolk?"

Lutz nodded enthusiastically. "You bet! We have a lot of fun! Last week we played scouting games and learned how to use a compass. And on Monday evening there's going to be a big bonfire and grilled sausages on the Schönenberg. Then in summer we're going to the Party rally in Nuremberg and staying in a big tented camp. Oh, Erich, it's a real shame you can't be there. You'd love it too!"

Erich gave him a wry grin. "Quite apart from the fact that they would never have taken me, do you seriously think I'd join such a bunch of losers?"

Lutz flushed. "Oh, you mean Kampmann and his friends. He's crazy, that's all. I mean, I couldn't care less about you being Jewish. To be honest, I didn't even really know until recently. And I don't know what people have against Jews, either. My father always says you're honest, decent folk, you Levis and the Heinrichs and the Neuburgers. Last week Kampmann gave us quite a lecture, saying all the Jews would have to get out of Germany because they've brought misfortune on the country. And afterward I told him I didn't see how that could be true, because, after all, your families have been here so long." He looked straight at Erich. "Then Kampmann was furious, and he shouted, 'You get out!' But honestly, I don't have anything against you."

No, you just keep your mouth shut and look away when Kampmann and the others are bullying me, that's all, thought Erich. You and the rest who don't have anything against us. Suddenly he couldn't stay any longer. He rose to his feet and reeled his line in. "Somehow they don't seem to be biting today," he said over his shoulder.

Lutz rose too, brushing his trousers down. "Coming to the gymnasium with me?"

"I kind of think your leaders wouldn't be glad to see me."

"I couldn't care less. After all, we're old friends." He looked defiantly at Erich.

Erich said slowly, "I really wouldn't want to get you into

trouble. Anyhow, I'm going the other way. Thanks all the same."

Lutz turned, his head bowed, and picked up his bicycle. "Good-bye, Erich," he called as he rode away, but Erich didn't reply. He watched him go for a while, his face expressionless, and then set off in the direction of the Kugelberg. Would Lutz really have turned up in his company? How far would his sudden flicker of heroism go? Probably until Kampmann next bawled him out, thought Erich, and he felt angry with himself because he'd been glad of what Lutz said all the same. But I'm not a beggar looking for charity, he thought, and he reached the top of the hill and the Benzenruhe woods out of breath. He'd run all the way as if he had to sweat the anger out of himself. It was up there in the gnarled old oak that little Lutz had once been stuck, wailing miserably. How they'd laughed at the time, and how they'd teased Lutz later!

Erich went to the edge of the woods and looked down at the town. Below him rose the mighty silhouette of the Collegiate Church, with houses surrounding it like sheep clustered around their shepherd. And people go on living there the way they did before, acting as if nothing's happened—like Lutz—while so much is changing all the time, thought Erich. Suddenly he was reminded of the poem they'd read with old Professor Wagner in their German class, the poem about Germany sleeping on downy pillows.

The May Day celebrations were staged as a great spectacle. Erich and Erwin had walked at the very end of the long line of students making for the gymnasium hall, as if that were the only natural place for them. Once there, they sat at the back, although Helmut had insisted that they ought to be with the rest of the class. "That gang won't have time to bully you now," he pointed out, watching Kampmann running about and directing his friends, who had assembled with banners around the speaker's lectern. Gremm, too, was busy, and had gathered some of the younger boys around him. They were probably going to perform something later.

All the same, Erich had turned down Helmut's suggestion. "I don't want to join in anything like this," he whispered in Erwin's ear. His cousin looked blankly at him, and glanced longingly at Rudi, who was sitting a few rows in front of them with Kurt, obviously exchanging jokes. Then it suddenly went quiet, and the clear voices of Gremm's group of boys, trying hard to keep in time, rang through the hall:

"Believe in ancient German pride, as now
the land revives again. Oh, never let your faith
subside, let none your German honor stain . . ."

Do they understand what they're talking about? Erich wondered, looking at the tall figure of Gremm conducting the chorus of speakers. German pride and German honor, what was that supposed to mean to Helmut, Kurt, Lutz, Kampmann, Erich himself . . . ? His eyes fixed on Gremm, and suddenly it seemed as if his gaze was returned and held, even over such a distance, by those pale blue eyes.

"Well, aren't we in luck!" exclaimed Father at lunch, crumpling up the newspaper.

"What do you mean, in luck?" asked Mother, handing Fanny the stacked plates. They had just finished eating, and Julius had picked up his midday cigar and the paper.

"As of yesterday we're living in Hindenburgstrasse, Hindenburg Street. When the town council met yesterday it decided to rename the main streets in Ellwangen. Suppose we'd been living in Lange Strasse, we'd have to give our address as Adolf-Hitler-Strasse now. As it is, we've been given good old Hindenburg. Not too bad at all. And I see that Haller Strasse is Bismarckstrasse now—even better. I'm sure your grandmother will be happy with her new address."

"But why are they renaming the streets?" asked Max.

"The Nazis have a majority on the new town council," Father explained. "So of course they have to show off. Ellwangen's main street renamed after Adolf Hitler . . . If anyone had told me a few months ago that such a thing could happen . . ."

He puffed at his cigar, raising clouds of thick blue smoke, and Mother rushed to open the window.

"But that's not really what I was going to tell you. Max, you go to your room and do some homework. Erich, I want you to come into the living room with your mother and me. We have something to discuss." They all rose, and Max sulkily left the kitchen, followed by the rest of the family. Fanny closed the door behind them and began doing the dishes. In the living room, Erich dropped into one of the deep leather armchairs and looked up at his father. Julius and Mother sat down on the sofa. Ever since the day Julius went to see the headmaster with Sigmund, and they came back without achieving anything, Erich and his father had discussed only trivial matters.

"Erich," said Julius, clearing his throat, "it's about your bar mitzvah. We went to see Uncle Sigmund and Aunt Lea yesterday to discuss it. As you know, your cousin will be celebrating his on the same Sabbath."

Erich nodded. The family had always regarded it as providential that his cousin was born only two days after him; and old Herr Neuburger, who would be ninety next year, was always saying how much it would mean to the tiny Jewish community of Ellwangen for two young men to become adult members of it on the same Sabbath.

"Next week you're going to old Kugler to be measured for your suit. I had my own first tailored suit for my bar mitzvah. I still remember how proud your grandfather Elias was then. And I shall be proud when I see my eldest son in his own suit for the first time." Julius Levi cleared his throat again. "But that's not all we wanted to say to you. The fact is, business is worse and worse these days. I needn't discuss the reasons. So we'll be holding the bar mitzvah here at home and not in the Golden Cross, as we'd planned. Mother and Aunt Lea will make it a good party. The inn is just too expensive, and anyway, we can't invite as many guests as we wanted to in the first place. But of course you can ask your best friends to the party. I hope you'll understand our decision, Erich."

The boy had to swallow several times before he could utter a hoarse "Of course, Father." He and the family had been looking forward to this bar mitzvah so much. It was to be a big party, Father had always said, and his relatives always teased Erich about it.

"I'll take care not to eat anything for three days before your bar mitzvah," Uncle Louis had said several times, adding with a twinkle, "And I can't wait to see you drink your first glass of wine."

Erich called himself to order and swallowed the lump in

his throat. It would be good all the same. The close family would all be there, even if the table in the Levi household was rather smaller and would probably be less lavishly laden than if they were at the inn. Mother's brothers Karl and Ludwig would be there with their wives. Aunt Betti and Uncle Samson, Grandmother and Aunt Mina with Ilse, and of course Uncle Louis would attend as well. You couldn't feel gloomy while he was around. And his friends . . . ? Erich heard himself saying, "I'm sure it will be great, and I'm really looking forward to it. But I don't want to ask any friends."

Melanie Levi looked inquiringly at her son. "Not even Helmut?"

Erich shook his head. "Not even Helmut." He himself couldn't exactly say why he didn't want his best friend there, but he insisted, "Only the family. That will be enough."

As he rose to his feet, Julius clapped his son on the shoulder. "It will be a really good party, you wait and see. We'll celebrate properly in spite of these bad times. I still can't believe that I'll be the father of a grown young man in October. And how pleased the rabbi will be! Perhaps some time we'll have a minyan* in the community without needing outside help."

That evening Erich lay in bed awake for a long time, listening to Max's regular breathing. His brother was enjoying the vocational high school, and so far he'd been spared the worst of the teachers there. He still hadn't told them what that "bad word" was, and Erich didn't press him to say any more. He was glad that Max didn't notice Erich's own problems.

The next day Erich went straight to his room after lunch. He was glad that Max seemed to have left the place to him; his brother's textbooks and homework exercise book were lying on the table untouched. He couldn't get the bar mitzvah out of his head. Why don't I want my friends there, wondered Erich, particularly Helmut? Did he still have any friends at school except for Helmut? Many of the boys he used to play with were in the Hitler Youth organization now, and spent their free time there. And the others, including Kurt, had recently backed out of several dates to meet, on flimsy excuses. Kurt of all people. Kurt, with whom he'd gone through so much, was keeping noticeably aloof. Erich could see his friend's face in front of him, lower lip drawn in, saying a hasty "Sorry, I really can't make it today, Erich. I'm having trouble with my old man just now."

"He's right about that," Helmut told Erich next day as they were strolling down what was now Adolf-Hitler-Strasse. Erich was taking some of Melanie's home-baked marble cake to his grandmother, along with a dozen eggs that Father had been given by a friendly dealer last market day. He had happened to meet Helmut, and Helmut had said he'd go part of the way with him. "He really is in trouble if he spends time with you," Helmut continued. "His old man has joined the Party now, one of what my father calls the opportunists who joined after the elections. And he'd like his son to be a proud member of the Hitler Youth. 'Let me introduce my son and heir—a good Nazi. Career all planned out!' You have to hand it to Kurt, so far he's managed to resist that idea, particularly because Kampmann and his gang get on his nerves so badly. But how much longer . . ."

Helmut didn't finish his sentence, but Erich knew what he was going to say. How much longer could Kurt withstand pressure from home? "Of course no one can be friends with a Jew," Erich exclaimed, clutching the handle of the basket so hard that the wicker cut painfully into his hand.

"That's about it," Helmut concluded.

What kind of answer had Erich expected? At least Helmut was honest. How much longer would *he* want to have a Jew as his best friend? Perhaps a time would come when Helmut's father would tell him it wasn't good for the legal practice for him to be friendly with Jews. Perhaps some of his clients had already said so; possibly veiled or outright hints had been dropped by the local Party leadership. Helmut himself had told him that attorneys in other towns and cities had received many threats for representing the interests of Jewish clients, or of people who criticized the Nazis. This was the kind of thing that Erich feared.

And he wouldn't really belong with us, not on the day of my bar mitzvah, he thought defiantly that evening, with his head buried in his pillows. He imagined what Helmut's face would look like if he gave the invitation. Perhaps his friend would be embarrassed, thank him effusively, and then look for some excuse. "Terribly nice of you, Erich, and I'd really love to come, but . . ." And then there'd be some reason why he couldn't, perhaps a family visit, important guests from out of town . . . and they'd both know that those were only excuses, they wouldn't be able to look each other in the eye. I couldn't bear that, thought Erich. And I couldn't bear to know the truth either, so that's why I'm not even going to invite him. With this thought, he finally fell asleep, as a pale moon cast a narrow strip of light through the gap between the curtains as they billowed gently in the wind.

Your Race

OVER THE NEXT few weeks, Erich and Max sensed another almost intangible change. Father's footsteps were slower, his hair was going gray, and his face looked even thinner. He often shut himself in the living room with Mother. Then Erich could hear their murmuring voices through the door for hours on end. He knew that Father's business difficulties were getting worse and worse, which was confirmed by Peter, who went about his work with increasing gloom.

"Business is bad these days," he confided to Erich, who was helping him muck out the cattle shed one afternoon. Peter thrust the pitchfork angrily into a steaming heap and drew on his cigarette. "If things carry on like this, I'll soon be getting fired. The boss is turning very odd too. There's no saying anything to him these days."

"What about Father's old customers? They were always

happy with their cattle, so he must have plenty of people who still buy from him."

"Not anymore. They're staying away. They're scared. Kolbe up and spoke at the last farmers' meeting. Folk weren't to buy from Jews, he said, and those who did needn't be surprised at what was coming to them. They'd all be on a list. And many of them really do believe the stupid stuff the Nazis talk. Jews are bloodsuckers and so on. Talking to them is like talking to a brick wall."

"Is it really that bad, Peter?"

"Oh, well, I guess I'm just angry." Peter pushed back his cap and scratched his forehead. "There's still a few decent men among them. Schlosser's coming by next week to look at the calves. Then maybe there'll be some money coming in."

Erich leaned the hay fork up against the wall and patted the calves' heads as he went past them. "Good-bye, Peter. I'll look in again tomorrow."

"Thanks for lending a hand, Erich. And don't take what I said badly. Better times will come again."

Erich went the short distance down to the Jagst and looked at the water for a while as it sluggishly flowed by. It hurt to see the spring landscape in bloom and feel nothing but black depression himself. Last year he'd still been playing Indians with his friends in the Benzenruhe woods, or catch in the Rübezahlweg cave. How they'd laughed when old Köberle the forest warden, tanned by wind and weather, had suddenly turned up and shone his flashlight over the walls of the cave, bellowing, "Come out, you young ruffians, come out at once! You know very well that's forbidden!" They'd been hiding at the far end of the cave behind some rocks, and they watched, giggling quietly, as he went away again grumbling and muttering, because Köberle was something of a coward and never ventured far into the cave. It was mainly Kampmann's fault that Erich's old friends were avoiding him these days. He had seen Kampmann a couple of times speaking to anyone who'd been talking to him or Erwin. Helmut was the only one Kampmann didn't dare approach; and he'd been leaving Kurt alone recently, ever since Kurt shook a clenched fist in his face a few days ago. All the same, the bond between Erich and Kurt was broken, and Erich often thought of what Helmut had told him.

Suppose my own father told me I couldn't be friends with certain people, Erich sometimes thought. Suppose I could only go around with Catholics and I wasn't supposed to mingle with Evangelicals, how would I react? Kurt was Evangelical, but the question of which church he went to had never been important. Again and again he wondered if it were possible to believe something so firmly that you were ready to do the stupidest and most unjust things for it. A man like Gremm, for instance, who was so clever and knew so much—why was he so inflexible? Erich could have listened to him forever when he talked to them about *The Lay of the Nibelungs* in class. The others grumbled about "that old stuff," but Erich immersed himself enthusiastically in the world of the legend, and spent hours thinking about the betrayal of Siegfried, and Brünhilde's revenge; Hagen of Tronje; the fair Kriemhild; and the fall of the Burgundians. He bought a book of the old Germanic sagas of gods and heroes with the money his relatives had given him at Pesach, and devoured the fascinating stories for several afternoons on end.

But then they had several lessons in German class as well about *The Lay of the Nibelungs*, and it began to seem that this pleasure too would be spoiled for him. For instance,

Gremm made casual remarks in passing about the "vigor of the Nordic race," as illustrated by the poem, and another lesson turned into a long monologue on "the relationship between the races in our country today," which Gremm, hovering over Erwin and Erich, delivered in his characteristic drawl, emphasizing the salient points. There were some smirks and malicious whispered comments when he made such remarks, although Erich couldn't quite make out what was really being said. But he faced them down and bravely tried to contribute to the discussion, putting his hand up all the time, although Gremm almost always ignored him. However, he didn't give up; he wanted to show the new teacher what he could do. After all, he'd been best in the class at German with old Wagner, and one of these days Gremm must surely realize that he had misunderstood him.

In a lesson on a very hot, sunny Monday, when the fragrance of the blooming chestnut trees in the church square came in through the open classroom windows, Gremm turned to Hagen of Tronje's decision to kill Siegfried. He asked the class whether that decision was logical and unavoidable. The students said nothing and shuffled awkwardly, although some assumed expressions of great interest, hoping they wouldn't be called on to answer. Others looked longingly out of the window, probably wondering when it would be warm enough to swim in the Jagst this year. Glancing behind him, Erich saw Helmut, whose bowed head and constantly moving right hand showed that he was doodling on the cover of his exercise book. He always did that when he was bored. But the question had electrified Erich. He had often thought about the question when he lay in bed in the evening, arms linked behind his head, while twilight darkened the narrow rectangle of the bedroom window. In the midst of the long silence, his hand shot up, and to his surprise he heard his name. Gremm had actually called on him to speak!

He stammered slightly as he began, but then his voice grew firmer, and he spoke faster and faster, realizing to his own surprise how the words were pouring out of him. He thought there could have been other ways around the problem, he said; for instance, why didn't Hagen ask Siegfried to explain himself? And why didn't he challenge him to single combat, man to man? Then the matter could have been decided in an honorable duel. As it was, Hagen had acted with malice, said Erich, adding that he thought the treasure he sank in the Rhine afterward had played a part. Hagen of Tronje was envious and treacherous. Erich stopped abruptly, suddenly feeling that all eyes were on him. Gremm was standing in the corner of the room, leaning against the wall, one leg casually crossed over the other. After a moment, the eyes of the boys all moved to him. Gremm remained silent, apparently giving his undivided interest to the contemplation of his shoes. Then he raised his head, and a thin smile curled his lips. He went up to Erich and turned those pale blue eyes right on him.

"Just the kind of answer I would have expected from a member of your race."

That was the word he always used in class. This time, however, he emphasized it differently. "*Your* race."

And then came his verdict, brief and cutting. He said that Erich completely failed to understand the Germanic concept of loyalty; the fact that Hagen had sunk the treasure in the Rhine symbolized the warrior's purity of mind. The un-German, rapacious, profit-seeking spirit of certain other races was completely alien to him, said Gremm. Then he took out his much-feared little black book and wrote something in it.

"This special contribution of yours, Levi, will earn you a special mark. A very bad one, I am afraid, because your contribution to the discussion shows that you understand nothing at all of German culture. I am grateful to you, all the same! You have shown us how important it is to pursue the development of our national spirit, while firmly disassociating ourselves from the blood of an alien race and rejecting it. Sit down, Levi!"

Erich obeyed. It wasn't until he sat that he noticed how his knees were trembling. He couldn't make much sense of what Gremm had said. He had understood only one thing: he was bad and he didn't understand anything because he was a Jew. The Jews were bad. An alien race . . . *your* race. And the others had taken it that way too; he could see that from their malicious expressions and all the whispering and murmuring. He was right, all the same. What kind of loyalty and honor did you show by murdering a defenseless man? And Helmut at least thought so too, he was sure of that. But Helmut didn't say anything; he had propped his chin on his hands and was looking out the window. As for Kurt, he was sitting with his arms crossed and a dark expression on his face, while Lutz was glancing uncertainly from Erich to Gremm and back again, looking as if he might burst into tears. Erich sneaked a glance at his cousin. Erwin was white around the nostrils as he sat there rigidly. Then he leaned toward Erich and hissed in his ear, "Keep your mouth shut next time. He only wants to tell us off, and you're giving him the chance."

Erich swallowed. Perhaps his cousin was right. Perhaps it was better to lay low and play dead, hoping that it would all pass over some time. But I *am* right all the same, he thought defiantly. Never mind what Gremm says.

After school he hurried home across the square and shut himself in his room without a word to Mother or Fanny. He went to his bedside table, took his treasured book of stories from the sagas, and began to tear it up systematically. It was hard work, because it was well bound, and he had to cut up the cover with scissors and a paper knife, but Erich was thorough, driven by a rage that he could hardly understand. Finally the floor was covered with snippets of paper both large and small. Erich dropped onto his bed, feeling more tired than he had ever been, burned out. After brooding for a while he fell asleep, and was woken by his mother knocking at the door and calling him.

Confused and disorientated for a moment, he opened the door, and Mother came in. She said nothing about the sight before her, nor did she ask any questions. Hugging her son close, she sat with Erich on the edge of the bed for a while. Then she looked lovingly into his eyes and said calmly, "Clear all this up, Erich. Ask Fanny for a dustpan and brush. And then come to eat."

She left the room, and Erich kneeled on the floor to collect the scraps of paper. Sometimes names looked up at him, and he knew which stories they came from. Without really knowing why, he began trying to put the snippets of paper together like a jigsaw puzzle, and the stories came into view again on the carpet, or at least parts of them. Lost in thought, he read the quarter pages or half pages that he had roughly fitted together. There was the bit about Beowulf fighting the dragon, and there was the saga of Walther and Hildegund, part of the episode when Walther reaches the court of King Attila.

Then he found some snippets from the very beginning of the book, about the gods and the creation and end of the world. With difficulty, he deciphered them:

> *. . . the bright stars fell from the sky.*
> *Smoke and fire was everywhere,*
> *And great heat.*

For a while he stared at these laboriously reconstructed lines, and tried to find the missing pieces of paper. Then he swept them all up and threw them in the waste bin.

A Trick

THE FOLLOWING WEEK, Gremm announced that the class was to write an essay on *The Lay of the Nibelungs* as a test in school next Friday. As the boys groaned, he said quietly but very firmly, "And I expect each of you to do his best with this of all subjects. A German boy must know what it means to put loyalty and self-sacrifice ahead of all personal interests. So don't disappoint me!"

"Gremm and the garbage he talks!" said Helmut crossly as they walked over the square after school. Kurt followed a little way behind, looking upset and kicking small stones.

"Why would I want to know about those old Germanic heroes? I'm in trouble now," Kurt grumbled. "I haven't even really read that stuff. Can I copy from you next week?" he asked Helmut.

Kurt had recently gone to sit next to Helmut because his

previous neighbor, Kühnle, a sturdy boy with a round face, had joined the Kampmann gang too. Like the others, he attended Hitler Youth meetings and strutted proudly in the uniform. Since his missionary talk was getting on Kurt's nerves, Kurt had asked permission to sit next to Helmut, and it was graciously granted. "Though not willingly," Gremm had said. "In fact, very reluctantly." And he added, with his sharp gaze turned on Helmut, "But I hope you will be able to avoid certain negative influences." Now Rudi, who used to sit next to Erwin, sat beside Kühnle, and Kampmann and the gang were trying hard to recruit him.

By now the boys had reached Helmut's house and said good-bye to Kurt, who went off sullenly when no one took any notice of what he had said. Erich was going on home too, but then suddenly stopped and went back to his friend.

"Helmut," he said, in a quiet voice, "your father has a big library. Do you think I could borrow a book about *The Lay of the Nibelungs?*"

"What do *you* want with that old stuff?" Helmut asked. "Okay, then. Come on in and I'll ask him."

They entered the large, cool hall of Helmut's parents' house together. It was one of the finest buildings on the church square. Erich loved the huge, curving staircase with its forged iron handrail and the beautiful stucco work on the ceiling, showing chubby-cheeked putti smiling at visitors at regular intervals as they climbed the stairs. Up in the Nolls' apartment, Kati the maid told them that Dr. Noll was in an important meeting and mustn't be disturbed, but Frau Noll was in the living room.

"Right, we'll go and ask Mother," said Helmut, giving Erich an encouraging nudge. They entered a large room with

windows looking out on the square. Through the fine net curtains you could see the outline of the church, looking different
and far away from this angle. Erich hadn't been to his friend's
home many times, for the Nolls and the Levis didn't mix in
the same social circles. But he liked the atmosphere here very
much—that cool distinction, and a certain aura of withdrawal,
had always made a great impression on him. That was what
he'd like for himself someday—a house with a cultivated
atmosphere. He admired the Nolls' cherrywood furniture and
the curving armchairs with their sloping legs, the high chairs in
the dining room with their carved backs, and all the things
standing on the chests of drawers around the walls—cande-
labras, silver picture frames with portraits of Helmut's fore-
bears and family wearing fixed smiles, brightly colored vases—
he gazed at them all with reverent awe.

Kurt didn't share his feelings, and said he was terrified
to move about the place because you could break something at
any moment. "At the Nolls' it's like being in a museum," he
said.

Frau Noll, a slender, thin-lipped woman with carefully
waved hair, gave him a friendly but distant greeting. She didn't
like it when Helmut brought friends home, disturbing her
domestic peace and quiet, as she put it, and that was another
reason why the boys seldom visited. Erich often wondered how
she spent her days; after all, she had several servants, and
Helmut was her only son. But he preferred not to ask his friend.
At Helmut's request, she decided, speaking in a quiet voice
with a slightly nervous note, that his father probably wouldn't
mind if they used the library. "But be quiet and don't leave it
untidy."

"We promise," said Helmut, who made faces as he led

his friend out of the sitting room. Erich had seen the library only once before, when he was visiting and Helmut's father had shown them a particularly valuable first edition with a title that he couldn't remember now. Herr Noll had bought the book at an auction and was very proud of it, but his lecture only bored Helmut and Erich. He now let his eyes wander again in amazement over the walls with bookshelves going up to the ceiling. Helmut found the wooden ladder and climbed up to one corner. "Let's see. My father and his neat and tidy habits! There must be something here. What exactly are you after?"

Erich shrugged. "I don't really know. A book about *The Lay of the Nibelungs* or something."

Helmut moved the ladder a little way. "Let's try literary history. There's sure to be something about it there. Oh, look, here we are!" He climbed down again with two fat books, which looked very old and had leather backs, already very worn. Erich read the titles out loud, stumbling over them slightly. "'*Weillmar: History of German National Literature. Von der Hagen: Preface to the Lay of the Nibelungs.*' That sounds just right. Thanks, Helmut."

He put the books carefully in his school satchel, promised yet again to look after them, and said good-bye to his friend, who stood at the top of the stairs. He ran the short way home, feeling elated. It was obvious that Helmut thought his behavior was odd. He had looked sideways at him several times, and seemed to have a great many questions on the tip of his tongue. But he hadn't asked them, and Erich was grateful to him for that.

He ate a fast lunch, barely noticing that Fanny had remarkably swollen eyes today and was silent. Erich hardly reacted to Max's questions, and was thankful when his brother said he was going to his friend Willi's that afternoon. Willi had recently been given a bicycle too, and Frau Levi was afraid the two friends would go racing down the Alte Steige, where Willi lived, and have an accident, but Max assured her they wouldn't.

So Erich had the boys' room to himself that afternoon, and buried himself in the two books, which did indeed contain long essays on *The Lay of the Nibelungs*. He'd show Gremm he knew something about German culture even if he was a Jew. He'd write the best essay of all. Gremm would be amazed. He could already see him, leaning on the teacher's lectern, Erich's exercise book open in his hands. "Levi, you have surprised me," he'd say, and then he, Erich Levi, would be asked to read the essay aloud, and the others would be astonished; even Kampmann would keep his mouth shut. He fantasized as he studied the essays in the book. There was a good deal that he didn't understand, but after a while he noticed that the ideas Gremm had mentioned were in here too. He copied some passages out and learned them by heart. "Masculine loyalty . . . friendship unto death . . . self-sacrifice . . . the heroic cast of mind . . . pride in the Fatherland and its people . . ." He read, wrote, fitted it all together, and found that he had something like the draft of an essay there.

Very pompous, but it does somehow sound like Gremm too, he thought, pleased. And these are old books, they must be written by authorities on the subject, so Gremm can't object. He put away the draft of his essay in the back of his desk drawer. Over the next few days he learned it by heart. He could hardly wait for the day when the essay was to be written in school.

On Friday morning Gremm entered the classroom with

a stack of exercise books under his arm, and began writing the subject on the blackboard in ornate letters. Erich was inwardly delighted—the phrasing of the subject instantly leaped to his eye. "The Nibelung Concept of Loyalty"—just as he'd expected. Gremm wanted to know what they understood by that concept, taking into account the characters and action of the story. Twenty-two heads bent over their exercise books, and there were some dismayed groans and quiet whispering, to which Gremm immediately put a stop.

Erich looked around. Lutz was scratching his ear with his penholder, Kurt was drawing squiggles on his blotting paper, and Erwin was biting his nails. All was still now, and you could only hear the pen nibs scratching the paper. Erich bent his head over the exercise book and began writing down what he had memorized. Gremm, walking around the classroom, suddenly stopped beside him and leaned on the desk, his arms folded, one leg in front of the other. It seemed to Erich as if his eyes were burning a hole in the back of his neck, and he suddenly felt hot all over. Beads of sweat ran down his neck, and he bent over his exercise book to hide what he had written from that gaze.

Suddenly a hand took his own left hand, which he had been holding over the writing, with gentle pressure. Gremm leaned over his shoulder and read, frowning. The boy looked up at his teacher, and his left hand—which Gremm was still holding—shook. Gremm drew in his lips just for a short moment, and then moved the corners of his mouth in a small, ugly smile. He let Erich go and rubbed his hands together, as if the touch had tainted them. Then he went to the front of the class again and sat at his desk. Erich continued to write. Sweat was still running down his neck, but he calmed down as he wrote on. One thought was hammering away in his head: I'll show you, just wait, I'll show you. . . .

When he had written the last sentence he closed the exercise book without reading the essay through, as if he were afraid of the words he had been writing down so industriously. He was the first to hand in his essay. Hesitantly, he went up to the desk, laid the exercise book on the front right-hand edge, and looked timidly up at Gremm, who didn't look back at him, but just nodded his head to indicate that Erich was dismissed.

Outside, Erich sat down on the steps and took a deep breath. A few passersby were crossing the church square. It would soon be midday, and the sun was already high above the green-gold tops of the chestnut trees. A few boys were standing on the square in front of the gymnasium, where the ground sloped down, smoking and exchanging pictures, looking at the photos and grinning. To Erich's right, the gable of the gray building where he lived rose into the blue sky of noon. Smoke was rising from the chimney. Fanny would be preparing lunch. Any moment now his father would appear to the right of the square in front of him, coming from the cattle sheds. Lean and of medium height, immaculately dressed as always, Julius Levi would take off his hat in a friendly greeting now and then, and anyone coming toward him would nod, or perhaps turn his head away, or even cross to the other side of the street. Fewer and fewer people greeted the Levis these days.

Erwin had told him, whispering during one of the last lessons, that his mother had been crying because her best friend had asked her to stop speaking to her openly in the street. Erich could just imagine it. And farther off, hardly visible from where Erich was sitting, there was that notice board in the showcase, the one he wouldn't look at—but other people did.

Kübler, a thin boy with a slight stammer who had some-times joined Erich and his friends in their games, had been told off in the last math lesson. Bönninger the math teacher had taken away his exercise book, in which he had been scribbling for some time. But then he had given it back without further comment, showing the fateful page to the class first. Many boys giggled, some looked at their desks, embarrassed. The picture, though poorly drawn, was easily recognizable as a fat man sit-ting on a globe with his legs apart and holding a bag of money. The nose was grotesque and hooked, the eyelids drooped heav-ily over the eyes, and there was no way anyone could mistake the Star of David above his head.

Just like the pictures in that showcase, Erich had thought, clenching his fists when Bönninger didn't say any-thing to Kübler. He was another who knew how to go with the flow, Helmut had once said mockingly. But now I've shown them, thought Erich. I just can't wait to hear what Gremm will say.

For the next few days he waited impatiently for the essays to be given back. He was hoping for some remark from Gremm, a hint, a sign. But Gremm preserved that icy, wounding civility of his, and still ignored Erich when he put up his hand. On the day after they wrote the essay in class, he had taken the books back to the Nolls', and returned them to Helmut's father him-self.

"Helmut has just gone to see his grandmother," Herr Noll told him. "But do come in, we can have a little talk all the same." He led Erich into the sitting room and took the books from him. "I've heard about your interest in German literature.

It does you credit to be reading such weighty tomes of your own accord, my boy!" Erich felt ashamed of himself. If Herr Noll only knew the real reason. . . .

Helmut's father began telling some anecdotes of his own school days, and Erich laughed dutifully. After a while, however, they began talking about their favorite books, and Herr Noll said that when he was Erich's age he too had been fascinated by the old sagas. Erich felt himself go red, and in his enthusiasm he talked a lot about the hero tales, while Herr Noll listened attentively. When the boy cautiously mentioned what he and Gremm had argued about, Herr Noll rose to his feet and went to the chest of drawers to get himself a cigar. Erich thought he saw a vein pulsing at his temples.

"Yes, Helmut told me about that argument. Not that it can really be called an argument. Listen to me, my boy, you're thinking along the right lines. Don't let all this talk of Nordic races and heroic courage and ancient Germanic virtues lead you astray. The stories of Siegfried and Hagen and Kriemhild are wonderful tales. They have everything—love and treachery, courage and death, all that goes to make up human life. And of course there are alternatives to murder—there always are. In fact the poet shows just what happens when we give way to evil, greed, and envy, and lack the courage to change and forgive. So don't let this stuff delude you," and as he spoke he slammed his hand down on the stacked books that he had put down on a delicate little antique table in front of him, making dust fly. "This stuff that they're flinging in the faces of you young people these days. Let me tell you what I always tell Helmut: I think poorly of any kind of honor and loyalty that means I have to kill other people, or go and get myself killed either. You want to live, and to live a good life, and that means respecting fellow human beings and their opinions!"

Erich's heart felt lighter. As long as there were people like Herr Noll, no one really had anything to worry about. If only more people thought the way he did. And he had said that he, Erich Levi, was right!

On the way home, however, his heart sank again. In his enthusiasm he had betrayed his own opinion! Hadn't he poured out the same stuff; even worse, hadn't he copied it and cheated, adopting other people's ideas, ideas he himself didn't believe in, just to impress Gremm? What was he trying to prove? That he, a Jewish boy, could feel, think, and write that way too, be just as wrongheaded in his ideas? As he climbed the creaking steps to his parents' apartment, he felt like a traitor, except that he wasn't quite sure exactly who or what he had betrayed.

Disaster struck next day. The last lesson was German, and Lutz, posted by the door as a lookout, announced to the class, "Here comes Gremm! With the essay exercise books!" The boys stood by their desks as Gremm entered the room. For a moment his eyes wandered over the class; they lingered on Erich for a fraction of a second, and then his outstretched right arm shot up in the Hitler salute, and he said curtly, "Heil Hitler! Sit down."

He put the stack of exercise books down on his desk, then picked up book after book to return it to its owner with a brief remark. Kurt had just scraped by with a "Fairly satisfactory." Gremm said he had been plain lazy. Others looked glum too. Even Kampmann hadn't done particularly well, which surprised the others, because he was the one who had been championing this very subject.

Even stranger was the fact that Gremm gave the second to last exercise book back to Helmut, with the brief comment, "The best essay. Well done, Noll. Fluently written and logically argued, even if I don't agree with everything you say. However, I am always able to respect independent thinking." The class whispered, and many were surprised. Helmut was always among the best, yes, but everyone knew that he and Gremm didn't exactly get on well. Appreciative glances were cast his way, although Helmut didn't seem to notice them, but just put his exercise book away in his satchel.

Meanwhile, Erich's heart was thudding. There was only one exercise book left on the desk, his own. It couldn't be the best essay, Helmut had written that, but it could hardly be coincidence that theirs were the last two essays to be given back.

"And now for you, Levi!" Gremm picked up the exercise book in his fingertips and went over to Erich. Suddenly all was perfectly quiet in the classroom. The boys were staring at the front row and holding their breath. Gremm held the exercise book by one corner between his thumb and forefinger, as if it were something he didn't like to touch. "I have been wondering whether to read aloud some passages from this shoddy piece of work, so that the class could hear what you have written for themselves. But I can hardly ask that of any of you." So saying, he suddenly let go of the exercise book and it dropped on Erich's desk half open, with crumpled pages and a piece of blotting paper falling out. "Our Herr Levi here has been copying, copying whole passages from books which he presumably did not think I would know. He was wrong! And he made a pitiful mess of the whole thing. You have given conclusive proof of what today is the usual opinion of your race, my dear fellow. Unable to create anything of your own, you lie and cheat.

Exploiting and battening on others has become second nature, so to speak, to your people. But now, thank God, there is an end to all that! Even the worst mark, Levi, is too good for you."

As if numbed, Erich listened to this diatribe, unable to take it in but understanding the essence of it. Gremm had realized that he was cheating—and yes, it *had* been cheating. And he had talked about "race" again. Had said terrible things about "his race." Liars and cheats, exploiting others. The words echoed on and on in his ears.

He felt as if he were in a fever for the rest of the lesson. He noticed Erwin moving away from him; he kept hearing whispers behind him. Then a crumpled piece of paper hit the back of his neck, and another and another. All the same, he kept his head bent over his book, dared not look up, hardly dared to breathe. Gremm, unmoved, went on talking and didn't seem to notice the volley of paper. At last the bell came to set him free, a long, shrill note that went through him like a knife. Now he had to cover the endless distance from the classroom along the corridor to the way out, then over the church square, and then home into the sheltering dark of the stairway, where it was cool and quiet, and the heavy front door kept the outside world away. He slowly packed his satchel. Apart from him there were only a few boys left in the room, and they looked at him sideways and then hurried out. Erwin had already slipped through the door, and Kurt had been one of the first to rush out of the classroom. But the worst of it was that Helmut hadn't waited for him.

The Bad Name

LEADEN-FOOTED, he went down the stairs to the big porch, and there they all were, standing in two rows at the bottom of the steps, legs apart, hands on their hips or in their trouser pockets. Their satchels lay in a heap between the steps and the wall of the gymnasium. Kampmann and Heidt, fat Müller and Kühnle, thickset and knock-kneed, Schluffi and Gabler, his former friends from elementary school, even Lutz was there, though hanging back slightly in the second row. Other boys from the class were standing undecided to the left and right of the steps.

From very far away, Erich heard the noise of the market traders taking down their stalls and wheeling their carts away. He remembered that Father was at the market today and could come around the corner any minute. This thought kept him going. He stopped for a moment on the last step, took a deep breath, and then tried to push past Kampmann, who was standing at the very front. Kampmann stepped to his left, barring Erich's way. Then he raised his right hand and hit Erich in the face as hard as he could. Curiously, Erich felt nothing at all at first; he just noticed something warm running over his mouth. He raised his arm to wipe it off, and looked in surprise at the sleeve of his jacket, which was now all red. Kampmann stepped aside, Heidt came forward and punched Erich in the stomach. Erich staggered, hands pressed to his belly. Someone kicked his shin, his calf, and suddenly a voice broke the silence that had been weighing on them all, saying loud and clear, "Jewish swine."

Then another boy said it, and yet another; all of a sudden it was a whole chorus. Erich ran away from them, heading for his home across the marketplace, still bent double and bleeding. "Jewish swine, Jewish swine!" The words rang in his ears. Several passersby stopped, shaking their heads; many of them laughed. Frau Bieg came running out of the Golden Cross in alarm, crying, "Erich, for heaven's sake, what happened to you?" But Erich took no notice of her, he just ran on until at last he had reached the heavy iron door that led to the back entrance of his building, and pushed it open with his last remnant of strength. Up in the apartment he barely made it to the bathroom before throwing up in the basin. Then he felt something cold being laid over the back of his neck. Someone gently wiped his face with a washcloth and led him with gentle pressure to his room, where he was carefully guided to the bed. After a while he opened his swollen eyelids and saw Mother and Fanny standing at his bedside.

"Don't talk, Erich," said his mother, placing her forefinger on his lips. "Just lie there and rest. I'll bring you a cold cloth." Only now did the boy notice the dreadful burning on his cheek and mouth and the dull pressure in his stomach. His legs hurt too. Fanny laid a fresh cold compress on the swollen half of his face. He gave her a grateful nod, and managed to get out, "I'll be all right."

Mother kept putting fresh compresses on, and after a while the worst of the pain went away. "It's not so bad. I was just in a fight."

"Martha says several of them set on you all at once." Martha was Frau Bieg, the proprietor of the Golden Cross.

"Then she wasn't looking properly."

"She said they were calling names too." Julius looked inquiringly at his son.

Erich lowered his head. "That's right. A . . . a bad name."

"What did they say, Erich?" The question came from Max. Unnoticed, he had come in and was standing in the doorway, eyes wide as he looked at his brother.

"Go away, little pest. None of your business," said Erich.

"But I want to know."

There was silence for a moment; then Julius Levi said quietly, "They said 'Jewish swine,' Max. We have to tell you, because you could hear that too some time."

"I already have." Max had come closer and was clutching the edge of the bed. "That's the bad name they called me at elementary school that time. I didn't want to tell you."

Julius picked up his younger son and sat down on the edge of Erich's bed with him. "People who call such names are stupid, remember that, Max. Stupid, simpleminded people."

"Are they bad people too? I never would have thought some of them would be like this."

Julius hesitated. "Some of them are bad. But mostly they're just stupid. Now, tell us what happened, Erich. You've been badly beaten up."

Erich let himself lie back again and pressed the cloth to his face to gain time. He was in a bind. There was no way he wanted to tell Father about his essay. But how else was he going to explain why the Kampmann gang had attacked him? Trying to sound calm, he said, "It really wasn't that bad, Father. Just a fistfight. And I came off worst, but don't make a big deal about it. What they said . . . well, I don't think they knew what they were shouting about. Like you said, a lot of them are plain stupid."

Julius Levi didn't seem convinced. He sat with Erich for a while, indecision on his face, and then took Max's hand and said, "Come on, Max, we'll leave your brother in peace now. Try to eat something, Erich."

They ate lunch in a subdued mood. Julius cracked a few jokes, trying to dispel the gloom. He compared Erich to the famous boxer Max Schmeling, and speculated on the success he'd have with women with those injuries, which made the family laugh, though mainly out of consideration for Father's feelings. Erich knew they were skating on very thin ice. His father didn't believe him, he knew that, and his mother, too, seemed to guess that there was more behind the incident than he admitted. After lunch he slunk off to his room again, grateful to the family for leaving him alone. He sat down at the big table where he and Max did their homework and tried to concentrate on an arithmetic exercise. But he couldn't do it. Restless as a caged tiger, he paced up and down the room, and stared down at the hurry and bustle on Hindenburgstrasse. Everyday life as he knew it was going on down there: cars drove along beeping at pedestrians crossing the road, women hurried past with shopping baskets; he recognized boys from school coming away from afternoon coaching in small groups, and the girl apprentice in the bookshop opposite was putting up a poster, probably an invitation to attend one of those rallies that were being held all the time these days.

Erich was deep in thought when Fanny opened the door without knocking and said, "Helmut's here!" Erich spun around, heart thudding, and saw his friend standing in the doorway.

Helmut came in. "You're quite a sight! They really beat you up."

"How did you know?"

"Kati told me. She was shopping in the Golden Cross. Poor Martha Bieg was in a terrible state. So many against one— she said it was shocking."

They were both silent for a moment. Helmut had taken his cap off when he came in and was kneading it in his hands. Erich, still standing by the window, looked at the floor. But then he came out with the question that bothered him even more than being beaten up outside school. "Why didn't you wait for me?"

Helmut looked at him, held his gaze, and then said firmly, "Because I was furious. To be honest, I was really furious with you!"

"Because I copied out of your father's books?"

Helmut nodded. "Exactly. After all, you deceived us too—Father and me. But what really makes me mad is you making yourself look bad like that. It must have been just what Gremm and Kampmann wanted. Of course it's bad that they beat you up, but . . ." Helmut didn't finish his sentence. It hung there in the room, echoing, and made the distance between the two boys seem greater.

In his head, Erich finished the sentence: ". . . but you were asking for it." And that was even worse than his burning cheek or the ache in his stomach—his friend didn't understand, perhaps even despised him.

Helmut seemed to sense the gulf that had opened up between them too, because he came closer and said, almost pleading, "Why did you do it? Explain, Erich, please. I mean, I know you. I'd like to understand, that's all."

Erich shrugged his shoulders. How could he explain something that he didn't really understand himself? How could he talk about his experiences, the hurt that his friend knew nothing about, that would always be alien to Helmut? How could he explain his longing to be liked and respected again? And how could he talk about the shame that was a part of his life now, and the animal fear that something was happening to his family and how they had no power over it? He just shrugged and said in an offhand tone, "I don't exactly know why either. But it's not as bad as all that. Other people copy too."

Helmut looked disappointed. "Yes, we copy from each other. That's fair enough. But what you did is different. You prepared it way ahead. I call that cheating—cheating the rest of us too. If Gremm hadn't noticed, if he'd given you a good mark, I'd have—well, I'd kind of have felt it wasn't right."

Erich stared at his friend incredulously. "After today I'm not sure whether I'll ever get a good mark from Gremm. Or rather, I *am* sure! You heard what he said."

"But I got an 'Excellent' too, even though I didn't put any of his drivel in."

"Yes, well, *you*!"

"Erich, it still wasn't right. You of all people have to be especially careful!"

Suddenly Erich felt very hot. Rage rose within him, uncontrollable fury. "What do you mean, I of all people have to be careful? What are you trying to say? Do I have to be nice and good just because I'm a Jew? Don't attract attention, that's what you mean. Keep ducking, keep knuckling under, right?"

"Erich, you're crazy! I didn't mean that at all."

"Then what *did* you mean?"

Helmut hesitated. "You want to watch out because Gremm has it in for you, that's all I meant."

"And why does he have it in for me? Because I'm a Jew. And you're still defending him. Him and the others. I can tell you one thing: he bought your support today with that good mark. There can be other opinions, you'll say? Don't make me laugh! You just don't get it."

"Oh, garbage!" Helmut put his cap on with a brusque movement. "It's no use talking to you today. You could at least say you're sorry you did it."

"I'm not sorry. Maybe that's just the way I really am!"

Helmut looked at him, baffled. "What do you mean by that?"

"Maybe I really am a cheat. Gremm said it's in our blood. Did you ever think about that?"

Helmut stood there rooted to the spot for a moment, then turned and left the room, slamming the door behind him.

Soon after that Fanny put her head around the door

and asked, "What's the matter with young Noll today? He's usually so polite. Now he just marches out without a word. Have you two been quarreling?"

Erich didn't answer right away. He stared out at the street, where Helmut appeared a moment later. Hands dug into his trouser pockets, he was almost running into the town. Only when Fanny came closer did Erich say, looking at her over his shoulder, "Nothing too serious. Perhaps he just doesn't feel comfortable here anymore."

Fanny was astonished. "What on earth do you mean? He's your best friend. What's going on today?"

Instead of giving her an answer, Erich asked, "Fanny, you've been with us for a long time. What do you think of us?"

Now Fanny was really puzzled. "What kind of a question is that? You're almost like my family."

"But suppose you compare us with the Christian families you know?"

"Erich Levi, I can swear to you I've never in my life met better people than your mother and father. I won't mention you and Max, though you *can* be real scamps sometimes. . . ."

Amazed, Erich saw that Fanny had started to cry. Her last few words were interrupted by sobs. She sat down on the edge of the bed and sniffled into her apron. Erich sat down beside her and put a comforting arm around her shoulders. "Oh, Fanny, Fanny, don't cry. I'll stop asking you such silly questions right now."

"It's not that." Fanny was sobbing harder and harder. "I really shouldn't tell you. Your parents wanted to tell you only just before."

"Before what? What is it, Fanny?"

She blew her nose with a determined sound, then

smoothed a strand of fair hair back from her forehead. She took Erich's hand and held it very tightly.

"I have to leave you on the first of next month, Erich. Your parents can't pay me anymore. It's not easy for them, I know. Your mother and I have cried over it a lot. But it's no good. I offered to work for lower wages, but I have to earn something—I don't get anything from my parents. But your mother said she couldn't take the responsibility for that. They have to keep Peter on, because your father needs him to work with the cattle, so I'm the one who has to go."

Erich listened to her, incredulous. He stared at the pattern on the rug, feeling as if he were caught up in a nightmare.

Fanny seemed to sense what was going on inside him, for she said in a very cheerful tone, "But as soon as business is better again I can come back! Your mother promised."

Erich laid his head on her shoulder and whispered, "But what are you going to do now?"

"I already have a new job. Your mother found it for me. With the Wolfs in Stuttgart." Erich nodded. He knew the Wolf family. Herr Wolf was a poultry dealer and a business friend of Father's. They had visited the Levis a few times. They were nice people, even if their three giggling daughters got on his nerves. Odd that business was obviously still going well for Herr Wolf. But he was glad for Fanny, because they really *were* nice people, and he told her so.

She nodded. "Yes, I'm sure, but there's no one as nice as my Levis. Listen, I sometimes go to see my parents up in Neunheim on the weekends, and then I'll visit you."

"Promise?"

"Promise!"

"And you'll come to my bar mitzvah anyway?"

"Word of honor, Erich. I'll buy myself a pretty dress for it in Stuttgart, just to do you proud!"

They sat there in silence for a while. Erich remembered her standing in the doorway when she first arrived, with a cardboard box in her hand, hair smartly arranged, and with a beaming smile. Her name was Franziska Werner, Father had told them. "But you must call me Fanny," she had added at once. "Everyone does." The boys had been just waiting to meet the new housemaid Father had told them about. He had hired her on the spot when he did a deal with her father one day. "It was so clean in that house you could eat your dinner off the floor," he had told them. And old Werner had said proudly that it was all due to his Fanny, she was a really good girl. She was looking for a place with a family to learn how to run a high-class household, he added. So they'd soon agreed, since the Levis had been looking for a new maid for some time—after Anni, their last one, married and went to live in Bavaria. Fanny would be very happy to go to Frau Levi, said her father, for nothing but good was heard of her, so she had moved into the Levis' home and captured the boys' hearts.

In spite of his misery, Erich had to smile when he remembered how Max used to get on Fanny's back and cling to her when she was kneeling down to scrub the floor, and how the brothers used to argue about which of them would marry her when they grew up. She had been their adviser in troubles great and small, and their ally, too, if a plate was broken, or there was a tear in a trouser leg to be mended, or they wanted something sweet to nibble in the evening though it wasn't really allowed. Life without Fanny, their merry, smiling Fanny, was simply unthinkable!

Erich could have burst into tears too, but he wouldn't let

himself. Instead, he tightened his arm around Fanny, and after a while she got up and said, in a cheerful voice, "There, that's enough crying. Now I need to make supper. Your father will be back from Lauchheim any minute. And we have to eat something, because all this moping about won't get us anywhere." She ran her hand through Erich's hair, as she often did. He had to grit his teeth when he thought how much he'd miss that.

After a while he went into the living room to find his mother. Melanie was sitting at the piano, and had just played a few bars on it. It occurred to Erich lately that Mother hadn't used her beloved instrument much, so he said quietly, "Play some more, Mother, do. I like to hear you."

His mother smiled and shook her head. "You all run away when I play Wagner! And I don't want to bother you in particular today, Erich."

Now Erich had to smile too. It was true, Wagner wasn't the kind of music he liked. But then he remembered his conversation with Fanny, and he told Mother about it.

"Oh, so she's told you. We didn't want to burden you children with it yet. We were going to tell you just before she left. But you yourselves must have noticed how sad Fanny's been recently."

"Isn't there any way she can stay, Mother?" asked Erich, although he already knew the answer.

His mother shook her head. "No, there isn't, Erich, believe me. We wouldn't let Fanny go unless we had to. But business is worse and worse these days."

"All the same, she offered to work for lower wages."

Mother shook her head. She looked very grave. "First, that just wouldn't be right, Erich. Fanny needs her wages. And she ought to be able to save something, for instance, for her trousseau when she gets married some day. And second . . . well, I'll tell you perfectly straight, we have to count every last pfennig ourselves now. I'm so worried that we may not be able to pay Peter soon either. What's more," said Mother, lowering her voice at this point, "I'm glad for Fanny that she'll be out of here. She hasn't said much, but I know a few things, from Martha Bieg among others. Our dear Fanny has been called names quite often recently, just for working for a Jewish family."

"Oh, you mean Frau Heeb," said Erich dismissively.

"Not just her, there are others too. So let's be happy that Fanny may be spared that in future, Erich. The Wolfs are Jewish, I know, but they've converted, they're baptized, so I'm sure it won't be so bad for them. Even if it's difficult for us, we must be glad for Fanny's sake that she's leaving."

There was no more to be said. Heavyhearted, Erich got up and gave his mother a brief hug. He went back to his room and sat down at the table. After a while, through the closed door, he heard music, soft music as if it were drifting away. Mother had begun to play again. It did sound like Wagner, whose music Mother liked so much, for reasons that Erich just couldn't fathom, but against his will the notes fascinated him.

He sat there, staring at the opposite wall, where some of his and Max's childish drawings were pinned up. One of them showed five little stick figures, but you could tell they were a man, two women, and two children. The man wore an enormous hat, the women had very full skirts, and the bigger boy was leading his little brother. The striking feature of their circular faces was their wide, smiling mouths, with the corners turned up. They were all laughing as they followed each other over a meadow full of brightly colored flowers. Underneath the drawing, a child—it must have been Max—had written in clumsy handwriting and with some spelling mistakes, "Papa, Mama, Fanny, Erich, Max." Erich stared at the picture, and didn't realize that as he did so, tears were running down his cheeks.

Just before supper, Father had come into the room again, asking him not to tell Max that Fanny was leaving. "He's already upset about his brother being beaten up. It would just be too much for him all at once."

Erich nodded. He didn't want to talk about it either. All he really wanted to do was sleep and forget today's nightmares. With some hesitation, his father had offered to write him an absence note for tomorrow. "We can see that you wouldn't want to go to school looking the way you do. Maybe you should stay at home for a few days until the worst of it's healed."

Until the worst of it's healed? I can't wait that long, thought Erich, but he gave his father's hand a grateful squeeze. "Thanks, but I'll have to go back eventually. I'd like to get it over with as soon as possible."

Julius Levi nodded. "Yes, that's what I thought too. I'm proud of you, Erich. And remember, we'll survive all this."

Then he went out. Soon after that, Max came into the room. Hesitantly, he approached his brother and asked in a strained voice, "Does it still hurt a lot?"

"It's okay. I can hardly feel a thing anymore."

Max swallowed. "Everyone in town knows how they beat you up. A lot of people asked me about you, but I didn't tell them anything. And . . . and people know they called you that name too. Some of them shouted it after me today when I was playing with Willi. But I pretended I wasn't listening."

Erich nodded. "Good idea, Max. We just won't listen to

them. Come on, time for supper." But Max hadn't finished yet. He was tracing the intricate pattern on the rug with the toe of his shoe.

"And Willi said you did something bad in school and that's why they beat you up. Is that true?"

For a moment, Erich thought about it. "Yes, Max, I'm afraid it is. I did a very, very stupid thing. But that's no reason to hit anyone."

Max nodded eagerly. "That's just what I told Willi. Lots of them against one of you, too. And I told him my brother Erich wouldn't do anything bad. My brother doesn't need to do anything bad, I said."

Touched, Erich nudged him in the ribs. For some time, they'd been too old to express affection for each other, but all the same Erich would have liked to give his brother a hug now, the way he used to when Max was still a little boy, and sometimes ran to him, flung his arms around his knees, and whispered, "Erich nice!"

To Go or Not?

THE NEXT MORNING, Erich looked at himself hard in the mirror. His right cheek was still slightly swollen and very red, and bruises had come out on his calves, shin, and stomach, so he put on a pair of long trousers, although it was almost as warm as midsummer outside. He couldn't eat anything at breakfast, but managed to swallow a few sips of milk. The short walk to school seemed endless today. He thought he felt eyes staring at him everywhere, almost as if he were running an invisible gauntlet.

Kampmann and the others were already at their desks, talking with Reger, the class spokesman, and several other boys. But when Erich came in the conversation stopped, and all eyes went straight to him. There was silence for a moment and then, when Erich sat down at his desk, apparently unconcerned, and took out his textbooks, exercise books, and writing things, the normal everyday noises started up again very slowly, though it was rather more muted than usual. Erwin gave him a timid sideways look, and a few others glanced back at him too. There was one boy absent this morning: Helmut. That was the first thing Erich had noticed on entering the room. Kurt was with Reger, and the others now quietly continued their discussion with Kampmann. Erich could make out a few words. It sounded like some people in the class weren't happy that Erich was beaten up.

Erich strained his ears and listened hard. Kampmann was just saying something like, "Well, your turn next, then!" in a nasty tone of voice, when the door swung open and the geography teacher Dr. Fetzer came in. Fetzer was one of the older teachers, nearing retirement. Erich liked him, although his lessons were little more than monologues, accompanied now and then by rhythmic taps with his walking stick on the map on the wall. But he could be amusing and ironic, and didn't mind making jokes at his own expense. Most important of all, however, he was fair and perfectly straight, and that, Erich thought, was what really mattered most in a teacher, particularly these days. Fetzer sat down at the teacher's desk and looked at the class over the top of his pince-nez. His gaze came to rest on Erich. Without any preamble or even a "Good morning," he launched straight into a condemnation of yesterday's violence.

"Unseemly and shameful!" he thundered, and went on to say that violence seemed to be the fashion these days.

In a sharp tone, Kampmann asked, "What do you mean by that, sir?"

Everyone looked to the front of the class and at Dr. Fetzer, who sat there for a moment, then rose to his feet and strolled around the classroom, hands linked behind his back as usual. Without mentioning names, he said that violence in general and beating people up in particular were no way to solve problems. As he talked he took his pince-nez off and cleaned them thoroughly with his handkerchief. Then he went on, in a quiet voice. "On the contrary, they create even worse problems. And most important, much that is very valuable is destroyed by violence, lost beyond recall."

There was a deathly hush in the classroom. Everyone knew that Fetzer's only son had died young in the trenches of Verdun. Kampmann knew too, and for a moment it seemed as if that would keep him sitting at his desk. But instead he shot to his feet again and snapped, "Sir, that doesn't answer my question!"

"Oh, Kampmann!" Fetzer looked at him over the top of his pince-nez. "Sit down, Kampmann, and open your atlas. You still have a lot to learn. So do the rest of you. The lowland plain of the Upper Rhine, if you please, gentlemen." As he passed, he laid a hand on Erich's shoulder, and then sat down at his own desk again.

Erich stared at the atlas in front of him, open at the map showing the lowland plain of the Upper Rhine, but heard none of what Fetzer was telling them. For the first time in ages he felt something like happiness. Only a small, subdued happiness, but it did him good, flowing through his whole body and warming it. Fetzer's encouragement, indirect as it was, Reger's criticism of Kampmann, the others who had backed Reger— that somehow helped him through the difficult beginning of this day at school. The rest of the morning passed slowly but without incident. The other teachers acted as if they didn't know anything about what had happened, ignoring

Erich's swollen face. At break, however, Erich noticed that Kampmann was very worked up. He was gesticulating wildly and talking to his friends, who surrounded him.

Erich, standing not far off with Erwin, caught the words, "Old fool . . . I'll show him!"

Reger had come up to him and Erwin at the beginning of break and said rather awkwardly, "I'm sorry, Levi. About yesterday, I mean. A few of the others and I have had a word with Kampmann. We didn't think it was right, so many against one. But you know what he's like! And I can hardly complain to the teacher. . . ."

The sentence hung in the air unfinished between them, but Erich nodded. No, he certainly couldn't go to Gremm about it. He thanked Reger, and soon after that, felt even better when Kurt came up to him.

"Do you know what's the matter with Helmut?" Erich asked, but Kurt just shook his head.

"No idea. Haven't seen him since yesterday." Kurt even walked back to the classroom with him and Erwin after break, which Erich thought was greatly to his credit, because Gremm was on supervision duty that day and was watching them out of the corner of his eye.

After school, Erich stood about undecidedly in the middle of the church square. He would have loved to go into the handsome house where the Nolls lived, to find out what had happened to Helmut. But he didn't dare. How could he look Herr Noll in the face? Helmut's father was sure to know how he'd cheated by now. Suppose Frau Noll wouldn't let him in because Helmut didn't want to see him, not after he'd let him down? Then he suddenly spotted Kati making her way to the front door with two heavy shopping bags. He hurried over and politely held the door open for her, taking his chance to ask what was wrong with Helmut.

"Out sick," she said curtly. "Sore throat and a temperature, but nothing serious, the doctor says. He can go back to school in a few days."

Erich thanked her, said a hasty, "Tell him I hope he's better soon," and then ran home.

There was a large, brand new, brown leather suitcase just inside the front door. "Our good-bye present to Fanny," said Mother as Erich walked rather warily around it. "So she doesn't have to go away with her things in a cardboard box again. How was school?"

"Not bad," said Erich, casting a last glance at the suitcase. He could have kicked it. He followed Mother into the kitchen, where she had just been chopping onions, and their sweetish, pungent aroma still hung in the air. Something was sizzling in the casserole on the stove. It'll always be like this now, he thought. Fanny will never be here again when I come home from school, and Mother will have to do all the work.

"Where's Fanny?" he asked, and Mother said she had gone to the town hall to fetch papers of some kind. "But tell me about school," she asked, and Erich told her about Fetzer and Reger and the others.

"Good." Mother was visibly relieved. "But didn't anyone else apologize to you?"

"Apologize!" snorted Erich. "What on earth do you think, Mother? I expect I can be thankful if they leave me alone."

"All the same," Mother insisted, "I can't make out those teachers. But your father thinks there's nothing to be done about it. I begged him to go and complain, but he says we wouldn't get anywhere. He lost heart, you know, after that time he went to see the Head. I just don't understand him." She dropped into the kitchen chair, looking very pale.

"I'm really not bothered about it," Erich assured her, thinking what a downright lie that was. But Mother looked so despondent that he just had to cheer her up. "Papa realized last time that Nazis run the school now, that's all it was. And you don't really get anywhere with someone like Gremm."

"But they can't allow things like that to happen!" Mother seemed unable to grasp it.

"Looks like they can. But maybe Uncle Süssel is right after all, and it will all die down again after a while."

His mother just shook her head. For a few moments they said nothing, Melanie sitting at the kitchen table and looking at her folded hands in her lap, Erich leaning against the sideboard with one leg over the other.

Suddenly, Mother said, "I've been wondering for some time whether it wouldn't be better to go away."

Erich started and looked blankly at his mother. "What do you mean?"

"Well, Aunt Mina wrote saying that Siegfried's been trying hard to persuade them and Ilse to go to America. He's very worried about them. And Erna, Herta, and Trudel are begging them just as hard to emigrate to Spain and join them there."

Siegfried was Aunt Mina and Uncle Louis's only son, a successful businessman who had been living near Chicago for several years. Their three other daughters lived in Barcelona, where Erna, the eldest, and her husband ran a small steel wares factory.

"And you want us to go to America or Spain too?" asked Erich, still astonished. "But this is our home. And Papa has his business here. And anyway . . ." But he couldn't think of any more reasons. All he knew was that in spite of Kampmann, in spite of Gremm, in spite of all the others he didn't want to leave Ellwangen. This was their home, no one could drive them away.

Mother became restless. She jumped up and passed a hand over her forehead as if shaking off a bad dream. Then she set to work at the stove, saying as she looked over her shoulder, "Never mind, Erich, it was just a silly idea. You think up all sorts of ideas when you don't know what to do. And everything's happening to us all at once right now."

Erich stared for a while at her back as she leaned forward. Imagine Mother thinking like that! Maybe it was all even worse than it seemed, maybe the grown-ups were keeping something from him. Maybe there were things he knew nothing about. He decided to read the newspaper more regularly, although Father said you couldn't believe everything the local paper said these days.

"The journalists are under great pressure. There's censorship everywhere," he had said at breakfast the other day, while he skimmed the headlines. And when Max asked what censorship was, and if those journalists were given marks like the kids at school, he had explained that yes, it really was a bit like that, only with much more serious consequences. "News stories that the Nazis don't like don't get printed, and journalists who write them can expect to be fired. Schlosser told me that the editor in chief of our local paper has actually received threats. There was even something in this new Nazi rag about a likely arrest soon."

Erich knew the new "rag," as his father called it. Recently the editorial offices of the local paper had moved to a brand new place in Oberamtstrasse, and there was a showcase up outside it. It contained the latest issue of the *Nationalzeitung*, and Kampmann's father printed the "rag."

Although Mother had made a delicious goulash for lunch, they all picked at their food with little appetite. Fanny's imminent departure lay over the family like a shadow. Only Max was unaffected, and told a funny story about his English lesson at school. The next few days passed in the kind of tense atmosphere where you wait for something you fear, knowing that it is inevitably coming your way. The day before Fanny left, Father took Max aside to tell him she was going. They went into the living room, while Erich helped Fanny do the dishes— for the last time, he thought sadly.

Then they heard Max screaming; there was a clatter like a chair being knocked over, the door was flung open, and there stood Max, white as a sheet. "I don't want you to go, Fanny!" he howled, flinging himself into her arms. Fanny crouched on the floor, running her wet hand soothingly over Max's head.

"I want Fanny to stay!" he repeated, amidst loud sobs.

Erich stood there rooted to the spot. The tea cloth had slipped out of his hand, and his mother was standing in the doorway looking upset as she watched the scene. At last Father came along, pulled Max away from Fanny and slapped his face. Erich jumped in alarm, but obviously the method worked, because Max stopped bawling instantly. He stared at his father for a moment, with grief and defiance all over his face, then ran past Mother and into his room.

"I didn't know he'd take it so hard," Father told Fanny,

sighing. "Please forgive that performance, Fanny. He's very fond of you."

Then Fanny and Mother burst into tears. I'll be howling, too, any minute now, thought Erich, and he fled to the attic, where he buried his head between his knees. Crouching on the dusty floor, he waited for the burning sensation in his throat to subside. Then he went downstairs to comfort Max.

As it happened, the last supper that Fanny shared with the Levis was on the Sabbath eve. She and Mother had made all the preparations as usual: they had laid the table, baked the challah loaves, prepared the food, lit the candles. Julius had gone to the service in Bergstrasse; he had asked Max and Erich to go with him, but they both refused. They wanted to spend every last minute they could with Fanny. After the meal, as lavish as ever on Sabbath eve, Father made a little speech thanking Fanny for all she had done for them.

"I'm going to miss all this so much," Fanny sighed, letting her eyes pass over the table, the good china that she had always looked after so carefully, the silver candlesticks, and the Sabbath platter with the challah crumbs still lying on it. "The Wolfs are baptized, so there won't be any more Sabbaths for me. I always felt it was such a lovely, festive idea, Frau Levi. And I've learned so much from you. . . ." Her voice faltered, and she had to search for her handkerchief.

Now we're all going to start bawling again, thought Erich in alarm, and he quickly launched into a funny story in which Fanny and a door-to-door salesman played the leading parts. Soon they were all exchanging reminiscences. "Oh, Fanny, do you remember how . . . wasn't that funny! . . . And remember when . . . ?" Erich did his turn as a mimic, and

Fanny and the others had to smile or even laugh, little as they really felt like laughing.

The next morning, Father put the new suitcase on the hand-cart. The family stood together in the front hall of the building, surrounding Fanny, who looked very elegant, going off to her new job in a flowered dress with a lace collar. She had bought it from Fräulein Klara Österlein, who had a little dress shop in Apothekergasse. "You have to think of your appearance in the city more than out here in the country," Fanny had confided to Erich, and she showed him two new blouses and a skirt that she had also bought from Fräulein Österlein.

Erich couldn't help grinning. "You'll soon be turning the heads of all the young men in Stuttgart. They'll be standing in line outside the Wolfs' apartment!" And she dug him in the ribs, laughing, just the same as always when they teased each other.

They now shook hands without a word. Fanny embraced Frau Levi, gave Max a quick hug, and then followed Julius, who had set off with the handcart in the direction of the rail station. The other three watched the handcart trundling away with the new suitcase on it, and Fanny walking off with her curls bouncing and her skirt swaying, until they had passed through the archway near the high school and finally disappeared from their view. Maria the apprentice came out of the china shop on the ground floor of the building and joined the three of them as they stood there motionless. "What's all this about Fanny?" she asked Melanie. "Why is she going away?"

"Maria, don't be so nosy, it's nothing to do with you." Auguste, the younger of the two Fräulein Pfisterers who owned the shop and the building had joined them. She snapped at Maria to go back into the shop, and briefly squeezed

Mother's arm. "What a pity Fanny is leaving. I always liked her so much. Such a nice, hardworking girl! But times aren't easy now. I'm sorry for you, Frau Levi."

Mother nodded to her thankfully. "Times certainly aren't easy. All the same—thank you, Fräulein Pfisterer."

Together with Max, Erich went up the slight rise to the high school porch. They'd be late for the first lesson today, but they didn't mind that. Lafrentz the history teacher entered Erich in the register and made a sarcastic remark of some kind, but Erich didn't really take it in. He sat down at his desk and noticed in passing that Helmut was finally back. Kati's optimistic prognosis had turned out to be wrong. Kurt had looked in at the Nolls' place a couple of days ago and came away with the news that Helmut had angina and would probably have to stay in bed for some time. Erich had walked around the Nolls' house again and again with a letter for Helmut, but he never plucked up the courage to go in. So he tore up the letter every evening and wrote another one the next day. And now Helmut was back!

At break, he waited with his heart thudding, watching Helmut out of the corner of his eye. Helmut came over, putting out his hand. "Hi there, long time no see!" he said in a fake cheerful tone.

Erich beamed, but he also noticed that his friend was looking rather drawn and very pale. When he asked, Helmut said casually, "Yes, it was no fun, but at least I have my appetite back now." Hesitantly, he added, "Let's do something this weekend, shall we, Erich? My parents are going to Stuttgart. Father has some boring old meeting of his fraternity. How about it?"

"Sure!" Erich felt as if a great weight had been lifted from his heart. The quarrel was over, his friend wasn't angry with him anymore. They agreed to meet late on Saturday afternoon, because Frau Levi liked everyone to eat a good lunch on the Sabbath. Almost like the old days, thought Erich as he went home, and he nearly forgot how sorry he was about Fanny.

That afternoon they met outside the church and then cycled up the steep rise of the Schlosssteige, the road leading to the castle. Once at the top, they cycled over the bumpy cobblestones, through the gate in the outer castle wall, and left their bikes. Going through a small door, they started along the narrow path around the castle. There were lawns and gardens here, and the town lay spread out like a box of toys down below. They sat on a low wall and began throwing pebbles at imaginary targets.

Erich hoped that Helmut would bring the conversation around to their quarrel on his own, but after a rather awkward silence he started telling a story of a distant relation who was going to work for a German firm in Buenos Aires. "Argentina, think of that! They'll be leaving from Bremerhaven in three days; it's a direct crossing to South America."

Helmut sounded enthusiastic, but Erich's heart sank like a stone. It reminded him of Mother's idea of leaving Germany. Trying to broach the subject of their quarrel himself, he mentioned old Dr. Fetzer and what he had said the morning after the attack on him, but Helmut only said casually, "He'll have to be careful what he says. My father has already heard something about early retirement—that'd probably be the best thing for him. He really gets to some of the people around here. I'm worried about him."

Erich spun around, surprised. "What do you mean, he'll have to be careful? He never says anything straight out against the Nazis."

"No, but he does indirectly, very loud and clear. Grimminger's in his eleventh-grade class; he's just been made Hitler Youth leader for Ellwangen, and Kampmann is his deputy. They're lying in wait for everything Fetzer says, and when Grimminger turns up in his Hitler Youth uniform, Fetzer really speaks his mind. He's been relatively restrained with us."

Now it was Erich's turn to grin. "Well, Dr. Fetzer certainly makes it clear that he thinks we're pretty dumb. And he thinks the Nazis in particular are super ultradumb. You should have seen Kampmann's face. . . ."

Helmut had to smile at this too. "I like the old fellow. He's a bit cranky, but otherwise he's okay. And he has guts, you have to give him that."

Suddenly the boys were serious again. "I really am worried about him now that you say that," said Erich, looking at his friend. But Helmut didn't react, just gazed at the town below and began throwing pebbles again.

A little later Kurt came along at a run, breathless, and said that his father hadn't wanted to let him come with them. He'd had to promise to keep away from that boy Levi in the future. "No offense, Erich, but my old man is scared to death. He's expecting a promotion, and he needs to be in good standing with the Party Comrades."

"So you told a little white lie." Helmut grinned.

"Kind of, yes. Well, in fact I didn't say anything about Erich. I just said I was meeting you up here, Helmut. And that's not a lie."

They rode on down to the castle ponds. As Kurt had no bike with him, he perched on Helmut's handlebars. Erich went ahead of them. Disappointment and shame were churning inside him, and he rode so fast that Helmut, who had to brake harder, couldn't keep up. He didn't react to his friend's shouts, but grimly rode his bicycle along the steep road down. He felt he'd like to ride on and on forever, far away, even away from his friends. The gulf was there, you couldn't miss seeing it. Helmut wasn't talking frankly to him anymore, and Kurt, well, at least he was honest.

When they reached the fishponds they watched the fat carp swimming through the muddy green water for a while. Kurt made several halfhearted suggestions about what they could do next, until Erich announced that he had to go home. He mounted his bike and rode away at top speed, sensing the eyes of his surprised friends watching him go.

I wonder what they're thinking now, he thought as he rode through the streets around the castle. It's just not like it used to be. It'll never be the same again.

The following week, Gremm told the class that there was going to be a big school sports day and other festivities at the end of June, with a procession all through town, too. The class greeted the prospect with excitement, and through the rising noise Gremm said curtly, "Erich Levi, Erwin Levi, you will not be taking part in these events."

Erwin gave a little start, and shot an inquiring glance at Erich, who whispered, "Well, what did you expect?"

After this last announcement the class had fallen silent for a moment, but then the conversation started up again, as if it were only to be taken for granted that the two Levis couldn't join in school events.

In their sports lesson, Kuhn, a wiry young teacher, was picking the teams for the relay races and the soccer tournament at the sports day. He was a pleasant, rather naive young man, popular with the boys who were good at games—although those who weren't hated him, because he was fanatical about all-round physical fitness. In general he never thought about politics at all—as the boys had soon noticed—but he enthusiastically welcomed "the movement" as he called it, because under the Nazis, sport was a very important school subject. Erich wasn't the least bit surprised when Kuhn called out his name for the soccer team. He was Kuhn's best forward, and that was all that counted to the sports master.

"Levi, Erich, you'll play outside left. Keep trying to get past the wings and pass the ball to Heidt at center."

"Sorry, sir . . ." Erich gave a wry grin. "I'm not allowed to participate in the sports day."

"Why not, are you sick or injured?" Kuhn looked surprised. "Hey, this is no good. I can't do without you."

Erich looked straight at him. "I think you'll have to, sir. Dr. Gremm specially said that I can't."

"But what the . . . ?" At this moment Kuhn looked almost simpleminded. The Kampmann gang was smirking, the rest were looking awkwardly at the ground. Suddenly Kuhn seemed to understand. "Oh yes, now I . . ." Kuhn began stammering, but he quickly recovered his self-control and decided that Lutz would play on the outside left.

Lutz of all people, thought Erich. They'll lose every game with him playing. He was a little proud that Kuhn thought so highly of him. It had even made him forget that he was a Jew.

The first letter from Fanny arrived in mid-June. She was very well, she told them. The Wolfs were nice, but she was homesick for Ellwangen and her Levis all the same. There was a lot of work to do in the Wolfs' big house, and much of it was new to her, so she wouldn't be able to pay a quick weekend visit just at the moment. The letter ended with special good wishes to "her two boys." Mother read it aloud at lunch.

Erich let his eyes wander through the kitchen, saw the sink where he had stood with Fanny so often, helping her to do the dishes, and saw the chair where she had sat at meals. Then he looked at Mother, who was putting the letter back in the envelope. She had grown paler and thinner these last few weeks. No wonder: there was more work to do now. She had to run the whole household on her own, and in the evenings she often sat with Father over his accounts books.

Julius had taken his two sons aside on the evening after Fanny left and told them, speaking very gravely, that they must help around the house more in the future. Erich and Max had always had chores to do, but now there were to be a good many more, Father explained, and they drew up a weekly plan including such unpopular tasks as shoe-cleaning, floor-polishing, and shopping. Both boys did try to stick to this plan, although sometimes they forgot a chore, or one brother left it to the other— who could then defend himself by saying it wasn't his turn. When Erich came home from school one day to find his mother kneeling on the floor, energetically scrubbing the tiles and straightening up from time to time with an expression of pain because her back hurt, he felt ashamed. He resolved to stick to his own timetable of chores more conscientiously and have a word with Max about it too.

At school it seemed to Erich as if they were giving him a respite. Not being allowed to take part in the school festivities still hurt, particularly when he saw the others training hard, but he was glad that after he'd been beaten up they had left him alone except for the usual remarks and insults. They're all very busy, that's what it is, he thought when he had to march off with Erwin and the others to one of the many public celebrations in the gymnasium again. It might be the anniversary of the death of some Nazi big shot Erich had never heard of, or something to do with an association that was attracting many members these days called the Battle League for Germany Abroad, but the boys were always faced with the same scenario: bloodred banners, brown uniforms, choral recitations, and endless speeches.

Gremm had started a drama group, and almost all the students who were in the Hitler Youth belonged. Kurt had told him recently—at one of their now rare meetings—that his father was putting pressure on him to join too. "It's the latest thing to be in Gremm's drama group," he said through clenched teeth. "I did go once to please my old man, just to take a look. I'd rather have a thrashing than go back again."

"What are they going to perform?" asked Erich.

"It's a play called *A People Without Room*.* I don't really understand what it's about. They keep carrying on in it about how Germans need more room to live in because we're 'spilling over.' Can *you* make anything of that?"

Erich let his eyes wander over the town and the green hills. "Not really, no."

"See what I mean? And anyway—me, acting in a play! With half of Ellwangen sitting there gawking. Not at me, they won't."

The boys cut twigs with their knives and began carving them into whistles. Kurt asked casually about Helmut. "I don't understand what happened between you two. He doesn't want to talk about it. Was it that business over your essay?"

Erich nodded. "He didn't take it well. Because I borrowed his father's books."

"I didn't think that was so bad. Gremm had it in for you anyway. I thought what Kampmann and his gang did to you was much worse." They both carved away. Soon wood shavings were covering the ground around them.

Erich wondered if he ought to tell Kurt more about his quarrel with Helmut. But how could he make him understand? Instead, he asked how Kurt and his father were getting on.

"He keeps wanting me to join the Hitler Youth. He joined the Party himself, he loves it. Hitler has saved Germany, he keeps saying." He lowered his knife and stared at the toes of his shoes. "Listen, Erich, I hope you won't mind if I don't go about with you at school or in town anymore. They'll go right to my father if I'm seen with you, and then I'll be in trouble."

"Who'll go and tell your father?"

"How should I know? Party members, like Gremm, for instance; people we know . . . Look, Erich, I hate this too. After all, you're still my friend, but . . ." Kurt stopped short, looking so upset that Erich suddenly felt sorry for him. "Oh, Erich, what's going on? I'm not supposed to see my best friend anymore! Hitler's saved Germany? Don't make me laugh!" He looked sideways at his friend, but Erich didn't react.

Instead, he picked up the whistle he had nearly finished and tried to get a couple of notes out of it. It sounded so shrill and discordant that Kurt made a face. "See, we can't even do that right," said Erich, with a wry grin.

They sat there together in silence for a little longer,

looking at the trees swaying in the evening breeze, and the shimmer of the red sky breaking through the green leaves and casting its light on them. They were out much too late, and both boys knew it. All the same, they just sat there, as if they would miss something irretrievable if one of them left now. But after a while, Kurt rose without a word, put his whistle and his knife in his pocket, and ran home in the direction of Rotenbach, calling a good-bye back to Erich over his shoulder.

Erich stayed there a moment longer, and then he also went back into town by cutting to the Kugelberg.

The next morning the apartment doorbell rang very early. Mother, who was still in her dressing gown, sent Max to answer the door. He came back with Helmut in tow. Helmut looked pale and upset. Erich jumped up and went toward his friend.

"Fetzer's dead," said Helmut without any greeting. "He died last night. They've just fetched the coffin. I came over right after my father told me."

Melanie Levi dropped into a chair. "But what did he die of? I mean, surely he wasn't all that old?"

"Almost sixty. Dr. Uhl thinks it was a heart attack. He called my father first thing this morning. Fetzer was an old Center Party man, like my father and Uhl."

Erich looked at the breakfast table, and his plate with the slice of bread and butter he'd been eating. Over these last few days he'd often seen Fetzer clutch the left side of his chest. He'd looked tired; tired and somehow—well, somehow *nauseated*. The word had occurred to Erich when he was listening to an argument between Kampmann and Fetzer in their last geography lesson. Ever since Fetzer had stood up for Erich, openly showing his contempt for the Nazis, there had been more or less open warfare between him and the members of the Jungvolk and Hitler Youth. Provocative questions, interruptions in class, failure to do homework, along with threats about "reports to higher authorities" had been made by some of the boys. It was even worse in Fetzer's own eleventh-grade class, because Grimminger, Ellwangen's Hitler Youth leader, was the leading figure there.

These thoughts went through Erich's head as he ran downstairs with Helmut, ignoring his mother as she called after him to finish his breakfast. Together, they ran along Hindenburgstrasse to Adolf-Hitler-Strasse. The Fetzers lived opposite Grandmother Babette. The two boys stopped a little way from the building. The door was just opening, and the Head, Dr. Kaiser, was leaving. He was all in black, and his white hair stood out on all sides as if he'd been in too much of a hurry to comb it. Without noticing the boys, who retreated behind a projecting wall, he marched off in the direction of the school. His thoughts seemed to be somewhere else entirely; he didn't even notice the civil "Good mornings" of passersby, and many of them looked at him in surprise as he walked on.

The first lesson would begin in a few minutes, and it was obvious that they were going to be late, but Erich couldn't have cared less just then. He and Helmut stared at the dark brown front door of the building, and then up at the first row of windows with their white lace curtains. He half expected the familiar face to appear at one of those windows any minute, or perhaps the door would open and the figure of Fetzer would hurry out, as always leaning slightly forward with his hands clasped behind his back.

They've broken his heart, thought Erich bitterly. They've literally broken his heart. He couldn't get over seeing everything he'd clung to so desperately since his son's death destroyed—his ideas of honor and decency—all that he'd preached to his students again and again. And then the insults and threats—it had all been just too much for his weak heart.

"Why are we standing around here?" he whispered after a while to Helmut, who was still staring at the building.

"Fetzer was the bravest of all the teachers. He told the Nazis straight out what he thought of them," said Helmut. "And he of all people . . . I just keep thinking that that door will open any moment and he'll come through it."

"Me, too. And we'd have been having geography with him today, third lesson." They set off for school in silence. As luck would have it, it was Gremm's German lesson they were going to be late for.

Expecting to be berated again by Gremm, maybe with an afternoon's detention too, Erich climbed the steps. The classroom door was open, with Reger on watch looking down the corridor. "Staff meeting," he told the two friends briefly, when they asked. "Old Fetzer died last night. How come you're so late?"

"None of your business," said Helmut, pushing his way past Reger into the classroom, where the others were standing around in small groups. There had obviously been a heated discussion, judging by the way the loud voices slowly died down when Helmut and Erich came in.

"Ah, Messieurs Noll and Levi, no doubt in deep mourning," barked Kübler, as Erwin, who had been standing alone by the window, beckoned Erich discreetly over.

"Keep your mouth shut—they want to wind you up. Kampmann was saying there's one fewer enemy of the movement now, and then of course some of the class were furious."

Helmut seemed to have an angry remark on the tip of his own tongue, but at that moment Reger shouted, "Here comes Gremm!" and they all ran to their desks. In a few brief words, Gremm told them that Herr Fetzer had died last night, and the funeral would be on Saturday. The school would of course take a proper part. Otherwise, attendance was voluntary.

What a charming prospect—the men in brown uniforms as mourners, thought Erich, wondering whether he was really allowed to go to a funeral on the Sabbath. He decided to ask the rabbi later, but he was definitely going to be there.

Unfortunately, Gremm said in the same breath that until further notice, he himself would take over the class's geography lessons.

There were a great many people lining the street leading to St. Wolfgang's Cemetery on Saturday. Some were just there as onlookers, but others really seemed sad, for Fetzer had been widely admired in Ellwangen. Erich could see a great many familiar faces, most of them former pupils, and some outstanding local people, mainly from the Center Party, crammed into black coats and wearing top hats. Frau Fetzer walked behind the coffin, a frail little figure who seemed to be almost extinguished by her black hat with its widow's veil. The family members and local worthies were joined by a procession of teachers and students from the high school, and Erich was glad to see that a great many of his own class had come, even some of Kampmann's bunch—Lutz, for instance—and not in uniform.

The coffin, as usual in Ellwangen, had been put on a carriage with black drapes, and the horses wore black headdresses with nodding plumes. When Erich as a little boy had seen such a funeral procession, he had thought it very amusing, almost like a circus show, and he had always wondered why the people were making such solemn faces. Now he walked beside Helmut with his classmates—no one had said he couldn't, not even Gremm, who was there with the other teachers. Kampmann and his gang hadn't come, nor had Erwin.

Coward, thought Erich scornfully, and after a long time he felt something like a silent agreement with Helmut, the unspoken understanding that was at the root of their friendship. Yet the invisible barrier between them would still be there, and Erich's own words still echoed in his ears, his helpless, furious cry of anger at his friend's lack of understanding. "Perhaps that's the way I really am!"

When the coffin was lowered into the grave, he asked Helmut quietly, "Do you think people can die of a broken heart?"

Helmut didn't take his eyes off Frau Fetzer, who was crying at the graveside, supported by the Head and a man from her family. A strong wind had risen and was tugging at her black veil, and the banner of the Alemannia student fraternity, held by a young member over the open grave, billowed in the wind.

"Yes," said Helmut between his teeth. "Yes, I do."

And after a while, during which the teachers had gone up to the grave, he added, "My father told me this morning that Fetzer was terrified of the future, because of us young people. And his own son's death never seemed pointless to him until now. Do you understand that?"

Erich didn't answer, for just then Gremm stepped forward. Erich waited, holding his breath—and sure enough, Gremm's hand shot up into the Hitler salute, and he stood there for a moment without moving. Insulting Fetzer even in death, thought Erich. He tugged Helmut by the sleeve, and they slipped away from the crowd and went back into town without a word.

The Bundle

THE FOLLOWING MONDAY, the sports day and other festivities took place out at the barracks, and from an upstairs window Erich and Max watched the other schoolboys march past, long lines of them going into town. The Jungvolk and the Hitler Youth had their banners, of course, and the SA band led the procession, along with the local Party big shots. Many of the teachers had turned up in uniform too, as they often did on such occasions, and Gremm—Erich craned his neck to find him in the crowd—yes, although Gremm was wearing a suit as usual, he had his Party badge conspicuously pinned to his lapel. Max nudged his brother. "It looks kind of horrible," he said.

"How do you mean?"

"Always banners and uniforms. I don't like it at all."

Erich nodded. "Neither do I. Let's be glad we're not

with them." Secretly he was surprised that his little brother didn't seem to mind much. Max wasn't particularly athletic, and he'd always hated gymnastics, but Erich had expected that being left out of the rest of the fun would hit him hard. However, Max had just shrugged and said he'd rather have a day off from school.

"Besides," said Erich, pointing to the gray clouds moving over the blue sky from the north, "it's going to rain later, and that'll literally put a damper on the party. You wait and see." Sure enough, it did begin to rain early in the afternoon. Little cascades ran down the windowpanes, and suddenly the rising noise in the street told the boys that the festivities had broken up in a hurry.

On his way home that evening, Helmut hammered on the back door of the Levis' building, and told Erich what had happened, as the two of them stood in the dark front hall among the empty cartons from the china shop. "They ran like rabbits when it started to rain. Gremm had just been making one of his bloodcurdling speeches about ancient German virtues and so on, and right on cue there was thunder and lightning. . . . Oh, and another thing: we lost ingloriously in the soccer tournament. Eliminated in the first round. Kuhn was very glum. Wouldn't have happened if you'd been playing."

The next Sabbath, the first in July, was a hot, dry day. Erich and Max had gone swimming in the boys' pool in the Jagst that afternoon. These days Erich expected to find problems there too, so he had scanned the area carefully before changing into his swimming trunks. There didn't seem to be much going on, though, and none of the Jungvolk or Hitler Youth boys were there. "They've gone off to camp in the Hohenlohe countryside," Helmut told him, when he came along later. "And Kurt's gone too, by the way."

"Is he a member?" asked Erich. His heart was thudding.

"Not yet. But it won't be long now, if you ask me. His father keeps pestering him to join. He was made to go along this time to see what it's like."

Erich floated in the green water of the river. Now and then he felt a light, cool touch on his legs. Fish swimming nimbly among the bathers. The alders and willows stood motionless on the bank, dipping their branches into the cool water that reflected them, and there wasn't a cloud in the sky. There was a slightly musty smell, overlaid by the scent of new-mown hay, and it sometimes seemed that even the flickering sunbeams had a smell of their own. It all smelled of summer. Erich thought back to last summer, when everything had seemed as weightless as he now felt in the water, light and yet safe in a familiar scene. Why couldn't you just shut off your own bit of the world from everything else, he wondered: the bit of your world as it had once been, as he felt it now, looking at the slowly flowing river, the alder and willow trees, and surrounded by the smell of summer?

Summer vacation would soon be here, and that meant Oedheim, Aunt Mina and Uncle Louis, another part of the old familiar world. It also meant no school, no Gremm, no Kampmann. But what after that? Erich didn't want to think about it; he just wanted to let himself drift, light and weightless, in the cool waters of the Jagst.

That evening, after they had celebrated the end of the Sabbath, Father read aloud from the paper as usual. Max and Erich had to clear the table, and Erich worked slowly so he could hear what his parents were talking about. Soon he wouldn't be able to read his beloved paper anymore, Julius was complaining.

"These days that Nazi rag, and it's fast becoming a smear-sheet, is about the only source of news," he was saying. "Bieg told me in confidence that Gabele keeps getting threats of arrest. The day before yesterday they broke the windows of the paper's editorial offices. 'Well-deserved popular justice,' it's called in their new Nazi gazette. But everyone knows who did it!"

Herr Gabele was the editor in chief of the local paper that Erich's parents had subscribed to for years. Erich had seen him in the Golden Cross, where he went now and then for a glass of wine or a snack: a friendly man, Father liked talking to him. The paper would be closed down soon, Father went on.

"And do you know what will be the only papers we can buy anywhere in Ellwangen then?" Father counted them off on his fingers. "The *People's Observer*. The *SA Man*. The *Stinging Nettle*—which certainly lives up to its name. Not forgetting that poisonous rag they have hanging outside Schuster's house. All of them as bad as each other."

Erich felt sorry for Herr Gabele, and thought of his wife and children. Luckily they were still quite small. The eldest had only just started school, but perhaps they would sense something of their mother's fears and their father's anxieties.

As he washed dishes, he remembered that about two weeks ago, even in Herr Gabele's paper, school statistics had been published, and for the first time ever mentioned the "racial origin of the pupils," as it was put. After lunch Erich had looked quickly for the paper and found the story. There it was, in black and white: 339 school students at the prep school and the vocational high school, of whom three were "non-Aryan." "Non-Aryan"—of course everyone knew that meant the Levi boys. The statistics also said that non-Aryans made up half of one percent of all the students; perhaps Dr. Kaiser the Head had made sure that that was added, because it was important these days for a school not to have too may Jewish pupils. So Uncle Ludwig had told Mother in a letter, adding that many schools in Pirmasens were refusing to take Jewish children now. Half of one percent—Erich clung to that fact. It wasn't many, and there wouldn't be any more for the time being.

He and Max were counting the days until summer vacation began. The plan was for them to spend the last three weeks of vacation in Oedheim and the first part of it at home. That meant sleeping late, no homework, no tests—and above all, no bullying. Helmut was going away with his parents for the last part of vacation too, somewhere on the North Sea coast, he told Erich, and the way he said it suggested that he wasn't necessarily looking forward to it.

"We could go for a few bike rides, or swim together," he suggested a little hesitantly, and for the first time in ages Erich felt really glad of something. The prospect of having to spend the vacation with only Max and Erwin hadn't been particularly attractive. Perhaps he and Helmut could still patch up the rift between them! Kurt, when asked about his vacation plans, wasn't very forthcoming. He didn't know yet what his parents had in mind, he said; he'd probably have to go to his godmother's again. And he wouldn't say much about that camp in the first weekend of July, when Helmut asked him.

"We'll be seeing him in uniform very soon now. Bet you anything," Helmut said to Erich.

But at any rate he wasn't yet marching in the big SA procession to the "dedication of banners" ceremony, as the newspaper and some handbills had called it. A large crowd once again lined the streets, down which lines of people paraded between the Church of St. Wolfgang and the gymnasium, where it became a huge, festive procession. A platform had been put up outside the church, and a whole forest of flags was waving on it. Erich, watching the spectacle with Max and Helmut from a remote vantage point up by the cemetery, kept wondering which banners were going to be dedicated, and how it was going to be done. Kolbe, the loudmouth-in-chief, made one of his dreaded speeches again, and his pithy sayings could be heard half the way over town, accompanied by enthusiastic cries of "Heil!"

"Those who are not National Socialists are our enemies and will be crushed," he shouted, and, "There's no room here for opposers to the movement!"

"He needs extra instruction from Gremm—he is a terrible speaker," whispered Helmut, in a failed attempt to be funny.

Erich responded to this remark with a wry smile. Max kept tugging at his sleeve, looking scared. Erich decided to get his little brother out of there as fast as possible.

That afternoon, a thunderstorm dispersed the crowd, and Julius, who was sitting comfortably, looking out the window and watching the groups hurrying home, gave his opinion with a broad smile that "someone up there" didn't like the Nazis too much. The following Sunday, the same thing happened to a different assembly.

Early that morning, Erich and Max were woken by bells ringing peals for the churches. Ellwangen was celebrating its seven hundredth anniversary. Days before, all the buildings in the town center had been decorated with evergreens; flags were waving everywhere, including the bloodred swastika banners. When a sudden torrential downpour fell on the candlelit procession in the evening, Erich asked his father why the powers that be didn't seem to look kindly on this occasion either. This time, Julius replied much more seriously, "I expect there are too many brown uniforms and too many red flags in the crowd. And too many hypocrites!"

The next Saturday came the much anticipated end-of-term ceremony. The days before had been almost entirely given over to history lessons, and not just the "normal" kind. Gremm and Lafrentz and the others had sounded off for hours about the World War, "The Betrayal of Versailles,"* and the "Emergence of the German Nation." Erich, who would much rather have heard something about prehistoric man and the Stone Age—subjects they'd normally have been studying—let all this just wash over him. He preferred to think of what he and Helmut would do during vacation, and wondered if they could really go and see Fanny in Stuttgart.

In the first week of the vacation, Helmut came around on his bicycle and suggested an expedition upriver along the Jagst, to find a remote place to swim. Erich breathed a secret sigh of relief. He was afraid that during vacation, when the boys' swimming pool would be very full, he would be called names or even worse. He couldn't quite shake off the suspicion that Helmut was thinking along the same lines and wanted to protect him from it. Or perhaps he didn't want to be seen around with Erich too often. But Erich didn't say anything about that. These days, there were things it was better not to discuss with his best friend.

They set off in the morning. Erich had brought plenty of picnic food and a flask of peppermint tea, because they were planning to be out all day. It was going to be a hot day too; the heat could already be felt almost like a solid wall among the buildings in town. At home, Mother had closed the shutters early in the morning to keep the sun out, and as they cycled through the town center Erich noticed that shutters were closed in other people's houses too—as if Ellwangen had closed its eyes and was dozing. There weren't many people out and about, and those who were hurried along the street so that they could get back to their cool, darkened rooms. Erich remembered that poem about sleeping Germany, the one they'd read with old Wagner. He found that he couldn't remember the poet's name, and thought briefly of Wagner. It was said that he had gone to live with his daughter in Schwäbisch Gmünd. Erich thought he must remind himself to ask Helmut about that.

They looked for a place in the shade off the path leading to Schwabsberg. It was isolated here. Only now and then did they hear the sound of a car approaching along the road and dying away again, or the rattle of a horse-drawn cart. They dangled their feet in the cool water of the Jagst and drank the tea, which was still lukewarm.

After a while Helmut stood up, saying he had to pee. But he very soon came hurrying back. Erich heard his gasping breath first; the soft grass on the bank swallowed up his footsteps. Then he saw his friend coming through the willows that grew on a bend in the river, and he realized at once that something was wrong. It was the expression in Helmut's eyes, one he had never seen there before. His face was white as chalk, and when he reached Erich, who had leaped to his feet in alarm, he couldn't speak at first. Then he managed to say, "There's . . . there's something over there!"

"Helmut, for heaven's sake, what's wrong?"

"Come with me!" Helmut grabbed his sleeve. He was starting to get control of himself again. "But don't be afraid. It's a man. I think he's drowned."

Erich stared at him. The words weren't getting through to his brain properly. "Drowned?"

"Yes, come on. We have to do something. Anything."

"Are you sure he's dead?"

"Of course I am." Helmut began running again. Beyond the bend he suddenly stopped and pointed to something lying on the bank.

"There! But don't go too close. It . . . it's not a pretty sight."

Erich took a few steps and suddenly realized that he felt weak at the knees. There was a bundle of something ahead of them—a bundle of something human! It was a man, no doubt about it from the outlines of the figure. Its torso was lying where sand had silted up at the slight bend in the river; its legs were in the water, swaying in the ripples.

As if part of it were still alive, thought Erich, and he flinched when he noticed the swarm of fat black flies that had settled on the corpse's face. Disturbed by the two boys' arrival, the flies began buzzing frantically and circling the dead man.

"Come on, let's get out of here!" Helmut grabbed Erich, who was still rooted to the spot.

"Is he really dead?" Fascinated, Erich watched the gentle movement of the man's legs. "Maybe he's only unconscious."

Helmut tightened his grip. His upper lip was raised so

that it looked as if he were baring his teeth. "Good heavens, can't you smell it?"

There was indeed a strange smell in the air. In some indefinable way it now dominated the familiar fragrance of summer. A sweetish smell, strange, yet familiar. When Fanny made meat broth it smelled a little like this. Suddenly Erich felt sick. He retched, and couldn't breathe.

Without knowing exactly what they were doing, the boys suddenly ran for it—ran to their bicycles and didn't even pick up the things they had left on the ground. They just wanted to get away from that smell, the lifeless bundle on the ground, the flies. They pedaled away like robots, not even stopping to decide which way to go. Just before they reached the boys' pool, Köberle, the weather-beaten warden, came along in the other direction. He was pushing his bicycle leisurely along the path beside the Jagst and looked with disapproval at the two boys, who let their bicycles flop to the ground and started disjointedly and breathlessly talking about something strange; a bundle, flies, legs in the water. He didn't believe them at first; they were naughty boys, and one of them was that Levi, the son of the Jewish cattle dealer. . . . But he finally got on his bike and told the two boys to lead the way. They dismounted just before the bend in the river.

"It's over there, Herr Köberle," said Helmut, and he and Erich shook their heads vigorously when Köberle ordered them to go first and show him where. Not for the world did they want to see that scene again or smell the stench of it. Both boys shuddered. The wind must have turned, for they could smell it where they stood now.

After a little while Köberle came back. He too was very pale under his weathered brown complexion. "You boys stay here and wait until I come back. I'm going for the doctor and the police, and you'll have to make statements."

It sounded so threatening that the boys stayed put, and only after some time did they venture to move a little farther from that dreadful place, away from the stench and the buzzing of the flies. They waited for what seemed to both of them an endless length of time, and then a car came jolting along the path by the river, followed by another, and several men jumped out. The boys recognized the local police chief and the doctor among them. They didn't spend much time with Erich and Helmut, but, led by Köberle, made their way straight to the spot on the bank. Farther off, a horse and cart appeared, and came closer rapidly. With horror, the boys saw that there was a coffin in the cart.

"Who found the body?" Police Chief Maier snapped at the two boys as they watched the coffin being unloaded, transfixed.

Helmut said he had. In stumbling words, he described their expedition and then how he had found the "bundle"—he still couldn't bring himself to say "body." It sounded so final.

"Right." Maier took out a notebook. "Name and address." When Helmut gave his address, Maier nodded briefly. The name of Noll was well known in town. Maier's manner became just a little friendlier.

"Well, Herr Noll"—yes, he actually called Helmut "Herr"—"we may have to ask you some more questions later." Helmut nodded.

Then Maier turned to Erich. When he heard the name Levi, he lowered his pencil, and shot a distrustful look at Erich from under frowning brows. Suddenly another car drove up, and two men in brown uniforms got out. Erich knew one of them: Hofer, who had been recently appointed local leader of the Nationalist Socialist Party when Kolbe went off to pursue his career in Stuttgart. Maier and the others stood at attention. Hofer nodded briefly at them, and Maier, with a slight nod too, described events. Erich heard murmured sentences, scraps of words: ". . . male corpse . . . drowned . . . the Jew Levi . . ." and felt a suspicious glance on him.

He went alternately hot and cold. Suppose he found himself involved in this case in some way? To people like Hofer, Jews were bad; they could be held responsible for anything. Could a person his age be sent to prison? Dr. Uhl interrupted his confused thoughts. In spite of the heat, the doctor was wearing a black suit, appropriate in view of the circumstances.

"Probably fell into the river. I dare say he was drunk, but it could have been suicide. He's been in the water at least two weeks. I guess he was washed up here because the water level is low."

"Anyone else involved?" asked Hofer sharply.

Dr. Uhl shook his head. "I don't think so at all. He was a strong man, a manual laborer, I'd say from his clothes. A man like that doesn't just go under if he's pushed into the water, and there are no injuries on him as far as I can tell at present."

For a moment Hofer looked very dissatisfied, but then he dismissed Uhl with his usual nod of the head, and snapped at the boys, "You two go home! But be ready to see us again, because we may want to ask you more questions."

That evening Erich badgered his mother to let them go to Oedheim earlier than planned. "And maybe we can go to Stuttgart next week, too, and see Fanny?"

Melanie shook her head. "Fanny hasn't replied to my last letter yet. We can't drop in on her just like that. And the arrangements for you and Max to visit Aunt Mina and Uncle Louis are all made too, we can't change them now. What's the matter, Erich?"

Not for the world could he have told her about that bundle lying half submerged in the water, about the flies . . . He just didn't want to be here, not at home! He wanted to get away from the memory of that sight and that smell. Nothing was right anymore! Even the little part of the world that still belonged to him had been spoiled. It was everywhere, that sinister beast fear—fear, and now death too. Perhaps if he were somewhere else he could forget the images, perhaps they'd fade and then go away. All he had left now was his home: the familiar walls with all the traces of their life, the pictures, the little stain on the wall above the sofa, the pattern of the rug, the glass-fronted cupboard with the candlesticks and the plate . . . all the things that were theirs.

On the following Sabbath, Erich helped Mother set the table. As usual, she got out the good china and the linen napkins, and put fresh candles in the candlesticks. Erich fetched the plate and put it in the middle of the table, on the embroidered tablecloth. For a moment he scrutinized it, as he had done so often before.

No, he thought, it's only an ordinary plate with boring colors, nothing special about it, it's worthless. And those—the eyes of God—they're just little triangles, that's all. The eyes of God! What a joke!

A few days later, without a word, Julius showed his elder son his open newspaper. "Body of Unknown Man Found in the Jagst," said the story.

Erich nodded. "Helmut found it. Then we told Köberle, and then the police came. How do you know that . . . ?"

His father carefully folded up the paper again. Without looking at Erich, he said, "A rumor came my way. Was it bad?"

Erich nodded again.

"What about the police?"

"They asked how we found him. They may come here too, to ask me more questions."

Strangely enough, Julius did not ask why his son hadn't told him the story before. Instead, he said, "I doubt it. It says in the paper he committed suicide. They'd found out who it was. A workman from near Crailsheim."

So Dr. Uhl was right, thought the boy. He'd have liked to know if the man had any family, people who'd be mourning him now, but his father couldn't say. Suddenly Erich burst out, "Papa, I can't get it out of my head. I'm scared to go to sleep because I'm afraid I'll dream of it. And I'm not going to swim in the Jagst ever, ever again."

His father put a hand on his shoulder. "I can understand that. That's why I phoned your aunt and uncle in Oedheim yesterday evening. You can go earlier. The day after tomorrow we'll take you and Max there and Mother and I will stay two days too. Oh, and Ilse's looking forward to seeing you, and I'm to give you her love. By the way, Aunt Mina told me she has a boyfriend these days."

The handcart jolted over the paving stones, past the mighty building of the high school, where it towered into the sky. Max was sitting astride the suitcases, as he always did when they were meeting someone or taking someone to the rail station. They passed the black notice board with pictures of hook-nosed men and the ugly headlines that positively jumped out at you. Old Schuster was standing in the doorway of the building. When he saw the Levi family coming he spat on the cobblestones and looked challengingly their way. The Levis ignored him, the handcart rumbled past him, and then at last they were at the station, where Peter had been waiting for them. He would take the handcart back, because Mother and Father were going to Oedheim with their sons.

Deep Cracks

UNCLE LOUIS was waiting for them at the little station in Oedheim. He had harnessed two horses to his cart in honor of the day. Erich recognized them at once: Rosi the brown mare and fiery Mali, whose black coat shone so beautifully in the sun. They drove uphill into the little town, for the station was just outside, by the river Kocher. Everything here was smaller, more cramped, and the buildings were lower than in Ellwangen; there were no grand residences, only small half-timbered houses with pointed gables, crowded together. But that didn't bother Erich. He was glad to be here, because this was a part of home too. He looked at their surroundings attentively, ready to point any changes out to Max. The familiar buildings, his old acquaintances, still stood in the little marketplace. The names over the shops, as usual, were crumbling away, and a large black-and-white cat was dozing in the sun outside the premises of "Johann Fuchs, Painter and Decorator." Ahead, the gray church with its mighty bulb-shaped towers rose to the sky, but opposite, a banner now hung on the town hall—the bloodred swastika banner. Over the next few days, Erich noticed increasingly that this paradise too, his vacation paradise, had cracks in it, deep ones.

On the morning after their arrival, he and Max went looking for the friends they'd played with in the past. Usually those children turned up on the first day of the Levi boys' visit, calling for them to go and swim in the river, build dams, or play hide-and-seek up at the castle. But today no one came. All was quiet. A hush hung over the alley between the house and the stable where the neighboring children used to jump out laughing and shouting, because everyone knew that Aunt Mina couldn't stand "all that sudden jumping about the place," as she called it. Sometimes Erich had a glimpse of a skirt or a braid flying through the air—that would be Lina and Marie, his oldest friends here—and heard them giggling and whispering softly, but that was all.

"There are a number of shops where they won't serve us anymore," Aunt Mina said on the second day, as they sat comfortably together after supper over a bottle of Heilbronn wine. The Levi parents nodded. It was just the same with them. They exchanged stories—stories of humiliations and betrayals, menacing stories.

"All the local council members are Nazis now," said Julius. "And they kicked the old mayor out."

Aunt Mina stared at her hands folded in her lap and asked sadly, "But what are we to do? If I only knew what to do! The children keep writing, urging us to leave, but how would I manage in Spain, maybe even America? Louis and I are getting older, we're like two deeply rooted trees. It's not so easy to transplant us."

Erich could understand that. I'm still young, he thought, but I have roots too. It would hurt me to leave home, even though nothing's right anymore and we don't belong.

"Ilse has a boyfriend now, a Christian," Uncle Louis went on. "We were sorry about that at first, Mina and I, sorry and a little worried. A different family, maybe grandchildren baptized Christians—how would it all work out? And supposing Ilse abandoned the faith of her forefathers . . . but now we're glad! If Martin marries her she's sure to be safe. Even though his family is against it. But young Martin is a good fellow."

They were sending Martha away, they went on. Martha was their maid, really more like another daughter to them. She always reminded Erich a little of Fanny, because she was so pretty and amusing. "She's going to Herta in Spain. Herta's second child is on the way, and she can use some help. We want to get Martha safely away from here, I'm sure you can imagine why. It was the same with your Fanny."

Mother and Father left next morning, and over the next few days Erich tried his hardest to enjoy the vacation in spite of everything, and to cheer up Max, who kept asking where their old friends were. They often went out into the country in the horse-drawn cart with Uncle Louis to see the farmers he did business with. He was still doing better than Father. A few of his old regular customers still came to him—but for how much longer?

"Thank God your aunt and I have some savings, and I can retire soon; I'm getting near that age. But everything else . . ." He left the sentence unfinished, but Erich knew what he meant. Everything else was uncertain. He spent most of their vacation in Oedheim with Max by the Kocher—but only for his brother's sake, because the riverbank where alders and willows grew, and the green waters of the river itself, reminded him of the Jagst. Sometimes Erich felt so frightened that he leaped out of the water in panic, particularly when a cold, slippery fish touched him. Then Max would laugh at him and shout, "Coward!" or "Scared of the water these days?" and splash him. And Erich laughed and splashed him back, but it was forced laughter; he hardly knew what he was doing. In the evenings when Ilse came home from Heilbronn, they would sit in the living room and play board games. They usually let Max win; he was so pleased, and didn't seem to notice what they were doing. Martin would be there too, Ilse's fiancé, a smart young man with a jaunty mustache.

One evening when Erich couldn't sleep, he was sitting on the windowsill looking at the silky dark blue night sky, when he heard giggling and soft whispering downstairs. Holding his breath, he leaned out and saw Ilse and Martin standing at the front door, kissing passionately.

Erich stared at the two closely entwined figures and their faces, two pale spots in the dark that seemed to be melting into each other. Suddenly he had a brand new feeling, a sense of excitement, a breathless expectation of something that life had waiting for him; something unknown, new, deeply seductive. And there was a touch of envy in it too, envy of the two carefree lovers. Martin doesn't mind that she's Jewish, he thought. They love each other, that's all that matters.

Suddenly it struck him that it wasn't right to be watching them doing something that was no one else's business.

He crept back to bed and listened to Max's breathing. The full tones of the clock striking on the nearby church could be heard at regular intervals, and Erich counted along with them automatically. He lay there with his arms folded behind his head and conjured up a picture of the lovers. In his imagination he took Martin's place; and the girl—well, the girl had no face and even in his first dreams, as he slipped into sleep, he was trying to give her features and remember her, until at last she eluded him entirely.

Erich and Max went home in the last week of August. Mother and Father fetched them from the station, and Erich noticed that his parents looked well and relaxed. "Ah, when we don't have you two pests here to bother us . . ." When Erich replied with a similar remark, Father tapped him affectionately on the nose. On the way home, Julius told him they had made themselves as comfortable as possible while the boys were away.

"We've been going out in the evenings again, almost like in the old days, to the Golden Cross or Café Schimmel. The Biegs and old Schimmel were glad to see us." Those were the places where they had been regular customers. Both owners had kept up their friendship with the Levi family even after January 1933*, although Herr Schimmel had had problems because of his hospitable welcome to "that Jewish rabble," as Father told Erich.

"He's been trying to get a license to serve alcohol for a long time," Julius said. "And he's just had a rejection again, more or less hinting that he ought to choose his customers better."

"So what will he do now?"

"He says the town council and the whole mob of Nazis

{ 161 }

can go to the devil, he'll just carry on as before without serving alcohol. We were and are old customers, he said, and that's that. Our picture hangs in the café and it's staying there—I just hope it doesn't give him more trouble." The picture was a wood carving in relief that Herr Schimmel had had done some time ago. It unmistakably showed his two regulars, Melanie and Julius Levi, with the police officer Rathgeb telling them that closing time was coming up. Father used to have a reputation for staying late, often until his wife had to remind him gently that it was time to go home. Some of Julius Levi's old mischief, so well caught in the carving, twinkled in his eye again as he leaned over and whispered in Erich's ear, "And Bruno always has a good bottle ready for us, license or no license."

Erich grinned wryly. "He'd better not let himself be caught at it."

Julius grew serious again. "It's an odd feeling to be getting old friends into difficulty just because you want to stay in touch with them. But I told Mother that we won't be intimidated all the same, or we'll soon be unable to go anywhere anymore. Tomorrow you're off to see old Kugler and try your suit on. I met him the other day, and he told me he's nearly finished. But I think you've grown again."

Sure enough, Kugler the master tailor had to let the sleeves out and make the trousers a little longer too. When Erich tried his suit on, he looked at himself in the mirror and was surprised. He thought he looked really grown up in that suit, and old Kugler even made an appreciative remark. Invitations to his bar mitzvah were sent out, and in the evening his mother went through her old cookbooks to decide on a meal worthy of the occasion.

"How about roast duck, Erich? Or do you think stuffed breast of veal would be better? With vegetables, noodles, and dumplings?"

"I don't mind," grunted Erich. "Has Fanny replied yet?"

Sighing, Melanie closed a shabby old book that had belonged to her grandmother. The gold lettering on the cover said KOSHER CUISINE, and the margins inside the book had been scribbled on by three generations of Süssel women, adding handwritten comments or additions to the recipes. "Your wife or Max's will inherit it one day," Mother had once said. "Whoever marries first will get the book."

"Fanny? Not yet, no," said Melanie quietly. "She is very busy." After the first letters, there had been only a picture post-card of the Old Castle in Stuttgart, and not another word from Fanny since, although Mother had written several times. Erich had sent a long letter to Stuttgart inviting her personally to his bar mitzvah—with extra scrawled greetings from Max too—but there had been no reply to that either.

And there was another thing that made him uneasy. On one of Mother's shopping trips, Martha Rieg had whispered to her in confidence that Fanny had been home to Neunheim for the weekend twice now. Melanie had told Julius that evening, and Erich had inadvertently overheard their conversation. He had just taken his shoes off, and when he heard Fanny's name he suddenly sat up straight and listened, holding his breath. She didn't like it very much with the Wolfs, Mother had gone on, and was going to look for another job. But why doesn't she come to see us? Erich wondered. She promised she would.

And now Mother didn't seem to have a good answer.

"Suppose Father went up to see her family in Neunheim some time and asked about Fanny?" he suggested.

"Oh, Erich, what good would that do? We just have to be patient. She's a young girl, perhaps she's met a boyfriend in Stuttgart."

"All the same, it's not a bit like Fanny."

But the day of his bar mitzvah was coming closer, and still there was no sign from her. Erich often thought of the new dress she'd been going to buy specially for him, and of the moment when she left, with her skirt swinging and her curls bobbing. *So she's walked out of our life too,* he thought, *like so many other people.*

School began again in early September, and the Kampmann gang, like several other students, had turned up in uniform. Erich waited apprehensively for Kurt, but to his relief he came in perfectly normal clothes. In break periods the Jungvolk and Hitler Youth boys sounded off at the top of their voices about the Party rally they'd been to in Nuremberg last week. They had seen the führer. Heidt and Müller had even been within a few meters of him as he passed the enthusiastically applauding Party members. They were in ecstasy over the marching, the music, everything. . . . Erich glanced at Kurt, who was standing a little way off with a dark, brooding expression on his face as he ate a sausage sandwich. They hadn't seen each other since the beginning of the vacation.

Erich took a deep breath and then walked up to him resolutely. It wasn't far to go. "Hey, what have you been doing?" he asked with assumed cheerfulness.

Kurt didn't answer right away. He stared absently at his sandwich, and then wrapped it up in its paper again.

"I'd better tell you straight out. I'm in the Hitler Youth now. Well, the Jungvolk. I won't be in the Hitler Youth until next year when I'm fourteen." He avoided looking at Erich as he said this.

For a long, long moment there was silence between them, an oppressive silence that Kurt obviously couldn't stand for very long, because he suddenly began to talk, stumbling, looking for words. He couldn't hold out anymore, he said, his father had put too much pressure on him. And what did it matter, anyway? Better to have a few sensible people in the organization too. And it wasn't that bad, well, okay, Kampmann and Grimminger were a couple of fanatics, they really got on his nerves, but there were other boys too who were different. . . .

Erich couldn't make out what his friend was trying to tell him. He kept on just hearing the same words in the same order. "I'm in the Hitler Youth now. . . ."

Kurt suddenly stopped. He had become all tangled up in his last sentence. What others, Erich wondered, and how are they different?

Suddenly Kampmann came up to the two of them. As if from far away, Erich heard his grating voice. "I see you're pestering our friends, Levi."

Erich didn't answer. It occurred to him again that Kurt wasn't wearing the Jungvolk uniform; he needed to ask him why he he had decided not to. Perhaps that meant something, perhaps he was only in the Jungvolk on probation, perhaps he could still back out. . . .

Suddenly he felt himself being grabbed from the front. Hands seized his shirt in such a tight grip that two buttons popped off. Kampmann's face came close to his; he could feel his breath; it smelled slightly of onions, not unpleasantly, but still it smelled of onions.

Erich suddenly remembered a line of verse from a book that he often used to look at with Mother when he was little. The author was called Wilhelm Busch, and right after the story of Max and Moritz, which Erich loved, there had been pictures illustrating the alphabet, and the picture for the letter O had shown an ugly man with a hooked nose, looking like the men on the notice board in the showcase outside old Schubert's house. There was a line of verse under it that Mother never read aloud. She had always closed the book at that point and started on Busch's story of Plish and Plumm. Later, when he could read for himself, he had deciphered that line, but he didn't understand it. *Onions are food that Jews enjoy.* He thought of it now, smelling Kampmann's breath with that not unpleasant aroma of onions. *Onions are food that Jews enjoy.*

"Answer when I speak to you, Levi!"

Beside him, Erich heard Kurt's voice, low and rather weary. "Leave him alone. He hasn't done anything."

Kampmann took no notice. Meanwhile the others had gathered around them in a circle, most of them boys in uniform, some of them from the older classes, while the others stood to one side, whispering excitedly. Kampmann was still holding Erich by the shirt. Where was the teacher supervising the break? Who was on duty today?

Grimminger the Hitler Youth leader from the eleventh grade stepped into the circle. The memory of old Fetzer briefly passed through Erich's mind.

"This Jew-boy is pestering our friends," Kampmann told Grimminger, without waiting to be asked.

"Oh, yes?" Grimminger planted himself in front of the two of them, hands on his hips. Then he punched Erich in the stomach, making him slump forward. Kampmann let go, and

Erich fell on the asphalt, where he lay writhing. "That's for today. There'll be one more each time, remember that, Jewish swine. Where are the others? There are two more somewhere." Grimminger's eyes searched the boys. Erwin was dragged forward amidst much shouting. He had been hiding behind Reger and the others.

Suddenly Helmut came between them. "That'll do, Grimminger."

Grimminger looked at him with contempt. "Better keep your big trap shut, or it'll be your turn next." And turning to Erwin, who was wriggling as he tried to free himself from the merciless hands holding him, he added, "Once and for all—you Jews keep to yourselves. A decent German doesn't want anything to do with the likes of you. I repeat, a *decent* German. Anyone who doesn't remember that must take the consequences, understand? And you two—just remember, every time you pester someone, there'll be an extra punch."

Erich, still fighting the urge to vomit, rose to his feet with difficulty. When he straightened up, it seemed to him for a moment as if they all took a step back. Staggering slightly, he looked around the school yard. Where was Max? Just so long as they left Max alone. Thank God, he was on the other side of the yard with the vocational high school boys, and Grimminger seemed to have forgotten about him, for he turned and went back to his friends. Somewhere far away, the bell rang for the end of break, and Erich dragged himself up the steps, accompanied by Helmut and Erwin.

"You go on ahead or you'll have problems," he whispered unevenly to Helmut, but Helmut just shook his head. In the distance Erich could make out Lafrentz, strolling at his leisure to the school entrance after the last groups of pupils.

So Lafrentz had been on duty. No wonder no one had intervened.

After the last lesson the other boys in the class hurried past Erich and Erwin, their faces turned away. Erich had experienced the lessons after break only through a misty barrier, a barrier of pain and shame. Not even Gremm's venomous remarks could penetrate it. He usually ignored Erich's offers to answer questions; today he asked him to answer several times, and Erich, rising with difficulty and standing beside his desk, apathetically said the same thing each time. "I don't know, sir." Then he sat down again. There was low, derisive giggling in the background, but curiously enough he kept hearing just one thing going around and around in his head—*Onions are food that Jews enjoy*—and seeing Kampmann in front of him, Kampmann with his mouth wide open.

He waited at the foot of the steps for Kurt and, ignoring the angry or horrified faces of the other boys, took his sleeve and asked hoarsely, "Why aren't you wearing your uniform?"

Kurt stood there for a moment, then grabbed Erich's wrist and pushed his hand away. Shaking his head, he ran through the square outside the church as if someone were after him.

Someone else walking out of my life—no, *running* out of it, thought Erich as he dragged himself back home, to the safety of the dark front hall and the familiar sounds.

Over the next few days, it turned out that the threats made by Grimminger and Kampmann had worked. Erich and Erwin were on their own at break, at first with the others watching them in shy embarrassment, later completely ignoring them. Only Helmut still joined them at first, until after a few days

Grimminger and some others from the eleventh grade—tall, strong boys—came up to him and threatened him.

"What good does it do anyone if they beat you up too? You'd better stay away from us," Erich almost begged his friend. They had met up at the Benzenruhe woods again, and were sitting at the foot of a tall oak. From here they had a fine view of the town and the woods around it. This had been where they had taken refuge recently, for their former friends at school were avoiding their old places these days, and they didn't like going to the Jagst water meadows because the memory of the dead body, the flies, and the stench was still too close.

"I can't see any reason to let Kampmann and Grimminger decide who can stand where on break. Suppose your father . . . ?"

"Forget it, Helmut!" Erich remembered his father's stooped figure, dragging steps, and haggard face that time when he came away from the headmaster's office, after Gremm had intimidated Dr. Kaiser. "That's a very dangerous man," he had heard him say, and Erich rubbed his eyes to rid himself of the picture of his father, powerless and humiliated. "We can't do anything. Gremm and the others will tell the Head some lie or other about us disturbing everyone, and so on. And you know yourself that Kaiser is afraid of them. You just have to listen to him when he addresses the school."

Helmut said nothing. He sat there with his knees drawn up, head down on them. After a while he said, so quietly that Erich could hardly make out the words, "My father and most of all my mother have been begging me not to go out in public with you anymore. The way my father put it, there've been hints dropped."

Erich lay back in the grass. It was already dry and had a

late summer smell of hay. The tops of the trees above him glowed red and gold in the light of the September sun. He lay motionless. Now and then the light, shining through the leaves, touched his face, and he closed his eyes. This was the moment he'd feared more than anything.

A good thing I didn't invite him to my bar mitzvah, thought Erich. It's worked out just the way I expected. Now Helmut's going too. . . . He suddenly realized that his friend had gone on talking.

"I'm sorry, I didn't hear what you said." Erich turned over on his front and began pulling up blades of grass and tearing them apart.

"I was saying my father has to be careful. The Nazis have him in their sights. Everyone knows that as an old Center Party member he's not the sort they like. And he still doesn't mince his words. Yesterday there was a knock on the front door first thing in the morning. My mother almost went crazy. We thought they'd come to take him away—"protective custody" is what they call it. But thank God it was only the coal merchant delivering briquettes—what a laugh! And the law office isn't doing so well anymore either. Several clients have left. Right now it's not much of an advantage to be represented by Noll." Helmut tried to grin, but he looked on the point of tears.

"And if Noll's son is a close friend of the son of Levi the Jew . . . that makes the situation even more difficult. Please try to understand, Erich."

The boys avoided meeting each other's eyes. Silence became a wall between them. Both of them wanted to say something, but didn't know what. After a while Helmut broke the oppressive silence, and his voice sounded desperate.

"I really don't know what's going to come of all this. Oh, damn it, I'm scared, Erich. Scared for my father, for you, scared of whatever happens next. My great-uncle Hertwig was saying the other day, 'The mob rules,' and he's right. Erich, I'm really scared."

Erich had never seen his friend like this before. He felt like putting his arms around him, but that would never do. After all, they were nearly grown men. He sat up and then said quietly, more to himself than Helmut, "Not so long ago my mother was saying we ought to leave Germany."

Helmut stared at him. "And go where?"

Erich shrugged his shoulders. He began arranging the ripped blades of grass around him in a circle. "I don't know. Maybe America. We have relatives there." Suddenly he could picture his mother, looking so small and helpless, slumped on the kitchen chair. He heard her talking about *going away*, and remembered how angry he had been. How could she even think of such a thing? This was their home! Home . . . He went up the gentle rise of the hill and stared down at the town, at the churches, the low-built houses, the mighty rectangle of the castle on top of its hill opposite. It was as if he had to burn that picture into his heart and his soul.

Helmut had come up with him, and together they walked downhill in silence. When they reached the Jagst they stopped for a moment.

"Do you remember . . . ?" Helmut began, and Erich interrupted.

"I can't stop thinking of it. The way he was lying there. I don't think I can ever swim in the river again."

Helmut nodded. "I dream about it sometimes."

"Me, too."

"The police never came back. My father asked about it. It was probably suicide."

"My father told me that too. It was in the paper. He was a workman."

"What do you think was the matter with him?"

The boys looked at each other for a moment, and then Helmut asked, "I mean, can you understand it?"

"What?"

"Doing a thing like that."

Erich thought for a moment. "I never really thought about it. But yes, I think I can."

To their right lay the town, with the first buildings rising beyond the slope of the riverbank, and suddenly they both stopped. They looked at each other, and then Helmut said hoarsely, "We can meet in secret. What do you think?"

Erich shook his head slightly. "Suppose someone sees us? Köberle, for instance, or people in our class?"

"But we could have met just by chance."

"No one's going to believe it."

"All the same, Erich, there must be some kind of way."

Erich did not reply. He wasn't as optimistic as his friend. But perhaps he had to encourage himself, cling to something, even if it was just a vain, foolish hope. They said good-bye as usual, as if nothing had happened. Tomorrow they'd see each other in school.

Bar Mitzvah

IT WAS FALL. Fairs were held in the town's inns, and the landlords announced that there'd be meat broth and hotcakes. Erich's parents went to the Café Schimmel and the Golden Cross as usual, but not nearly as often as they used to. Mother kept saying she had a guilty conscience because she didn't want to get their friends, the owners, into trouble. They tried to keep a little bit of normality in their lives as much as they could, but it was getting more and more difficult. The newspapers were full of more or less open attacks on "the pernicious Jewish spirit."

Erich had taken to picking up the newspaper in the morning, so as to look at it in secret before breakfast, and he also passed the showcase outside the editorial offices where the Party newspaper was on display, skimming quickly through the articles, with his bike propped against the wall. The texts all followed the same pattern; they were about the "swindles perpetrated by Jewish profiteers," and told tales of Jewish tradesmen who had cheated their customers. Much was made of the cattle dealer from Oberdorf who had sold a local farmer a cow that was blind in one eye and always coughing. As Father had said, there are always a few bad apples in a barrel. And even an experienced cattle dealer could find that he had sold an animal which wasn't in perfect health. However, the newspaper kept on publishing such stories and linking them with dark threats.

One day Erich read an article stating that "The Jewish question is the question of Germany's survival." It was full of long-winded phrases. Erich noticed some particularly pompous examples, for instance about "the German spirit" and how it was "falling victim to an un-German, rapacious ruling class of capitalist usurers." Without understanding in detail what all that meant, he felt that the tone of such stories was getting shriller and more venomous. He kept hearing Helmut's, "I'm scared, Erich," uttered with difficulty, and seeing his mother sitting on the kitchen chair and talking about going away. All the same, he tried to show that he was happy about his coming bar mitzvah. Mother and Aunt Lea were going to so much trouble with the preparations.

On the morning of Tuesday the third of October, his birthday, there was a large cake with thirteen candles on the table. It was Mother's wonderful hazelnut cake, baked only for special occasions. The table of birthday presents wasn't as lavish as over the last few years, but that was only what he had expected. There were new knitted socks and a gray-and-white pullover with a Norwegian pattern, some chocolate, a present of money from Granny Babette, and a book from Max with gold lettering on the leather spine. *German Hero Sagas*. He was touched, and swallowed hard, trying not to cry.

"I saved up for it." Max was obviously proud of that. "You like reading those stories so much, and the old book's ruined."

Granny Babette, Aunt Lea, Uncle Sigmund, and Erwin all came to coffee in the afternoon. Erwin's birthday was two days later. They avoided discussing politics and all the things that were now troubling them so much. This was Erich's day, and they were going to celebrate it as cheerfully as possible in spite of all their fears.

On Saturday morning, the day of his bar mitzvah, Erich woke early. He lay there in bed for a while, looking at the narrow rectangle of light on the floor drawn by the sun coming through the crack between the curtains, growing lighter and lighter. It was going to be a sunny, dry day. There in the wardrobe hung his suit, specially made for the occasion by Herr Kugler. It looked elegant and festive, and Erich had seemed strange to himself when he tried it on for the last time. Old Kugler had made him stand in front of the full-length mirror on the wall, and said proudly, "You look really distinguished, Erich. It's a perfect fit."

Herr Kugler had used the polite, grown-up form of the pronoun "you" to him, and perhaps it was the suit that did it. After all, he was a grown man now, at least by the laws of his faith. The suit had been delivered punctually yesterday evening, just before the festive meal for the Sabbath eve, which was in Uncle Sigmund and Aunt Lea's home. But Julius and Melanie were giving the supper for the bar mitzvah itself. In the afternoon they had pushed all the tables in the apartment together to make one big one. The whole family had come: Aunt Mina and Uncle Louis with Ilse; Aunt Betti and Uncle Samson from Ulm; the two Süssel uncles from Pirmasens and

Wanne-Eickel; and Aunt Lea's relations from Markelsheim. They had brought a great many crates of wine, which they stacked in the bathroom. Father had put the bottles of white wine in the bath and kept running cold water over them. And of course Granny Babette was there, in her usual black silk. Erich had always thought the rustle and swishing of her black silk dress was a very good sound.

Erich slipped out of bed and went down to the bathroom, which was crammed not only with crates of wine but with platters of carp in aspic, filled rolls, and cold meat sliced paper thin. He made his way over to the mirror, where he looked at himself long and hard. He saw a thin face with the Levis' unmistakable jug ears, though they weren't as bad as Father's or Max's. His best feature was his eyes, he thought. Big brown eyes. And his hair, thick and dark, which he now damped down slightly so that he could part it neatly and then comb it carefully back. As Fanny had always said—he was the vainest boy she knew.

Oh, Fanny! The day before yesterday a letter had come, more of a note, really. A few hastily scribbled lines, as if the writer had been in a great hurry. Or wanted to write the letter quickly, unseen by anyone. No, she had said, she couldn't come—she gave no reason—she was sorry, and there had been a dozen white handkerchiefs with the letter. She had embroidered "E.L." on them in delicate, curly letters. Mother had read the note without comment, and firmly crossed Fanny's name off the guest list. And to Max's anxious question, "Why isn't she coming?" she had replied only with a brief, "I don't know," then added, "We'd better not count on her coming to see us again."

And that, I suppose, is the end of that chapter, thought

Erich, as he carefully put on the new white shirt that Mother had bought him. But Fanny, our Fanny! Was she afraid, like so many others? He slipped into his trousers and jacket, and looked at himself in the mirror again. He really did look grown-up now—well, *almost* grown-up, he corrected himself. Dark down had begun forming on his upper lip recently, but it still grew only sparsely, as he had to admit whenever he inspected it. And he would never be as tall as Kampmann, although he had grown some more over the last few months. All things considered, however, he was satisfied. The suit was a perfect fit, and he'd do the family credit today.

Other people were beginning to stir in the apartment. Mother poked the fire in the kitchen stove and called for Max. The squeal of wardrobe doors came from Fanny's old room, where Aunt Mina and Uncle Louis were sleeping, and someone knocked softly at the bathroom door. It was Father.

"May I come in?" He looked his son up and down. "Well, I must say you're looking good. Really elegant. You always were a vain fellow! Now all you need is a tie." And he handed Erich a pale silk tie.

"Oh, thanks, Father. Now you must show me how to tie one of these things! Today I'm grown up, after all."

Julius wagged a finger at him. "Not quite yet! But yes, I really must teach you how to tie a tie. Although you won't be having so very many occasions to wear one just yet. Come here." He put the tie around Erich's neck and then, standing in front of the mirror, took him through the process step by step. "Look, now you pass this end over the knot—no, this one—and you feed the other end through the loop here."

Erich fidgeted impatiently, but finally they had the job done, and father and son looked gravely at each other in the mirror. "Not bad at all. You look good, son." Then Julius took Erich by the shoulders, turned him around, and looked hard into his face for a moment.

"Listen to this, Erich. Years ago, when your mother and I were telling each other how proud we would be when we celebrated our sons' bar mitzvahs, we never dreamed that this occasion would have to take place under such circumstances. You know what I mean. And you boys—you in particular, Erich—are feeling so many of the effects of it. You have a lot to put up with. That's what troubles us the most, especially your mother. But do you remember what I said to you back in spring, when it was beginning? On our way to the cattle sheds?"

Erich nodded, and tried desperately to hold back the tears prickling at the back of his eyes.

"We won't let them get us down. And we will let nothing take our pride and dignity from us, do you hear, Erich?"

Oh, Father, he thought, they've taken so much from us already: our friends and Fanny too; we've lost so much. All we have left is our hopes and a few dreams, at least we have those. But he couldn't say so to Father, who was looking at him straight, almost pleadingly; Father, who seemed to be clinging to his convictions like a drowning man to a rope.

"Yes, Father," said Erich, taking a deep breath. "I promise I'll always remember that."

"Good," said Julius, kissing his son on the forehead. "And my best wishes for your great day. We are very proud of you, my boy."

After breakfast they went to the prayer hall in Bergstrasse. They were a festive little procession, the men in black suits and starched white collars, the women elegant in coats with fur collars turned up, their hats worn low over the forehead in the current fashion. Mother looked best of all, along with Ilse, of course, thought Erich proudly. She might be wearing last year's skirt suit and coat—there hadn't been enough money for new clothes for her—but with her tall, slender figure and carefully arranged dark brown hair, she looked lovely. He and Erwin brought up the rear of their group, followed by his grandmother, walking with great dignity on the arm of her eldest son, Uncle Siegfried.

A few passersby stopped and whispered quietly, but most of them looked the other way and hurried on. A group of Brownshirts was standing outside the inn next to the rail station, obviously going for an early drink. They shouted insults at the little group. Erich saw mouths wide open, grinning, spitefully distorted mouths, hands pointing at them; he heard words that he didn't want to understand. Curiously enough he kept thinking of the same sentence, a staccato rhythm in his ears, that childhood memory from when it was still an innocent remark, as he took it in his ignorance *Onions are food that Jews enjoy.*

Now I know, though, thought Erich. We're just dirt to them, onion-eaters, stinking dirt, and he looked fearfully at the faces of his grandmother, his mother and father, all the others walking steadily on. Only Uncle Samson once seemed on the point of turning around, his fist clenched, but Aunt Betti stopped him. Max kept turning and seemed to want to ask Mother something now and then, but Melanie held his hand tight and led him on, and so they arrived in Bergstrasse at last.

Dr. Berlinger, the rabbi, who had come specially from Schwäbisch Hall, was waiting with the cantor and met them at the door. All the Jewish families in Ellwangen had come, the Heinrichs, the Neuburgers, even old Herr Neuburger with his walking stick, his head shaking slightly. They were a small, lost-looking group, but now they formed a guard of honor for him and Erwin, the two youngest members of the congregation, their hope for the future. Old Herr Neuburger always used to say that they were doing well in the little community, even if they had no minyan of their own and had to invite guests from outside to make up the number. Suddenly Erich felt as if everything was all right, at least in this part of his world, where they belonged together and respected each other and were glad of one another's company. Mother and Aunt Lea had decorated the prayer hall with leafy branches and late summer flowers. The sweet, heavy fragrance of the flowers hung in the room like a distant memory.

Then Erich, as the elder boy, was called forward to the bima,* where the scroll of the Torah lay before him. He felt the eyes of the family on him behind his back as he slowly walked forward, very carefully, trembling at the knees. He mustn't do anything wrong now, mustn't stumble over his words or get them mixed up. Slowly and solemnly he read the scripture for the day, hearing the words echo in the room:

> *In the beginning God created the heaven and the earth.*
> *And the earth was without form, and void,*
> *and darkness was upon the face of the deep.*
> *And the spirit of God moved upon the face of the waters . . .*

It moved him strangely that the text was from the beginning of the Bible, the story of Creation, and it was strange, too, that the last sentence he read was the same as the inscription on the family's Sabbath plate: "And the evening and the morning were the sixth day."

The rabbi gave him a friendly nod when he stood up after reading the lesson and went back to his place very slowly, so as to enjoy every moment. He saw the pride in his parents' faces, he saw Ilse's lips silently blowing him a kiss, saw Uncle Louis smiling, and Aunt Mina wiping away a tear. He saw his brother Max gazing at him respectfully, and Herr Neuburger nodding with benevolence. Now he was grown up; he really belonged. He felt proud and for a moment happy—he, Erich Levi, a member of the Jewish community of Ellwangen, and he stopped thinking about the world outside the door of the little prayer hall.

After he and Erwin had received congratulations and the envelopes with cards and presents of money, they went home again.

There was an enticing smell in the apartment already. Martha Bieg, red in the face, was at work in the kitchen. She had brought one of her salesgirls along to help, and the girl was just putting the big pan of soup on the stove. Melanie hadn't wanted to accept Frau Bieg's offer at first. "We wouldn't like to get you into any difficulties, Martha," she protested. But Martha had dismissed all protests, and in addition said she would bring her best girl, Elli, along to lend a hand. "Suppose she doesn't want to?" Mother had hesitantly asked, but Martha was having none of that.

"She has to want to, I'll see to it." Elli was in fact looking a little sullen. She didn't like being made to come along and help out "at the Jews' place," and her little bob to Melanie and the others when they came in was only a sketchy one. But Martha was really glad to see them, pinched Erich's and Erwin's cheeks, and asked jokingly if she ought to address them both as "Herr Levi" now. Erich dutifully laughed and then clinked glasses with everyone.

It was his first glass of wine, and a particularly good wine brought along by Aunt Lea's relations, one that was usually drunk only on special occasions, as Aunt Lea's brother proudly told everyone. The wine, heavy and sweet, ran down his throat and was soon spreading comfortable warmth all through his body. A slight, pleasant weariness came over him, and only when he had eaten some of the appetizers and had some soup did his head clear again.

It was a good party. They tried to leave all their anxieties and fears outside, clung close to each other and their memories, to everything they shared and that kept them together. They drank toasts to Erich and Erwin, cracked jokes, told stories of the old days, and then Ilse sat down at the piano and played music for dancing. Erich danced in turn with Mother and then Aunt Lea, who was livelier than Erich had ever seen her. He danced clumsily, without knowing the steps, but the rhythm of the music had entered into his body, and his mother and aunt, laughing, adjusted to his movements. When Uncle Ludwig took over from Ilse and struck up a polka, Erich danced with Ilse too, a wild, unruly dance, and he suddenly thought of that night in Oedheim, the whispering and the quiet laughter and the two faces merging. It was a strange and new feeling to hold a woman's body so close, such a strong feeling that he felt afraid of it, and suddenly let go of Ilse.

"What's the matter?" she cried, laughing, but then there was a sudden hammering on the front door of the apartment. They all stood rooted to the spot for a moment. Uncle Ludwig looked particularly funny, with his hands hovering over the piano keyboard where he had been just about to strike a chord.

Into this deathly silence, Julius said quietly, "I'll go and see who it is." He shook Mother's hand off as she tried to hold him back. Slowly, he went to the living room door and along the passage.

Erich was standing close to Ilse. Little beads of perspiration had formed on her upper lip. She was breathing fast and looking at the passage, like all the others. Grandmother had dropped into one of the leather armchairs. Aunt Mina went up to her and began stroking her hand.

Slowly, Father opened the front door, and in the dark of the landing outside they could see the outlines of two figures, policemen, but that was all they could see. However, Erich recognized one of them; he had been out by the Jagst on the day that he and Helmut found the body. The family was standing close together in the doorways of the living room and kitchen. Max and little Heinz-Viktor, Aunt Betti and Uncle Samson's son, were trying to wriggle past all those bodies and arms and legs.

The larger of the policemen, the burly man whom Erich had seen before, let his eyes wander over the company, who looked at him with anxiety and caution. No one but Julius dared go into the passage; they stayed by the doors as if an invisible line had been drawn and they mustn't cross it. The other policeman, who was younger and thinner, kept behind his colleague. He seemed to feel embarrassed about it all.

Without so much as a "Good evening," the bigger man began talking. There'd been complaints, he said, some of the neighbors had called the police. Whatever they were indulging in here was much too loud. He talked about disturbing the peace of the neighborhood at night, and possible legal proceedings, and finally his voice grew loud and threatening. Erich wasn't really listening; he was watching the man's mouth opening and closing, fascinated by it. Curiously enough this burly policeman had a soft, curving, almost feminine mouth that didn't suit the rest of his appearance at all, or what he was saying either. Small bubbles of spit sprayed out of that mouth and collected as narrow rivulets at its corners. When he had finished what he had to say, the man instinctively took out his handkerchief and wiped his face with it.

Julius tried to explain that this was a special family party, a happy occasion. "And officer, it's not ten yet, and I can assure you we won't be playing music after ten. We'll keep very quiet. It's Saturday evening, remember." As if in confirmation of this remark, bawling and laughter rose from the street below, where several drunks were probably on their way home from the nearby inns.

The taller policeman adjusted his uniform jacket. "Well, now you know. Not a sound out of here, or else . . ." That "or else" was like a huge post rammed into the floor of the room. You had to watch out for the post or you might bump into it and hurt yourself. It augured no good. Even your own four walls were no protection anymore; you were being watched. They were carefully registering what went on within those walls, and at the slightest excuse they could come back, representatives of the power that had the say about everything these days. The uniformed men went to the door without a good-bye, as it seemed at first, but then the smaller officer turned around and said, very quietly and awkwardly, "Good night."

Those words were like a magic charm, breaking the spell on the family as they stood as if frozen in the doorway.

They moved apart and went back into the living room, but everything remained muted. There was no music anymore, no laughter, even when they talked, they kept their voices down, and Mother quickly checked that all the doors and windows were closed. After a while the visiting relations said good night; they were tired, they said, and they had to get up early tomorrow to go home. Only Aunt Mina and Uncle Louis stayed sitting in the living room a little longer, drinking cognac from the brandy glasses that Mother had silently taken out of the glass-fronted cupboard. Max was sent to bed, although he sulked, but Erich was allowed to stay up a little longer. After all, he was one of the adults now. They talked about this and that, and admired Erich's presents again. The Nolls and a few others had remembered his bar mitzvah day and sent something. The Biegs, of course, and the two Fräulein Pfisterers, and also Frau Österlein, who owned the shop where Mother bought her dresses, and Dr. Schlegel from Sebastian-Merkle-Strasse, who had been the family's dentist for many years.

Erich's glance lingered on the table beside the piano where all his presents were piled up. It had been only a small table, and over these last few days he had wondered what it would have been like if his bar mitzvah had been a year before. Perhaps—no, certainly—they'd have needed a bigger table, and it would have been piled high! But today the little one was enough. And in the middle of the presents, lovingly displayed, were Fanny's handkerchiefs. Every time he looked at those handkerchiefs he felt a dull pain, a pain that he didn't want to acknowledge, but it was there deep inside him.

After a while, when Uncle Louis and Father had begun talking politics, despite the best efforts of Mother and Aunt Mina to stop them, Erich went over to the table and slipped the book that Max had given him on top of the handkerchiefs. As she said good night, Aunt Mina hugged him and whispered in his ear, "It was a lovely bar mitzvah, Erich, in spite of everything."

Erich nodded. Yes, his parents and the whole family had gone to a great deal of trouble. And the little prayer hall had been so festively decorated. But all the same—you could never get away from it, never get away from the power, the fear, the shame.

Chanukah 1933

TWO WEEKS LATER, on a Monday, Father came into the kitchen to find Mother. He looked very pale. Melanie was making sandwiches for Max and Erich to take to school for break while the boys sat at the kitchen table eating their breakfast, looking tired and listless. Julius held the newspaper out to Mother. He had just collected it from their box in the front hall of the building. "Here, read that!"

Mother wiped her hands on her apron and took the paper. "'Germany Leaves the League of Nations,'" she read aloud. Melanie lowered the paper and looked inquiringly at Father. "Julius, what does it mean?"

Father paced up and down the kitchen. "Ultimately it means what I've always thought those fellows were after. A number of others think so too. Schlosser told me the other day it would end in this."

"In what? Julius, what do you mean?"

Father stopped and looked at his sons, then drew Mother aside and said something to her quietly. Erich, his curiosity aroused, stared at Father, watched his lips, and realized that he was saying only a single word. He could lip-read it rather than hear it, that soundlessly breathed word. "War."

To Erich, war was something nebulous, you couldn't quite put your finger on it. He linked it to ideas of men fighting each other like the heroes in his beloved sagas. And of course war meant death. He briefly closed his eyes and thought of the man in the river, but as the teachers were always saying, especially Gremm, dying in war was self-sacrifice and special. "To die for the Fatherland," someone had written up on the blackboard recently, was "sweet and honorable." And now Father was talking about Hitler wanting to start a war. But what's the difference? he thought bitterly. Hitler is already at war with us Jews.

Gray fall days began—usually there was dense mist above the Jagst in the morning, and mothers put out their children's woolen socks, because it had turned cold. At the end of October, the "loudmouth-in-chief" really did become the new mayor of Ellwangen, as Helmut had predicted a long time ago; that infallible oracle, his father, had told him about Kolbe's plans. The news didn't particularly upset Erich. The Nazis were everywhere now, and there was nothing anyone could do about them. He had other anxieties: he had to get through the daily battle for survival at school, ignore gibes and insults, bear his loneliness at break when he stood in a corner with his sandwich, overcome his fear of being attacked when someone suddenly came up to him—a strong Hitler Youth boy, for instance, calling him and Erwin names to provoke them. He had to avoid the deliberate pushing and shoving as they hurried up and down stairs and along the corridors to their classroom. He had to put up with injustice, with teachers tormenting him, with bad marks that he didn't deserve and were purely arbitrary. He had to accept the thoughtlessness of the other boys, the fact that they all avoided him and left him alone in the yard at break like a half-forgotten piece of furniture, an unwelcome memory that you put out of your mind.

On the last Monday in October, Gremm assembled his class in the church square. "The führer will be flying over Ellwangen on his way to Stuttgart," he had solemnly announced, and so they were standing around, hands dug into their trouser pockets, caps well down on their heads because a cold fall wind was sweeping dry chestnut leaves all over the square, blowing dust and grains of sand into their faces. At every distant sound the boys raised their arms and pointed excitedly at the gray October sky, but there was nothing to be seen, and finally Gremm decided that they could go back indoors.

Erich, who had been standing apart from the others with Erwin as usual, kept exchanging secret glances with Helmut, who was on the edge of the larger group, and was making faces to tell Erich how stupid he thought all this was. They had a private game of watching Kampmann and the others—their faces looked so silly with noses raised aloft and mouths wide open—and the way they frantically raced back and forth. "There—there he is! . . . Where? . . . Look, look up there . . . !"

You'd think it was the Messiah coming, thought Erich, amused, and then, with a small shudder, he realized that to

Gremm, Kampmann, and a great many other people, Hitler probably *was* something like their Messiah.

Fall went by in an endless series of torchlit processions, banner dedication ceremonies, rallies, memorial ceremonies in the gymnasium hall. There was always something to be celebrated through that fall of 1933, and Erich stopped listening when long speeches were made on the faintest pretext. Several of the others seemed to feel the same. Much more important was Eisele's biology test, which almost everyone failed miserably, or the question of whether the boxer Max Schmeling had false teeth, as claimed one day at break by fat Müller. The subject aroused such heated argument that it ended in a fight between Müller and several fanatical Schmeling fans. "Watch out or you may soon need false teeth yourself," Schluffi had hissed at fat Müller before he went to the Head's study along with several others to be given their punishment: four hours' detention that afternoon. The teacher on supervision duty at break had reported their scuffle at once.

At such moments Erich longed passionately to belong again, to be able to hang around with the others, shout support for his friends, make comments to Helmut about what was going on.

Helmut—that was the worst of all, the loss of that friendship. In spite of the difficult circumstances, they still tried to keep it going, or at least parts of it, like the broken fragments of a valuable vase that might perhaps be glued together again some day. It was dark very early in the evening now, and Helmut sometimes slipped past the buildings on the marketplace at that time of day and over to the building where the Levis lived, to meet Erich at the back entrance.

Soon after his bar mitzvah, Erich had moved into

Fanny's old room. He did it in a spirit of defiance: she was never coming back, he was grown up now, so why shouldn't he have a room of his own? Then Max could read in the evenings until his eyes fell out without bothering Erich. And he'd finally have some peace from his brother's endless questions. So he moved into Fanny's room and suppressed his memories. He changed the position of the chest of drawers and wardrobe and asked Mother to put up some new drapes. "Not as girlie as the old ones," he had muttered to Melanie, who swallowed a sharp retort with some difficulty, but did in fact take down the pale blue flower-patterned drapes in silence, searched her linen chest, and finally found some that Erich liked. They were made of linen in a strong, brown shade, and he thought they were better for a boy's room whose occupant was almost grown up.

After supper he usually went off to his room and left the window open for a while, in spite of the cool fall air. And on many evenings he heard the familiar whistle, their secret signal, and ran down to open the back door. Then he and Helmut sat on the narrow stairs leading down to the cellars, among the crates and boxes from the ironmongery and china shop, and if one of the two Fräulein Pfisterers came along to lock the cellar door, she would give them a conspiratorial wink and go away, coming back to lock up later.

The two sisters were nice, though they seemed quite old to Erich—proverbial old maids with braids of hair pinned up on their heads, and long skirts. But the younger one, Marie, had youthful, twinkling eyes; and Auguste, who usually looked very grave and stern—which was quite enough to give you a guilty conscience on the spot—had a big, generous heart. Julius had recently told the family that certain "upright citizens," as he ironically called them, had told the two ladies in fairly plain terms that they ought to evict the Levis from the apartment they rented. Both ladies, in equally plain terms, had let it be known that they wouldn't dream of turning the tenants they had known so long out into the street, and they would thank other people to mind their own business.

Erich always remembered that when he saw either of the Fräulein Pfisterers, and he knew he must be cheered by people like them, who stayed friends with his family despite all the hostility. They made life more bearable. And Helmut's occasional visits helped too, even though there was so much they couldn't share any longer. But it felt good to talk about the day's events, large and small, for Helmut was still very close to him. At such moments, safe in the darkness of the back hall, Erich at least had the illusion that it might all be back the way it had once been.

Then, when he went upstairs again, Mother would be sitting at the kitchen table in the lamplight, darning socks or sewing on buttons. She had much more to do now that Fanny wasn't there. Sometimes Mother and Father still treated themselves to a meal out, in the café or at the inn, but hardly anyone would share a table with them these days, and Julius, who used to enjoy a game of cards at the Bunch of Grapes, couldn't find anyone to be his partner now, so he generally stayed at home.

Christmas was coming; the shops decorated their windows with evergreens and glass baubles, which meant Chanukah was imminent too. Mother took the menorah out of the glass-fronted cupboard to polish it until the tarnished silver shone. During lessons at school Erich's eyes wandered more often than usual to the window, where a leaden gray sky hung over the towers of the Collegiate Church. But yet again it refused to snow; mud in the streets splashed up and made your socks damp. It was truly filthy weather, as even the newspaper said. A Christmas tree went up in the middle of the marketplace this year for the first time ever, and the local Nazis made a big deal of it. Christmas had not originally been a Christian festival at all, Gremm told them in class, but had originated with the old Germanic tribes, so the Christmas tree was their legacy too. Erich wasn't really listening, just thinking to himself that the Nazis didn't even balk at rejecting the good old Christmas tree, which Gremm insisted on calling a Yule tree instead.

There had always been a Christmas tree in the Levis' apartment in December, even though they were Jewish, but Erich decided to ask his mother not to have one this year. If even the Christmas tree was of old Germanic origin, then it had no business in a Jewish household. His parents agreed, but Max went on whining until, a few days before Christmas Eve, Julius went out and came back with a small tree, which they stood in a corner of the living room as usual. "The others were much bigger," Max complained, and he was cross about his presents too. They were far less lavish this year.

"Just keep your mouth shut, will you?" Erich hissed at him on the first day of Chanukah, when Max, visibly discontented, was opening his packages that were piled up between the Christmas tree and the menorah.

But all the same, Chanukah, which usually fell a few days before Christmas, was very good. The evening before it, the rabbi came over specially from Schwäbisch Hall and held a lovely service in the prayer hall. Herr Silbermann sang during the service. Dr. Berlinger reminded the congregation of the origin of the festival and the miracle worked by the Almighty when he gave his oppressed people a sign. Erich, standing in the front row between Father and Uncle Sigmund, thought privately that they could do with another miracle like that now. However, he felt comforted by Dr. Berlinger's sermon, and when they sat together in the evening by the light of the menorah candles, along with the wax tapers on the poor little Christmas tree, it was almost like the old, cheerful, happy Chanukah atmosphere. Erich opened his packages more slowly and thoughtfully than Max, of course, since he was almost grown up now and didn't make a great fuss about presents. There were more practical items and fewer fun things than usual: knitted socks, pullovers, warm underclothes. What he liked best was Grandmother's present. When she went away to spend the festive season with Aunt Betti in Ulm, she had left both brothers a generous sum of money.

On the day after Christmas, Max came into Erich's room. He was wearing his coat and his Norwegian cap. "Coming?" he asked his brother, who was lying on his bed reading.

Erich stretched and yawned. "Coming where?"

"To Willi's place, of course, to play with his train set." A visit to Max's friend was an established Christmas ritual. Years ago, Willi's father had given him a Märklin train set, adding very generously to it every year, so he now had a magnificent collection, and a room up on the attic floor had to be specially cleared for it at Christmas. Erich suspected that, to judge by the time and enthusiasm he devoted to playing with it, Willi's father was really giving himself presents. For the Levi boys a visit to Willi's was always a great event, since his train set was infinitely better than their own. They always admired the new additions with just a touch of envy, and then they played trains all afternoon until the gathering dusk darkened the room, and the little lights on the trains themselves twinkled brightly.

For a moment Erich paused to think, but then he jumped up. So maybe he *had* celebrated his bar mitzvah, but playing trains still hadn't lost its charms. Anyway, it would be better than lying around here on his bed all day. "Okay, wait a moment."

When they were trudging up the Alte Steige, he asked Max, "Are you sure Frau Mendler really invited you for today?"

Max nodded without looking at him.

"Then why didn't you tell me?"

"I just forgot. Anyway, we do it every year."

Erich began to get suspicious. There was something about Max's manner that he didn't quite like. When they rang the bell, the door opened after a while, and Willi's little sister, Erika, looked out through the narrow crack. She had the end of one of her braids in her mouth and was chewing it. Undecided, she looked at the two visitors, then turned and shouted, "Mama, Mama, come quick!"

Frau Mendler appeared in the doorway with a coffeepot in her hand. When she saw Max and Erich she pushed Erika aside and barred the boys' view of the front hall by placing her ample frame full in the doorway. She was red in the face and obviously embarrassed. "Oh, my word, it's Max and Erich! I'd forgotten all about you. But I'm afraid today is really no good, we have visitors at the moment, and . . ."

Erich interrupted her, tightly squeezing the cap he had politely taken off when the door was opened. "I'm so sorry, Frau Mendler. We really didn't want to disturb anyone. It was just about the train set—but Max probably misunderstood something."

Frau Mendler nodded so vigorously that her pinned up hair wobbled. "Yes, a misunderstanding. Just a misunderstanding, I'm sure. But it's really no good this year, we told Willi so too. Do please understand. Perhaps next . . ." Now Frau Mendler was stumbling over her words.

Erich put his cap on and took hold of Max's arm. "Forgive us for bothering you, Frau Mendler. And happy Christmas to you."

Frau Mendler was visibly relieved, although still rather embarrassed. "Oh yes, thank you, and the same to you. Would you like a few Christmas cookies to take with you?"

"No, thanks, really!" called Erich as they walked away. He still had Max in an iron grip. His brother hadn't said a word. In silence, they walked a little way down the road. By now it had begun to rain again, a cold rain mingled with snow that covered the street with a dirty gray film.

Suddenly a violent rage seized upon Erich, a blind, furious rage that made him feel as if he were bursting. Without really knowing what he was doing he grabbed Max, threw him into the gray, greasy dirt, and then kicked him several times. He had to vent his feelings now, at once, trample on everything, break and destroy it, the way their lives were being trampled on, broken, and destroyed. He stopped kicking and hitting only when he saw the expression on Max's face. Max hadn't made a sound but was just staring straight at his brother. The look of horror in his wide eyes and his unnatural silence finally brought Erich to his senses.

He got down in the road beside his brother and began awkwardly stroking his hair. Max suddenly began crying, a soundless, mute weeping, and now and then a convulsive sob shook his body. Erich noticed tears running down his own cheeks all of a sudden, falling steadily onto the back of his hand and his brother's hair. Max had buried his head in Erich's jacket.

"Why did you do that to us?" Erich whispered, still stroking Max's head. There was silence for a while, as sobs went on running through Max, but then he freed himself and looked at Erich.

"I wanted to play with the trains so much. I just didn't think. I wanted it to be the same as always. Willi hadn't said anything. But I did want to so much. Erich, why can't things go back to the way they used to be? Why not, Erich?"

Erich looked at his brother. Tears were still running down Max's face, mingled with snot; his eyelids were swollen, and there were red marks on his left cheek where Erich had hit him in the face. Suddenly Erich remembered the picture that hung over his mother's dressing table in his parents' bedroom. Father had had it painted from a photograph. It showed Erich and Max as little boys in front of a traditional landscape of spruce trees and Alpine huts. They were wearing traditional costume, lederhosen and jackets, and Erich still vaguely remembered how the picture had been taken. They had gone to spend a few days in the Alps—it seemed ages ago now. His parents had bought the traditional costumes then, and Father had a local photographer take the photo because he was so charmed by the sight of his two boys standing hand in hand in a flowery meadow. In fact the Alpine meadow had been artificial, just like the mountains and spruce trees; they were part of the stage settings in the photographer's studio, but that didn't spoil Mother and Father's pleasure. Erich suddenly remembered every detail. Once again he saw the photographer before him, hidden under a big black cloth, and the curious smell of paints and chemicals. He felt the pressure of his brother's small hand trustingly clutching his own, and for a moment he closed his eyes to rid himself of these images.

When he opened them again he saw that Max was still looking straight at him. He felt the cold damp seeping through his clothes, and with difficulty clambered to his feet, helping his brother up, too. Without looking at him, he said firmly, "It will never be the way it was again, Max, or at least not for a long time. You'd better get used to that idea. Come along, let's go home or we'll catch cold. And another thing," he added, stopping to look at his brother's tearstained face. "We won't tell Mother and Father anything about this, right? I'm sorry about what happened, but it would be better if you didn't mention it. It would make Mama very sad."

Slowly, Max nodded. As they picked their way down the sloping road, taking care not to slip in the slush, Max suddenly put his hand into Erich's. For a brief moment, Erich thought of the picture of the two little boys in the Alpine meadow again. Then he pressed Max's hand very hard, just for a minute, and they walked back home through the town, at peace with one another.

Belonging

HE COLD MARKET, held in Ellwangen at the beginning of January, was a large horse and cattle market with hundreds of years of tradition behind it. It was always a great event for Julius Levi and his family. Father was constantly out and about on the days of the market and often brought friends home, customers or cattle dealers from outside Ellwangen, who sat in the living room drinking the local wine and smoking fat cigars until smoke hung in the air. Mother would always open all the windows in the evening in spite of the cold weather. "Just so that we can see where we're going," she used to say, only half joking.

The group that came home with Father this year on Monday evening, after the first day of the market, was smaller than usual, and it included none of his own customers, just colleagues who happened to be Jewish.

Erich also noticed that most of them looked graver and more anxious than usual. They cracked jokes with the boys, and yes, they gave Erich money as a late bar mitzvah present, but then they quickly went off into the living room, talking quietly together. Mother gave them red wine and glasses, and carefully closed the door. This time there was little of the usual laughter and exuberant talk.

Mother had told Erich that old Herr Neumeister from Oberdorf had given up cattle dealing entirely and moved to Stuttgart with his children. In the end he'd had almost no business at all. And Salomon Hirsch, who owned a large cattle-dealing business near Gaildorf, was speaking openly of selling up while he could still get something for it, and then emigrating. Erich felt a pang when Mother mentioned that, for it reminded him of the unwelcome idea that they too might have to go away some day. But he tried to push the thought out of his mind, and kept busy helping his mother bring up more wine from the cellar. When he entered the living room with fresh supplies, the men had their heads close together.

"Those bastards are everywhere now," he heard young Bamberger saying as he came in. Bamberger was the only man smoking cigarettes rather than cigars. He had recently taken over his father's cattle business in Bopfingen, and was starting a family. Father had told Mother the evening before that his wife was expecting their first child.

"Uniforms and banners all over the place! And the SA bandsmen played for the opening ceremony instead of the good old town band!" Salomon Hirsch brought his fist down on the table, making the glasses clink, and the men nodded.

"The SA reserved almost all the tables at the Lamb for this evening," added young Bamberger. "There's nowhere for us to go now. I'd really have liked to see Haase's show, too." A quiet murmur of agreement greeted his words.

Erich had read in the newspaper that Paul Haase, the famous comedian from Saxony, was to perform at the Lamb inn when the Cold Market opened, and he knew how disappointed Father must be. He would have loved to see the show, Erich felt sure. But surrounded by SA men? He couldn't possibly go. "We wouldn't feel much like laughing," said Isidor Schlossberger, with a wry grin. He was distantly related to the Levis, and when Erich refilled his glass he clapped him on the shoulder. "Well, my boy, and when are you going into your father's business? I'd be glad to see you join us here some day."

"I really want to study at university, Uncle Isidor. I'll be taking my high school diploma in five years' time," said Erich, biting his lower lip.

"I'll be taking my high school diploma in five years' time." The words echoed inside his head. He had a long way yet to go, but he'd do it in spite of all the bullying. Another five years.

"Oh yes, that's right, you're at the prep school. I'll bet you're a bright lad. And how's things at school, then?"

"Okay, Uncle Isidor. But it's not all that easy for us these days."

Isidor Schlossberger and the others nodded thoughtfully.

"Erich is a very brave boy, even though they bully him and he's met with violence," Father suddenly said, his voice calm. "So far Max has been luckier. His class is taught only by the older teachers, and they leave him alone. Some of his friends don't invite him to their houses anymore, but on the whole he's rather better off than Erich. But as I said, Erich stands up to it courageously." Julius looked affectionately at his son. "We're proud of him."

Standing in the doorway, Erich felt himself go red. The men looked at him kindly, and exchanged tales of similar experiences relating to their own children and grand-children.

Erich stacked the empty bottles away in the kitchen and then went to the window, where he pressed his forehead to the cool pane. It was already dark outside, and he could see noth-ing but the lighted windows in the houses opposite. He thought of last year's Cold Market and its cheerful atmosphere; he also remembered Fanny in the kitchen, her face flushed, making sandwiches. And Mother had worn a lovely new dress with a brooch at the neck, and everyone had admired her. Today she was wearing a housedress and looked tired and careworn. He thought again of the five years still to go until he took his diploma, those endless five years. And then what would things be like? What would they be like in *one* year's time, at the next Cold Market?

He opened the window and took deep breaths of the keen, cold air, drawing the familiar smell of smoke and snow into his nostrils, a smell known to him since childhood, and thought that it was about all that hadn't changed.

During the next week Gremm seemed very edgy. The premiere of the play he was directing was coming up. A few days before the great event, on a Friday, they had only half a morning of lessons before Gremm marched his class off to the gymnasium hall for the dress rehearsal. All the members of the Jungvolk and the Hitler Youth in the class were in the play, including

Kurt. He was only an extra standing around onstage, but he was in it all the same, and Erich thought bitterly how he'd seemed to hate the mere idea only a few weeks ago. They hadn't spoken to each other much since the morning when he had told Erich how he'd given way to pressure from his father. At school, like most people, Kurt avoided meeting Erich's eyes and kept him at a distance, as if he were afraid even of being physically close to him. They did meet now and then in town, and once or twice Erich felt that Kurt was going to come up to him and say something. But every time, he passed quickly, eyes fixed firmly on the ground. So now he was up there with the others onstage. The female lead, a big blond girl, was declaiming her lines in a stilted voice, and Gremm, holding the text of the play, stood among the seats in the auditorium concentrating hard. He was so tensed up that he must have forgotten the presence of the Jewish students, or he would probably have sent them out of the hall, thought Erich, for being unable to understand what he'd called "this masterpiece of German culture."

And the masterpiece was enough to bore anyone rigid. The actors were very unnatural, spoke their lines overtheatrically to the empty hall, and Erich, who had made his way to the far side of the auditorium with Erwin, noticed some of his classmates hiding yawns. All the same, everyone crowded around Gremm and their friends who had been in the play when it ended, full of praise. "Fantastic, sir, that was really good! You put on a great show!"

Erich, glad that nothing of the kind was expected of him, slipped out of the hall with Erwin and set off for home. No one tried to stop them.

Tuesday was the first night of the show, and Erich stood at the living room window to watch crowds of spectators streaming toward the brightly lit gymnasium. Mingling with a few black SS uniforms were the brown uniforms of the SA men—more and more of them around these days—who dominated the scene. Practically all the members of the local Party were on their way to the hall, including the "loudmouth-in-chief," although he came in a car that pedestrians respectfully made way for as it clattered around the corner of Hindenburgstrasse. Erich could see many of the boys from his class, and a number of adults who he didn't think were particularly fond of the Nazis. But it was probably advisable not to miss a show supported by the Fighting League for German Culture and directed by Dr. Gremm. And it would certainly be a great success. Erich was sure of that. Who was going to criticize a play that followed all the guidelines of Nazi propaganda, and had also been staged by one of the most prominent Party Comrades in town?

With a violent movement, he closed the drapes and then went to his room, where he flung himself on the bed. He really ought to be doing homework: several arithmetic exercises and a German essay. His open German exercise book lay on the table, and whenever he saw the blank pages and the heading like a black bar at the top of the left-hand page, he felt a pang.

"Loyalty Means Self-Sacrifice," was the subject that Gremm had written on the board a few days ago. "The best essay will be read aloud on February the twenty-third," he had added, almost like a threat. "I hope that each and every one of you knows what *that* date means." Of course they did; they knew it by heart. Even in their sleep they could have recited the dates of all the new "great national heroes," people of whose existence they had known nothing at all until recently, dates of events that had been meaningless and obscure until January 30,

1933. February the 23rd was the anniversary of the death of Horst Wessel, a young SA man who had been murdered in the political turmoil at the end of the Weimar Republic. Gremm had told them his story many times, making it clear that he was a martyr and they must take such men as an example. And now came this slogan about loyalty and self-sacrifice.

Nonsense, thought Erich. And he knew what stupid stuff the others would be spouting. All lies and hypocrisy! He jumped up from his bed, reached blindly for his pen, and scored a deep black line right across the empty pages, making the ink spurt and leaving little black spots on the immaculate white paper. His mark for German was already settled anyway, maybe he wouldn't even get a "Satisfactory" from Gremm this year. He wasn't going to do the arithmetic homework either. And next Wednesday, the 31st of January, he was just going to stay in bed. There was to be another big commemoration ceremony at school; this time, of course, in honor of the Nazis' rise to power. Yet again there'd be endless speeches, spoken choruses, and singing. "Raise high the flag . . ." Always that endless, resonant shouting and singing. He was going to stay away from all such celebrations from now on, never mind what Mother said. After all, he didn't belong with the others anymore.

Kurt had been a leading light in the class's Jungvolk group for some time now, and loved to brag about it. He and the others had been to the pictures in January. The movie they saw was called *Hitler Youth Quex*, and obviously it had left a lasting impression.

"Suddenly he's all enthusiastic about the good things he says the Nazis have done, telling people they'll finally put an end to old-fashioned ways," Helmut confided at one of his secret evening meetings with Erich on the steps down to the cellar.

"Just what does he mean by that?" asked Erich.

Helmut shrugged his shoulders. "I don't exactly know either. But he keeps saying we're all one community now, and that family background makes no difference. Poor or rich, it comes to the same thing, and now he'll have as good a chance in life as people like me." Although it was dark, Erich knew that his friend was smiling slightly, but it was a bitter smile.

"So I told him it was more than likely," continued Helmut, "that he'd have considerably *better* chances than me in the future if he's such a staunch Party supporter. And I told him I'd prefer it if we didn't discuss you."

"What did he say about that?"

"Nothing. He ignored me on purpose. Oh yes, and then he said our local Nazis were planning something else amazing, and it will be in the paper soon."

Erich looked up at his friend, who let several seconds go by, smiling wryly at him.

"Well, come on, what *are* they planning?"

"They're going to stop having segregated swimming pools this year. There'll be a mixed family open-air pool on the Jagst. They're even going to have new changing cubicles and all kinds of other stuff, or so Grimminger announced at one of their last group evenings."

In spite of everything, this made Erich laugh. "Remember how much we always wanted mixed swimming, because there'd be girls and so on?"

"Sure. Now we don't have go slink off to the girls' pool in secret to spy on them. And risk getting caught and thrashed by old Köberle."

Erich nodded. "A pity really, if you look at it that way. It was kind of exciting. But he's right about one thing. Kurt, I mean. That segregation really was old-fashioned."

Helmut said thoughtfully, "I wonder how they'll celebrate it. As a victory for 'the healthy National Socialist view of the world' or something like that, I guess."

Erich said nothing. He felt depressed. Suddenly he was wondering what it would be like this summer. Would he and Erwin and Max still be allowed to go swimming at all? Uncle Ludwig had written the other day saying there were notices up in many places in Pirmasens saying "Jews Not Welcome." Great-Uncle Otto, who had run a butcher's shop in Speyer for years, had wanted to go to a spa town on the North Sea coast for the good of his health, but the brochures from many of the seaside resorts actually boasted that they were "free from Jews." The hotel where he and Aunt Hanna had often stayed before suddenly wouldn't take his booking. There were no rooms vacant, he had been told curtly—and that was in the middle of March, right out of season. Suppose notices like that went up in Ellwangen! Suppose they were kept away from the swimming pool and told "Jews Not Welcome"!

He swallowed the lump that had come to his throat, and tried hard to make his voice sound firm. Hoarsely, he told Helmut, "I didn't know it bothered him so much."

Helmut turned to him and asked, bewildered, "What do you mean?"

"Well, Kurt. I didn't know he minded so much about his family background. I mean, we Levis had more money than his family too, once, and compared to you Nolls, well, socially you were way above him."

Helmut sat there, pensive for a while, running his

forefinger along the joints in the steps of the stairway, then said uncertainly, "But we never made him feel it."

"It was there all the same. We just didn't mention it."

"But what I really can't understand," Helmut insisted, "is the way he's fallen for their Nazi propaganda."

Neither boy said anything for a while. They were both puzzled. Then Helmut said quietly, "But I think we just have to put up with it. He seems to like it with the Nazis. He's respected there. And he belongs."

He belongs, thought Erich. Yes, he belongs. Look at it that way, and I can almost understand how Kurt feels.

A Small Revenge

SURE ENOUGH, in two days' time, the newspaper ran a big story about the plan to do away with segregated swimming pools on the Jagst. Next day the *National-zeitung* published a letter from a reader describing himself as "A Local Teacher" who wished to remain anonymous. He congratulated the town council on "this bold decision," which he described as "a victory over local prudery." Gremm, you bet your life, thought Erich, sitting on his bike and propping himself up against the *National-zeitung* sales kiosk to study the copy on display. The massive figure of one of the paper's reporters appeared at the window, a man Erich had seen several times in the distance on official occasions. He was wearing the brown SA uniform and leaning against the window with a coffee cup in his hand. At the sight of Erich he gave a start. He flung the window open and slammed his cup down on the outside sill, making the coffee slop over.

"Hey, you, Jew-boy!" he shouted, both hands down on the sill. "Clear off, Jew-boy, or I'll make you!"

Erich couldn't help it—he stuck out his tongue, and then pedaled away fast to get out of the man's sight. The reporter shouted a few more angry threats after him, but Erich didn't hear them, or didn't want to. Chuckling quietly, he turned onto Adolf-Hitler-Strasse to ride home. It was small revenge, very small, but it made him feel good all the same.

A few days later the newspaper announced another great event. Everything else paled beside it. "Heinrich Himmler Coming To Ellwangen. The Reichsführer-SS* will visit our town!" Gremm seemed over the moon about the coming event, and went on at great length about the "special honor" of "this historic moment." Erich listened impassively to Gremm's remarks, which seemed set to go on forever, and tried to exchange glances with Helmut, but Helmut was looking out the window with a gloomy expression on his face. Gremm said that the solemn day would open with a great rally, with music and marching in the marketplace. All the buildings would put out flags, and there was to be a fireworks display and a torchlight procession organized by the Jungvolk and the Hitler Youth. "I expect all of you to give of your very best on this special day," Gremm ended his address, letting his glance sweep over the whole class.

It came to a brief halt on reaching Erich and Erwin, and Gremm opened his mouth as if to say something, but Erich calmly returned his glance. Gremm seemed to think better of it, and finally began the lesson. With a sigh of relief, Erich opened his book and began reading along with the lines that Lutz, at Gremm's request, was reading out loud.

"'Nor shall all joy be lost while I rule Spain. You too shall have the freedom, in full view, to show your human side!'" said the old King of Spain to the audacious young Marquis Poa in Schiller's verse play *Don Carlos*. Lutz stumbled over the words as he read, making mistakes.

Erich shook his head. That wasn't the way to read those lines at all. The king was tremendously impressed by the young marquis. His words ought to be read with far more warmth, and heartfelt feeling. It was pathetic, too, to think of a king with so much power promising a happy life worthy of a human being to just one man! So how about all the others? Erich thought, feeling empty and sad.

The following Friday the town was in an uproar. Erich was visiting Granny Babette, who had just recovered from a nasty attack of the flu and was still rather shaky on her feet. Mother had made her some good strong beef broth, and Erich had taken it carefully to her in a lidded can. He and his grandmother stood at the window while she sipped the broth from a cup, looking out in silence through her fine lace curtains at the sea of banners on both sides of the street. The Jungvolk and Hitler Youth boys were standing at the roadside with their torches, and now and then curious bystanders craned their necks and looked toward town to see if the convoy of cars escorting Ellwangen's famous guest was in sight yet.

Granny had grown thin these last few weeks. There were still circular red patches on her sunken cheeks. A feverish look, his mother called it, and she had already said to Julius several times, sounding concerned, that they ought to take more care of Granny. She wondered aloud whether it might not be better to take her to Aunt Mina in Oedheim. Aunt Mina's children were grown up, and she could look after Babette better. "It's probably a little quieter in Oedheim too," Mother had told Julius. "Oedheim is a smaller town. All this going on in Ellwangen is upsetting your mother far too much."

"I doubt that it's any better in Oedheim, judging by what Louis tells me over the phone."

Father seldom contradicted his wife, but this time he was firm. "And it's not so easy to transplant an old tree. That might be an even greater strain on her. You and Lea must take turns, and we'll all lend a hand."

Erich thought of that conversation now as he stood beside his grandmother. Putting his arm around her, he tried to draw her small, frail figure away from the window. "Come on, Granny, you'll just get upset again, and the doctor said you have to think of your heart."

Sighing, Granny dropped into an armchair. Suddenly loud cries of "Heil!" came in from outside. Her face twisted, and she put a hand to her left breast. "My heart medicine, Erich, over there on the little table. Give me twenty drops in a spoon."

Alarmed, Erich did as she said. As he hurried to the table he cast a quick glance out at the street. By now the shouts of "Heil!" had died down again. Obviously a false alarm. He sat with Granny Babette for a while, holding her hand, which felt remarkably steady as it lay in his. She had closed her eyes, and there were a few little beads of perspiration on her forehead. Suddenly she said, out of the blue, "I'm so worried about all of you."

"All of who, Granny?"

"You young people, my dear. You and Erwin and Max. And Ilse and little Heinz-Viktor too. Thank God my other grandchildren have all grown up and left home. But you're still so young, what's to become of you?"

Erich didn't reply. What could he say? They sat in silence for a while, grandmother and grandson, and then they heard the noise swelling outside again, and more shouts of "Heil!" Evidently the great man was on his way.

It was dark outside now, and Erich went over to the door to switch the light on. A warm glow spread over the large table and the chairs upholstered in red velvet in the middle of the room. Erich remembered how they all used to sit around Granny's coffee table. He and Max had to sit on the cushions from the sofa with its tall legs and curved back. Max always needed two cushions more than Erich, and still he could only just see above the tabletop. Erich was always teasing him about it.

The shouting and cries of "Heil" outside were getting louder and louder, frightening the old lady. "Come on, Granny," said Erich, "let's go to the back of the apartment. You can lie down for a while in your bedroom." He led his grandmother to her room, where she wouldn't hear all the noise, and maybe could sleep a little, at least until the crowd had dispersed and it was quieter. After he had settled Granny on her bed and put a blanket over her, he went quietly downstairs and opened the back door. Thank goodness it wasn't locked, or he would have had to go out onto Adolf-Hitler-Strasse, right into the middle of the jubilant crowd. He hurried through the empty streets of the old town and passed the offices of the *National-zeitung*.

There was a bicycle propped beside the entrance. It belonged to the reporter who had chased him away the other day; Erich had seen him riding it a few times. He was sure to be with the crowd now, right in front of the town hall, where there was to be another ceremony. "Ellwangen Gives Heinrich

Himmler the Freedom of Our Town!" the newspaper had said, and the entire editorial team would certainly be present to record the great moment. Erich stood there for a moment, and suddenly he heard that rasping, "Clear out, Jew-boy!" in his ears again.

He looked around. Darkness had swallowed up everything but the gray shapes of the buildings, where few windows were lit. In the distance he heard shouting and applause, and—drowning out the rest of the noise more and more now—the rhythmic sounds of drums and trumpets. The band had marched into the church square to play for the big rally. Erich ducked down and fiddled with the valve on the back tire of the bike. He cautiously pulled it out, looked around quickly, waited a moment, then rose and strolled on at his leisure. He almost started whistling, but stopped himself. Grinning, he imagined the reporter's stupid face, and heard him swearing.

Once he reached the church square he would have to make his way through the crowds, and he was afraid of being recognized and called names. But everyone was much too busy watching the spectacle in the square to take any notice of him. By now the Jungvolk and Hitler Youth boys had marched in and formed a large circle outside the Collegiate Church, which was bright with the quivering light of their torches. Without looking back, Erich hurried on, but instead of going straight home he went on to the river. He sat down on the sloping bank. The grass was cold and damp. The sounds of the cattle in Father's premises behind him came to his ears, quiet and muted. There weren't many of them now, just a few calves and two dairy cows. A light was on in the little apartment above the cattle sheds. Peter was still up. So he hadn't gone into town. "I'm not having anything to do with that bunch!" he had growled once, spitting contemptuously on the ground.

How much longer will Father be able to pay him? Erich wondered, searching his pocket for the bicycle valve. He finally found it among some string and his handkerchief, clutched it for a moment, and then threw it, soaring high, into the river Jagst. "That's for the 'Jew-boy'!" he murmured under his breath, feeling a grim pleasure.

A week later, the end of term came. Erich looked indifferently at the report booklet that Gremm had handed him without comment. How excited he had been a year ago! Excited and proud and full of happy anticipation. Now all that mattered was to have this school year behind him. One year fewer on the way to his great aim. University studies in Tübingen and Berlin and Leipzig—he still believed that his future lay there. Of course his mark for German was poor, as were history and mathematics. One ray of light was his mark for Latin. A "Good" from old Richter the Latin teacher was uplifting, and so was his mark from Immig for music.

Helmut had come up beside him, unnoticed, and whispered, "Well, how did you do?"

Erich looked around the classroom, where most of the boys had gathered around Kampmann and Kurt, both of them obviously shooting their mouths off. Erwin was sitting hunched up, sniffing.

"As expected. I got through, that's the main thing. How about you?" Erich replied.

Helmut gave a little grin. "Much the same. Amazing what a national revolution can do. Looks like we have some new intellectual giants in the class." And Kampmann and the others did indeed seem very pleased with themselves. Kurt was positively bursting with pride.

Suddenly Erich sensed his former friend's eyes on him. Kurt was looking challengingly at Erich, who quickly pulled Erwin to his feet. "Come on, let's get out of here. I don't want a fight."

Erwin gave one more noisy sniff, but obediently went with his cousin. Out in the square, the schoolboys were gathering around the recently erected flagpole. The flag was fluttering in a cold spring wind that stung their faces. Erich, shivering, kept close to the gray wall with Erwin, nodding his head to suggest that they'd better go in the direction of Hindenburgstrasse. At the far end of the square some of the twelfth-grade boys were singing, "To the east we now will ride . . ." Any moment the flag would be lowered, and then they'd break into the inevitable Horst Wessel Song again. Better get away first, better avoid the others, in particular Kampmann and Kurt, who'd want to relish their triumph. Erich breathed a sigh of relief when he reached the heavy brown front door of their building.

Next door, in the Pfisterers' ironmongery and china shop, there was a lot of activity. Marie, the younger Fräulein Pfisterer, had just come to the door to show a customer out. "Ah, it's you, Erich. You had reports today, right? Are you happy with yours?"

"It . . . it was okay. Thanks, Fräulein Marie." Erich opened the front door and stepped into the familiar darkness of the hall.

Aunt Mina and Uncle Louis didn't come for Pesach this year. Instead, Julius took Granny to Oedheim, where she was to stay a few weeks. She was still very weak, and couldn't eat properly. Aunt Mina was planning to "fatten her up," as she wrote in her last letter, and Julius had finally agreed. He came home from Oedheim depressed. Ilse and Martin's wedding had been put off indefinitely. Martin's family was being difficult about it, Julius said, adding that he couldn't see anything ever coming of that engagement.

"But they love each other so much," protested Erich, picturing the couple embracing under the window.

Julius laughed derisively. "As if that would bother *them*," he said, leaving anyone to guess whether by "them" he meant Martin's family or the Nazis in general. "Perhaps such things will actually be forbidden some day. . . ."

"What things, Papa?"

"Well, marriage between Jews and Christians. It wouldn't surprise me in the least, the way that gang is talking."

Erich was horrified. "People can't be forbidden to love each other because they have different religions."

"Oh, yes they can, my boy. That's how it once was, and we're on the way right back there, or that's how it looks to me. Maybe we'll be exiled to the ghetto again some day . . ." Julius saw his son's wide eyes, stopped short, and then said, "I'm sorry, Erich, I got carried away. It won't be as bad as that. Don't take any notice of me; I'm just in a bad temper. Aunt Mina and Uncle Louis are so worried, and as for Ilse . . . well, you can imagine."

So it was a quiet Pesach. They spent the Seder evening with Uncle Sigmund and Aunt Lea. Erich would rather have stayed at home in his room that evening. The carefully laid table with the Seder food, the bone, the herbs, and the egg suddenly struck him as ridiculous, symbols now meaningless binding them to a tradition that meant nothing to him anymore. He dimly remembered how happy and solemn he had felt last Pesach, and he smiled ruefully. Very well, they were Jews: there was nothing to be done about that, and anyway he was proud of his family. But he suddenly felt an indeterminate anger with these rituals from the distant past, these words and set phrases—old-fashioned nonsense, he thought. That was what made them "different," that was what distinguished them from other people. Perhaps they ought to give it all up—and give up the idea of Jerusalem too, an unknown place far away, more distant than the moon. This was where he wanted to live, this was where he wanted to belong again.

Gertraud

ONCE AGAIN Mother sewed a new ribbon to his cap at the end of the Easter vacation. Soon his grade would be among the older boys who were so much admired. On the first day of the new school year he stood half hidden behind the flight of gray stone steps leading up to the main high school entrance, watching the others, hearing them laughing, shouting, asking questions. He saw Kurt, wearing his uniform in honor of the day, like almost all the boys now. Erich's glance swept across the square. Here came Helmut walking across it, shoulders high, hands in his trouser pockets, making his way through the various groups. He nodded slightly to Erich. Erich strained his eyes to see if Erwin was coming along Hindenburgstrasse yet. So far he hadn't turned up. Erich felt worried. Perhaps his cousin was sick again. Or perhaps he too was scared of this first day back at school, the uncertainty that lay ahead of them, the insults, the humiliations.

Then Erich saw the girl. Like him, she was standing a little way apart from the rest. A group of the oldest boys had run to the flagpole, where Kampmann, Grimminger, and a few of the others had just hoisted the bloodred flag, leaving a clear view of her. She was small, shorter than Erich, and very slender. Her dark brown hair was caught back by a barrette, and fell softly waving to her shoulders. She wore a gray jacket and pleated skirt with a purple pattern. She was holding her school satchel to her breast like a shield, timidly watching the noisy, boisterous crowd. Erich had never seen her before. She must be new to the school. Perhaps her parents had only just moved to Ellwangen, like Kurt when his father, who came from near Heilbronn, had been transferred to the regional court here.

Erich couldn't take his eyes off her; he felt as if he knew her, as if he had seen her face somewhere before, but a long time ago. When a group of twelfth-grade boys, strolling proudly along with measured step in their white caps, cut off his view of her, he determinedly made his way through the crowd. Close to the church doors he met a group of his own class who hadn't come in uniform. Reger was among them, and Erich buttonholed him, although Reger was obviously reluctant to talk. "Suppose anyone sees us, Erich!"

"I couldn't care less. Just tell me who that is." Reger looked around. Unobtrusively, Erich turned him to the place where the girl had been standing. "The small girl with the brown hair. Over there." She hadn't moved.

Reger looked at her for a few seconds, then turned away, shrugging. "No idea. She must be new."

"Do you think she may be in our class?" Erich felt his heart in his mouth.

"How should I know? What's the matter with you?" Reger looked sideways at Erich.

He felt himself go red as a beet. Hastily, he turned his face away. "Nothing. I just thought I knew her from somewhere."

She wasn't in their class, as Erich had hoped. Instead, Gremm came in to announce that he was their class teacher again this year as well as their German teacher. "We'll carry on the good work we began last year, and it will continue to be my aim to keep harmful alien influences at bay." As he said that he gave Erich and Erwin a venomous look. The other teachers were almost the same as last year, too. At least they had old Richter for Latin again, so there was a gleam of hope there. But they had Eisele for biology too this year, which boded no good. Their old biology teacher Herr Stölzle—a bit of a heavyweight but a kindly and jovial man—had struggled a good deal with the new subject of racial theory, which was now on the curriculum and was clearly important, since it was almost all they'd studied last year. Stölzle had talked at length about the Nordic, Eastern, and Western types, and had them studying drawings, skulls, profiles, and bone structure. His mind was not entirely on the matter, that was clear. He kept passing his handkerchief over his shining red face during his monotonous lectures, and his eyes would go to the classroom door longingly, as if he'd rather be anywhere else.

But at least he left Erwin and me in peace, thought Erich gratefully. We didn't have to listen to stuff about the inferiority of the Jewish race. You can bet your life it will be different with Eisele.

After lessons, he hung around the courthouse building. Perhaps *she* was still in school, perhaps he could see her again, maybe even find out which class she was in. He waited for quite a while. Most of the students had started for home, and there were only a few small groups still standing around in the square. He was just about to give up and go home too, when he saw her. She was coming down the steps with Lotte Richter, the Latin teacher's daughter. Lotte was the only girl in Class Five. So the new girl was one class above him. He had to find out her name and where she lived. As the girls walked straight toward him, he pressed very close to the wall of the courthouse. Then they stopped, and the unknown girl, smiling a bit, gave the taller, sturdier Lotte her hand. Then she stood waiting for someone, letting her eyes wander around the square, as if trying to memorize the various buildings. Erich found that he had to swallow several times because his throat had suddenly gone dry. Suppose he walked past her now, very casually, as if just by chance? Perhaps he could just say, "Hello," and then ask her if she was looking for something.

Perhaps he could . . . but in the middle of his reflections, something unexpected happened. The door of the main school entrance opened and Gremm came out, followed by Eisele, Gumprecht, and Lafrentz. They were all in uniform except for Gremm. They stopped at the foot of the steps for a moment; Erich could hear them laughing—Lafrentz's laughter a hoarse bleat, Gumprecht's deep and full. Only Gremm didn't join in, but just raised the corners of his mouth. Then they shook hands, said good-bye, and separated. But Gremm didn't go his usual way over the church square. He seemed to be making straight for Erich. The boy's heart almost stopped. Had Gremm seen him, even though he was keeping very close to the wall? Erich hardly dared to breathe. Any moment he'd hear that cold, smooth voice. "What's all this, Levi? Skulking around spying on people? Just what I'd have expected of the likes of you. . . ."

Endless minutes passed, but nothing happened. Erich turned his head to the right, trying to see the square out of the corner of his eye. For a moment his heart seemed to stop once again. Gremm was some way off, quite far enough, he hadn't seen him, but he was talking to the girl. And after he had exchanged a few words with her, he took her arm in a light grip and they both walked on together, side by side, right across the church square. The girl belonged with Gremm! The realization was like a blow to his stomach.

Suddenly he heard the familiar voice of Martha Bieg, who had appeared in the doorway of the butcher's shop. "Hello, Erich, what are you doing slinking along the wall like a robber? Oh, no offense meant!" she said soothingly, seeing the boy's pale face as she came closer. "I was only wondering. What have you seen? You're so pale!"

"Nothing, Frau Bieg. Everything's okay."

Martha Bieg thoughtfully watched the figures of Gremm and the girl growing smaller and then disappearing behind the chestnut trees of the square. "Looks like you were hiding. Admit it, now. He's a real fanatic. I can imagine you have a tough time with him. Well, your mother's told me a thing or two."

Erich bowed his head. Martha Bieg meant well, but suddenly he felt so ashamed he'd have liked to turn and run.

Taking no notice of his reaction, she went on, "I'm just sorry for that girl."

Erich's head shot up again. "You know her?"

"Well, not exactly. But I know from Frau Munk, who

cleans for the Gremms, that she's his niece. She's from Stuttgart, I believe, staying with the Gremms now. That's all I know. Frau Gremm doesn't buy from me, I expect you can guess why. I dare say he told her not to." And she winked at Erich in what she probably thought was a conspiratorial manner, adding, "Would you like a piece of sausage, Erich?"

A piece of sausage, that panacea on days good and bad alike! In spite of himself, Erich couldn't help smiling. She was a kindhearted soul, Martha Bieg. "Thank you very much, but I need to go home now. It's nearly lunchtime."

"Yes, I understand. I quite forgot that you're a big boy now after your confirmation." Martha Bieg sensibly called it a confirmation because she just couldn't remember bar mitzvah—"that funny word," as she called it.

Erich moved away from the wall of the building and went the few steps to the back door. Martha Bieg called after him to give them her regards at home. In the hall he met Maria, the apprentice, just about to carry some crates down the cellar steps. He chivalrously held the door open for her, and looked at her so long that she went slightly pink and began giggling. She wasn't to know that he had suddenly seen *her*, the new girl, in his mind's eye, that slender, delicate figure with chestnut-brown hair. And her eyes—she'd had large, sad eyes! But the color . . . no, he didn't know, he just had to find out what color her eyes were.

At his next secret meeting with Helmut he asked him about the girl. Helmut didn't know much. "Seems she's Gremm's niece. Living with him and his wife. I saw her yesterday evening with her aunt, going into the meeting of the National Socialist Women's Association. Keep on doing crochet work for the führer! If she's as fanatical as her uncle, too bad! But why do you want to know?"

Erich was glad that his friend couldn't see him very clearly in the dark hall, because he could feel his cheeks burning. "She reminds me of someone," he said, trying hard to make his voice sound firm. "It doesn't matter," he added, and began talking about their last German essay.

When he was in bed that night, he wondered why he had lied to his friend. Why was he so interested in this girl? He'd better not waste time thinking about her if she was Gremm's niece. And if she thought the way her uncle did, then he, Erich Levi, a Jew, wouldn't exist at all for her. Making up his mind never to think of her again, he turned over on his right side and tried to get to sleep. It was a long time before he succeeded.

Two days later, on Wednesday, he saw her again. The students had been rounded up for a commemoration ceremony, something to do with the German colonies, and were walking in long lines to the gymnasium. Although he had sworn never to take part in such ceremonies again—never mind what disciplinary measures he brought on himself—he brought up the end of the procession with Erwin. He had seen her pass, wearing the Bund Deutscher Mädchen* (BDM) uniform today, and for a moment he had thought she gave him a shy but interested glance. Just imagination, he told himself, but that brief moment had been enough to make him throw overboard all his good resolutions of the last two nights.

After the ceremony, which he ignored as usual, the students gathered outside school for a roll call with flags. As they assembled, he saw Kampmann talking to her and putting his hand on her shoulder. Erich clenched his fists. He would have liked to go over and push that hand—Kampmann's great paw with the little blond hairs on the back—and hit him in his grinning face. He was being very familiar with her. But that wasn't surprising. Erich felt sure that her uncle would heartily approve of such a friendship. Clenching his teeth, he turned and hurried home, taking no notice of the bewildered Max, who was panting as he ran after his brother and crying, "Erich, Erich!" again and again. He caught up just before Erich reached the front door.

"What are you running like that for? Wait a minute— I have to tell you something."

Erich turned and saw that Max was very upset. The corners of his mouth were twitching as if he might burst into tears any minute. "What is it?" he asked, drawing his little brother into the hall.

Max sat down on the bottom step of the stairs. "Lafrentz said I have to walk with you and Erwin now, behind everyone else. I can't be with my friends in my class anymore. And he's moved me away from Willi too. I have to sit all by myself at the front of the class from now on."

Wearily, Erich sat down beside his brother and put an arm around him. So it's caught up with him too, he thought. This is a fine beginning to the new school year. No wonder, with Lafrentz as his new teacher. Max sniffed noisily, and Erich handed him a handkerchief. "Max, listen. That's just the way it is now. There's nothing to be done about it. Don't show that you mind, and do as you're told." Knuckle under, he thought, don't attract attention, knuckle under. And endure the years. Maybe it will work out. He added aloud, "You'd better come and join me and Erwin at break too. You know where we always stand. I guess that will be best."

Max hung his head. "Willi said we can't see each other so much. He only plays with the others at break. And I'm not to visit his home anymore. Because of the neighbors, his mother says."

"That's why you'd better join me at break. We don't need anyone else." Erich gave his brother's right hand a little squeeze and helped him to his feet. "Come on, and don't let them notice anything upstairs. We can get through this."

At the end of the week, Gremm read out a decree saying that from now on everyone must salute the SA banners. "They are symbols of faith and loyalty," he droned on, and stopped as if by chance at Helmut's desk, accompanying his last words with short, sharp blows of the palm of his hand on the desktop.

Gremm's threatening him, thought Erich uneasily. Someone like Helmut isn't going to obey the decree, and he knows it.

Gremm also announced that Labor Day, May 1st, was to be a new feast day for everyone, "Thanks to the führer's heartfelt love for the working people." This year there would be large-scale celebrations in Ellwangen. There were plans for a torchlight procession up to the Schönenberg, and young people were invited to the church square to welcome May at midnight, with dancing and singing into the small hours. The class greeted this announcement with applause and cries of appreciation, and most of the enthusiasm seemed to be genuine. A day off school! But Gremm damped the jubilation down to some extent when he continued, "And I shall have the great honor of making a speech on this occasion. I naturally expect every German boy and every German girl to take part in the rally outside the church after divine service." As he uttered the words "German boy," he looked sharply into Erich's face.

I'm a German boy too, thought Erich defiantly. You can't say I'm not. But don't worry, Dr. Gremm, I certainly won't be turning up for your rally.

On Tuesday evening, however, when the sounds of the band echoed in the air, and laughter and cheerful voices could be heard through the open window, Erich couldn't stay at home. He slipped out of the apartment carrying his shoes, and put them on only when he was down the stairs so that the sound of their heels wouldn't give him away. He had told Mother that he was tired and was going to read in bed. Julius had withdrawn to the living room, muttering, and slammed the door after him as if that would silence the noise coming in. They would have been sure to forbid him to go to a Nazi occasion. But something drew the boy out there to the noise, the music, and the laughter. He knew that most of the others from school would be there, except for Helmut, probably. And of course, so would *she*. Erich wouldn't let himself think about it, but his heart beat faster at the thought of seeing the girl he was trying in vain to put out of his mind.

There was a great crowd in the church square. Many uniforms, black and brown, dominated the scene. A platform decorated with evergreens and flowers had been put up in the square, and the band was sitting on it, moving on now from marching tunes to waltzes. Erich thought fleetingly of Ilse and their dance together at his bar mitzvah. He could see some of the others from his class, most of them in Jungvolk uniforms, the older boys already members of the Hitler Youth. In the distance, Kampmann was trying to organize a large group of Jungvolk into a neat line; he was one of the leaders now, Lutz had told Erich. Dusk had fallen, casting long shadows over the square, and the sky above was velvety blue. The flowering chestnuts lining it had a sweet fragrance that mingled with the smell of food and beer. By now the leaders had managed to form the boys and girls into a long column, and what seemed like an endless line of young people carrying torches marched over the square on their way to the Schönenberg. Erich retreated into the shadows behind one of the mighty trees. He mustn't be seen or there would certainly be nasty remarks; he'd be threatened with violence and then chased away. And if *she* saw that . . . no, unthinkable! So he kept in the background, but after a while, when the cries and laughter of the boys and girls marching past could no longer be heard, he set off on the way up to the pilgrimage church on top of the Schönenberg. Even Erich himself couldn't have said why.

Darkness had now fallen over the town, and under its cover Erich hurried up the hill, careful to keep a good distance behind the others. He walked to one side of the trodden path, passed through the trees and bushes, and then stopped, breathing hard, at the side of the large square in front of the twin towers of the pilgrimage church on the hilltop. He could go no farther; the whole square was swarming with boys and girls who made a lot of noise as they crowded around the large stack of wood that was going to be set on fire. Erich withdrew further into the bushes, and a few minutes later loud shouts told him that the May Day bonfire had been lit. A flickering golden light came through the trees, and Erich strained his eyes, but could see only dancing shadows beside the huge fire. For a while he stayed there, holding his breath, and then, sighing, started downhill again, still taking care to keep off the more visible path.

Suddenly he heard strange sounds. They didn't come from the hill above, where shouts and laughter still rose and died away in waves. These were quite close, the breathing of someone walking fast, the slight scraping of pebbles coming loose. Erich stopped in the cover of a flowering hawthorn and had to force himself not to sneeze at the acrid scent of the blossom. The other person must have stopped too, for there was total silence for a moment, and then Erich heard an anxious voice whisper, "Is anyone there?"

It was a girl, and she had probably heard his suppressed sneeze. He didn't want to scare her, for she seemed to be on her own, so he parted the branches of the bush and said as calmly as he could, "It's me, but there's nothing for you to be afraid of."

The girl was still standing motionless on the path, looking at him with her eyes wide open in alarm. Erich thought his heart would stop—it was *her*, that mysterious girl, Gremm's niece. He stepped out from the bushes and stopped a little way from her.

He had to clear his throat before, with difficulty, he managed to get out a couple of sentences. "It's only me. You really don't have to be scared." What a silly thing to say, he told himself furiously. She doesn't even know me.

But the girl didn't seem to mind. She smiled, as far as he could see in the dark, and even went a few steps closer to him. "So who are you?"

Erich swallowed. She would know from his name that he was Jewish. The Jew Levi. She might even have heard of him. He could just imagine Gremm talking about him over lunch, about Levi, that dirty, deceitful Jew. . . .

"My name's Erich. Erich Levi," he whispered.

"Oh, so that's you!" She didn't turn around, didn't

turn her back on him and walk away. Instead she looked at him curiously. Even the smile on her lips stayed in place.

"You know me?"

"Well, kind of indirectly. I have to confess something— I read your essays." Erich, completely taken aback, said nothing. After a moment's hesitation, she went on. She had probably been waiting for him to answer. "Of course Gremm mustn't know. Please don't give me away. But I like looking through the essays he brings home to correct. On the quiet, when he's out. I specially liked yours. Particularly that last one, about *Don Carlos*. What you wrote about the lonely old king —I mean, I thought it was really good. And *he* gives you such bad marks. I don't think that's fair."

"I'm Jewish."

"Yes, I know." She said it in a perfectly ordinary way, as if it were just an obvious statement of fact. "But that's no reason for him to give you bad marks. You write so well. But Gremm is inflexible. My father says so too."

She speaks of her uncle as if he were a stranger, thought Erich. She doesn't like him! Suddenly he felt happy, as if a burden had fallen from his shoulders. He could have jumped in the air. Instead, he stood there rooted to the ground, staring at her with his mouth open. Come on, say something, he told himself. Say something, anything.

"Are you angry that I read your essays?" she asked uncertainly.

"No, no," Erich quickly assured her. "I'm really glad if you liked them." They walked slowly down the path, which dropped steeply at this point. Erich kept close beside her. After a while he asked, his voice halting, "You're Gremm's niece, aren't you?"

"Yes. I'm sorry, I haven't even told you my name. I'm Gertraud. Gertraud Seidel."

Erich hesitated for a moment. Then he asked, "And you've come to live with your aunt and uncle?"

She stopped abruptly. Little stones tumbled downhill, and you could hear the small, crunching sound they made in falling until they came to rest. Halfway down the hill there was a bench with a fine view of the town. A few lights were winking down there. It was perfectly quiet except for the muted noise from the top of the hill, and the flickering firelight still shone through the bushes. Gertraud made for the bench and, after a moment, Erich sat down beside her. Gertraud was sitting very upright with her hands clasped in her lap. Her thoughts seemed to be very far away, and her voice seemed to come from far away too. "My mother died, you see. At Christmas, well, on Christmas Eve. She . . . she'd been ill for a long time."

Erich kept silent. He didn't know what to say.

"That's why I came away." She pointed to the hilltop. "Away from there. They're all having such a good time. I'd . . . I'd have had to look cheerful myself, and I find it so difficult. I'd rather be alone."

Erich nodded. "I can understand that." After a moment, he added, "It's the same with me. Because of course other people don't notice how you're feeling. They don't know what it's like."

She looked attentively at his profile for a while. "And they always expect you to be able to pull yourself together."

Erich nodded again.

"My father is away a lot, traveling. He's a businessman. And he didn't want me to be left alone at home with Monika."

"Monika?"

"Our maid. Although the two of us had been on our own all the time while Mama was ill. But now he worries about me." She sounded almost angry as she said that. "So I had to come and live with my uncle and aunt. Gremm is Mama's brother," she added almost apologetically.

"And you didn't want to come?"

She shook her head firmly. "I'd rather have stayed in our old apartment in Stuttgart. Going to my old school."

"So you don't like it here," said Erich, stating a fact.

"It's all new. And Gremm . . ." She stopped, and then went on in a quiet voice. "Well, you know him. He's very . . . very strict. And my aunt, she's nice, but she can't stand up to him. He even said she mustn't go to church. 'Don't keep running to the Holy Joes,' he keeps snapping. And then she cries in secret. She's very religious, she really needs the church. They lost their little boy years ago—he drowned."

Erich looked at her in astonishment. So Gremm, the stern and unapproachable Gremm, had known grief too, in fact great grief.

Suddenly she jumped up. "I should go back down to the church square. The others will be there soon, and there'll be trouble if Gremm realizes I wasn't with them." They both began running; they passed the foot of the castle hill and then turned, panting for breath, into one of the narrow alleys leading into town. The street closest to the church square was empty, but you could hear music and laughter. They stopped in the shelter of one of the old houses that had belonged to the priests of the Collegiate Church, where there was a jutting bay window.

Erich said hesitantly, "I'd better go now. I don't

want to be seen in the square—you understand, I guess."

Looking at the ground, she said, more to herself than him, "Dr. Rosenfeld was our doctor at home for years. He looked after Mama so well, he took such good care of her. From the moment when she first fell ill. Then all of a sudden Gremm wanted her to go to another doctor instead. An Aryan doctor, but she didn't like him at all. And poor Dr. Rosenfeld has hardly any patients left." She looked Erich in the face. "I'm so sorry," she added, not saying whether she meant for Dr. Rosenfeld in particular, or for him, Erich Levi, who couldn't go into the church square with her and join the others. She was still looking straight at him, and Erich realized that in the dark here he couldn't see the color of her eyes.

He heard himself suddenly saying something, and realized how fast his heart was beating. "If you like somewhere to go and be alone . . . I know some good places where no one can disturb you. I'll show you if you like."

He felt her take his right hand and press it. "Thank you. I'd like that. But . . ." Erich felt his heart drop like a stone. Of course, how could they do such a thing? If it came to Gremm's ears there'd be dreadful trouble.

Then she said, "But it would work on Friday, next Friday. Gremm wants to take my aunt and me to a Comrades' social evening in Aalen. I'll just say I have a headache."

Erich asked quickly, "What time?"

"They'll be leaving about six. How about six-thirty? Where can we meet?"

Erich thought for a moment. "You know where the gymnasium is?" She nodded. "Behind the building. If anyone's there we'll pretend we don't know each other. Then I'll walk a little way on and wait. Okay?" She nodded again.

{ 234 }

They parted in silence, Gertraud on her way to the brightly lit church square, he into the darkness of the surrounding streets. Then Erich stopped again and called to her, in a low voice. "Hey—what color are your eyes?"

"What?" She stopped too, staring into the darkness where she had heard his voice.

"What color are your eyes?"

"Blue. Why do you want to know?"

"Oh, just asking." There had been a hint of a smile in her voice just now; he had heard it quite clearly.

Secrets

WHEN HE REACHED home and tried opening the apartment door as quietly as possible, he was suddenly dazzled by bright light. There were lights on in all the windows at the front of the apartment. Coming in through the back door, he hadn't noticed that. Mother was standing in the living room doorway, her face gray with anxiety and exhaustion. "Erich, where on earth have you been? We were so worried!"

Father appeared behind her. Erich noticed at once that he had been drinking rather more than usual. His face was flushed and he spoke in a slurred voice. "Erich, tell us where you've been this minute! Your mother is sick with worry. I've searched the town for you three times."

Erich felt guilty. He had been sure no one would notice his absence. But of course Mother often looked in to see if everything was all right. The door to his old room opened, and

Max appeared. He looked sleepy, with his hair tousled. "Is Erich home?"

"Yes, Max, you go back to bed now." At that moment twelve heavy, hollow strokes of the clock rang out from the Collegiate Church. There was shouting from the marketplace. And then the cheers were drowned out by clearer notes, the bells ringing for May Day. The Levis listened for a moment, then Julius went into his bedroom, his feet dragging. Melanie gently propelled Max back into his room. Erich, glad to have escaped more questions or a lecture, slipped into his bedroom. The windows were wide open, and he sat down, rested his arms on the windowsill, and laid his head on his arms. He could hear the music of the band playing for the May Day dancing in the distance now. Staring at the velvety blue sky, he thought again and again: Friday, I'll be seeing her on Friday.

Next morning, Julius sat at the kitchen table with reddened eyes. The sound of a cannon being fired had woken them early in the morning, and when Erich quickly got up to close the windows, Gremm's voice began booming out. Tinny and distorted by the loudspeakers, it echoed back from the fine old Baroque buildings around the marketplace. ". . . have faith in the future of the Fatherland . . ." it was proclaiming when Erich joined his father at the table. Neither said anything for a while, and Julius seemed embarrassed, perhaps because of drinking too much wine yesterday evening. As if I minded about that, thought Erich with a faint smile, handing Mother his cup to be filled with cocoa. Gremm was now spouting something about ". . . our love for the führer," and Julius made a face as if Mother's coffee were a particularly disgusting brew.

"Listen, Erich. You're not to go out anymore without asking our permission first, is that understood?" Julius said at last into the awkward silence. "We were desperately worried."

The booming speech from the marketplace went on. ". . . hoping for victory in the true German style . . ." said Gremm, his voice almost cracking as he shouted into the microphone. Who does he want a victory over? wondered the boy wearily. And what is a victory in the true German style anyway?

"Are you listening to me, Erich?" asked Julius sharply.

Erich shrugged. "Yes, Father."

"And do you promise?"

Promise what? Oh yes, not to go out without permission. He nodded, thinking that he would probably be breaking that promise very soon. Next Friday.

Gremm's voice was rising now. "Germany must live, even if we die!" he bellowed. And many voices shouting "Heil!" answered him.

Julius rose to his feet so violently that his chair tipped over backward. "Can we never have any peace?" he cried, his face turning an alarming shade of red. More quietly, he added, "I'm off to the cattle sheds. You can't get away from them anywhere, not even at home."

The door swung heavily back, closing behind him. In silence, Melanie went to his place, stood the chair up, and began clearing Julius's breakfast dishes away. Erich put the roll he had begun eating back on his plate.

"You can't get away from them anywhere," Father had said, and once again fear rose in Erich like a wild animal, devouring even memories now, his memories of yesterday evening. You can't get away from them anywhere. . . .

For the next few days Erich tried to avoid any meeting with Kampmann, Kurt, and the others. He and Erwin kept to the side of the church square near the school entrance, so that in an emergency they could get away along Hindenburgstrasse, although the school students were strictly forbidden to leave the school yard. But he didn't want Gertraud witnessing any of the bullying and humiliation he suffered; she must not know about it, he had to avoid that at all costs. If only Max would join them—but in spite of Erich's persuasions he preferred to stay with his classmates, although he had already come home several times with a nosebleed and torn trousers. He had told Mother it was just ordinary scuffling, but Erich knew better. Helmut had told him that several of Max's classmates and some much older Hitler Youth boys too—boys a great deal bigger than him—would beat him up sometimes, and Mother herself, as Erich could tell from the look on her face, didn't believe a word of it. She went to bed early on evenings when that happened, and through the bedroom door Erich could hear the soft sobbing that she was trying hard to stifle.

Then came Friday evening, the evening he had been looking forward to so much. He had told a white lie, saying rather uneasily that he was going over to Erwin's to help him with some math homework. His mother had given him a suspicious look—it seemed to be saying, "But you hardly ever go to see Erwin, you don't really get on so well with him." However, Melanie said nothing, just paused for a moment, scrutinizing her son, and said, "But you'll be home in time for the beginning of the Sabbath, won't you, Erich?"

He nodded. The sun set late at this time of year, and if by any chance he wasn't home in time, well, he'd think of some excuse or other.

Breathless, he ran off, although he was much too early. At least he could start out in the direction of Uncle Sigmund's house, which was useful if Mother was watching him from the window, and once he reached the bridge over the Jagst he'd be out of her sight. Peter was leaning on a pitchfork outside the cattle sheds, blinking at the bright May sunlight. Erich made himself as inconspicuous as possible, keeping close to the balustrade of the bridge, and then ran to the gymnasium at top speed. Once there, he sat down where he could keep an eye on the bridge.

Suppose she didn't come? Perhaps the Gremms hadn't gone away after all. Or perhaps she'd been made to go with them in spite of her headache. The clock of the Collegiate Church struck six. There weren't many people about; most had finished work for the day, some were hurrying home. Here and there you could see a few schoolboys in Jungvolk or Hitler Youth uniforms hurrying past, going into the town center. There must be a meeting there this evening. Good, that meant there wouldn't be many of his fellow students out and about. He waited endless minutes. Then a small, slender figure emerged from behind a bunch of noisy Jungvolk boys near the railroad. Erich watched with his heart beating wildly as she came closer. In spite of the summery weather, she had put on a knitted jacket, wrapping it around her as if she were freezing. She stopped by the gymnasium and looked around.

Erich emerged from the shadow of the building and called quietly, "Gertraud, Gertraud!"

She didn't react at first. Only when he formed his hands into a trumpet around his mouth and called again, a little louder, did she turn to him. Uncertain, she came closer, and Erich looked around briefly, feeling some alarm—thank God no one had seen them. She was pale and seemed rather run-down, but when Erich asked in concern if she was all right she said, "It's nothing. It's funny, but I do have a bit of a headache now, but I have headaches quite often; they're not serious." Then she told him that Gremm had been badgering her—"Not that he wanted to take me to Aalen at all, but he wanted me to go to a big Hitler Youth and BDM meeting this evening in town. It's because of the Mother's Day celebrations."

Erich suddenly felt guilty. Mother's Day in a week, and he hadn't even thought about it!

"They're making a big occasion out of it this year," she went on. "With a large-scale celebration at our school next Saturday, too. He doesn't seem to mind that I'm not really in the mood for any kind of Mother's Day festivities. I pretended I was going, that's why I'm wearing this." She undid her thick knitted jacket, and Erich saw that she was wearing her BDM uniform: black skirt, white blouse, black cravat.

"Suppose it comes out that you weren't there?" asked Erich.

She smiled. "Oh, it's sure to come out. Kampmann will see to that. He's probably making his fingers sore ringing the doorbell. He insisted on calling for me. I'll just say I'd already started out, but on the way I felt so sick that I had to turn back."

"Will they believe you?"

She shrugged. "They'll have to prove I wasn't telling the truth first." Then she laughed, and Erich was captivated by the sound of her laughter, merry and lighthearted. Then she gave him a conspiratorial glance. "They may think all sorts of things, but you can bet your life they'll never guess I was having a secret meeting with Erich Levi."

Erich had to laugh too. Now he felt cheerful himself. All his fears were gone, the wild animal was driven away. They shared a secret, something that was theirs alone. And she trusted him! With a slight nod of his head he indicated the slope of the Kugelberg rising behind the gymnasium. "It's up there."

She followed him, and just for a moment Erich felt worried as they set off along the path leading to the Benzenruhe woods. Suppose they were seen after all? It was usually deserted here during the week; on Sundays a few hikers used the path, but all the same, suppose old Köberle were doing his rounds? But then he shook off his anxiety. Gertraud was running ahead of him in high spirits, and now and then a sunbeam stealing through the dense growth of the trees shone on her chestnut hair, bringing out its red-gold glints.

When they were at the top of the slope, Erich pointed to the little area of woods. "That's it."

"Lovely." She let her eyes wander over the old oak and beech trees, and Erich told her how Lutz had once been stuck in that oak. Chuckling, she sat down on the lush, bright green grass covering the woodland floor. Erich sat beside her. Below them stretched the familiar outline of the town. They sat there in silence, watching the white clouds that resembled a well-fed, lethargic flock of sheep as they slowly moved over the castle on the opposite hill. She told him about her mother. "I was just about living in the hospital for her last few weeks. I went there straight after school, did my homework there, and in the end I even slept there. She was so scared of being alone. And my father doesn't have much spare time." He traveled a lot on business for a large mechanical engineering company, she said. And then, after some hesitation, she talked about her mother's cancer and how it had slowly eaten her away—like an animal devouring her, that was how her mother had described it.

Erich thought of that animal-like fear that had eaten its

way into him, and how much worse it must be if you knew for certain that the animal was killing you. They discussed death too, and Erich told her about the body he and Helmut had found in the Jagst last summer, and the flies, and the stench of it.

"She looked very peaceful at the end," said Gertraud thoughtfully. "And she wasn't afraid anymore. I held her hand. Are you afraid of dying?"

"I don't know." Erich hesitated. "Since that time— when we found the man, I mean—I do think about it sometimes. I'd really like to get old and have a good life before I die!" They both laughed. "But all the same," Erich went on, "the way things are right now . . ." He stopped and bit his lower lip. For God's sake don't start crying, he thought. And please, Gertraud, don't say anything. Just don't say anything now.

Gertraud was quiet. After a little while he felt her put one of her hands on his and press it gently. They sat there in silence, looking at the white mountains of clouds. It was meant to be, he thought, just the two of us here in the whole world, just the two of us and those clouds. He showed her the Rübezahlweg cave, and told her the adventure stories they used to think up back in the old days—he and Helmut and Kurt. Suddenly Erich saw that the rays of the sun were already slanting low through the leaves. "I have to go," he said. "The Sabbath will be beginning, and if I'm not back there'll be trouble. And Mother would be sad."

"I thought the Sabbath was always on a Saturday." Gertraud said, and to his delight, Erich heard something like disappointment in her voice.

"No, it begins on Friday evening. At sunset." He hesitated briefly. "Will we meet again soon?"

She nodded. "I'll let you know as soon as I can find out

when Gremm and my aunt are going away again." She looked straight into his eyes. "That was lovely, Erich. Thank you." And once again she quickly pressed his hand.

"Yes—yes, it *was* lovely," Erich said. "And thank you too. There's . . . there's hardly anyone I can talk to now, except Helmut. And not always to him."

She nodded.

Erich added, "I'll wait here for a little while until you're down the slope. Then I'll follow slowly. So good-bye for now."

She nodded to him again and then quickly went down the hill, a slender figure in a knitted jacket too big for her, clutching it closely around her. And she really does have blue eyes, thought Erich. As blue as . . . as . . . He tried to think of a comparison, but nothing seemed to fit. She just had lovely blue eyes, beautiful blue eyes.

The family had just sat down at the table, and Mother was lighting the candles. Erich expected awkward questions after staying out so long, but Father just gave him a brief nod and then began to recite the blessing in a rather gloomy voice. So thank goodness they hadn't checked up on him at Uncle Sigmund's and found out about his deception. Breathing a sigh of relief, Erich reached for a piece of the challah bread lying on the Sabbath plate, and couldn't help smiling when he thought of the superstitious awe of the child he had once been. The eyes of God looking at you—what nonsense stupid, ignorant children will believe!

They couldn't meet again for two weeks. Gremm was watching Gertraud closely, and her aunt usually went to the BDM meetings with her, or sometimes Kampmann escorted her there, as she told Erich later. He grimly clenched his fists. Kampmann had his eye on her, that much was obvious. Think of the way he'd looked at her in the church square! In those two weeks Erich had waited with increasing desperation for some sign from her. He couldn't go up and speak to her himself— where could they be alone? Certainly not in school, under the suspicious eyes of Kampmann and the others. In the end it was Helmut who, with a grin, gave him a little note folded over and over again at one of their evening meetings. It was addressed to "Erich Levi" in rather clumsy letters, as if the message had been written in a great hurry or even in the dark.

"I never expected to be a go-between," remarked Helmut, still grinning. Then, suddenly turning perfectly serious, he asked, "Look, are you out of your mind? You do know she's Gremm's niece, don't you?"

Erich wasn't going to answer that question. He eagerly snatched the note from his friend's hand. "When did she give it to you?"

"After school yesterday. Very clever, the way she did it. Waited for me as I was just opening our front door, acted as if she wanted to ask me something, and pressed this little love letter into my hand. Don't worry, I haven't read it. For heaven's sake, Erich, do be careful!"

Erich patted his friend soothingly on the shoulder. "Don't worry. Anyway, what do you mean, love letter? That's not what it is."

Helmut looked at him. "What is it, then?"

Erich hesitated, for he didn't know himself. He knew just one thing, that he had to see her again, speak to her. And he knew that something had happened since she had come to Ellwangen. But how could he explain that to his friend? "We like talking to each other," he said. "She . . . she's not very happy with the Gremms. Her mother's dead."

Helmut was still looking steadfastly at him. "Once upon a time there was this couple deep in love—famous for it, in fact. In Italy, to be precise, Verona. Name of Romeo and Juliet, you may remember. Sad to say, they didn't survive." He clapped Erich on the shoulder and added in a low voice, "I'll say it again, Erich, be careful. This isn't a game you're playing." Then he turned away, quietly closing the door behind him.

No, thought Erich, it isn't a game, and he heard his father saying, "You can't get away from them anywhere these days."

Then he hastily unfolded the note and deciphered it, with difficulty, in the light from the streetlamp outside. "Saturday evening at seven, but *not* at the gym. At the bench on the Schönenberg." The word "not" was underlined three times, and suddenly Erich knew where Gremm would most likely be. Willy Reichert, the famous comedian, was putting on a show in the gymnasium hall, at the invitation of the Strength Through Joy organization.* He'd certainly be going to that. Erich thought, fleetingly, how disappointed his father would be. He thought highly of Reichert and hardly ever missed one of his radio programs. And now he couldn't go and see him in person!

On Saturday, Erich was on tenterhooks. The sun was nowhere near setting at seven, so the meal to celebrate the Havdalah* would be late. What could he say? The family had always regarded the meals at the beginning and end of the Sabbath as sacred. Only real illness was an acceptable reason for missing them. But if he went to bed, Mother would be sure to look in on him later. Gertraud didn't know about Jewish family customs.

He wanted to see her; he absolutely *had* to see her. Erich thought desperately all through the day, but he couldn't come up with anything. Finally he went into the kitchen, to find Mother carefully lowering a carp into simmering water. That would once have been a job for Fanny. Mother should not have to work on the Sabbath, but what could be done about it?

Erich clung to the door frame and whispered in a weak voice that he hoped made him sound sick, "Mama, I feel just terrible. I have a dreadful headache, and I can't look at the light properly." He had learned this from Aunt Lea, who sometimes suffered from what Julius dismissively called "Lea's usual migraines." Erich didn't know if men could suffer from migraines too, but he had to risk it. He did know from his aunt that the patient needed absolute peace and quiet and must not be disturbed.

Alarmed, Melanie came close and laid a hand on his forehead, as she always did when he or Max complained of feeling sick. "You don't have a temperature. That's odd. Can you be starting to have migraines all of a sudden?"

Erich felt guilty when he saw his mother's worried face. But at least he was able to go straight to his room, and Melanie promised that none of the family would disturb him, although she left it an open question as to whether that meant her too. Never mind, he must risk it. He couldn't climb out of the window, which was too high, so he had to take the dangerous route along the corridor and downstairs. And supper hadn't even begun yet! Then a piece of good luck came to his aid. Uncle Sigmund dropped in for a few moments to discuss something with Mother and Father, and they all went back into the living room. Max must have been to be deep in one of his books; there was no sign of him, and no sound from him either. Erich thought of making a dummy of clothes under his bedspread, but that would have seemed too deceitful. If they did come looking for him he could always say that he hadn't felt well indoors and had to get some fresh air.

He ran all the way to the Schönenberg and didn't stop until he saw her on the bench. She saw him too, and ran to meet him.

"I thought you weren't coming!" she cried, but it didn't sound reproachful, just relieved. They walked uphill together, along the cemetery beside the pilgrimage church, and turned into a little area of woods with a soft, mossy floor that swallowed up their footsteps. They would certainly not be seen here, not on a Saturday evening, though sometimes farmers drove their tractors or horse-drawn carts past the woods to reach their fields. Erich listened now and then, but all was still except for the agitated twittering of the birds they disturbed.

When he got home at nine thirty, all seemed peaceful. Julius's voice came from the living room, where he was reading the paper to Mother. Erich caught the familiar smell of the big cigar that Father allowed himself on the Sabbath. Breathing heavily, he dropped onto his bed. His absence had gone unnoticed!

He closed his eyes and thought of how Gertraud had walked close to him, talking about Stuttgart; her old school; her favorite teacher, who was fired because the Nazis said that married women couldn't work in such jobs anymore. "I asked Gremm if that's fair, if we women are really worth less under the National Socialists than we used to be. And do you know what he said?" She had turned suddenly and stood right in front of Erich, her eyes very dark at that moment. "He said, 'On the contrary!' At last we were being allowed to fulfill our real purpose, he said, which was to be mothers. That's the noblest career of all, according to him. In fact he doesn't like it that I'm at the high school. He accepts it only because that was my mother's wish for me, and my father wants it too." She had thought for a moment. "Well, I do want to have children some day. But first I want to study, and go to university." She had sat down on one of the many clumps of moss, and there was a smell of resin and rotting wood.

"What do you want to study?" he had asked, and she hesitated for a moment. But then, as if remembering a distant and half-forgotten dream, she said more to herself than him, "I want to study medicine, I want to be a doctor. When I was at the hospital with Mama I saw how the doctors help people. And I watched Dr. Rosenfeld too. I think it's the best profession of all—making other people well. Or at least keeping their pain under control. But I can forget about that now."

"Why?"

"Because since last year only ten percent of university students can be women. How am I ever going to make it into that ten percent?"

"How do you know that?" he had asked, bewildered.

"Gremm told me. But I'm going to stay on and take my high school diploma all the same, I told him, at least I'll do that!"

I guess I can forget my own dream too, then, Erich thought. What percentage of Jews are allowed to go to university? Five percent, three percent, none at all? He had told her about his plans. "And I want to study law and get to be a judge. For the sake of justice. I want to be a fair, incorruptible judge!"

She had looked sideways at him, thoughtfully. "I like that idea—being a judge! I'm sure you'd be good at it. You see so much so clearly." He had gone very red, and couldn't look her in the face.

Now, back in his dark room, he thought that the both of them could forget their dreams. And the future was so uncertain! Another five years, another four years—and then what? They had sat there side by side in silence for a long time, until Gertraud finally whispered, "Perhaps it will all change!"

"How do you see that happening?"

She had shrugged her shoulders. "I don't know. Perhaps Hitler will die. Do you think it's wicked to pray for someone to die?" She had leaned over to him and put her mouth very close to his ear. "That's what I do. Every evening I pray for him to die."

He had looked at her in astonishment. "I . . . I don't know. There are others as well as Hitler." But she had shaken her head.

Perhaps I ought to pray for Hitler to die too, he thought, but would Herr Silbermann approve, or the rabbi, and what would the Almighty think? He closed his eyes and imagined her face close to his, again, with him breathing her scent of flowers and the sun.

Suddenly he was aware of a movement. His mother had come into his room without a sound and was standing beside his bed.

"Where have you been, Erich?" she asked sternly. "I looked in to bring you a headache tablet and something to drink, and your bed was empty."

He half turned to the wall and buried his teeth in his lower lip. What could he say? He didn't want to lie to his mother, and it would have been ridiculous to say he just went for a walk. She wouldn't believe him.

She sat down on the edge of the bed with a faint sigh and tried to take his hand, but he pulled it away. "Erich, look at me! I'm so worried. I haven't said anything to your father, he has far too much on his plate already. But why won't you look at me?"

Instead of answering, he turned to the wall and left her with a view of his back. She sat there waiting. He couldn't stand it anymore. Between clenched teeth, he got out the words, "Leave me alone!"

As soon as he had said it he was horrified at himself. He'd never spoken to his mother like that before. He waited for her reaction, a violent outburst, punishment, perhaps even a slap in the face, although Melanie had never once hit her children. She sat there for a moment longer, then went with dragging footsteps to the door, which closed almost without a sound. Erich turned and opened his mouth to say something, but it was too late. She wasn't there.

He dropped back on the bed, staring at the ceiling. He was ashamed. It wasn't right to speak to his mother like that. But deep inside him there was something else, too, a thought that he didn't want to think all the way through, that he tried to suppress. Finally, however, he had to admit that he bore them a grudge, both of them, his mother and his father. He was angry with them and didn't know why. And here it came, the thought that mustn't be entertained but was now forcing itself through his lips. Soundlessly, he spoke it. "And what if I wasn't a Jew?"

Fragments

NEXT DAY, SUNDAY, Julius went off to the bed-
room after lunch without a word, and then came out in his best
double-breasted, dark gray pin-striped suit. He was holding
his best hat too, a soft, gray felt hat, and he kept running the
back of his right hand over it, as if to remove invisible lint. He
avoided looking at Mother, who was just putting the coffeepot
on the table, and said casually, "I'm going over to the gymnasium. Willy Reichert is giving another performance this afternoon. I thought I'd really like to go."

Erich, who was just coming out of the kitchen with
what was left of the Sabbath hazelnut cake, nearly dropped the
plate.

"Papa," he cried, horrified. "It's a Nazi show. You can't
go to it!"

"Why not?" Julius's tone became very aggressive. "Why

not, may I ask? I am a respectable citizen of this country. I can go where I like. They've announced it everywhere, after all, and invited citizens of Ellwangen. And that's me—a citizen of this town!"

Melanie was rooted to the spot, still holding the coffeepot in her hand. "Julius," she asked, almost pleading. "You can't go there! Do be reasonable!"

With an abrupt movement, Julius put his hat on and marched to the door, past Erich and Max, who had just come out of his room. "I am going there now! And I'm not having anyone tell me what I can and I can't do. After all, I have nothing on my conscience!" He slammed the front door of the apartment, and Max began sobbing.

"Shut up!" Erich snapped at him, hastily putting the cake plate down on the table.

"Erich, Erich, run after him. Quick, or something terrible will happen. Try to stop him!" Melanie ran into the living room to watch Julius from the window.

Erich quickly tied his shoes and ran down the stairs two steps at a time. Hindenburgstrasse was very busy. There were a great many people out for a Sunday walk, and some were probably on their way to the gymnasium with the bloodred banners waving outside its main entrance. Erich ran a little way toward the bridge over the Jagst. Where was Father? Then he saw him walking over the bridge with a firm tread. Erich jostled several of the passersby as he made his way through the crowd. "Papa, Papa, stop! Wait for me!"

Julius stopped and looked at his son. "What are you doing here? Go home!"

"Papa, do be sensible. Please come back. Mother is so scared!"

"Erich, for the last time, go home at once. I am going to see this show, never mind what the rest of you say!"

"But they won't let you in, Papa!"

"We'll see about that," said Julius through his teeth. "We'll see about that." He went on walking.

Erich kept close behind him, pulling his sleeve from time to time. Julius angrily resisted, but Erich wasn't giving up. "Come with me, please, Papa."

Suddenly he felt a hard blow on his cheek, knocking his head to one side. Shocked, he stared at his father, who stood there with his hand still raised, looking pale. Several passersby stopped and began whispering or even laughing. Erich caught a few words. ". . . the Jew Levi . . . typical . . . what riffraff. . . ." For a moment father and son stared at each other, then Julius abruptly turned and went on his way.

Erich stood there as if rooted to the spot, feeling his cheek burning. He realized that several people were still staring at him. Instinctively he turned to run home, to get away from here, but then he thought of his father again, thought of him with resentment and rage; but he also thought of his mother's anxious face and heard her urging him to follow Father.

He ran back to the gymnasium, where Julius was now waiting at the entrance. Some SA men with their legs planted wide apart stood at the open doors. Erich recognized a few of them, and was horrified to see that one of them was Bartle, Max's former elementary schoolteacher.

"Well, Herr Levi, and where do we think we're going?" asked one of the guards, leering, and Julius replied that he wanted to see Willy Reichert's show.

"And do you have a ticket?"

"No, but I heard there were still plenty of seats." Julius pointed to the inside of the hall. "I'll buy one in there."

"Too bad, but we're sold out." Part of the hall could be seen through the open doors. There were still several rows of empty seats.

Without a word, Julius pointed at them and was about to walk in, but the SA man pushed him aside. "Didn't you hear? It's sold out! Or let's say, it's sold out for the likes of *you*."

Julius took a step back. "Kindly let me in at once, or else . . ."

"Or else?" The SA man stood in his way again, derision in his face, and the others laughed and nudged each other.

Bartle, who obviously found the whole thing embarrassing, went up to Julius and took his arm. "Do see sense, Herr Levi!"

But Julius wasn't listening. He shook off Bartle's hand and went on staring at the SA man stationed in front of him. Then he took a step forward, determined to force his way past the guard.

Everything happened very fast. The other SA men lunged forward, seized Julius, and threw him to the ground, where he lay motionless for a moment, doubled up.

"Papa!" screamed Erich, running to him. "Papa, are you hurt?"

Slowly, Julius rose to his feet, leaning on Erich's arm. He was retching and coughing, and Erich was afraid he might throw up, but he only spat out the dirt that had got into his mouth, and finally stood there, swaying. The SA men were back at the entrance to the hall, rubbing their hands as if they had just touched something filthy. Bartle had gone to the back of the group. Some of the people going into the hall passed, shaking their heads; several others had stopped to enjoy the spectacle.

"Come on, Father!" Erich picked Julius's hat up from the ground and handed it to his father, who was laboriously brushing the dust off his clothes. Then they went home, father and son together.

Julius still seemed dazed and was walking unsteadily. For a moment he took Erich's hand, as he used to when he was leading him around as a little boy, but then he let go, and, supporting himself imperceptibly on Erich's shoulder, he let his son take him home.

None of the family ever mentioned this incident again, not that day or ever. It was as if it hadn't happened. Erich sometimes watched his father out of the corner of his eye, saw the lines around his eyes and mouth growing deeper, saw his sunken cheeks and thin figure, which wasn't held as upright as before. Julius walked with a stoop, as if carrying a heavy burden. The dignified cattle dealer Julius Levi had grown old and weak. And even though Erich was ashamed of himself for it, he couldn't forget the picture of his humiliated father lying in the dirt before him. He despised him, and he despised himself for doing so.

One very hot June day, Erich came home from school an hour early. Lafrentz was sick, so there had been no English lesson. He found his mother in the living room kneeling in front of the big oak sideboard. She had pulled out the bottom drawers, and their contents lay on the floor: two large boxes containing the heavy silver cutlery, some candlesticks, small dishes to hold candy, napkin rings—all solid silver. Some of it had been in the family for a long time. Mother was so proud of these things;

Erich remembered how she and Fanny would often take them out and polish them carefully. So at first he thought the annual spring-cleaning was about to begin, but then he saw the large suitcase lying open beside Mother as she put several silver dishes in it, wrapped in cloth. She was so absorbed in what she was doing that she hadn't noticed him coming in, so he cleared his throat.

Melanie turned in alarm. "Home already, Erich?"

"Yes, no English lesson today. What on earth are you doing, Mama?"

Melanie flushed. She rose stiffly and then dropped into one of the soft leather armchairs. "Oh, Erich. You and Max weren't really supposed to know. But you're almost grown up now, and . . . and we probably couldn't keep it secret much longer anyway. Your father is going to Würzburg tomorrow to the Jewish Aid organization to sell some of our silver. He . . . he's making hardly any money these days, and we still have to pay the rent, and buy cattle feed; we have Peter's wages to pay, and we have to eat too. We . . . we've been living on one of our savings accounts for some time, and Father doesn't want to touch the others. They're our last nest egg. So we're selling some of the silver. You can't eat silver, Father says."

Erich perched on the arm of the chair and laid his cheek against Mother's head. "Is it as bad as that?"

She nodded. "But Father doesn't want to face facts. He says it must change some time. He firmly believes it will. Business is in a bottleneck, that's what he says, and we just have to get over all this." Speaking with difficulty, she added, "I'm afraid he's entertaining false hopes. Oh, Erich, I'm so worried!" Tears were running down Melanie's face all of a sudden, and she wiped them absently away with her apron, just as Fanny had done when she told him she had to go away because of the money.

It never stops, thought the boy. It just gets worse and worse. And fear rose in him again—if things didn't improve, if everything was sold, if they couldn't pay the rent anymore . . . ? "Suppose I found a job to do? As well as school, I mean," he said to his mother.

Melanie hugged her elder son hard. "You're a good boy. But what kind of job could you do? I'd rather you concentrated on schoolwork, that's much more important. We mustn't give up hope."

He helped his mother pack the silverware and the boxes of cutlery in the suitcase. It was heavy when they'd finished, and Erich couldn't think how his father was going to carry it on his own. While Mother started making lunch in the kitchen, Erich sat in the deep leather armchair and stared at the ceiling. Mother was right: what *could* he do? If only there were some kind of part-time work he could take! But who was going to employ him? Perhaps the Fräulein Pfisterers, he thought. Perhaps he could carry crates, run errands for them, something of that kind. But the few coins he'd earn that way would be only a drop in the ocean.

Meanwhile, the aroma of crepes drifted out of the kitchen. It reminded him of Fanny; Fanny who hadn't been in touch for so long. He had to pull himself together, because Max would be home any minute. Max would complain about lunch again. He had grown a lot these last few months, and suddenly he didn't like the sweet crepes that had been his favorite for so long. Tuesday, "Dessert day," wasn't the only time they were served now. Max wanted more meat, but it was in short supply in the Levi household. Mother put a roast on the table only on the Sabbath. And if this goes on, Erich thought, what will happen next? But it was no good thinking of that. Mother was right, they just had to keep on hoping. Weary, he went into the kitchen to set the table.

Julius came back from Würzburg two days later. The suitcase was empty, but Julius stooped as much as when he had left with it. The banknotes and coins that he counted out in front of Mother on the kitchen table were obviously less than his parents had expected, because Melanie, gray-faced, had asked, "Is that all? But the silver was worth much more!"

Julius laughed sourly. "What do you think? Do you suppose we're the only Jews with difficulties? How many Jewish businessmen aren't selling anything now? How many Jewish lawyers don't have any clients left? How many Jewish doctors have lost their patients? And how many Jewish civil servants have been fired? We can think ourselves lucky to get anything for the silver at all!"

After that, Erich was obsessed by the fear of what would happen to them in the end.

Only in the rare moments that he spent with Gertraud could he forget his anxieties and laugh cheerfully. She had let Lotte Richter in on their secret, much to his alarm at first, and now Lotte carried letters between them. "Don't you think people will notice if I'm seen with Helmut?" Gertraud had defended herself against his protests. "Gremm dislikes him almost as much as you. And Lotte can be trusted." So now, when Lotte stopped close to him at break, for instance to tie a shoelace, she gave him Gertraud's notes. Now that it was high summer they generally met up in the Benzenruhe, which Gertraud particularly liked. It was shady under the tops of the mighty trees that spread over them like a vaulted roof, and if an occasional hiker or farmer came by they could disappear unnoticed into the dense bushes. They would sit down on the lush green grass there. Erich usually lay on his stomach so he could look at her as she sat in front of him with a blade of grass between her teeth. They counted the clouds drifting over them, gave them names, and wondered where they were going. They dreamed of all the journeys they would like to take, and imagined a life where all their dreams came true. However, it was more difficult for them to meet in summer because Gremm wanted Gertraud to go swimming with her aunt as often as possible. "A German woman must have a healthy body," he liked to say, and Gertraud often repeated with a giggle. And then there were all the BDM meetings that she couldn't really miss, because Gremm would find out. When Gertraud shyly asked if he didn't go swimming in the Jagst sometimes, Erich had firmly rejected the idea. "I'd only provoke people. What do you think Kampmann and the others would do with me? And we couldn't talk then either."

Helmut had asked him a few times, halfheartedly, whether they might not meet away from the open-air swimming pool sometimes, in a remote corner of the Jagst, but Erich sensed that his friend had reservations, and always refused. Helmut's father was still under close observation, or at least so Helmut had told him, and the threats and attempts to intimidate him had actually increased. He didn't want to cause his friend extra problems. And then he kept thinking of the dead body lying in the river too, and probably so did Helmut.

Early in July the catastrophe that Erich had secretly feared all along happened. He and Gertraud had made a date to meet one hot Sunday, the first Sunday in July, and the sun was already very low in the sky when she finally came running away from town along the path. He was full of alarm as he stood on the outskirts of the woods, keeping an anxious lookout for her. When he saw her he ran part of the way to meet her, and she was just beginning to explain breathlessly that she had had to go to a ladies' circle meeting with her aunt, when a motorcycle came clattering up from below.

Frozen with horror, they stayed put. There was nowhere to hide, and they had probably been seen already. The motorbike came closer fast, and Erich could see the rider. He was a friend of Grimminger's, of all people. Erich had seen the two of them together in town a few times. Grimminger's friend didn't go to the high school, but worked as an apprentice in Aalen. The motorbike was obviously brand new, and the young man was probably trying it out in this remote place, although it was only a footpath. He stopped when he drew level with Erich and Gertraud and shouted something at them, but the roar of the engine swallowed up his words.

Erich seized Gertraud's arm and pulled her away. They ran down the path together without looking back. Only the fading of the engine noise made them stop. Gasping for breath, Erich turned around. "He's gone," he managed to say, and saw Gertraud staring at him wide-eyed.

"He saw us," she whispered, as if numb. "He saw us! Suppose he tells people . . . ?"

Erich tried to reassure her. "He won't have thought anything much of it. His mind is on his motorbike."

"But he stopped. And he shouted something at us, Erich!" In her agitation, she took hold of his arm. "Erich, I'm so scared. If my uncle hears about it . . ." She gazed at him pleadingly. What was he to say? He was so helpless himself.

All the same, he tried to calm her. "We could easily have met by chance."

"But I lied and told Gremm I was going to see Lotte, and instead I'm here with you," she whispered.

"Look, you go home now and don't let them notice anything. Just say Lotte was out and you went for a walk instead." He carefully removed her hand from his sleeve, which she was still holding tight. "Keep perfectly calm, okay?"

She nodded, then went off toward the town, but she kept turning to cast him pleading glances. It had been a long time since Erich had felt so utterly miserable.

On Monday morning he watched the Kampmann gang closely, and kept a sharp eye on Grimminger at break. But they acted normal; no one came up menacingly and shouted, "Levi, you Jewish swine, listen to me!" Gremm behaved the same as usual, too. Erich went home that day feeling better. Perhaps the motorcyclist really wouldn't mention it. On the other hand, it was still too soon to feel safe.

As soon as he opened the front door he heard that Father had turned the radio up loud. An agitated, rasping voice met him the moment he entered the living room, where Julius was leaning forward in his armchair with his ear close to the loudspeaker. "Goebbels is making a speech," he told Erich. "Listen!"

Reluctantly, Erich sat down on the sofa. What did he care about Dr. Goebbels? He had enough troubles already.

"They're murdering each other!" cried Julius above the screeching voice on the radio.

"Who, Father?"

"The Nazis. Hitler had a number of top SA men shot

yesterday, and Röhm is under arrest. It seems they were planning a putsch against Hitler.* Who'd have believed it?" His father was as excited as a child. "Now they're turning on each other. That's the best news in a very long time."

Erich rose abruptly and went to his room. Oh, Father, he thought, you and your hopes. A few less Nazis—what did that mean? It wouldn't change anything.

Two weeks later, loudspeakers were put up in the marketplace. A speech by the führer was to be broadcast countrywide. Probably about this Röhm, thought Erich that afternoon as he watched people streaming toward the marketplace, where the inevitable brass band was already in place. The bloodred banners waved around the scene, and indeed all over town. A little later the voice was echoing back from the proud Baroque buildings surrounding the square, that slavering, screeching, cracking voice. Erich hurried home, went upstairs, and resisted the impulse to go all the way up to the attic, where he had always fled as a child. He used to crouch in the corner there, eyes closed, hands over his ears, so as to see and hear nothing, to shut out everything he was afraid of. But there was no getting away from that voice. It made its way into the apartment, somewhat muted but still impossible to ignore.

"... In which fate has taught me again that in dire need we must cling with all our might to the most precious things that are given us in this world, the German people and the German Reich." Just for once he has a point there, thought the boy, staring down into the empty street without seeing it, forehead pressed to the pane. He's certainly clinging to Germany for all he's worth!

The next night, he was woken by a whirring sound, and

soon after that he heard breaking glass. Erich leaped out of bed and hurried to the window. He strained his eyes, looking down, but in the darkness he couldn't make anything out.

Suddenly he heard a loud crack very close to him. Something flew through the pane and past him. The glass broke and fell on his bed in pieces. He stood there rooted to the ground, unable to move. At that moment the door was flung open and Julius rushed in. "Erich, get back from the window! They're smashing the panes!" He pulled him toward the doorway so hard that Erich cut himself on one of the pieces of glass lying around. Limping, with one heel bleeding badly, he made his way into the corridor, where Mother stood with her hands over her mouth, as if suppressing a scream by force. "Quick, quick, get Max!"

Julius ran to the door of Max's room, which looked out on Hindenburgstrasse, and came back the next moment with a sleepy Max rubbing his eyes. "We'd better stay in the corridor. Who knows what else they may do?"

Julius tried the handle of the front door to make sure it was really closed and locked, and, breathing heavily, leaned against the paneled wall. For a few moments there was deathly silence. The family were all straining their ears, but no more sounds came from outside.

Suddenly the voice of the landlord of the Crown Inn rang out. "What the devil's all this racket in the middle of the night? Calm down or I'm going for the police!" Then another window was broken with a crash, and after that it was quiet again. The horrific incident seemed to be over.

Erich limped into the bathroom to find a bandage—a small puddle of blood had gathered around his foot while they waited in the corridor. Melanie followed him, with one hand still pressed to her mouth. Erich saw that she was trembling. "It's okay, Mama, I can do it myself," he said soothingly, when he saw her shaking fingers emptying all kinds of items out of the bathroom cupboard at random. He sat down on the edge of the tub, realizing that he felt weak at the knees. He was sick to his stomach, too. He felt dreadful.

Julius leaned down to him. "Is it very bad, Erich?"

He shook his head, gritting his teeth. Melanie had finally found a bandage and was trying to put it over the injured place on Erich's foot.

"They threw stones at all the windows looking out on the backyard. From catapults, I think." Julius was holding a stone in his hand; it was not particularly large, but it had sharp edges. "Suppose it had hit you on the head, Erich—it doesn't bear thinking of." He looked at his father without a word. Julius was wearing striped pajamas, and his hair was tousled. How small he is, thought the boy. Small and thin. And he looks so tired.

"Who do you think it was?" asked Erich, but he knew already.

Julius laughed bitterly. "Who do you suppose? I think that question answers itself."

Troubles

THE NEXT MORNING the two Fräulein Pfisterers
came to inspect the damage. Julius had waited for them early in
the morning when they came to open up the shop, and now they
were standing in Erich's room, gazing in silence at the left-hand
side of the window, where irregular, jagged glass still stood
around the frame. Melanie had swept up the splinters
overnight—no one could think of sleeping anyway. Max was
grumpy due to lack of sleep as he set off for school, but Erich
had stayed at home. He could hardly walk; his foot was throbbing and badly swollen. Mother had removed a few splinters
of glass with tweezers, and said that if the inflammation didn't
go down soon they'd have to visit the doctor. Erich lay on the
living room sofa with his leg propped up on cushions, and
Mother came in from time to time to change the cold compress
on his foot.

Through the half-open living room door, he could hear the voices of Julius and the two ladies. Auguste was saying out loud and very audibly, "I call it outrageous, Herr Levi, absolutely outrageous!"

Erich couldn't help smiling. Fräulein Auguste spoke her mind, and she had courage enough for a whole artillery regiment, or so Julius always used to say, half joking, half critically. "And she's as stubborn as twenty mules," he generally added. These qualities turned out useful for the Levis just now.

"Fräulein Auguste and Fräulein Marie are going to complain to the police. And then the glazier will fit new windowpanes," said Melanie, who had come in to change the compress again.

"Good," said Erich, looking anxiously at his mother's pale face. "But will the police catch whoever did it?" I ought really to ask if they'll *want* to catch whoever did it, he thought, but he didn't say so.

Melanie sat down beside him. "Thank God the Fräulein Pfisterers are going to have the damage repaired. Fräulein Marie says she thinks the insurance will pay for it. Oh yes, and she sends you her love and this." She put her hand in her overall pocket and brought out a milk chocolate candy bar, which she gave Erich.

He felt tears come to his eyes. No bullying or insults had been able to make him cry recently—he had had to stand firm, harden himself to all the bad things going on—but this affectionate gesture broke down his defenses. He turned his head so his mother couldn't see his tears. There are still good people around, he thought, clutching the chocolate so tight that it softened under the pressure.

The glazier, a sullen young man who hardly said a word,

came around midday. When Melanie asked if he would like a coffee or anything else to drink, he answered only with a decided gesture of refusal. All the same, he was thorough and worked fast, and when he left the apartment without another word, the windowpanes shone as usual. Mother had cleaned them carefully, and Erich was able to move back into his own room that afternoon.

He lay down on the bed and tried to get some sleep, for he was exhausted, but he just tossed and turned, as much as his injured foot would let him. Certain thoughts kept going through his mind, tormenting him, and he couldn't shake them off. It hadn't just been some boyish prank, as his father had rightly said. It had been an attack on the Levi family because they were Jewish. On the other hand, nothing of the kind had happened to the Heinrichs, the Neuburgers, and Uncle Sigmund. Suppose the incident was connected with him and Gertraud? Suppose the motorcyclist had been talking after all? Grimminger might have passed it on to Kampmann—and then it was easy to put two and two together. And if Grimminger and Kampmann knew, then Gremm certainly knew as well. Erich clenched his fists. He was so worried about Gertraud. What made it even worse was that now he was tied to home, with his injured foot still painful and throbbing. And there was no one he could send to ask her; he just had to wait, hard as that was for him. Perhaps Helmut would come by this evening. He would have heard about the broken glass last night, he'd have noticed Erich's absence from school. Maybe Helmut could help. . . .

With this thought in his mind, he dropped off to sleep after all, and didn't wake until he heard the old whistle down on the street. Bewildered, he sat up. He didn't know how long he had been asleep, but the night sky was blue above the Collegiate Church and the marketplace. Once again a whistle came from down there, louder this time, and Erich limped to the window. He could put some weight on his foot again, although only very carefully, for the cuts still hurt. He peered down into the dark backyard, and could just make out Helmut's figure crouching among the crates and cartons.

"Hold on, I'm coming," Erich called softly, and he limped out into the corridor. The apartment was dark and quiet; his parents and Max had probably gone to sleep. He went downstairs barefoot, carefully dragging the injured leg. It wasn't cold, and he couldn't have fitted a shoe on over his swollen heel anyway.

Down below, Helmut met him, but was very agitated. "What happened here? And what's the matter with your leg?"

Whispering, Erich told him about last night's incident. And he saw all his fears suddenly confirmed when Helmut replied soberly, "Kampmann and company, you bet your life!"

"How do you know?"

"I picked up this and that during the break this morning. How they'd shown the Jewish swine a thing or two last night. You most of all. They thought it was a very good sign that you weren't in school. I was beginning to think you must be at death's door, but then I saw young Max, so I knew it couldn't be as bad as that."

"And what else?"

"I didn't hear any more. They kept putting their heads together and whispering. Oh yes, and Gremm was in a particularly good mood today—he came down on your cousin so hard that Erwin ran howling to the bathroom at break. And one of the eleventh-grade boys grabbed him there and shook him, shouting that he didn't want to pee along with a Jewish swine; your cousin could darn well wait till he'd finished."

Helmut told him all this in a perfectly neutral, indifferent voice. But suddenly he took hold of his friend's arm, and Erich realized how upset Helmut really was. "Erich, there's something up, I can sense it!"

"What about Gertraud?" Erich interrupted him.

"Wasn't in school today. And I only saw Lotte at a distance. I didn't get a chance to speak to her."

"Gertraud . . ." whispered Erich, dazed. Fear seized him worse than ever, constricting his throat and eating into him. It could be just coincidence that she'd stayed at home, perhaps she was really sick, perhaps she had a headache . . . but he knew that that was mere wishful thinking. Their secret meetings had come out, and Helmut was thinking exactly the same, he probably just didn't want to say so. If I only could speak to Gertraud, he thought. If I only knew what they've done to her.

"Erich!" Helmut was still holding his arm firmly. "Erich, my father told me the other day that Kaiser is retiring at the end of this school year. So far he's prevented the worst from happening, says Father, for all the saber-rattling speeches he has to make. And the next headmaster . . ."

"Do they know who it'll be yet?" whispered Erich uneasily. But he already knew the answer.

"I've heard that Gremm is a likely candidate. What that means . . ." Helmut didn't finish his sentence, but Erich knew what he'd been going to say anyway.

"But he can't just throw us out. Not if we don't do anything wrong!"

Helmut laughed briefly. "You must be joking! You

ought to have seen which way the wind's blowing by now. They can do anything they like!"

Erich was dazed. He forgot about his throbbing foot and the cold from the asphalt seeping into him as it grew chillier. Of course he had known it, had secretly feared it, but he had tried to forget, clinging to a vague hope. Keep out of sight, lie low, perhaps he could get by somehow that way. . . . Oh, what a fool he'd been! Foolish, naive, and stupid. The business with Gertraud might mean the end. He'd have to leave the high school, his school, Gremm would make sure he did. He thought fleetingly of yesterday's dreams; he thought of Tübingen, saw himself sitting by the Neckar River, there with a stack of books under his arm. Books like Helmut's father's— big fat law books. And in the distance he saw Gertraud coming toward him, laughing and waving, her hair swinging in time with her footsteps, and now she was running faster and faster, running to him. . . . He put his hands over his eyes as if to press that image out of them, destroy the dream forever.

"I have to see Gertraud, I absolutely must speak to her," Erich said. "I have to know what's going on."

Helmut loosened his hold and clapped him on the shoulder. "I'm sorry, but much as I'd like to, I can't help you."

Erich clutched his friend's hand. "But you can have a word with Lotte. Please try. I'll be back in school again on Monday even if I have to use a cane. If you hear anything, let me know first."

Helmut just nodded, and they parted in silence.

On Monday, Erich went to school, limping laboriously along. He could put a bit of weight on his foot, but it still hurt badly. Melanie had been against his going and insisted that she wanted to take him to the doctor. "I'm afraid you may get blood poisoning, Erich!"

But he had firmly refused. Whatever it cost him, he had to see if Gertraud was there today and if she was all right. And he had to see Kampmann's face, and the faces of the others; he had to see Gremm too, and find out for himself how they were all acting.

All fell still as he entered the classroom. Most people turned away, looking embarrassed when he came in, and no one asked about his injured foot. Helmut was standing by one of the windows, and seemed to be staring into space. Kampmann and the others put their heads together. Erich feared malicious comments and venomous remarks, but it was strangely quiet, almost deathly quiet. Then Kurt moved away from the group and sat down at his desk, and the others followed suit.

Suddenly Erich felt someone grab his collar and pull him to his feet. He felt Kampmann's hot breath on the back of his neck and heard what he was hissing in his ear. "I've a score to settle with you, Levi. Your sort don't know where to stop. But I'll finish you, I'll do just that, you swine. Last week was only the beginning!"

At that moment Gremm entered the classroom. The boys rose. Kampmann suddenly let go, and Erich fell forward over his desk. They know, he thought. They all know. Oh, Gertraud, I'm so afraid. And *he* knows too. But Gremm seemed to be ignoring the incident. He began the lesson in his monotonous voice.

Erich was sitting at his desk, dazed, still feeling Kampmann's breath, hot and slightly redolent of onions. And he waited like a delinquent for the inevitable punishment.

There'd be a remark any moment, he'd be summoned to account for himself this afternoon . . . but he might have been air so far as Gremm was concerned. The teacher acted as if he weren't there. Suddenly Erwin unintentionally trod on his foot, the injured one, and pain flared up, bringing tears to his eyes. They were to open their textbooks, and there he sat, unable to do it, now of all times when he absolutely couldn't make any mistakes or attract attention.

But Gremm didn't seem to notice that Erich Levi was still searching his satchel while fat Müller, stumbling over his words, had already begun reading a poem aloud. "'We are the noble ones—make way there, make way!'"

Suddenly Erich realized that Gremm was standing right beside him. He kept his head bent over his book, but Gremm did not move on. He was standing so close that Erich could smell his aftershave, very clean and soapy.

"'Make way for good German men or you must die!'" read fat Müller, and then sat down again with a sigh of relief. The class remained silent. *Or you must die!* The words echoed in Erich's ears.

Suddenly he could bear it no longer. He raised his head with a jerk and met Gremm's eyes. They were looking down at him; cold, pale, and blue. And there was a glint in those eyes that Erich couldn't describe, but it was something dangerous, boding no good. Like a cat playing with a mouse, thought the bewildered boy, that's how he's looking at me, like a cat playing with a mouse before it kills and eats it. He couldn't withstand that gaze. He looked down at his book, at the poem that fat Müller had just been reading. *Make way for good German men or you must die!*

* * *

After school he went home as fast as he could. He had to think of a plan right away; he had to think of some way to help Gertraud. But what could he do? As he turned the corner of the Crown, out of breath, to cross the backyard and get into the building, Lotte Richter appeared in front of him all of a sudden, as if she had sprung out of nowhere. Without a word, she tugged his sleeve, and the two of them pressed close to the wall, half hidden by garbage bins and empty wine crates. He felt Lotte's hand in his, hot and trembling as she passed him a small, much-folded note.

"Here, this is for you. Gertraud's under house arrest until further notice. She gave me that in school this morning." As she spoke, she gazed around with a hunted look.

"Thanks, Lotte," whispered Erich. "What about you?"

"Gremm has his suspicions. He even spoke to my father. But of course I'm denying everything. I have to go now. Take care, Erich."

"Thanks again. You're . . ." Erich hesitated, and then whispered, "You're a really good friend."

As she moved away, she said over her shoulder, "That's okay. I'm doing it for Gertraud. And you." With these words she gave him a rather enigmatic look that baffled Erich for a moment, but then he hurried on. He didn't have time to think about Lotte Richter just now.

In the apartment, he hastily greeted his mother. Melanie was in the kitchen, lost in thought while she stirred the contents of a pot. His father was out in Rosenberg, where one farmer was still willing to do business with him. Perhaps he might be able to sell one of the calves, she told Erich, but he was only half listening.

"I'm going to do homework," he muttered, impatient to get to his room at last.

"Lunch in an hour" she called after him. "We'll wait for Father. Eat a roll if you're hungry." But by now Erich was in his room, carefully unfolding the crumpled note. He had a guilty conscience—Mother had looked so stricken since the incident of the broken windowpanes. She wasn't sleeping well either. Sometimes he heard her wandering restlessly around the apartment by night. She kept going to the door to check that it was locked, and adjusting the drapes over the windows. Often she sat huddled in the living room for hours on end, taking fright at every sound. In spite of her protests, Julius had sent her to see Dr. Uhl, who diagnosed alarmingly high blood pressure and prescribed her some drops. As she was about to leave his consulting room, the doctor had stopped her and started to say something in obvious embarrassment. He would rather she didn't come in during normal surgery hours, he said; she and the whole Levi family. If there was anything urgent they could let him know and then visit his consulting rooms in the evening, coming to the back door after dark. Mother had described this conversation in a trembling voice. So no one was supposed to get sick!

I ought really to have stayed in the kitchen talking to her, taking her mind off things a bit, telling jokes, imitating teachers the way I used to, thought Erich uneasily. But this was more important. He just had to find out how Gertraud was now. He laboriously deciphered her letter. She had made her handwriting tiny so as to get as much on the paper as possible.

Gremm probably knows everything, she said in a hasty scribble, letters crooked. He had put her through several interrogations, she said—she actually used the word "interrogations." But of course she had not said anything—she underlined "not" three times. Instead, she insisted that they had met entirely by chance on the path.

"Kampmann has asked me about it too," she went on, "but I gave him the brush-off, I asked what right he thought he had. And Lotte has been questioned about the 'company' I keep! But Lotte is great—she made out she knew nothing. Her father was furious after Gremm left. He threatened her with all sorts of punishments if he found out she was lying. Gremm told me I'd have to go to a boarding school if he heard anything else, but I'm not afraid of that, because it's Father who makes the decisions. I just don't want to leave Ellwangen because of you! My aunt keeps crying so much. I do feel guilty about her, because Gremm is so angry with her. It's her fault, he says, she didn't keep a close enough eye on me. Erich, I have to see you! I'm under house arrest, but there's a Party Comrade coming from Stuttgart on Saturday, one of the top brass, so he and my aunt have to go to that event, Gremm says. They'll lock me in, but I can climb out through the kitchen window. Can you get away even though it's the Sabbath? We can meet on the Schönenberg where we went the first time. Let Lotte know at break tomorrow. I need to see you. Love from Gertraud."

Erich lowered the letter. So the worst had really happened, and the motorcyclist had talked. But what was ever really the worst? Whenever you thought it had happened, something even worse came along. What was Gremm going to do? He'd looked at him so oddly this morning. Then, Erich thought of what Helmut had told him. Despite the fear burrowing ever deeper into him, there was something else, something that felt really good, an indescribable feeling. What was it she'd written? "I just don't want to leave Ellwangen because of you!" *Because of you!* That almost made up for everything.

On Saturday evening he found a suitable moment to slip into the kitchen and see Mother. Julius had gone to the prayer hall with Uncle Sigmund, and Max too; it was time for him to begin preparing for his own bar mitzvah.

"Mama," Erich hesitantly began, "I have a great favor to ask you. It's really important, or I wouldn't ask."

Melanie, who was putting a pigeon in the oven, turned to look with concern at her elder son. Her face was flushed. "What is it, Erich?"

"Could I go out this evening just for once? Before the evening meal. I know you like us all to be together on the Sabbath, but this is really, really important."

Melanie looked hard at her son. Deep in thought, she pushed back a strand of hair that had fallen over her forehead. "Erich, won't you tell me just what is going on? Is it something to do with that girl, Gremm's niece? People are talking. Martha Bieg told me about it."

Erich went bright red. If people were talking about it . . . !

"Mama, I can't discuss it, not right now. But it's really very important. Please let me go out."

Melanie took him by the shoulders.

"Erich," she whispered imploringly, "I refused to believe it! How could you get together with Gremm's niece, of all people? But I'm beginning to think there's something to it after all. Erich, is it true? Do you know what you're doing?"

Erich bowed his head. He couldn't meet his mother's pleading gaze. Melanie began shaking him, gently at first, but harder and harder when he didn't answer her.

"Erich, please tell me it isn't true!"

He freed himself from her grasp and took several steps back. "So suppose it *was* true?" he said savagely. "Why wouldn't I make friends with a girl?"

"Not with this one! Or others like her, either. For heaven's sake, Erich, do I really have to tell you why it just won't do?"

Erich thrust out his chin. "Plenty of girls used to visit us in the old days. Max and I were always bringing them home to play. And you were glad to see them because you'd always wanted a daughter, or so you said."

Melanie dropped into a chair. "In the old days, Erich, in the old days." She seemed dreadfully tired. "That was different. Times were different then," she whispered. "But you know that yourself." Erich saw tears running down her cheeks, and she didn't even make any attempt to wipe them away. She just sat there looking weary.

Erich looked down. What a brute I am, upsetting Mother so much, he thought. Why did I begin this utterly pointless discussion? Perhaps because that rage was back in him again, that uncontrollable, furious rage. Suppose I weren't a Jew . . . ? He turned abruptly and heard her voice behind him.

"Erich, I don't suppose it's any use asking you not to go. You're going to meet her, aren't you?" Erich nodded, without looking at his mother. "Promise me to end it, Erich. Please, promise me to break with her. And then I'll tell Father some story to explain why you aren't here. But just today, just this one time. After that you must never meet her again, do you hear? And I'll do my best to make sure you don't!"

Without a word, Erich went to the door. He heard a

sound behind him, stifled and full of fear. "Erich, do you promise?"

He didn't look at her, but he nodded. At that moment he would have promised anything just to get away.

The Last Meeting

HE WAS AT THE Schönenberg much too early. With a sigh of relief he sat down on the bench to get his breath back, but after a while he couldn't sit there any longer, and paced down the steep path and then back up again. Whenever he reached the top he stood there for a moment with his eyes closed, and then turned abruptly, as if he could bend fate to his wishes that way, and Gertraud would suddenly be there. But he didn't notice when she did arrive. He had heard voices from farther above, and had walked toward the church in alarm. A small group of old ladies had gathered on top of the steep hill to look at the view of the town below. He watched them until they strolled back to the pilgrimage church.

When he turned, relieved, Gertraud was suddenly there in front of him.

"Erich!" For a moment she smiled at him, and then she

did something totally surprising. She put her arm around his neck and nestled close to him. "Erich, I'm so glad!" she whispered.

He couldn't help it—after a moment of astonishment and hesitation, he put his own arms around her and held her close. They stood like that for a little while, motionless. A thousand thoughts shot through his head, and then gave way to an entirely new feeling, one he couldn't describe. He breathed in her scent of flowers and sunlight, keeping his eyes closed all the time, as if that way he could keep this moment with him forever. Suddenly he realized why she had seemed so familiar to him at first! It was crazy, but she was the girl in his dreams, that time when he'd slipped into Martin's role and suddenly he was holding that other, faceless girl instead of Ilse. Gertraud moved out of his embrace, and they both stood there rather shyly, without looking at each other.

"I'm so glad you could come," she whispered. They sat down on the bench, just as they had when they'd first met there in May. Quickly, words tumbling over each other, she told him how angry Gremm had been, and about his interrogations and threats. And she said he'd forced her to promise to break off all contact with Erich. "In the end I promised everything he wanted," she said, sounding almost cheerful about it. "Promises you're forced to make aren't real promises. It's blackmail!"

For a moment Erich closed his eyes, once again hearing Mother's anxious, "Erich, do you promise?" Was that blackmail too? What did Mother know about the two of them?

Meanwhile, Gertraud had taken his hand and was talking earnestly to him. Maybe they could still manage to meet, with Lotte's help, and if they were very careful . . . Gremm was a busy man, and she could deal with her aunt. But they'd have to be very, very careful. Erich listened without really hearing her. He didn't believe they could go on meeting, not when he remembered the way Gremm had looked at him this morning. Like a cat playing with a mouse, he thought again. But he didn't feel afraid now. He was just aware of her being so close to him, and her hand in his.

Suddenly she jumped up. "I'd better go. After one of those meetings they usually sit around together having a drink, but better safe than sorry. We'll have to watch out!"

Sure enough, the sun was already much lower in the sky, and the trees and bushes were casting long shadows. Erich hadn't noticed how fast time had passed. They'd be beginning the evening meal at home now. Mother would have lit the candles, and the challah bread would be lying on the plate in the middle of the table, while Father said the prayer for the end of the Sabbath. What story had Mother told him? Gertraud slowly removed her hand from his and reluctant, went a few steps downhill toward the town. He stood motionless, watching her go.

Suddenly she turned around and ran the short distance back up to him. He spread his arms wide to stop her, and she ran straight into them and, to his boundless amazement, pressed her lips to his. Erich stood there for a moment, as if rooted to the ground, but then he held her even closer and returned her kiss.

They stood there without moving, and time didn't seem to exist anymore. But suddenly, beyond the vast happiness that was flooding through him, he sensed an unknown, lurking danger. It rose and overcame any other feeling, so that he pushed Gertraud away from him almost roughly. And then he was fully aware of that danger; he saw it with a horror that sent all his blood racing to his heart, and he could hardly breathe.

Gremm was there, a little way above them. He was standing perfectly still, wearing his usual gray suit with the Party badge on the lapel of his jacket, and holding a lightweight felt hat. Erich registered his presence, and Gertraud began to tremble. With a few rapid paces, Gremm came up to them, caught hold of Gertraud and pulled her toward him, while he raised his other hand as if to strike Erich. Erich instinctively ducked, and Gertraud uttered a soft cry, but then Gremm lowered his hand again and turned away. He hauled Gertraud uphill with him, and as they went, Erich could hear a few words hissed, but he couldn't make out what they were.

Soon after that, Erich heard a car door slamming on the forecourt outside the church, and then the noise of an engine slowly chugging away. Gremm had obviously come with some other people, for he had no car of his own. He had probably asked some Party Comrade to drive him up to the pilgrimage church.

How stupid and naive he and Gertraud had been! Suspecting nothing, they had fallen straight into the trap Gremm had set for them. He had probably been spying on Gertraud all along. He'd have seen her climb out of the kitchen window and run toward the Schönenberg, and then Erich supposed he had come after her in the car. How long had he been standing there watching them?

Erich never knew how he had made his way home, where the familiar smell of cigar smoke and candle wax met him. The radio was playing music quietly in the living room, a male voice was singing an aria. Probably the music of Wagner that Mother liked so much. The Nazis revered him too. Melanie put her head out of the living room doorway as he was about to slip into his room. She must have been waiting for him to come home all this time.

She closed the door and hurried after Erich. In his room, she sat down on the chair at the desk with a sigh of relief. "Thank God, here you are, Erich. I was so worried."

Erich had stood there as if blind for a moment, staring at his mother. Then he turned and pressed his face to the windowpane. New panes, he thought; how long are they going to last?

Melanie came up behind him. "Erich, you look terrible! You're as white as a sheet." She was about to put out her hand to stroke his hair, but he avoided it.

"What did you tell Father?"

"I said you were invited to supper with the Nolls."

Erich's head shot around. "And he believed you?"

His mother smiled faintly. "He wanted to believe me. You know Father."

Erich slowly nodded. Yes, that was just like Julius Levi: a man who didn't want to see what was really happening, who clung to his illusions like a drowning man clinging to a rope.

"Erich, what happened? You . . . you look dreadful."

He went on staring out the window. The sound of muted laughter came from the Crown Inn, a girl screeched, and a man's laughing voice drowned out the rest of the noise. "Leave me alone, Mother. It's nothing. I just have a bad headache again."

"What about your promise, Erich?" his mother insisted.

"Don't worry, Mama, the problem's solved." Erich

smiled, though his throat had tightened. "You really don't have anything to worry about anymore. I'll keep my promise."

Melanie slowly went out of the room. Erich dropped onto his bed and buried his head in the pillow. He had no choice but to keep his promise. He'd never see her again, ever! That realization shook his whole body, and he put his head under the pillows so that no one outside could hear him sobbing out loud.

When he set out for school on Monday morning he felt like a condemned man on the way to his execution. He was sure to be called to see the Head at once. He waited almost meekly to be attacked by Kampmann, Grimminger, and the others, although he wasn't sure how much they knew. Gremm was certainly not going to go around saying that his own niece and a Jew . . .

The first lesson was biology with Eisele, who told them at length about a lecture that had been given in the gymnasium hall on Saturday evening. It was the one that Gremm had said he was attending. A Party Comrade from Stuttgart called Stähle had spoken on "Racial purity as the first commandment of our nation," and said a great deal about those who "dishonored the race." Eisele picked up this subject and proceeded, with relish, to explain that "the inequality of races" rested on natural biological laws, and that cross-breeding between races, particularly the superior and the inferior kinds, was to be avoided because the resulting "racial mongrels" represented a real danger to "the healthy body of the people," and must be eradicated.

At this point Helmut spoke up, obviously angry, to ask what scientific proof there was for these theories. He finally had Eisele involved in a discussion, and drove the teacher further and further back on the defensive. In the end all Eisele could do was put a bad mark against Helmut's name in the register and give him three hours' detention that afternoon.

"Noll is obstinate and was disturbing the lesson," Eisele dictated to the class spokesman, who wrote it all down in the register—too hesitantly, it seemed, for Eisele, who soon afterward made some sarcastic remarks about Reger and several others in the class who were known to still be in the Catholic Youth organization. Eisele thundered denunciations of what he called "certified Christians," because they kept trying to evade the problem of offspring who suffered from hereditary disease. As he spoke he darted venomous looks around the class.

Erich listened with only half an ear. All he could think of was how ironic it was that this very lecture had been given on Saturday evening. According to the lecture, he had dishonored the race too! Perhaps Eisele already knew something about what had happened, and had talked to Gremm. But even the German lesson with Gremm himself passed without what he had feared happening. Gremm was in an even worse temper than usual, but to Erich's amazement he left him alone.

There had been no sign of Gertraud at break, and he couldn't see Lotte anywhere either, or not from the corner where he stood alone with Erwin and Max. At midday he ran up to the Benzenruhe to visit all the places where they had sat together. He couldn't rest; his thoughts tumbled over one another. How was Gertraud? What was Gremm going to do? It was dreadful waiting for something that you knew was bound to happen though you didn't know exactly when or how. The same idea kept going through his head: Gremm is playing with me like a cat does with a mouse. He's caught me, he lets me seem to get away for a moment only to pounce all the faster, just the way cats do. The only question is, when is he going to deliver that final blow.

Julius had assumed that Erich and Max would be going to Oedheim during the summer vacation, as usual. "Granny Babette is looking forward to seeing you," he announced at lunch, folding up the letter from Aunt Mina that he had just been reading aloud. Granny had moved to live with her eldest daughter for good; she had given up her apartment on Adolf-Hitler-Strasse and disposed of her household possessions. Some of them had gone to Oedheim: her favorite armchair, the pictures, a few other items that she was particularly fond of. The rest had been given away to the children.

Erich now owned Grandfather Elias's old-fashioned watch, which had always fascinated him as a child because its lid snapped open when you pressed a tiny spring. Since Granny Babette's eldest grandson, Siegfried, had been living in America for a long time, she had decided that the second eldest, Erich, who was her favorite grandchild anyway, should have the watch that she had so carefully preserved. It was lying on his chest of drawers now, and sometimes, lost in thought, he would pick it up, snap it open and shut again, and wonder how much it would fetch if he sold it. For he was well aware that some more valuables had gone to Würzburg to be sold, although Mother and Father did their best to hide it from him and Max.

To Julius's surprise, Erich now said that he didn't want to go to Oedheim this summer.

"And why not?" Julius asked. There was an angry undertone to his voice.

"Because I don't want to," replied Erich, looking

straight at his father. "I'm nearly fourteen, I don't have fun playing games by the river anymore. And no one wants anything to do with us anyway. It's just the same there as it is here!"

Julius looked belligerent for a moment, but then lowered his eyes. Since that incident when he was left lying in the dirt in front of the gymnasium, with the SA men calling him names, their relationship had been more awkward. Erich often felt as if his father lost his temper and spoke angrily only because it was expected of him. It was part of the role he had always played. In reality he was tired, and sick with worry. So Erich was not too surprised that Julius gave in almost at once. "Well, of course we can't force you. But Aunt Mina and Uncle Louis will be disappointed. You'll have to write and explain."

Erich nodded. He'd think of something or other.

"How about you, Max?" his father cautiously asked.

"I'm going anyway," Max announced, and muttered under his breath, glancing at Erich, "Spoilsport."

A few days later the long vacation began. Max packed his case and marched off to the station with Father. Julius would be coming back in a few days.

It sometimes seemed to Erich that Mother wanted to say something to him—something that was very much on her mind—but she didn't seem to trust herself to do it. So she kept to a whispered, "How are you, Erich?" morning and evening, to which he always automatically replied, "I'm fine, Mama, don't worry."

Then Julius came back, gloomy and morose. Grandmother was better, he told them. She was sorry that Erich hadn't come. And Uncle Louis's business was doing badly, almost as badly as his own.

"How about Ilse and Martin?" asked Erich expectantly, but Julius only shrugged his shoulders.

"They're talking of going to join the others in Barcelona, although the political situation there is deteriorating too. Trudel has written saying they're thinking of emigrating to South America."

"What about Aunt Mina and Uncle Louis?" Erich went on, and Julius shrugged again.

"They want to stay here, whatever happens. Particularly Mina. Although Siegfried is urging them to come to the USA. He says he'll even pay for their passage."

Soon after this another letter from Aunt Betti arrived. Heinz-Viktor, who was now in his second year at school, was always being teased and bullied. And he was having to learn some very strange things. She didn't say exactly what, but Erich could guess. He'll have to sing Nazi songs, he thought bitterly, and they probably teach even the little ones all that stuff about race. What was it Max had been told to write in his exercise book the other day? "Jews are bloodsuckers and exploit others. They are the mortal enemies of our nation." And that was in a dictation that was supposed to teach good spelling! His brother had shown him the exercise book in silence, and Erich, shrugging, had handed it back.

"Take care Mother doesn't see that." There was nothing else to say.

The vacation dragged on. Not knowing was the worst of it—not knowing what had become of Gertraud, or what still lay ahead of them. And there was no one he could share his fears with. Helmut had gone to one of the Baltic spa resorts with his parents. Herr Noll was going to be treated there, because he wasn't in very good health. "His heart," Helmut had explained when they said good-bye in their secret place in the cellar on the last day of school. "It's all been a bit too much for my old man. Dr. Uhl says he must take care and not put too much strain on his constitution. But that's easier said than done. Business isn't so good for us either, and that depresses him—that and now—well, you can imagine." The two boys looked wordlessly at each other. Erich knew exactly what his friend was talking about.

After the first week of the vacation, when Ellwangen was covered almost continuously by a leaden gray sky, and rain beat monotonously against the windows, he went down to the shop to have a word with the Fräulein Pfisterers. Could he help out at all in the shop, he shyly asked, and after a little thought Fräulein Marie said, well, yes, he could lend the girl apprentice a hand, carrying and unpacking crates, sweeping out the premises, going to the post, and he would even earn a few pfennigs. Erich felt relieved. It would be better than staying in his room watching the raindrops, which appeared to be drumming on the panes in a rhythm of their own. And when the rain stopped, it was better than going to the places that had been so important to him, for his memories always overwhelmed him there, so that he thought one day he wouldn't be able to bear the burden of them. He would rather work hard and not have to think so much.

As time went on, he heard a whispered question now and then, or a low-voiced remark wondering why the "Jewboy" was working in this respectable shop, but Fräulein Auguste in particular was short and sharp in her responses. And Fräulein Marie sometimes even gave him an extra coin and then said that he looked too sad, and what had happened to the cheerful Erich of the old days, always ready for fun and pranks?

On the first Thursday in August, all the flags were lowered to half-mast around the middle of the afternoon, and there was wild speculation in the shop. What had happened? Erich, who was just opening some crates, thought with a thudding heart how Gertraud had said she prayed for Hitler's death. But it wasn't Adolf Hitler who had died, it was old President Hindenburg, the newspaper headlines announced the next morning.

"And now the way is absolutely clear for Hitler," said Julius. A little later, Mother closed the windows, for the SS band was marching past down below on its way to the gymnasium, where there was to be a great mourning procession.

The old president's death left Erich cold. But how could things get worse? He was not particularly surprised when, at the end of August, his father read out from the paper that over ninety percent of Germans had voted for Hitler to become president, saying that he was now "truly the leader of the German nation." Father and Mother had not taken part in what was called a plebiscite*, since, according to Julius, the whole thing was "nothing but a joke."

All the same, 616 citizens of Ellwangen had voted against Hitler for president. That was more than anywhere else in the region, and gave the Levi family a little hope. Apparently it wasn't as bad here as in other places. Much more important than these events, however, was his daily visit to the mailbox around midday. Sometimes, when he was busy at the front of the shop, he waited for the postman, took the letters, and looked quickly through them; but there was never one from Gertraud. Now and then Erich tried striking a bargain with the Almighty, promising to unpack the crates that had just arrived in record time, to clean the sales counter particularly well in the evening, to help his mother on the weekend, but it never worked.

They'll be watching her, thought Erich, so she won't have a chance to write a letter or send it without anyone knowing. He had heard from Martha Bieg that the Gremms had gone away and wouldn't be back until the end of August. Whether that would be with or without their niece she didn't know, and the Gremms' cleaning lady, the source of her information, didn't even know where they had gone. Somewhere in the Black Forest, she thought, so in the evening Erich sometimes looked at the map in his atlas showing the Black Forest, and wondered where Gertraud might be now. A brief postcard came from Helmut: best wishes from Zingst on the Baltic coast. In the last week of the vacation Uncle Sigmund paid them a short visit, as he often did. Aunt Lea was still in Markelsheim with Erwin, visiting her parents. Uncle Sigmund looked even more careworn than usual, and gratefully accepted the cognac that Melanie handed him in silence.

"I was in Schwäbisch Hall yesterday to see Dr. Berlinger, along with the other community leaders," he told them. The rabbi had a large area to look after, so he relied a great deal on the cooperation of the leaders of the Jewish communities, and they all met regularly. "They all have the same complaints," said Uncle Sigmund, sipping the cognac. "Abuse, attacks, worst of all, severe financial losses because people who buy from us are just making trouble for themselves. Herr Lewkowitz, the cantor in Hall, said that in one village they've even put up a blackboard outside the village hall denouncing everyone who does business with Jews by name."

Melanie was indignant. "That's medieval!"

"But there's even worse to come." Uncle Sigmund took

another large sip and put the glass down on the table with deliberation. He ran his fingertips carefully along the stem of the glass and then said, without looking at his listeners, who were watching him in suspense, "We have concrete evidence that Jewish communities are to be dissolved. Our own prayer hall, for instance, is to be used for other purposes, as they so charmingly put it."

They all stared at him, shocked.

"But where are we to pray, then?" Melanie whispered. "Where can we celebrate our feast days? Max will be having his bar mitzvah next year! Are we supposed to go to Hall every time? Or is the synagogue there going to be closed too? It's impossible!"

Sigmund did not reply, but just went on running his finger up and down the stem of his glass.

Julius asked, his voice heavy, "So just what is to become of our prayer hall?"

Sigmund did not look up. "They want to give it to the Hitler Youth. It seems they need the space."

There was dead silence for a moment, then Julius cried, "Outrageous! Are they trying to make fun of us now too?"

With a shaking hand, Melanie poured more cognac, ignoring the few drops that fell on the carefully polished table. "Isn't there anything to be done?" she asked in a tremulous voice.

Uncle Sigmund shook his head. "Of course Dr. Berlinger will oppose the idea strongly, but what can he do? Ultimately it will be decided on another level. We just hope that the central organization will be able to do something."

Erich had only a vague idea what the central organization was. His father had once explained that as a body it represented German Jews. But what can German Jews do against the Nazis? Erich wondered as he tossed and turned in bed that night, unable to fall asleep. Now they're even taking our prayer hall away, he thought. And Father and Mother are secretly selling the household valuables piece by piece. If this goes on we'll soon have nothing left. He remembered what his father had once said when the two of them were on their way to the cattle sheds, and Father had still been so proud and confident. ". . . But we will never let them take our honor!"

How much honor is still left to Julius Levi's family? thought Erich. And when they've taken the last of it, then what? At last he fell into an uneasy sleep in which he dreamed of Gertraud. He was trying to reach her, but in vain; for however hard he tried to move forward, he was rooted to the spot.

Shame and Rage

ON THE FIRST DAY back at school after the long vacation, Erich looked around the yard with his heart beating fast, searching for Gertraud. He forced his way through the groups of young people standing close together, jostling some of them and risking insults and name-calling. He did get some of that, particularly from the schoolboys wearing the Jungvolk or Hitler Youth uniform, but it didn't upset him; he just thought that what had once been a colorful scene was now a dreary monotone, dominated by black and gray. Kampmann was leaning against the wall of the school building, surrounded by his cronies, and Erich sensed rather than saw the nasty looks being shot at him. Kampmann seemed to have said something, probably about him, for he thought he'd heard his name, but he didn't stop to bother about it. Roars of laughter greeted Kampmann's sally, but

Erich pressed on toward the entrance, still looking for Gertraud.

Suddenly he saw Lotte Richter standing on her own on the steps. When she saw Erich coming she shook her head, and almost imperceptibly nodded in the direction of the Collegiate Church, where Grimminger had stationed himself near the entrance, hands on his hips, surveying the teeming throng in the square like a victorious general. At last the doors of the high school opened, and long lines formed. The smaller pupils were shuffling impatiently, but the big ones weren't in such a hurry. Erich saw Helmut, who nodded to him. He had come home from vacation only the day before yesterday, and they hadn't had a chance to talk yet. Erwin pulled Erich's sleeve, and they both went to the very end of the line.

Gertraud wasn't here. Everything revolved around that thought. So they had sent her away, just as she'd feared. He absolutely had to speak to Lotte later on; she was the one person who could tell him anything. He scarcely heard a word when Gremm greeted the class and the next moment announced that there would be no regular lessons on Thursday because everyone was to listen to the broadcast of the führer's address from the Reich Party Rally in Nuremberg. A few particularly deserving members of the Jungvolk and the Hitler Youth—at this point he nodded to Kampmann and Kurt—were even going to Nuremberg to take part in the rally itself.

Erich's lip curled scornfully, and he glanced back so that he could look at Kurt. How quickly someone could change!

"Levi, eyes forward," came a sharp command from the corner where Gremm was standing, and Erich jumped. Be careful, he warned himself, be careful. He heard Gremm's cutting voice behind him, every syllable delivered staccato, words flying like knives. He said something about "the mortal enemies of our nation," and the "power of world Jewry," and Erich listened in surprise. He couldn't make much of the phrase "world Jewry" at all. Then Gremm told the class to take out their German exercise books and write a dictation exercise. There was the sound of rustling paper, desk lids slammed, and Erich nervously reached for his pen, dipped it in the inkwell, and immediately left a large blot on the cover of his exercise book. He quickly glanced up at the desk on its plinth where Gremm had seated himself, but thank heavens he hadn't noticed anything, and Erich carefully tried soaking up the ink with blotting paper. He'd put a new cover on the book later today.

Gremm began dictating in a monotonous voice. "From a speech made by Benjamin Franklin in the year 1789."

Erich breathed again. This couldn't be too bad, or anyway not what he'd expected after all that about the strange term "world Jewry." This Benjamin Franklin was an American, he knew that much; he'd had something or other to do with the founding of the United States. But then the rest of it came pelting down on him—stuff that he couldn't possibly write out.

He lowered his pen and listened incredulously to what Gremm was dictating. "'In whatever country Jews have settled, they have lowered its moral tone; depreciated its commercial integrity; have built up a state within the state . . .'"*

Erich heard the sound of scratchy pen nibs hurrying over the paper. Their echo was almost unbearable. Turning, he saw that all the others were writing, their heads bent over their exercise books; even Helmut was writing! "'. . . Why? Because they are vampires,'" Gremm ended his quotation, and then told the class to read through the text carefully and make any necessary corrections.

"Levi, why weren't you taking down the dictation?" Gremm was suddenly standing in front of Erich, who still sat there motionless, pen in hand. He leaned over and looked at Erwin's exercise book. Erwin too had written only the beginning of the dictation.

"Get up when I'm speaking to you, you two!" Gremm's voice, which had begun quietly, almost gently, suddenly cracked. Now he was shouting.

Erwin shot to his feet, followed by Erich, who struggled out of his daze. All was perfectly quiet in the classroom.

"Well, come along! Why didn't you write your dictation? I want an answer!"

Erich felt that Erwin was looking sideways at him. He swallowed several times, and then whispered, "We . . . we can't write that."

"Louder, please!" bellowed Gremm.

Erich cleared his throat and then said, in a firmer voice, "We can't write that."

"You forgot to say 'sir'! Again!"

Erich clung to the edge of his desk with both hands. Rage arose in him, a wild rage that he could do nothing about, overwhelming him. He said in a very loud voice, emphasizing every syllable just as Gremm did, "We can't write that, *sir*." The last word was positively flung in Gremm's face. It sounded like a declaration of war.

Gremm was standing so close to him that Erich could smell his aftershave. "And why not?"

"Because it's an insult to Erwin and me and all the others."

"All the others?" Gremm smiled. It was a small, cold, unpleasant smile. "You mean people of your kind?"

Erich said no more. He was waiting. The whole thing was a trap. They faced each other, he and Gremm, and he tried to withstand the teacher's gaze and that unpleasant little triumphant smile.

"Well, you two will write out the text twenty times this afternoon, and then learn it by heart. You can recite it to the class tomorrow. That's your punishment for insubordination. If you do not do as I tell you . . ." Gremm paused for some time, and looked around the classroom. His smile grew wider. "Well, then we'll see."

There was a moment's silence, and then the class began to laugh. They laughed and applauded. Not all of them, of course. Reger and a few others sat with their heads bent, and Helmut had clenched his fists and was staring at Gremm as if he'd like to leap at him. But most of them laughed, the loudest of all being Kampmann, and Kurt, who couldn't control himself. That was what hurt most.

Suddenly, in the midst of all this laughter, the bell went off for break, ending it abruptly. In the new noise that arose, Erich heard his cousin whispering, "What are we going to do, Erich? I can't write that out."

Erich was still choking on his rage. If only Kampmann had come up to him now, or someone else had said something! But they were all making their way past him. Only Helmut, hesitating, still stood by the window.

"We won't, either. Come on." He led Erwin out, and gave a curt nod to Helmut, who made a little gesture signaling that he had to speak to Erich today.

That afternoon Uncle Sigmund dropped in to say that

he had made an appointment to speak to Dr. Kaiser. He and Julius had agreed that he would go to see the Head alone, not only as Erwin's father but also as a representative of the small Jewish community of Ellwangen, whose leader, after all, he was. "That text for dictation insults us all!" he had said, slamming his hand down on the table so hard that Mother's crystal vase wobbled alarmingly.

After he had left, Erich went into his room. He didn't want to see Mother's face, which was still tearstained from her violent weeping. She had cried her eyes out in the kitchen after Erich told her what had happened at school. Don't attract attention, lie low: that had been his watchword so far. But this was more than he could take. They could not put up with this humiliation, whatever the consequences. He was used to insults; he'd heard about the inferiority of his race over and over again in biology, and in other subjects too. He had swallowed it all, hard as he found it to do so. But being forced to recite such insults out loud, humiliating and deriding himself, was just too much. Julius had seen it that way too, and something of his old fighting spirit revived when he hurried off to his brother's house after lunch to discuss what they should do. They had agreed to complain to the headmaster, whatever happened.

Erich went to the window. He was just in time to see Uncle Sigmund hurrying across the square and disappearing through the great porch of the high school. He sat down to do his homework. His English book lay open in front of him, but he couldn't concentrate on the text. The image of Gremm laughing kept coming between him and the pages.

After a while he put his pen down and went over to the chest of drawers. There was a small hand mirror there which he used to check the parting of his hair first thing in the morning. What was it Fanny always said? "You're the vainest boy I know." He looked in the mirror. A thin face looked back at him from large brown eyes—"dachshund eyes," Fanny had called them. "The way you look at a person would melt a heart of stone," she had added, and Gertraud too had sometimes said to him, "Don't look at me like that! You make me feel so strange." And his heart used to beat faster at such remarks. Now his hair, thick and dark brown, was carefully parted as always. He examined himself critically for a long time, and then thought: So what's different about me? I don't look like those hook-nosed men down in the display case outside Schuster's house. Max doesn't look like them either, and Mother most certainly doesn't. Perhaps Father's nose is rather large, but still ... What's so different about us?

He suddenly remembered an episode that had happened a long time ago, when he was still a little boy, just going into first grade at elementary school. At the time Mother and Father used to give a big dinner party for business friends and acquaintances every few weeks. It had always been a great occasion. The table was laid with a damask cloth, sparkling crystal glasses, and the family's old silver cutlery—the silver that was now with the Jewish Aid organization in Würzburg, or might already be on someone else's table. Days in advance, Mother and the maid would begin baking, marinating a joint of meat, and polishing up the china. When the great day came, Max and he used to look out of their room in the evening with shining eyes to watch the guests arrive. Mother always looked so elegant at that time, and Father was very dignified and distinguished too. The next day the boys would be given what was left of the special dessert. Mother always kept it for them.

Several times, Melanie had also invited families who were not so closely connected with them. They were people she particularly liked; for instance, Max and Erich's pediatrician, or the owner of the pharmacy where she went to buy medicines. These were distinguished families who had lived in Ellwangen a long time. Julius had looked over her shoulder as she wrote the invitations, briefly commenting, "But they won't accept, Melanie."

And he had been right. Refusals always came back, politely worded and written on thick paper of good quality, and after a while Mother stopped sending invitations to certain addresses. At first she had not wanted to do as Erich asked when he kept urging her to invite the Nolls. This was at the time when he and Helmut were first becoming friends. In the end she had given in, sighing, and Erich himself, beaming happily, had delivered the letter to the Noll family. And then the refusal had come back, also politely worded and written on thick paper of good quality, and no invitation had ever been sent to the Nolls again.

"But why don't they want to come?" he had asked his mother. "It's so nice here. Why don't the Nolls come? They're always so friendly to me. And why don't Gudrun's parents come? I mean, we play with her. And then there's the others . . ."

Mother had looked at him for a moment, and then, lost in thought, had patted his cheek, saying, "They're all delightful people, but they have their own circles of friends, and we have ours. I have to keep reminding myself of that."

This explanation had not satisfied him at the time, but now he understood. We probably never really belonged, he thought, or Uncle Sigmund either, or the Neuburgers and the Heinrichs. I just didn't realize it at the time. It had always been that way. Well, if Benjamin Franklin wrote something like that almost two hundred years ago! And he was a very clever man. He took another look at himself in the mirror. I just wish I knew why, he thought.

Uncle Sigmund came back in the evening. He looked both relieved and anxious. "There'll be no writing out that piece and learning it by heart," he told the family, who had gathered in the living room. "Dr. Kaiser agreed that it was more than should be asked of the boys. He reprimanded Gremm, though Gremm defended himself cleverly, saying that after all Benjamin Franklin wrote it, but the Head wasn't going along with that. However, you'll each have two hours' detention."

"Why?" Erich interrupted indignantly. "Why are we being punished? We did nothing wrong!"

Uncle Sigmund shrugged his shoulders. "Well, you didn't do as the teacher told you. I suspect that Dr. Kaiser upheld the detention so that Gremm could save face. There was nothing I could do about that."

"It's still not fair," grumbled Erich, although he secretly felt relieved. "Thanks all the same, Uncle Sigmund."

"However, there's something else." Sigmund Levi hesitated for a moment. "I . . . it's difficult for me to talk about this, but there's no point in burying our heads in the sand. As I was about to leave, Dr. Kaiser kept me back for a moment after Gremm had gone. He told me he's retiring at the end of the present school year. I think he's very glad of that, because he doesn't seem to like what's going on around him at all. 'I won't have to howl with the wolves any longer then,' he told me. But," said Uncle Sigmund, lowering his voice, ". . . but he also said he won't be able to do any more for us then. 'So far, I've protected the boys as best I could, Herr Levi; your son and his cousin. I don't yet know who my successor will be, but you can assume it will be someone who thinks more along the new, official lines.' That's literally what he said."

"So what's he trying to tell us?" Julius sounded hoarse. "Does that mean there'll be even more bullying and violence?"

Sigmund looked his brother in the face. "I think he was trying to hint that they'll have to leave the high school some time, and maybe in the not-too-distant future. When I met the other community leaders, they were openly saying that there are concrete plans to exclude Jewish pupils from the public schools. They're to go to special Jewish schools instead."

"But how's that going to work? There are only three Jewish children in all Ellwangen. It may be all right in big cities, but here . . . ?"

Sigmund shrugged. "I don't know, Julius. Perhaps it won't come to that. All the same, I think we have to be prepared for all eventualities."

Erich felt dazed. He thought of his conversation with Helmut a few weeks back. That fear had materialized now. If even Dr. Kaiser was talking about it . . . and there was Gremm, lurking in the background, biding his time, sure of victory. Suppose he had to leave school! He didn't even want to think about it.

That night Erich prayed for the first time in months. It was a very childish prayer, and he was almost ashamed of it. He prayed to the Almighty to make Hitler die. And he asked to be able to stay at school and see Gertraud once more. But most of all he prayed for Hitler to be out of the way.

Next day the class waited in vain for "the two Jew-boys

to perform," as Kampmann put it. Gremm said briefly that after consultation with Dr. Kaiser, their "outrageous insubordination" was to be punished by different methods. Sounds wonderfully dramatic, Erich thought. Just as if something even worse was going to happen to us. But he probably wants to hide the fact that he's had to back off.

On Saturday they had to attend another large rally in the gymnasium. It was a memorial service for the late Reich President Hindenburg. Erich and Erwin stood at the very back of the long line that moved along Hindenburgstrasse. The leaves of the old chestnut trees lining the marketplace were slowly turning color, and several chestnuts lay on the ground with their husks bursting; small, prickly green hedgehogs with the dull glow of the dark brown chestnuts peeping out of them. Erich thought nostalgically of the old days when they used to play naughty tricks, beating chestnuts down from the trees with large wooden clubs and snatching them up before they were gathered by the forest warden. Admittedly it was a rough-and-ready method of harvesting the nuts, but it had been fun when they all met afterward, red in the face from running, to see who had collected the most.

Once they reached the gymnasium, he and Erwin and Max settled in an unobtrusive corner right next to the door. After the usual speeches and spoken choruses, Dr. Kaiser swore the staff to be loyal to Adolf Hitler. It wasn't the constitution they were supposed to serve anymore, but the führer himself as the personification of the nation. That, as the Head put it, was "an entity of supreme importance." And Erich, hearing all this with a shudder, thought that at least the old headmaster had expressed something of his distaste, if only in veiled terms. He looked at the figure in the old-fashioned black frock coat with mingled respect and affection. He had sometimes resented Dr. Kaiser for his speeches in "the genuine Nazi tone," as Helmut had once sarcastically put it, but all the same he protected his Jewish pupils, perhaps preventing even worse from happening. But for how much longer? Erich thought, once again feeling a lump in his throat. He was one of the first to hurry out when the doors were opened; he had to get some fresh air. It was stifling inside there.

When he reached home he smelled freshly baked bread. The challah loaves were already on the table, crisp, brown, and sprinkled with poppy seeds. Melanie asked her elder son to go over to the Golden Cross butcher shop to fetch the joint of mutton she had ordered. Erich made a face. Recently they had started having mutton, and in spite of Mother's good cooking he didn't really like the meat with its coarse fibers and strong flavor. But he made no comment, took the shopping bag off its hook, and went over to the shop, where the landlord of the Golden Cross gave him a large piece of meat. He went home past the Crown Inn so as to come in by the back door, since a good many school students were still walking down Hindenburgstrasse at the front of the building.

Suddenly he heard a quietly spoken "Erich!" and saw Lotte standing at the corner. Erich's nod told her to follow him, and he pulled her through the back door by her sleeve. They stood by the cellar door, slightly out of breath. "No one comes here," Erich told her. "Only the apprentice now and then, and if she does we'll pretend you're looking for the front entrance. And the Fräulein Pfisterers won't tell anyone."

Lotte cast a hunted glance around her and then whispered, "Gertraud says to give you her love."

Erich held her arm so tight that she uttered a small cry. "How is she? Where is she? Is she all right?"

Lotte freed her arm from his grip, saying reproachfully, "You're hurting me!" But when she saw his pale face and the anxiety in his eyes, she said in a kinder tone, "Yes, she's all right, as far as anyone can be said to be all right under the circumstances. They sent her to a boarding school in the Black Forest."

"Who are 'they'?"

"Gremm and her father. Gremm gave her father hell, going on about bad influences that had ruined Gertraud entirely."

"And he believed such garbage?"

"Well, what could he do? Gremm won't have her here anymore, and she can't stay at home alone in Stuttgart. So they sent her to this boarding school. It's very strict there. They keep an eye on any letters, that's why she hasn't written. She's afraid Gremm may have said something, and they'll confiscate any letters she writes you and report it. And then you'll be in trouble."

"You mean they read other people's letters there?" asked Erich incredulously.

Instead of answering, Lotte only shrugged. "We worked out a kind of secret language," she said at last, after a moment of silence in which Erich laboriously digested all this new information. "That way at least I can tell how she *really* is. Anyway, I'm to give you her love and say she's thinking of you. She'll be back in Stuttgart with her father at Christmas, and then she'll get in touch." Lotte was impatiently making for the door. "I have to go now—better safe than sorry. My father's been watching me like a hawk for some time; I guess you can imagine why. 'It's *my* reputation at stake, Lotte,' he keeps saying. Good-bye, Erich!"

"Good-bye, Lotte. And thanks!"

"That's okay." She slipped through the doorway, and looked back at him for a moment. "Take care, Erich!"

He nodded, lost in thought, and slowly climbed the stairs. The bag with the mutton in it suddenly weighed a ton. So she was in a boarding school! And it sounded like a very strict one. She must be dreadfully unhappy, and there was nothing he could do about it. But at least he now knew where she was, and there was sure to be a letter at Christmas, and then he could write back.

When he opened the kitchen door, he saw Mother sitting at the table reading a letter. "Aunt Betti and Uncle Samson will be coming for the New Year," she said, without looking up. "They're staying with Uncle Sigmund. They have a lot to tell me, Betti writes."

Sullenly, Erich flung the shopping bag down on the table. He was fond of Aunt Betti, though he liked Aunt Mina more, but he felt bad-tempered now because the major festival days were coming. Rosh Hashanah* and shortly after it Yom Kippur* were days of grave ceremony. What an idea, celebrating New Year's in September, he thought, suddenly and inexplicably. The Christian New Year's is far more fun; there's fireworks and champagne and punch, and everyone looks forward to the year ahead. But at our New Year's we're supposed to do penance and think of death and sit around in the prayer hall forever, and we even have to fast all day on Yom Kippur.

Mother seemed to be reading his thoughts, for she looked hard at him. He turned away and opened the kitchen cupboard to cut himself a slice of bread.

"Erich, we'll be celebrating together as we do every

year," he heard Mother say behind his back, with some hesitation. "I don't want to hear anything about your being invited to go somewhere else."

"Who would invite me?" Erich turned abruptly. "Who'd invite me, I ask you? No one wants any more to do with us. And I'll tell you one thing: okay, I'll be there this time, but there's a time coming when I won't have anything to do with all that nonsense anymore."

"Erich!" His mother uttered a cry of indignation. "Erich, how can you say a thing like that? It's your religion. It's the most important thing we have. It's . . ." She struggled for words, and Erich completed the sentence for her in what he himself realized, with secret horror, was a very unpleasant tone of voice. "It's reactionary and totally outdated. So we celebrate the beginning of the year 5695 next week—I mean, it's totally ridiculous. No wonder other people look down on us."

"But, Erich . . ." Melanie seemed utterly bewildered.

"And what am I supposed to do penance for?" Suddenly Erich felt something like savage triumph. "Just what, I ask myself, am I supposed to do penance for? For being beaten up and called names and given bad marks I don't deserve? For not having any friends left? And where's our God, where's our sublime, almighty God when we need him? You can't help noticing that he's let us down!"

He angrily bit into his bread and chewed without paying any attention to the flavor.

"Erich." Suddenly Mother was calm again. "Do I really have to tell you what is important and sacred to us at this of all times? You're so self-righteous. You ought to repent of this scene, if nothing else, and of upsetting your mother so much. And let me remind you what we pray at Yom Kippur: 'But more particularly we remember the suffering of the house of Israel, a people of sorrows and acquainted with grief.' If we break with our religion and our customs, all those who despise and persecute us will triumph. Then they'll have won. You don't want that, do you?"

Erich marched to the door. As he went out, he snapped back at his mother, "Personally, I don't want to suffer or have sorrows or be acquainted with grief; can't you understand that?"

He slammed the door behind him and went to his room. His rage had left him, and he was ashamed of himself, but he wasn't about to admit it.

New Year

AUNT BETTI and Uncle Samson arrived the day before Rosh Hashanah. Julius and Uncle Sigmund went to the rail station to meet them. Erich saw them at the prayer hall in the evening. He had followed Father there, although still reluctantly. The little hall was well filled, for the Heinrichs and Neuburgers had visitors too. Dr. Berlinger the rabbi had not come from Hall, because he had many congregations to care for, so instead Herr Silbermann, Erich's old religious education teacher, and Uncle Sigmund recited the prayers.

Erich himself, as the youngest member of the community, was called up to the Torah to read the lesson. Exactly a year ago, on the day of his bar mitzvah, he had read from the Torah for the first time, and as he slowly walked forward to the lectern he remembered how proud he had been then. Herr

Silbermann gave him a friendly nod. Erich read fast, as if to get the whole thing behind him as quickly as possible, and stumbled over his words once or twice, but that didn't seem to bother the other members of the congregation. He was upset, it was easy to understand.

After the end of the service, when the little congregation was standing there for a short while to wish each other "*Shana tova*,"* old Herr Neuburger put a hand on Erich's head and gave him a coin. "All the best, Erich!" he said. "And I hope it really will be a happier new year, particularly for you young people."

"Happy New Year to you too, Herr Neuburger, and thanks." Erich gave him a conspiratorial wink, and old Herr Neuburger had to laugh. Then he nudged him affectionately. "You're getting to be a fine young man. It's a shame there are no girls of your age here in the community."

Erich thought that there were plenty of girls here in Ellwangen, but old Herr Neuburger was right—none of them were for him, a Jew. And anyway, there was only one girl he thought about, and she was even farther from his reach.

At supper, Aunt Betti did most of the talking. Mother had gone to a great deal of trouble, and the table really did look very festive, even if most of the silver had been replaced by ordinary everyday cutlery. As children, Erich and Max had always looked forward to the Rosh Hashanah meal, for according to tradition it began with apples and honey. "That's because we hope our new year will be just as sweet," Mother used to explain to them.

Now it was Heinz-Viktor who enjoyed the sweet start the most. He kept stuffing the slices of apple drenched in honey into his mouth, which was already sticky and smeared, and

Erich grinned to himself, thinking that his aunt and uncle would be having their sleep disturbed this New Year's Eve.

The little boy had been born late to his parents, when Aunt Betti had given up all hope of having children of her own. But then along came Heinz-Viktor, her coddled and spoiled only son, on whom all her fears and cares focused. Her conversation was all about him too, and now she hardly ever stopped talking about the way he was teased and bullied at school. "And he has to learn all those songs they're singing by heart, and last week he brought home a piece of paper with a . . . a man on it, a caricature, well, you can imagine what it was like, and he had to color it in and learn the verse underneath it—oh, such a ridiculous verse, I can't repeat it!" Suddenly there were tears in her eyes, and Uncle Samson put a comforting hand on hers. All the time she had been picking at the embroidery on the tablecloth, even pulling out some of the threads.

Her constant talk got on Erich's nerves, but now that he saw how upset she was, he felt very sorry for her.

Melanie said soothingly, "Have something to eat, Betti, do," and nodded slightly to Max and Heinz-Viktor, who were shoveling carp and potatoes into themselves, apparently taking no notice of the conversation. Mother's gentle reproach worked. Aunt Betti fell silent and began halfheartedly toying with her food. Uncle Samson began talking to Father about business, but Julius didn't really seem keen for that kind of conversation.

Suddenly Uncle Samson spoke into the silence that was broken only by the sound of knives and forks, "Our community leader thinks there will be attempts to withdraw Jewish children from public schools and send them to special Jewish schools. Old Goldberg told me that there are already inquiries being made about potential premises for a Jewish elementary school."

Uncle Samson talks so pompously, thought Erich. But perhaps he doesn't want the little ones to understand what it's all about.

"Yes, that's what they want, to exclude us from everything," Julius said. "A backward step, one of many, but a severe one."

Hesitantly, Uncle Samson went on, "Well, in the circumstances I'll be glad that Heinz-Viktor doesn't . . ."

Julius interrupted excitedly. "A backward step, I tell you . . ." And he would have worked himself up even more. The two smaller boys, Max and Heinz-Viktor, had stopped eating and were staring at him. Melanie hastily began talking about the religious service, but that started Aunt Betti off again. "The service is much more solemn and beautiful in our synagogue at home in Ulm. The prayer hall here is very unimpressive. They don't even blow a shofar* . . ." And so it went on, until Mother finally took her into the kitchen after dessert to have her help with the dishes.

Erich wandered off to his room once Max and his cousin had gone to play in the bedroom the two brothers had once shared. As he passed the kitchen, Erich heard Betti's high voice raised in complaints, and felt sorry for his mother. Once in his room, he opened the window wide and took deep breaths of the cool fall air. It already smelled slightly of wood and coal, for many people had begun heating their homes these last few days. The nights were unusually chilly.

So this was it, the year 5695, on which so many of the hopes and wishes of the Jews living here depended—probably more than in all the years before. Fleetingly, Erich remembered Herr Neuburger's words. "I hope it really will be a happier new year." He thought of Aunt Betti's fears, and Uncle Samson's careworn expression. That thoughtful, serious man had fought at the front in the World War, and had several shrapnel splinters in his shoulder, which sometimes made it ache so much that he walked bent sideways. He gave his health for his country, thought Erich, pressing his face to the cool windowpane, and now he has to watch his son—the apple of his eye, so carefully protected by his family—being teased and beaten. I wish I knew if it's the same for all Jewish children, he thought. And now here came the year 5695; in a few weeks' time it would be the Christian year 1935. What would the coming year bring?

Jews Out!

ERICH PUSHED PAST the steaming bodies of horses standing close together in the square outside the high school and the Collegiate Church, making movement almost impossible. White vapor rose from their nostrils, and from the mouths of their owners lining the square, arms folded against the cold, stamping on the ground now and then to warm their feet a little. It was very chilly this January morning in 1935, "a Cold Market that really deserves the name," as the newspaper had said this morning. The night before, it had snowed, and the spire of the Collegiate Church was powdered with white, just like the onion domes of the town parish church and the sloping roofs of the former priests' houses, from whose chimneys thin smoke curled. The horses were beautifully groomed, and some even had their manes woven into little braids, for the great parade was to be at midday, and after that there would be the traditional presentation of prizes. Erich loved the bustling atmosphere in town, the shouting and running about, the smells, and the excitement at home too, where Mother had begun arranging platters of cold meats early in the morning, for guests were expected again—Father's customers and colleagues.

A change seemed to have come over Julius these last few days: his figure was more upright, his eyes looked bright and energetic, and not as tired as they had for some months past. The Cold Market and Julius Levi went together somehow, thought Erich. At the same time Erich felt deeply apprehensive when he thought that Father's hopes of doing good business might come to nothing yet again this year. Julius had sat down to breakfast this morning rubbing his hands, enumerating all the people he'd be meeting. Business at the Cold Market, the contacts you made or renewed there—those things could make the difference between a good year and a bad one. It was a mystery to Erich where his father found the optimism to assume that this year could be better than last year. He knew many farmers owed Father money. Julius had helped a great many of them, particularly in the bad years after the worldwide economic slump; he had given them credit or lent them a young cow to raise free, so that the farmer could at least earn something from the sale of her milk. But now most were avoiding him, either because they were afraid, or because, despite knowing better, they themselves actually believed all that nonsense about bloodsucking Jews.

But the market is like a cordial to him, it does him good, thought Erich as he climbed the steps to the school entrance, casting one more glance at the gleaming black and brown coats of the horses where they stood close together. Melanie had seemed cheerful too; she had even been humming as she stood at the kitchen table this morning slicing cucumbers wafer thin to garnish her open sandwiches.

Involuntarily, Erich's hand went to his back pocket, for as he walked along he thought he could hear the paper rustling slightly. That was *his* elixir, *his* hope: two closely written sheets of paper, a letter from Gertraud, which had finally come with the mail last Saturday. He had unfolded the letter and read it again and again, so that in some places the ink was already blurred and illegible. He knew it by heart. She had gone skiing in Austria with her father, she wrote, and now at last she could venture to send him a letter. The boarding school was very strict, run by nuns who checked incoming and outgoing mail all the time. She wasn't sure, she said, whether Gremm might have instructed them to report any letters addressed to Erich, and she didn't want to make trouble for him.

"Gremm didn't like the idea that I was going to a convent school, but my father had his own way about that. Anyway, Gremm would rather I was here than still in touch with you. Somehow or other he managed to convince my father that my morals were endangered, as he put it. Papa doesn't mind if I'm friendly with a Jew, so Gremm thought that up as an alternative. I hope that as time goes by I can convince Papa that I'll be all right alone in Stuttgart, but unfortunately, he won't hear of it at the moment. At least I'm glad I don't have to stay with Gremm anymore, although I'm very sorry for my aunt. The worst thing of all is that I can't see you." At this point in the letter Erich's heart leaped.

She went on to say that she didn't like it much with the nuns, but at least she could go on to take her high school diploma; her father had said so. "When I'm sitting in the study room with the other girls in the afternoon, doing homework, my feet keep itching and I want to run out and a long way off. Most of all I'd like to run to you, Erich, so that we could go to the Benzenruhe wood again, or the Schönenberg, and count the clouds or think up stories. But I believe we'll see each other again one day, just as much as I believe that all our dreams will come true." Erich loved this part of the letter. He had read it again and again, and her words were still echoing in his ears as he reached the classroom and settled down, sighing.

After school he and Max and Erwin didn't go straight home. Instead, they strolled over to the Fuchseck where the cattle market was held, and there was a small carnival with shooting galleries and other amusements. During the Cold Market there was no regular lunch at home, so sometimes they could wheedle a few coins out of Father to buy some sausage and rolls at one of the stalls. They slid along the sidewalk down to the marketplace—"skidding," the boys called it—promptly earning indignant remarks from several passersby, because sliding in the streets was forbidden. But that didn't bother the boys. They cheerfully made their way through the dense crowds that had formed around the bulls, cows, and calves. Erich saw Isidor Schlossberger standing with some other cattle dealers, and he spotted young Bamberger, gesticulating extravagantly as he praised one of his dairy cows to the skies.

Thank goodness there were still some farmers who dared to do business with Jewish dealers. It was all the braver of them because they were under suspicious observation from the many men and boys in black and brown uniforms. The SA band had stationed itself right on the Fuchseck. It was probably about to give an open-air concert.

Young Bamberger had seen Erich and the other two

boys, and called something to them, but it was lost in the sound of the march that the band was striking up. So he made a speaking trumpet of his hands, and at last they could catch a few words. Father was in the Golden Lamb, young Bamberger told him, and Erich nodded to Max and Erwin to tell them to follow him.

It was very lively in the Golden Lamb. Red in the face, the waitresses were carrying beer tankards and deep plates of tripe and fried potatoes, the traditional Cold Market dish, while thick clouds of smoke wafted about the room so that you could hardly see the dark wooden paneling. Julius was sitting in the corner by the tiled stove along with several other cattle dealers, and two local farmers whom Erich knew: old Schlosser, and a farmer from Dinkelsbühl who bought his cattle only from Julius Levi. "You're an honest, down-to-earth man, Herr Levi," he used to say, as Julius had several times proudly told his family.

A good thing that some of Father's customers are still loyal, thought Erich, looking apprehensively at the other tables, where a number of men in the brown SA and black SS uniforms had made themselves comfortable. The mayor was sitting at one of the tables with his staff and the local Party leader Kolbe, holding forth. Beside him, in a black uniform, sat the commander of the local SS troops, a man with the extremely common name of Müller. He had a face that gave nothing away. He consists just of his uniform, thought Erich, and they really all looked the same, with little Hitler mustaches that seemed stuck on.

Julius waved to the boys, who were soon sitting beside him, and he did indeed give them some money to spend. He's enjoying the Market, thought Erich. He's almost his old self today. Let's hope there's no trouble with all these Nazis around.

In the afternoon Father came home, accompanied as usual by some of his colleagues. Once again they were all Jewish dealers, more or less the same visitors as last year. Taking the guests' hats and coats, Erich was shocked by the sight of his father's face. Something had happened, he could see that at once. Julius looked quite different, and when he invited his guests into the living room he did so with mechanical civility. It seemed to Erich as if his thoughts were somewhere else entirely.

Late that evening, Erich's fears were confirmed. When the door had closed behind the last guest, and only the aroma of cigars lingered to remind anyone of their visitors, Julius came to join Melanie and Erich in the kitchen. He was holding a piece of paper and put it down on the table in front of Mother. "There, read that. This is what it's come to."

Erich jumped up and joined his mother, who hesitantly took the paper as if she feared it might burn her. It was an official form—Erich could see that at first glance—a form to say that the recipient had to leave the town of Ellwangen. But that wasn't the worst of it. Right across the form two words were written in large letters, instantly catching the eye. "Jews out!"

Erich stared at the letters, unable to take them in at first. "Jews out!" His eyes lingered on them as if magnetically attracted by the black handwriting.

Melanie slowly lowered the piece of paper and put it carefully down on the table. Then she looked straight at Julius and asked, "Where does that come from?"

Father laughed briefly and then dropped heavily to one of the kitchen chairs. "Where does it come from? Oh, I can tell you that. I was in the Lamb eating a dish of tripe with Schlosser, Helfrich, and a few others. There were Nazis at all the other tables. I thought there'd be trouble, but strangely enough they kept quiet. That did surprise me, but I thought it was because of Toni; I thought they were keeping quiet because of him."

Anton Ackermann was the landlord of the Golden Lamb. Julius had once done a lot of business with him, and even now he sometimes did a deal with Toni, although the landlord was always complaining that it made trouble for him. And indeed that was why Father hardly visited the Lamb anymore; he didn't want to make problems for Toni, because the local Nazis now spent much of their leisure time sitting in the old, dark-paneled main room of the inn. Julius had always liked the beer there better than anywhere else.

"Oh, why on earth did you go there?" Melanie asked, with a faint hint of impatience in her voice.

"Why did I go there?" Julius brought his fist down on the table. The piece of paper was raised for a moment by the draft, and then fell gently on the kitchen floor. "Why did I go there?" Julius repeated, and the veins on his forehead swelled alarmingly. "I can tell you that too. When did they ever have the Cold Market without a Levi there? And part of the market is eating tripe in the Lamb. I'm not letting that Nazi gang stop me."

"But how did you get this paper?" Melanie persisted, suddenly sounding very weary.

"I paid, I said good-bye to the others, I went to the men's room, and when I came back it was all very quiet suddenly. They were all looking at where I'd been sitting. My plate was still there, and a piece of paper tucked under it. I thought at once that it boded no good. Then someone shouted out, 'Mail for you, Levi!' And suddenly they all began laughing. How they laughed . . . they roared with laughter, every last one of them." Julius's voice broke, and Erich saw, with horror, that his father was doing his best to keep the tears back.

It was only a few seconds before he had himself under control again. "I picked the rag up, put it in my pocket, went out. I'm not doing you the favor of getting upset now, I thought. I walked out very slowly. Toni was right behind me, apologizing. 'Nothing you can do about it,' I told him. And I said I'd better not go there anymore. . . ." Julius's shoulders began to shake, and he hid his head in his hands. Mother rose with difficulty, went over, and put her arm around him.

Erich went to the place where the paper was lying, picked it up and carried it over to the stove. "Jews out!" The letters hit him in the face. He opened the stove door, stuffed the paper in, and saw the red flame leaping up at it, until it quickly fell to a small heap of ashes. Then he took hold of Max, who was still sitting at the kitchen table looking at Mother and Father. His little brother's teeth were dug right into his lower lip, and a wet trail was running down his right cheek. "Come on, Max," said Erich gently, leading his brother to the room they had once shared.

By now it had begun snowing again, flakes falling thickly from the sky, as if magically attracted by the streetlight as they performed an intricate dance in front of them. In the distance you could hear the sound of the band playing in the Golden Lamb. Erich stared out the window, looking at the swirling snowflakes. The rooftops opposite were covered with white, and a thick layer of snow had settled in the street too, making it difficult for passersby to get along. He thought of a similar episode almost exactly two years ago, when that endless procession was on its way to the gymnasium hall, soon after Hitler came to power. There had been a dense snowfall then too. "Just like that time," he whispered, face pressed to the windowpane. "Just the same. And I feel—yes, this time too, I feel as if heaven wants to cover it all up. Under a linen shroud."

Over the next few days the young people of Ellwangen went up to either the Schönenberg or the Neunheimer Steige to toboggan down the slopes. Dr. Eisele's small son landed in the ditch and broke a leg, providing a subject of conversation for days on end. There was even a report in the paper giving young Hermann Eisele brief status as a celebrity. Another particular attraction was the new ice rink near the bridge over the Jagst, which was to replace the old one on the castle moat, deemed too dangerous now, especially when a thaw came. "Another achievement to chalk up to the credit of the National Socialists," Helmut had sarcastically commented.

On one of those January days, Max came into Erich's room. He had his cap pulled down over his face and was getting his gloves on. "Hey, I'm going up to the Steige to toboggan down. I might meet Willi there. I want to see where Hermann fell in the ditch. Are you coming?"

Erich didn't turn around. He kept on staring at the marketplace, where preparations for a large gathering were in full swing. You could hear the noise all the way up in his room. Any moment now that inevitable SA band would begin to play. Or was it the SS band this time? It made no difference anyway. This particular celebration would be about the Saarland, which had voted by ninety and a half percent to stay in the German Reich, as the newspaper had said this morning. That meant there'd be another ceremony at school tomorrow. Well, at least if there was no lesson with Gremm . . . He said out loud to his brother, "No, I'm not coming and you'd better not go either."

"Why not?" Max suddenly sounded very aggressive.

How like each other they are, Father and Max, thought Erich. They just won't see what's going on around them. He said very firmly, "You know exactly why not. Willi can't play with you anymore. And if there are certain other people on the Steige, you'll get beaten up. If you want to risk that, go ahead."

There was silence for a while. Then Erich realized that Max was leaving the room. He still didn't turn around. He heard Max's boots on the floor out in the corridor. Next moment the door to Max's room was slammed, hard. He was sorry for his little brother, but it was better to look facts in the face.

Erich kept a little box containing the treasures of his childhood in his chest of drawers: the first tooth he'd lost, a bird's egg, stones with a metallic gleam that he'd once taken for gems, and some photos. One of them showed him and Max with a whole lot of other children. Max and some of the others were sitting in sleighs, the rest were standing behind them. The father of a girl at their kindergarten had taken the picture. At the time Max was still in kindergarten, and Erich had started at elementary school. It showed him as he was at the time—"A bright, chirpy little fellow," that was how his old teacher had described him. He was challengingly holding a big snowball up to the camera, but it had a secret inside: a horse dropping. Such snowballs of course had an unexpected effect when you threw them. Erich still remembered getting a thrashing for doing it— even from Peter once, when he knocked a cigarette out of his mouth with the snowball, and Peter wouldn't say a word to him for days. He couldn't help smiling at the thought, although the thrashing had hurt like hell, since it had been administered in righteous anger. All the same, it had been good fun. He looked at the photo for a long time. How many years ago since it had been taken? It seemed to him it must be infinitely long ago—no, as if it had been taken in a different life.

Torrential Water

WHEN ERICH CAME HOME from school one day at the end of January, Herr van Wien from Frankfurt was sitting at the dining table, eating a bowl of Melanie's famous chicken soup. He was a sales representative for a firm selling fabrics, and had visited the Levis many times over the years, for Melanie was a good customer. He was no stranger in and around Ellwangen, where plenty of people bought his wares. "Very good customers," Herr van Wien always emphasized proudly. "From the best circles of society. Even the judge's wife buys from me."

Erich liked Herr van Wien, who was always ready for fun, and had a certain cosmopolitan air that the boy admired. He traveled widely and had many tales to tell.

Today, however, his smile when he greeted Erich seemed rather forced, and he didn't seem to be enjoying the chicken soup properly either, for after a while he pushed the plate aside still half full. "Nothing to do with your soup, Frau Levi," he assured Melanie. "It's as good as ever, but the times we live in are enough to spoil anyone's appetite." He was doing hardly any business, he said; even his most loyal customers were drifting away. "Yet everyone still says how good the quality of my fabrics is, and at a reasonable price too. But of course the real reason is obvious." He took a piece of paper from his jacket pocket. It was a column hastily torn out of today's *National-zeitung*, as Erich could see at a glance. "Read that, Frau Levi. One of my customers gave it to me this morning. It just about explains everything."

Melanie took the scrap of paper, read it, and then, with some hesitation, passed it on to Erich.

"Watch out, there's a Jew about!" it said, and then came Herr van Wien's name. The press cutting went on: "Those who have not yet learned to regard a Jew as a parasite on the German people should ask for information from People's Comrades who have fallen for their wiles. The Jew van Wien would be well advised to make himself scarce as soon as possible. And the illustrious customers who buy from this sinister tradesman would do better to remember their own German heritage."

"So it's the same here as everywhere," remarked Herr van Wien, with a melancholy smile. He put the newspaper column back in his jacket pocket, made an elegant bow to Melanie, and said good-bye. "And thanks for your hospitality, dear lady."

"How will you manage—what are you going to do?" Melanie called after him when he was almost through the doorway.

Herr van Wien turned once more and absentmindedly

stroked his little black mustache as if to reassure himself that it was still in place. "Some of us in the Jewish community in Frankfurt are saying it would be a good idea to pack our bags and go. But I'm not so sure . . . I'll tell you frankly, Frau Levi, I'm afraid. We are forbidden to do more and more, and the official language gets more vicious by the day. On the other hand, this country is our home. What would I do in America, or even Palestine, where so many are going these days?" Herr van Wien shrugged helplessly. "I admit, I really don't know. These last two years I've often thought that we ought not just to give up hope, but now . . ." He bowed again and quietly closed the door behind him.

Melanie and Erich watched him go. His last, unfinished sentence still hung in the air. Herr van Wien was right! They kept thinking that things couldn't get worse, but they always did. And we just duck as if it were a passing storm, thought Erich uneasily. What will happen next?

Early in February the Jagst River flooded. It was a "torrential cascade," said the newspaper, and on Saturday evening Father read out loud that there hadn't been such high water in or around Ellwangen since 1882. Snow had fallen for days; it was wet snow that settled in the streets only briefly and then turned to gray slush.

Despite the inhospitable weather, one Monday afternoon Erich decided to go and see Peter at the cattle sheds. He hadn't been there very often recently. Father had bought a cow and a calf at the Cold Market, and he thought he'd like to see them. He wrapped his woolen scarf tightly around his neck and trudged off through the slush to the bridge over the Jagst.

Where, he wondered on the way, did Father find the

money to buy more cattle? And what gave him any reason to hope that he could keep the business going? He's admirable really, thought Erich, for the way he refuses to give up. And somehow or other the business does go on, although not profitably, as he could see from Mother's weary face when she counted out the housekeeping money at the beginning of every week. Max urgently needed a new coat. He was wearing Erich's old loden jacket, but its sleeves were already much too short for him. And I could do with a pair of new shoes, thought Erich, as he trudged doggedly through the snow, feeling the wet cold penetrate his boots.

Peter was just mucking out the cattle, and was obviously pleased to see Erich. "It's a long time since you were here," he said, tracing a wide circle in the air with the handle of his pitchfork. "A busy time at school?"

Erich's answer was evasive, but then he admired the new purchases at length. He affectionately tickled the calf's neck, and it rubbed its head against his sleeve. Meanwhile Peter, who seemed to regard Erich's visit as a welcome distraction, lit a cigarette. Neither of them said anything for some time, and then Peter pointed to the scene outside the open door of the shed. "Don't like that at all. Let's hope the water don't rise no further or we'll have the whole shed flooded."

Together, they went to the door and looked at the Jagst, which raced past them gurgling and foaming. Pieces of wood and even uprooted tree trunks drifted in the brown, murky water. Flotsam and jetsam had caught in the hanging branches of a willow, and Erich could even see the corpse of a huge water rat. Nauseated, he turned away and went back to the shed, followed by Peter, who was drawing thoughtfully on his cigarette.

"What do we do if it does rise higher?" asked Erich uneasily.

Peter threw his cigarette end into a bucket of water, and then fished it out again. The boss didn't like him to smoke in the cattle sheds, and considering all the hay stored there, it was a wise precaution. Turning to Erich, he said, "How would I know? Hope and pray. Or take the cattle somewhere else."

"Like where?" Erich asked, but only a shrug answered him.

He slept very badly that night. The gurgling water had revived his memory of that body he and Helmut had found in the river, and he had confused dreams of it again. But suddenly it was Father being washed away by the raging torrent. Erich clung to him, full of fear that the water might swallow him up too, and then he suddenly heard the frightened cries of animals, and dreamed that the cattle shed itself was being carried away by the waters.

He woke with a start. For a moment, in that strange twilight state between dream and waking, he didn't know where he was. He lay motionless for a moment, and then he heard the knocking and cries that had stolen into his dreams and woken him. This was no dream; something had happened. Once again he heard noise down below, someone hammering on the front door of the building, and then a frightened voice. "Herr Levi, come quick, for heaven's sake. Can you hear me, boss?" It was Peter. From far away, Erich could now clearly hear screaming and shouting and the terrified lowing of the cattle. Something was going on down at the cattle shed.

Erich leaped out of bed, fished his trousers off the chair, and tried slipping into them even as he ran into the corridor. Now he could hear the calls and knocking very clearly. The door of his parents' bedroom was flung open, and Julius came out. He had hastily tucked his long nightshirt into his trousers and snatched his coat off the hook as he raced past. By now Erich had his own trousers on and was also reaching for his jacket.

"Stay here, Mama!" he urged his mother, who was standing in the doorway in her nightdress, hands to her left breast. She shook her head vigorously and picked up her own coat.

For a moment Erich, bewildered, wondered whether calming Mother or helping Father was more important just now. After a brief hesitation, he ran after Julius, who was already on his way up the street. Peter hurried after them, breathlessly uttering a few words that Erich couldn't immediately grasp. But something had happened—something bad, that much was clear. When he reached the railroad tracks, he saw flickering flashlights and clearly heard the cries of animals and people shouting. On the way, he caught up with Father and Peter, and they were now behind him.

Once they reached the bridge over the Jagst they stopped as if dazed. For a moment Erich thought he was still in the middle of a nightmare and would wake up any minute, safe in the warmth of his bed. He closed his eyes for a second as if that would get rid of the picture before his eyes, but it stayed there, and suddenly he felt the noise was so intense that he couldn't bear it anymore. And the picture burned itself deep into his soul. He would never be able to forget it.

About twenty men had gathered outside the cattle shed, all in SA or SS uniform. There were some people in civilian clothing too, but they were only onlookers, although they were egging the others on, making comments and laughing. The uniformed men had broken down the door of the shed and were driving the cattle out, hitting them with sticks. The two dairy cows—the best animals Julius had—were standing on the sloping riverbank, lowing anxiously, only a few feet from the water. An SA man hit the cow nearest to it, and she slipped in and was carried away by the torrential waters. The crowd shouted, "Encore!" and began applauding. A man in an SS uniform dragged the calf that Julius had just bought, ready to push it into the water too. The calf brayed and pulled frantically at its halter, but it was hauled mercilessly farther toward the river.

At that moment Erich heard a shout, a shout full of rage and torment such as he had never heard before. It came from his father. Julius ran forward, fought his way through the uniformed men, pushed several of them aside, and finally seized the halter and tugged the calf back again at the last minute. By now the second dairy cow had been carried away by the rushing water.

The men stood there stupefied for a moment as Julius appeared among them so suddenly, and that instant of surprise worked to his advantage. But now the circle of uniformed men closed menacingly around him, and the two who were closest to Julius grabbed him and tore the halter out of his hands.

"Hey, look, it's the Jew in person! Want to see what happens to your cattle? Come along, we'll give you a front seat!" shouted one of the men around him, taking a long pull at a brandy bottle which he then passed on to his neighbors. Roars of laughter greeted his words, and some of the men began hauling Julius toward the bank. Erich made his way in among them, kicking shins, hitting out, and finally got hold of his father's arm.

"And here's the little Jew, too!" shouted one of the men standing close to his father, as he tried to seize Erich. Next moment, however, the boy felt the man's grip slacken, while the others standing around drew back. Peter had come running up, striking Erich's attacker a mighty blow in the face that knocked him to the ground.

"Touch that boy, or Herr Levi, and you'll have me to deal with!" roared Peter, looking wildly around him. His conduct was ridiculous; the others outnumbered them, and it would be easy for them to be thrown in the river like the cattle. But Peter was undeterred. "Come on, then! Just you try attacking decent folk! Come on! I've known most of you a long time and you know me. I'm not afraid of you!"

For a moment there was a deathly hush. Erich watched the men around him with bated breath. He could see their faces for the first time. In the flickering torchlight, he saw that these uniforms did have faces above them. They were the faces of neighbors, faces of people he knew. There were some among them who had once been friendly to him, who had smiled at him. Now they looked malevolent and crafty and sullen.

But Peter's words seemed to have taken effect. The bystanders started shuffling their feet uneasily. You could hear a few quietly muttered remarks, and the more reasonable among them were saying it was time to go. Only the uniformed men didn't seem willing to give up their fun. They'd been planning to "give the Jew and his cattle a baptism," as someone encouragingly called out. Julius had taken the calf's halter firmly in his hand, in spite of the men, who again assumed a more threatening attitude. Peter, meanwhile, was trying to drive the remaining cattle back into the shed, and now they were impeding him only halfheartedly.

"Please, gentlemen," said Julius quietly—and far too humbly Erich thought. "Please, I still have a little money, I could give you that to redeem my cattle. It's at home, I'd only have to fetch it. Please let my son go, and then I'll bring you the money."

At that moment Erich realized, with horror, that he hated his father for what he was doing. He's demeaning himself, he thought angrily, demeaning himself in front of this rabble, calling them "gentlemen." But the word "money" seemed to exert a certain magical power, for the men let go of Julius and consulted together quietly. "How much can you give us?" one of them called.

"I could let you have five hundred reichsmarks. It's what we put aside for a rainy day, but if you'll leave us in peace . . ." Julius didn't end his sentence, but looked pleadingly around them.

Erich felt hot. Five hundred marks! They could live on that for a long time! And that wasn't taking into account the loss Father had suffered by the drowning of his cattle. He had seen all the calves swept away except for the little one still impatiently trying to get back to its shed, while Julius held it fast.

Meanwhile, the uniformed men whispered to each other. "Very well, Jew. A few of us will go with you and you'll give us the money. The boy stays here until you're back."

Julius handed Erich the calf's halter. By now Peter had come up, and he put an old blanket around Erich's shoulders. He hadn't even realized that he had begun trembling. His teeth were chattering, and his knees were giving way. He pressed close to the calf, which was still mooing anxiously, and felt some of the warmth of the animal's body pass into him. Most of the spectators had dispersed; the show was over. The uniformed men stood smoking and passing the brandy bottle around.

All of a sudden Mother quietly emerged from the darkness and put one arm around Erich's shoulders. They stood in silence.

"Where's Max?" whispered Erich after a while, in a croaking voice.

"At home. I told him to stay in the apartment. Aunt Lea and Uncle Sigmund are with him."

After what seemed an eternity, Father returned, surrounded by the men who had gone with him. One of them was triumphantly waving a bundle of banknotes, to be greeted by roars of applause from the waiting men. Father hurried toward them, and Erich really looked at him for the first time that evening. He's a ridiculous sight, thought Erich bitterly. His bare feet in slippers, his coat flung on over his nightshirt, his hair tousled and standing out from his head. It was unjust to think so, as Erich was well aware, but his sense of shame and humiliation won the upper hand.

Up on the bridge over the Jagst a few people, woken by all the noise, had gathered and were whispering together. Some of the neighbors were leaning far out of their windows to see the show, in spite of the cold night air. Erich walked past them, still wrapped in the blanket. His mother was carefully holding it in place over his shoulders. He would rather have walked by himself, but he didn't want to hurt his mother's feelings. His father, breathing heavily, had sent them home. "Peter and I will put things straight and try to get the sheds locked," he said. "You two go home now. You can hardly keep on your feet."

At his mother's side, Erich walked past the neighbors, past acquaintances who bowed their heads. No one looked at them. Perhaps none of them wanted to answer the question in Erich's eyes: "Why didn't you help us?"

When they reached the apartment Uncle Sigmund hurried to meet them. There was a silent question in his anxious gaze. Melanie answered it. "They drowned two dairy cows, and all the calves but one. Julius gave them money, and then they let us go." Mother's voice broke. Uncle Sigmund took her arm and led her into the living room, where Aunt Lea was still sitting with Erwin and Max. Max was still crying, and Melanie took him in her arms.

"I'll go to Julius. Perhaps I can help. And I want to look at my own cattle too," said Uncle Sigmund. Erich nodded. Thank heaven his uncle's premises had been spared, although they were next to Julius's. The uniformed men had probably forgotten it. But they might come back some time. Erich laid his head on the back of the sofa and closed his eyes. Tears ran down his cheeks. It wasn't just grief for the cows and calves that had been slaughtered so wretchedly, or shock over this surprise attack by night. What really upset him was the abrupt realization that other people wanted to destroy them. Wanted to destroy the family of the cattle dealer Julius Levi, who lived by their cattle, and therefore took good care of the animals and treated them well. The message was clear as day. They weren't safe here anymore; there was no place for them in Ellwangen. They'll do away with us, too, some time, thought the boy, just before he slipped into the uneasy sleep of exhaustion.

The Letter

ON THE FIRST Friday in March after their second lesson, students were told to go to the gymnasium hall in well-ordered lines. There was to be a "Saar commemoration," celebrating "the return of the Saarland to the German Reich." Erich and Erwin were the last to leave the classroom. The two of them were just wondering how they could get out of taking part when the school janitor came up to them and handed them two envelopes. "For Sigmund Levi and Julius Levi. Those are your fathers, right?"

They nodded apprehensively. Erich felt as if he were touching a red-hot iron, but he held the envelope firmly, and even managed to get out something like a thank you.

Alarmed, Erwin stared at him. "What do you think it is?"

Erich laughed bitterly. "Can't you guess?"

Erwin looked down. "Yes, I think so."

They set off for home without another word. It didn't matter anymore whether or not they took part in the ceremony, or whether they were punished for playing truant.

"Let's get it over with," said Erich with a wry smile and a nod for Erwin. He watched for a while, until his cousin was out of sight. He was a thin boy, smaller than Erich and not as good at schoolwork. In the old days Erich had often laughed at Aunt Lea and Uncle Sigmund's only son, coddled and spoiled by his mother. It was funny, they'd never talked to each other much. For instance, he didn't know what Erwin wanted to be when he grew up. He knew nothing at all about his dreams and wishes. And now they were companions in misfortune.

He set off for home, walking slowly, because his school satchel with the letter in it seemed to weigh a ton on his back. He found Mother and Father in the living room, sitting at the writing desk and bent over the account books. They spent a lot of time with the accounts these days, for the loss of four calves and two milk cows had been a severe one, quite apart from the five hundred marks that Julius had sacrificed to save the rest of the cattle, his son, and himself. He had gone to the police the next day to lodge a complaint. A little later he was told that the people he named had nothing to do with the incident. They denied everything, and had witnesses. Yet the whole town knew who had been involved in the nocturnal attack. But the Levi family hadn't seriously expected the perpetrators to be punished, or even asked to pay damages.

Now, without a word, Erich put the letter on the desk. Father did not look at him, but opened the envelope and scanned the few lines.

Finally he straightened up and said, turning to Melanie,

"Put my good gray suit out, would you, and a clean shirt? I have to go and see the headmaster. An appointment for two o'clock this afternoon." In passing, he gently patted Erich's head, a gesture that he hadn't ventured to make recently. And normally Erich would have flinched from such a show of affection, but today he was thankful for it. It was well meant, and the only thing they could do for each other was to exchange these small proofs of helpless affection and intimacy, a last bulwark against malice.

After lunch Erich couldn't stay around at home anymore. His father had set off for the high school without a word of farewell. A little later, finding it impossible to stay in his room doing nothing, Erich slipped out of the house. He thought briefly of going up to the Benzenruhe, but then decided against it. He'd rather go to the Schönenberg, which suited his mood better. And once there he could read Gertraud's new letter, which Lotte had given him that morning. Gertraud had put it in an envelope addressed to Lotte herself.

When he read it again, sitting on "their bench," he suddenly knew that he wasn't going to write back. He was never going to write Gertraud another letter. He was certain of that, even if the reasons weren't clear to him. It would hurt, he knew, but it was better this way. There was no point in dragging out something that had already ended. And it had ended, he had known that ever since February. Best not to prolong the pain. On the way back to town, he thought about his decision and whether he was right, or if he ought to tell Gertraud after all. But what could he say? It would be very difficult to find the words to make her understand.

When he reached the marketplace and was about to cross it, he suddenly saw Fanny standing at the entrance to the big stationery shop. She was deep in conversation with an elderly lady whom Erich knew, although he couldn't remember her name. He slowed down and retreated behind one of the huge chestnut trees to watch her. She was still the old Fanny, their Fanny, quite unchanged except that she had a different, rather shorter hairstyle. After what seemed to Erich an eternity, she said good-bye to the old lady and turned toward him. He looked around. There were no passersby in the marketplace, only a few children playing and fooling about in the middle of the square. She hadn't seen him yet, and when she was level with him he stepped out of the shade of the tree and said quietly, "Hello, Fanny."

She uttered a small cry, and put her hand to her heart. "Erich . . . ? My God, what a shock you gave me!"

"I didn't mean to, Fanny, honestly. But I was so glad to see you. How are you?"

"Erich, listen," she said, casting hunted glances around her like an animal looking for its pursuer. "I'm sorry, Erich, but we can't talk to each other here. Not here, of all places. Or . . . or we'll be in trouble." As she spoke she looked anxiously out of the corner of her eye at one of the finest buildings on the marketplace, diagonally opposite them. Erich knew why. That was where the top Nazi, the dreaded Kolbe, lived.

"What kind of trouble, Fanny? Why are you so scared? And why didn't you write anymore? We wrote to you so often," Erich persisted, acting as if he hadn't heard her last excuse.

"Erich, do try to understand." She took a couple of steps aside, and Erich was afraid she was about to walk away again. But then Fanny looked at him once more, saw the pleading expression that she'd never been able to withstand, and came closer again. She pressed against the rugged tree trunk, which half hid her from sight, and said, "I did want to write to you, I wanted to come and see you, but my father wouldn't let me. They threatened him, and my brothers too. . . ." She stopped short and looked imploringly at him. "You see, Father was so frightened because I used to work for Jews. . . ."

"But what did they threaten you with?"

She shrugged. "They just did. Nothing particular. Just saying we must watch our step. Father even thought they might burn the farm down." She swallowed a couple of times, and then said hastily, "Please believe me, it's bad for me too. When I'm in Ellwangen, and I pass the house where my Levis live, I . . . it always makes me cry. I cross to the other side of the street, I can't look."

Erich saw that she was indeed crying. She searched her bag for a handkerchief and dabbed at her tears. "I left the Wolfs, too. I'm with a Christian family now, but I don't like it there one bit. The other day they even claimed I'd stolen some money. Can you imagine that? But . . . but I'll soon be coming back to Ellwangen." She tried to smile through her tears. "I'm getting married."

Suddenly Erich had to smile too. "Oh, you can't do that, Fanny!"

She looked at him in surprise. "And why not?"

"Because *I* am going to marry you. Or Max is. Anyway, we're going to keep you in the family, don't you remember?"

She nodded, and for a moment they looked at each other in silence. So many memories linked them, memories of good times together that had been abruptly, finally, ended. And they didn't even have the comfort of a friendship that would survive this parting. Something had been irretrievably destroyed. Fanny seemed to feel the same. Without looking at him again she said, "I have to go now, Erich. Give your parents and Max my love. I really do think of you often."

Erich nodded. "Thank you. All the best to you too. And congratulations! Who's the lucky man?"

As she turned away she said, "You don't know him. Well, good-bye for the last time, Erich." And she walked away fast over the square.

For a moment Erich closed his eyes, and in his mind's eye saw her going to the rail station with Julius on the day when she set off to begin her new job in Stuttgart. Now Fanny's going out of our lives too, he had thought then in what was still a very childish way. And he had been right.

When he opened the front door of the apartment he could hear Julius and Uncle Sigmund talking in low voices, with Aunt Lea's high, agitated voice rising above theirs. So his father and uncle were back, and the family council had already begun. The decision had been made. He carefully opened the living room door, and suddenly it was very quiet. They all stopped talking and looked at him. He tried to keep calm, although he felt weak at the knees. Aunt Lea was sitting on the sofa with Erwin, who had been crying. Julius stood by the window, a lighted cigar in his hand. Uncle Sigmund and Melanie were sitting in two of the heavy leather armchairs. He went over to his mother and perched on the arm of her chair. Melanie put her arm around him, and for a moment he leaned his head against her hair. Her familiar scent rose to his nostrils, and his heart calmed a little.

"Where have you been, Erich?" asked his father. "We were getting really worried." Julius tried hard to make his voice sound firm, but Erich could hear the faltering undertones, the fear and helpless desperation behind it.

"I went for a walk," was all he said, looking challengingly at his father. "Well, say it. I know what's coming. So say it and get it over with."

Julius cleared his throat. "As you know, Sigmund and I have been to see Dr. Kaiser. He was very friendly and forthcoming, but he also made it quite clear that . . . well, you can imagine, Erich. We are to take you out of school, you and Erwin. That way we'll do it before you are actually excluded, and save you from the further harassment that is bound to lie ahead. That was what Dr. Kaiser was unmistakably saying."

Julius's words hung in the air. Yes, the message was clear. All the same, Erich asked questions. Although this was only what he had expected, a voice was whispering deep inside him, fed by his helpless rage at being the victim of outrageous injustice.

People are always making judgments about me, and it's not my fault, he thought, clenching his fists. But he said defiantly, "How can Erwin and I be excluded from school when we've done nothing wrong? We're good students, we behave well, so how come we can just be thrown out?"

For a moment no one knew what to say. Julius stared at his cigar as if he might find an answer in the rising smoke. In the end, Uncle Sigmund began talking. He sounded tired, and each of his words seemed to call for an immense effort. "That's what we asked the headmaster ourselves, Erich. But it seems there's a new law coming into force. In principle, it says that Jewish students can be excluded from schools at any time. What they call a flexible policy, Dr. Kaiser said, but it does give schools the chance of turning out their Jewish students."

"So what exactly does this law say?" asked Erich, trying to keep calm.

"Well, for one thing, that non-Aryan students must not come before Aryan students, whatever that may mean. And then—I hope I can remember this properly—there was something about students who are 'harmful to the national community' being expelled from schools."

"But—" Erich began indignantly.

"No buts," Uncle Sigmund interrupted him. "No buts, Erich. It does no good. You know yourself that in the eyes of the Nazis, Jews are automatically regarded as vermin. And there's more, too." He paused for a moment and looked at his nephew sympathetically, as Erich thought, but that sympathy made him even angrier. "Dr. Kaiser explained it to us. That last paragraph can apply to Aryan students as well. For instance, if they have any contact with Jewish students. Which means that practically anyone who mingles with you, speaks to you, can be excluded from school, too. I don't suppose I have to explain what that means."

Erich stared at his uncle. He was slow to take in the meaning of his words. Then that meant that Helmut also risked exclusion. Some time, someone was sure to notice him standing outside Erich's window in the evening and then see the two of them disappearing through the back door. It was only a question of time . . . and what about Gertraud? Suppose anyone found out they'd been writing letters? Then what would happen to Lotte? He had guessed it. He was not the only one in danger, he was also a danger to everyone who liked him, was willing to help him, loved him. How cruel and ingenious it was! Dazed, he listened to what Julius was saying.

"Believe me, Erich, if Uncle Sigmund and I had seen any chance . . . but Dr. Kaiser is right. His successor may not have been appointed yet, but you can be sure it'll be someone devoted to the Nazi cause. Very probably a Party Comrade, because here in Catholic Ellwangen they're taking particular care to ensure that all important positions are gradually filled by Nazis. At least, that's what Dr. Kaiser thinks, and I have to agree with him. Even Gremm is under discussion as the next headmaster. At any rate . . ." He hesitated briefly, and then went on in a firm voice, "at any rate, this afternoon we applied to withdraw you and Erwin from the school. You'll be leaving in three weeks' time at the end of the school year."

Erich leaped to his feet. "You've withdrawn us already?" He went up to his father, who had turned very pale. "Why did you do it? Why?" He wanted to take Julius by the lapel of his jacket and shake him.

"Erich!" Uncle Sigmund rose to his feet and joined them. Erich felt him place a soothing hand on his shoulder. "Erich, I think we've made it clear to you both that there's nothing else to be done. Erwin understands, and . . ."

"But I don't," Erich interrupted. "Of course I know they can throw us out anytime, but we're not going voluntarily! We've done nothing wrong. I'm not letting them intimidate me."

"Remember what Dr. Kaiser said. Remember all the harassment that would still be coming your way. The two of you will soon be completely isolated."

Erich heard his mother's voice behind him, gentle but with a pleading note in it. However, her words didn't reach him. He shook his head wildly.

Julius cleared his throat several times, looking past

Erich at Uncle Sigmund, who presumably nodded to him, for he turned his eyes back to his elder son. "There's something else, Erich. It concerns Max as well."

Of course Max was affected. Dazed, Erich mopped his brow. What was true of the high school must logically apply to all other schools in Ellwangen.

"What about Max?" he asked.

"Well, Dr. Kaiser has promised us that he will make sure Max can stay on until he's old enough to leave the vocational high school with a diploma. He's going to go to the authorities about it himself. However," said Julius, hesitating again and looking down, "however, Dr. Kaiser made it clear to us that in return, so to speak, we will withdraw you and Erwin voluntarily from school and make no fuss about it. They don't really want trouble. And as you two would have been excluded from school sooner or later anyway, we decided . . ."

"To go along with it so that Max can stay on!"

"Erich, please don't speak in that tone," his mother whispered in the background.

Julius tried to put an arm around his son's shoulders, but Erich angrily shook it off. Blinded by tears, he looked around the room for a moment, saw Aunt Lea dabbing at her eyes, and Erwin staring at him openmouthed. Uncle Sigmund stood with his head bent, and Mother rose from her chair to go to him. But Erich made a gesture of fending her off, and ran out of the room.

The clock on the wall was striking seven by the time Erich became aware of his surroundings again. He must have been sitting at his desk for hours, as if in a trance. First he had mechanically unpacked his satchel and neatly stacked his school books. Then he had begun his Latin homework, dipping his pen in the ink like an automaton, and he was about to start writing when he realized he was pressing the pen down so hard that ink was dripping on the paper in large blots. Trembling, he put his pen down and stared at the text until the words began to dance. What do I think I'm doing? he asked himself. He'd never again in his life need to know Latin; he wouldn't need to do any more homework.

It was over. He sat there, just sat there waiting for the tears to come, but they didn't. A soft knock on his door brought him back to reality. The door opened and Max slowly made his way in.

"Erich," he said uncertainly. "Erich, I'm to tell you it's time for supper, and—"

"Get out!" Erich cried wildly. "Get out of here and leave me in peace!"

Max gasped and closed the door with a bang.

What am I doing? Erich thought wearily. He can't help it. But there it was again, that ugly feeling of envy and jealousy. Max could stay on at school at his, Erich's, expense. At the same moment he told himself that was sheer nonsense, but he just couldn't get rid of that ugly, gnawing jealousy.

Later he did go to the kitchen, where the atmosphere was oppressively silent. Mother put a bowl of soup in front of him without a word, but he immediately pushed it away.

"I have one more question." His own voice alarmed him, for it sounded so spiteful and aggressive.

But Julius seemed glad that he was speaking at all, and even tried a small smile. "I should think you have a great many questions, and there are some things we have to discuss."

"What am I supposed to do now? The school year ends

in three weeks, and I need to do *something* after that. Do you want me to carry crates for the Fräulein Pfisterers, or help Peter muck out the cattle?"

"Erich, please," his mother interjected.

"Let it be." Julius put his hand on her arm. "Erich is right. Uncle Sigmund, your mother, and I had a long discussion about that this afternoon," he said, turning to Erich. "We agreed that you and Erwin had better go into business as trainees somewhere. We were thinking of some large firm with a good reputation where you can get a sound commercial grounding. Then there will be many careers open to you later."

What kind of careers? What careers was Father talking about? He wanted to go to university, study law, and become a judge. Or perhaps an attorney. All these thoughts shot through his mind. Out loud, he asked, "And where do we find this large and reputable firm that's going to take on Jewish trainees? Can you tell me that?" Suddenly Father's artificial optimism fell away. Erich saw that Mother had begun to shed silent tears.

"Not around here, of course, that's obvious," Julius said at last. "There's really only one opportunity, but it does have a number of advantages."

"And just what is it?"

"Uncle Ludwig," said Julius quickly. "Uncle Ludwig in Pirmasens. There are a good many Jewish firms there—he works for one himself, a large company. And you'd be comfortable living with the family. I phoned him just now, and he agreed; he's going to find out about a possible post as a trainee for you tomorrow."

"Is Erich going away?" Max jumped up from his chair so suddenly that it fell over with a crash. "Erich can't go! That's impossible!"

"Max, calm down and pick your chair up. It's in Erich's best interests," said Julius disapprovingly.

Erich was shattered. He had never thought of that. Going away from Ellwangen, leaving home . . . going away! And exactly where was Pirmasens? He had been there once to visit Uncle Ludwig with Mother and Father, when he was a little boy. That was soon after Uncle Ludwig's marriage. They had traveled forever on the train, but otherwise he couldn't remember anything about it. Suddenly a new idea came to him. "But if I have to go away anyway, then I could go to one of the big cities where there are Jewish schools, and I could take my high school diploma after all."

Julius waved this idea away. "Impossible, Erich. It won't work. The nearest big city with a Jewish high school would be Frankfurt. You can't go there all on your own—you're not even fifteen. Quite apart from the fact that we can't afford it."

Erich leaped up. The words kept echoing through his head. Trainee's post . . . Pirmasens . . . withdrawn from school . . . Uncle Ludwig . . . And now another realization dawned on him in all its significance: I have to leave home!

Worn out, he went to his room. Mother went to follow him, but Father held her back, and through his closed door he heard Max crying for a long time. "Erich can't go away! I don't want him to go away. I want Erich to stay here. . . ."

A few days later Uncle Ludwig called back. Erich could begin commercial training at the beginning of May with the company of Adler & Oppenheimer. It was the firm where he himself was employed, as the director's right-hand man, said Julius.

"It's good news, my boy!" Julius seemed genuinely

relieved. "Your mother and I are glad that your future is secured, and you'll be well looked after. Uncle Ludwig and Aunt Ruth will welcome you into their home."

Good news? What does good news mean to us now, thought Erich. I have to go off to a city I don't know and start working at something I don't want to do. I have to leave behind everything that means anything to me: my family, Helmut, all the streets and squares of the town where I grew up, and I have to leave my hopes and dreams behind too. Briefly, an image shot through his mind, a very distinct image that had taken up permanent residence there. He and Gertraud were sitting beside the Neckar River in Tübingen, two young students full of hope for the future. It would remain only a dream now, a hope that had come to nothing, a hope that still hurt, and was better to forget.

Mother had suggested that he might not go to school at all those last three weeks. "Father and I would understand, and so would Dr. Kaiser, I think," she had said that same evening. She had come to his room, quite late, and sat on the edge of the bed, holding his hand the way she used to in the past when he wasn't well. At first he was going to withdraw his hand from hers, but she held it tight. And in a way her familiar touch did him good. Neither of them could think of much to say, but behind that silence he sensed his mother's deep despair. However well meant her suggestion was, he wouldn't hear of it. "I have to go, Mama. I don't want them saying I'm wriggling out of it. Please, you have to understand me."

She thought about it, and then nodded. "You're the only one who can decide that, Erich." So he went to school as if nothing had happened. The others didn't know yet, he could tell from the way they acted. Even Helmut had no idea. On one of their evening meetings his friend wondered who their teacher would be next year. "We're sure to be rid of Gremm," he said. "Two years of him are quite enough. And with luck we'll be spared having him as Head . . . but better safe than sorry. Who knows what may happen?"

As Helmut thought aloud, Erich kept his head bent to prevent his friend from seeing the tears that had risen to his eyes. There wouldn't be any next year for him, but he couldn't tell Helmut that.

So he went on going to school, but hardly took part in the lessons. He just sat there apathetically. The teachers left him alone, and even Gremm ignored him. They must have known that he was leaving. Sometimes he glanced up at Gremm, to see if the victor's triumphant smile, which he had so often displayed after successfully bullying him, was on show. But Gremm didn't look at him, he just acted as if Erich were air, and wore his usual inscrutable expression. During these days it sometimes seemed to Erich as if he were functioning like a woundup clock, performing tasks precisely laid out for him. His thoughts and emotions seemed to have been switched off, and he felt as if he were underneath a gigantic glass dome. What had happened and what was going to happen hadn't yet entirely reached his conscious mind. It seemed to him unthinkable that in a few days he would be walking through the mighty entrance of the high school and into his classroom for the last time.

But that last day inexorably, inevitably came. After the bell rang for the last time, he packed his textbooks and exercise books into his satchel, taking particular care to put the report leaflet that Gremm had handed him between the pages of his

Latin book, and he placed Erwin's report beside it. His cousin hadn't been to school for the last week. Aunt Lea said he was ailing and that the whole business was too upsetting for him. Erich's classmates pushed past, shouting and laughing, taking no notice of him, although a few of them were hanging around the door looking embarrassed as they cast him curious and sometimes pitying glances.

Word had got around over the last few days that the two Levis were going to leave the school, and Gremm had announced it before handing out the reports. "At their own wish," he had said emphatically, and then that cold, unpleasant little smile had played around his lips again. Helmut stopped beside Erich for a moment as he left the classroom and whispered, "I'll drop by this evening around nine, okay?" Erich nodded. And taking no notice of Kampmann, who was smirking and gesturing in Erich's direction and darting venomous glances at him, Helmut suddenly added, in a hoarse voice, "Why on earth didn't you tell me?"

"What use would that have been?" Erich whispered back.

Then Reger and a few others actually came up to shake hands with him. "Good-bye and good luck, Levi." They stood there for a moment, looking helpless and awkward, and then that was over too, and he'd got through it without bursting into tears. He waited until everyone else was outside, and then, the last to leave, he slowly went down the massive staircase. With deliberation, he ran his fingers along the banister rail. How many hands had touched that oak rail, shaking, excited, sweating, cheerful, expectant hands—and now his own hand lovingly passed over the polished wood of the banisters for the very last time. Yes, it was a loving gesture, because he'd loved this building where he had spent part of his life, learning so much. He had learned things that were important and valuable, even if they didn't hold true anymore.

And he would so much have liked to have learned more. But it was all over now. Down at the bottom of the stairs, he let his eyes wander once more down the long corridor that, with its vaulted ceiling, had always reminded him of the interior of a church. He knew this was good-bye forever.

Leaving

ON SATURDAY May 4, 1935, the Levis' handcart rattled over the cobblestones on the way to the train station. Julius was pulling it along, and Erich and his mother walked behind, deliberately making the most of these last moments before they said good-bye. Erich's suitcase was on the cart, the big old family suitcase, full of shirts, socks, underwear, some of the things new, although heaven knew money was short. Mother had also altered two suits for him that Julius didn't wear often. Old Herr Kugler had tried letting out the seams on Erich's bar mitzvah suit, but it was no use. "Nothing to be done about it, Frau Levi," Herr Kugler had said apologetically. "Your Erich has just grown out of that suit."

So Max was to wear it for his own bar mitzvah, although he would rather have had a new one. But Father's suits now fit Erich perfectly, and he looked really elegant and grown up in them. "You'll have to look good at work," Mother had said as she lovingly packed the snow-white handkerchiefs and freshly starched shirts into his case. And she had asked him what pictures and other mementos of home he would like to take. After all, he was to have a room to himself in Pirmasens. Only a small room, Uncle Ludwig had written, for a few months ago their second baby had been born, a little boy, and they needed the other spare room for him and little Lucie. But their maid had recently given notice, so Erich could have her room.

"You must make it nice and comfortable for yourself," Mother had said, showing him some pictures he could take— pictures of the family and Ellwangen—but Erich had said no to all of them. He didn't want to make his room "nice and comfortable." It was a place where he would be living for the time being, where he was just in transit. Better not to begin feeling at home anywhere. The only mementos he had taken were a photograph of Mother, and his old German book containing the poem about a sleeping Germany that they had once read with Professor Wagner. He also took the little paperback edition of Schiller's play *Don Carlos*, because it reminded him of Gertraud.

The handcart bumped along Hindenburgstrasse, where passersby were hurrying from shop to shop. Some cast curious glances at the little procession. The Fräulein Pfisterers had given him a chocolate bar and ten reichsmarks yesterday evening, and Fräulein Marie had even shed tears. Now they were both standing in their shop window waving white handkerchiefs.

The landlord of the Golden Cross had brought a

present too, and on their last evening together, Helmut had awkwardly pressed a small rectangular package into his hand. "This is for you. Heine's poems, a really old edition. Father gave it to me specially for you, with his very best wishes." Then they shook hands in silence once more. "Write, Erich, keep in touch," Helmut said as he left, and then the door closed behind him. The volume of Heine was now carefully packed in Erich's rucksack. He would start reading it on the train. He knew why Helmut and his father had given him this particular book. Heine, too, had been a Jew, unwelcome in Germany, who had had to leave his native land.

You're in good company, Erich Levi, he thought with grim irony as they passed through the great archway leading past the high school. The big building stood there, silent and forbidding, its many windows looking dully down on him like blind eyes.

For a moment he thought of Dr. Kaiser the headmaster, respected and liked by his students. Erich hadn't wanted to go to the big end-of-year celebrations in the gymnasium hall on the day after reports were given out. It was also to be a good-bye to Dr. Kaiser. "Wild horses won't drag me there. I don't want to see any of them," he had told his mother, but when he heard the noise made by everyone on the way to the hall on Saturday morning he couldn't help it, he had to go too. In a way he felt he owed it to his old headmaster to attend his leaving ceremony.

The hall was crowded. Many visitors who had come too late to get seats were standing by the walls. Erich forced his way through the groups of people at the entrance, so at least he had a view of the platform, which was surrounded by a sea of blood-red banners. Poor Head, he thought, and then Kolbe, the top

Nazi spoke, having come especially for the occasion. Erich was hardly listening. Kolbe was blathering about "working for the interests of the Fatherland," and "the convictions of the nation." Erich was waiting expectantly for the headmaster's speech, although he didn't imagine it would be very impressive. All the well-known Nazis of Ellwangen were sitting down there, and he'd have to "howl with the wolves" again, as he had put it.

Then Dr. Kaiser stepped up to the speaker's lectern, and with every word he spoke he surprised Erich and the rest of the audience more and more. He would take as the starting point for his speech, he said, a quotation from the Roman poet Horace: "Have the courage to be wise." And then came the speech itself, an extraordinary speech such as hadn't been heard in this hall over the last few years. He had always hoped to educate his students to value freedom and to be more independent, said Dr. Kaiser. He had hoped to make them understand that they had "no right to show lack of restraint, to act by the law of the jungle, or to act ruthlessly as members of a master race," he went on. "I always hoped to give my students the freedom to learn for themselves on their way through life," he added. And then the speech was over. In his usual black frock coat and with his slightly untidy white hair, Dr. Kaiser went back to his seat, and then the applause began, at first sporadic and hesitant, then growing louder and louder. But some of the audience didn't clap at all.

I wonder what Kolbe made of that, thought Erich; is he clapping too? As they struck up the Horst Wessel Song, he slipped out.

Now, on the way to the station, he was thinking of those words of Dr. Kaiser's. He wouldn't forget them. He felt as if the

Head had made that speech especially for him. Of course it was highly unlikely that the headmaster of Ellwangen High School was thinking of his former student Erich Levi at that moment, but all the same Erich couldn't get the idea out of his head. He wanted to believe it so much, and he would take those words of the poet away with him, like a present. "Have the courage to be wise."

When they reached the station there was still a little time left. They had left home too early. Erich avoided looking at Mother's face. He knew she was trying to fight back tears. If he had looked at her, he would have broken down himself. Max hadn't wanted to come with them. He had shut himself in his room, and didn't say good-bye to Erich.

Julius kept talking all the time. That was his own way of coping with grief, by giving an impression of hectic activity. "Uncle Ludwig will meet you at the station in Pirmasens, but I put his address in your rucksack, just in case. And mind you behave well, particularly to Aunt Ruth. Keep your room neat and clean and mind you're always punctual. . . ." And so on, and so forth.

Erich was hardly listening. From the station, he took one last look at the towers of the Collegiate Church rising above the high school in the blue springtime sky. This had been his home for so many years, and now he must leave for a strange city. Maybe he could come back for the Jewish feast days in the fall; maybe he'd get a few days' vacation then. He'd have to discuss it with Uncle Ludwig. The train moved slowly in, and the steam of the locomotive escaped the funnel with a loud hiss. Julius opened a passenger car door and put the suitcase inside. Erich felt his mother clinging to him, pressing her wet cheek to his forehead. Then Father pushed him into the car, almost roughly. The doors were slammed shut and the train started to move off, jolting. He saw Mother and Father standing on the platform, getting smaller and smaller. The houses of Ellwangen flew past him, and for a moment he stretched out his arms as if to hold the familiar images of his childhood tight.

Farewell

ELLWANGEN, GERMANY, 1938
[THREE YEARS LATER]

ERICH WAS UP in the attic room trying to open the window so that he could look down at the buildings opposite and the street far below. The familiar view of his childhood—with a faint smile, he remembered how he could stand here on the sill as a child without ducking his head. Now, when he sat down and leaned against the sloping ceiling, he almost touched the opposite wall with his feet. After he had opened the little window, the sounds of the street came up from below, and he could watch the swallows drop straight down from the bright blue sky, only to reappear swooping over the rooftops. He had arrived from Pirmasens an hour ago; his suitcase was still standing in the corridor downstairs unpacked, and he hadn't touched the lunch that his mother had warmed up specially for him. He had gone through all the rooms, now empty, staring at the pale rectangular patches on the walls where the pictures once hung. He was thinking hard, trying to remember what it had once looked like here.

That was where the heavy glass display cabinet had stood, the leather sofa and deep armchairs were over there, but now all that the Levi family's living room contained was a rickety little table on which Mother had set out the silver candlesticks and the Sabbath plate. She was probably intent on packing those items away too in the suitcase that stood on the floor, open and almost full. However, Erich hadn't packed his own things yet. He would obviously have to leave some of them here. The big suitcase, four feet long, three feet high, and two feet deep, contained all the possessions that the Levi family still had. They could take only this one case with them on their long journey, the last journey taking them out of this country that had once been theirs, but where they were strangers now, hated strangers, rejected, persecuted, exiled.

He fished in his trouser pocket for a crumpled packet of cigarettes and lit one. Of course it was crazy to smoke among the rafters in this old attic on a hot July day, but he would be careful. His mother was always nervous the moment she saw him with a cigarette. And she had to avoid stress because of her high blood pressure, which was worse these days. Their upcoming emigration to America was too much of a strain for her to bear.

He stretched carefully and inhaled the smoke. The steamship would leave Bremen in a few days' time for America, that unknown and distant land that was now to be his home. It was a great stroke of luck for them, so Uncle Karl, Mother's other brother, had written in his last letter. "You can be thankful you're getting out in time!"

And Herr Wenzel, the clerk for the Ellwangen town

council, had said something along the same lines. Last year Julius had gone to see him in a fury, when the municipality sent a letter saying that Jewish dealers were banned from the Ellwangen markets as of March 10, 1937. Mother wrote a letter telling Erich about it. Father was so upset that she had been quite unable to calm him down.

And then he went off to the town hall and I couldn't stop him— well, you know your father. He went to Herr Wenzel, one of the few there who were still civil to us. "My business is completely ruined now," Father shouted. But Herr Wenzel kept calm and just said, "That was the intention, Herr Levi." Father was speechless. Then Herr Wenzel took him into a corner of the room and whispered to him. "Do you still not see what's going on here?" he asked. "Herr Levi, let me give you some good advice. It's all I can do for you now. Get together all the money you have before it's taken from you. And then leave this country, you and your family, before it's too late. There are even worse things coming your way, Herr Levi. Leave before it's too late."

Father had gone home white as a sheet, Mother told Erich. But one good thing came of the whole business: from then on Father worked energetically to organize their emigration. "He realizes that there's no future for us here anymore. What would we live on? And he can't get over that business with Vitus Bieg, any more than he can get over the way the Nazis drowned his cattle in the Jagst," said Mother in one of her next letters.

The business with Vitus Bieg had indeed been a terrible blow. Just before the episode with Herr Wenzel, Father had gone to the market as usual, although he did almost no business now, and there was only one cow and her calf in the stable. He'd had to fire Peter, who went on to find work with a local farmer. People didn't talk to Julius and Sigmund Levi anymore either, for fear of being seen mingling with Jews. On that Tuesday, however, Vitus Bieg, landlord of the Golden Cross, had gone over to Father, who was standing on his own in the big marketplace, and exchanged a few words with his old friend.

"Then little Lore came along to see us in the evening, pale and trembling. They'd been looking for Vitus for hours, no one knew where he was. Martha Bieg went everywhere, even to the town hall and the police, but they just laughed at her and made silly jokes," Mother had told him. After three endless days the landlord of the Golden Cross came home again, pale and saying little. He had been arrested for speaking to the Jew Levi, that was all they could get out of him. He never said just where he had been and what they had done to him. Martha Bieg suspected that he had been in the cells in an SS barracks; there had been an SS troop stationed there since 1935. From that day on the landlord of the Cross was a changed man, quieter than before.

After that, the Levis had been entirely isolated, and one day Melanie even sent little Lore home when she came in secret, bringing a few eggs from her mother. "Suppose someone saw you, child! Go home, and never come to see us again. It's better that way!" Lore began crying, and I couldn't help crying too, but there was nothing else for it," Mother had written. And she added something that was no news to Erich anymore. "It's painful, but we have to face facts: we are a danger to our friends."

Uncle Sigmund had recently made the same discovery. He had gone for a glass of wine and a snack in a small village nearby where he used to do business with several farmers, and the landlord of the village inn had served him and greeted him as an old acquaintance. Some local farmers had joined him at his table, enjoying a good chat as they did in the past. A few days later, however, a newspaper entitled *Flammenzeichen*, "Flame Signal," a particularly venomous Nazi publication that was read in and around Ellwangen these days, published a story containing open threats against the landlord for serving "national parasites," and even naming the farmers who "mixed with such company."

It's true, it's high time we left, thought Erich, stubbing out his cigarette on the masonry around the window and throwing it into the street. There's no life for us here anymore. He closed the little window and climbed down the narrow loft ladder to the apartment, where Mother was standing by the kitchen sink.

"Where have you been, Erich?" she asked, wrinkling her nose. "Oh, you've been smoking again, haven't you?"

Erich nodded, and pointed to the dishes that she had begun to dry. "Those were all clean. Why are you washing them again?"

"I'm going to give them to the neighbors over the next few days. We can't take any more than we've packed. And I won't have anyone saying Melanie Levi gave away china that wasn't sparkling clean."

Instead of answering, Erich gave her a hug and planted a kiss on her head. She had grown thin, and there was a good deal of silvery gray in her hair now. He was very worried about her health. She hadn't gone to the doctor again because slinking around by night in secret went against her grain. He would have to have a word with Julius about that. But standing there by the sink, energetic and ready for the fray, she was her old self again, their loving mother, a woman who prided herself on her reputation as an excellent housewife, even if only for the sake of a few plates and dishes, her last possessions in an apartment stripped bare.

In their time of need they had been obliged to sell almost everything, much of it well under its real value, to get together the money for their passage. Soon after the conversation with Herr Wenzel that had scared Julius so much, he had taken their last savings book to the bank. It was their final nest egg, carefully kept for the rainiest of days. Father had found out what the voyage to America would cost them. The nest egg, together with the money from the sale of their furniture and household equipment, was just enough. They couldn't take any of it with them anyway; large items of baggage were out of the question because of the high cost, let alone a crate to carry furniture.

And then he had waited in the bank, ignored by everyone at first, until finally one of the older bank clerks, a man who had known him a long time, took pity on him and asked what he wanted. When Julius produced his savings-account book and asked to have the money paid out in cash, the clerk reacted with an uneasy look, and then disappeared without a word into one of the back rooms. After a while the bank manager of the branch—a young upstart, as Julius described him later—came along with the savings book. He had drawn a line right across the last page and written "Account invalid" over it. He handed Julius the book back, saying, "Jews have no savings with us," turned on his heel and left. And there stood Julius holding the savings book, the Levi family's last possession. He had been robbed and cheated, and there was nothing he could do about it. Jews had no rights in this country anymore, he knew that only too well.

"We feel as if we're in a trap," Mother had written. "We must get out of here while we still can, and we have no money left now."

Erich had earned little as a trainee. In April 1938 he had completed his training, and at first he had hoped he could go on working for the company as a clerk on a fixed salary, saving it up for the journey. But Herr Kahn, manager of the Pirmasens branch of Adler & Oppenheimer, had been able to hold out little help to his employees in the spring of 1938. The company itself was doing worse and worse these days, and would soon be going out of business. It hoped to be able to pay its staff a small amount of compensation, but no one knew how much that would be. So Erich's hopes were dashed. And anyway, no one knew how much time was left. Perhaps all Jewish money would be confiscated, like the sum in the Levi family's savings book.

"There have been rumors for some time that the Nazis have plans of that kind," Uncle Ludwig had told him when they were walking home together along Lemberger Strasse after a meeting of the workforce. Uncle Ludwig had managed to draw his money out in time, and it was now lying in a metal box in the living room cupboard, a constant source of worry to Aunt Ruth, who feared burglars.

"We must make sure we get out of the country, and the sooner the better," Uncle Ludwig had said, his face grave. The image of the trap in which they were caught took firm hold of Erich's mind at this point, and more and more frequently he felt overcome by a sense of panic when he thought that they might be prisoners already, with invisible walls and bars being erected around them.

But then rescue came to Julius Levi and his family in the form, not surprisingly, of the Fräulein Pfisterers. The family's last hope had been the cattle sheds on the Jagst, which had been empty since the spring of 1937 but had some value, for the premises were solidly built, and there was Peter's old apartment on the upper floor.

Julius had not been hopeful. There were stories everywhere of Jews being cheated and robbed. "People can get Jewish possessions for a few pfennigs these days, and we can think ourselves lucky if we get paid anything at all for them. I don't like to think what we may get for the cattle sheds."

But in the end he did get a proper price, all because of Marie and Auguste, who one day expressed an interest in acquiring the premises. They would use the ground floor as a storeroom for their business, and they could rent the apartment on the upper floor to one of their employees. They had paid 8,000 reichsmarks, and that was the family's salvation. With the money their household goods had fetched, they now had just enough for the passage to America, with a tiny sum left over as capital for starting again in the New World. And so Marie and Auguste Pfisterer had helped them yet again, for the last time.

Late in the afternoon Father came home. He had greeted Erich briefly when his son first arrived home at midday, and then hurried straight off to the town hall. They had almost all the papers they needed for emigration—all but the police document certifying that they had no criminal record; for some inexplicable reason, it seemed that it couldn't be issued yet.

"Pure harassment," Julius had commented, but now, when he came in through the door, he was waving an official form, and cried in relief, "It's done!"

"That's a weight off my mind!" Melanie rushed out of the kitchen. "I was really afraid they might make difficulties of some kind for us at the last moment."

Julius went into the living room and put the certificate down on the rickety little table with the other papers that had been so laboriously acquired. There was confirmation from the American consulate that they would be permitted to emigrate to the United States. There was the "affidavit" from Uncle Karl in the States, along with evidence that he had property there and had deposited a sum as "security" for them in the bank in New York. Their future country would take them in, but also wanted to be sure that its new citizens would not be a burden on the state, so Uncle Karl had had to vouch for them. The tickets for the voyage were stacked neatly, and Julius put the police certificate ceremoniously down beside their passports stamped with the exit visas. That certificate was the very last of the necessary documents proving that they were honest citizens.

Those papers on the table are our salvation, thought Erich, watching his father as Julius stood by the table for a while, lost in his own thoughts. That's the way we have to look at it. No more sorrow and despair; we must be glad to be getting away. But when he sat in the kitchen with his parents that evening—it was furnished only with three old chairs and a table from the Fräulein Pfisterers' cellar—he suddenly realized how infinitely sad he felt. Every corner of this apartment was so familiar to him.

He had so many memories of it, and now he could count on the fingers of one hand the number of times he would be sitting here. It was getting dark, and shadows were slowly falling in the room, but Mother did not put a light on. They just sat there in silence, listening to the familiar creak of the floorboards and the noise in the street outside, rising and slowly ebbing again.

In spite of his mother's disapproving look, Erich lit himself a cigarette, and finally Julius lit a cigar too, and they watched the blue curls of smoke floating over to the open window.

Mother rose, moving slowly, and handed them a cracked old saucer as an ashtray. At the same time she fetched a picture postcard showing the Tower of London. "Here, from Max," she said. "It came the day before yesterday."

Erich took the postcard and turned it over. "Dear Mama and Papa, I am well. But the food in the home isn't very nice. When exactly are you going to America? Write and tell me when you get there. How is Erich? Love from Max." It was written in the rounded and still childish handwriting so typical of his little brother.

"He seems to be taking it well," said Erich, handing the card back to Melanie.

Julius nodded. "It almost broke your mother's heart when he left in February. But I always said that Max was tough. Anyway, he's safe now, and that's what matters."

Max had gone to England on one of the "children's transports." One day Uncle Sigmund had come in with the news that for some time now Jewish aid organizations had been offering the chance for Jewish children to be sent out of the country. "And it costs almost nothing," he had told Julius. "It's all financed by donations. I think we ought to see if Max can go. He isn't sixteen yet, so he falls within the age range."

Uncle Sigmund and Julius had embarked on a long exchange of letters, and then, at very short notice, their application had been accepted. Max had a place on a transport and in February he could go to London, where he would live in a children's home. Mother had resisted the idea for some time. "He's still so dependent, such a child," she wrote in a letter to Erich. But finally Melanie had to bow to the force of the arguments; the fact that Max would get out of Germany weighed more with her than her maternal anxieties.

"He didn't shed a tear when we took him to the station," Father told Erich proudly for the umpteenth time. "Quite the opposite—he was the one comforting Mother."

Erich had sometimes wondered how often his brother had wept into his pillow at night, and how he was getting on in a country whose language he had only just begun to learn in school. The vocational school began teaching students French first.

"How did you manage with school?" he asked now, for they had never really talked about it. But Julius told him that Max had left with a vocational diploma, even though there were still two months to go before the end of the school year when he left.

School—at that moment Erich thought of his second-to-last visit home to Ellwangen, in March 1936. That had been for Max's bar mitzvah. He had walked from the station that day with his heart thudding as he passed "his school," the old high school. It had been almost a year since he'd been back to the town. The first-year trainees didn't get vacation, and Erich had no money for the train ticket, anyway, but he had been able to take a couple of days off for this special family celebration. The next morning, he had thought, he would stroll, as if by chance, across the square just when it was time for break. He knew from Helmut's letters what had been going on in school. A few months after Dr. Kaiser's retirement a new headmaster had arrived, a "staunch Party Comrade," as Helmut had commented. So Gremm hadn't been appointed after all, in spite of those doom-laden prophecies. "He's been more insufferable than ever since then," Helmut wrote. "We have him for English now, and it looks as if the man will be dogging me all the way to my high school diploma. There's a lot of speculation about the reasons why he didn't become Head, but no one really knows anything for certain."

So Gremm hadn't made it! The news filled Erich with grim satisfaction. He and Helmut corresponded only sporadically, for they lived in different worlds now, and they were both well aware of it, but all the same, Erich had been looking forward to seeing his friend again. So he had felt both happy and excited when he strolled past his old school on that sunny March morning, the day after his arrival. How often he'd pictured this scene to himself! He was wearing Uncle Ludwig's best coat. Ludwig, whose figure was much the same as his, had lent it to him specially for the bar mitzvah.

He had stopped, looking around him. Not much had changed. The twelfth-grade boys with white bands on their caps were walking around with measured tread, the smaller boys were racing about playing catch or hide-and-seek. Groups of students stood around talking; there were shouts, calls, laughter, and the teacher on supervision duty was stalking back and forth. He must be new, for Erich had never seen him before. Then he saw Reger and a few of his friends standing in one corner. Helmut was with them. They had finally noticed him, and so had some of the other, older students. He could tell from the way they were glancing at him and whispering.

At last Helmut moved away from the group and came toward him, hesitantly followed by a couple of the others, though they cast timid glances at the teacher supervising break.

"Hello, old fellow," Helmut had said, rather awkwardly. "You're looking good."

"I'm fine." Erich took out a cigarette with a practiced gesture, lit it, and offered the packet to his former classmates, but they all said "No, thanks" and looked at him with a mixture of admiration and embarrassment. He began talking to them, told them about the company where he was employed—he actually said "employed." It was a big firm, he told them, with an international reputation. . . .

And as he went on, he suddenly realized that he was horrified by the way he was talking. It wasn't him standing here, it was a stranger showing off and talking big. Yet he couldn't stop, although he felt more and more as though he were outside himself, standing next to a stranger called Erich Levi who was saying all these things.

They had parted in haste; break was over. "Great, Erich! Really good to see you. Let's hear from you again." And then they had gone their separate ways.

Helmut's letters became few and far between, and the day came when Erich left them unanswered. He was ashamed of himself, but they had nothing in common anymore.

All this came back to him on that warm July evening in the family's kitchen.

It was the Sabbath, and they were sitting together at the rickety table, eating off cracked china—their last three plates— and drinking their wine from water glasses. Tomorrow, once they were gone, Peter would come for the last of the Levis' household goods. But the candlesticks were lighted as usual, and the white bread lay on the Sabbath plate, although it was bought and not homemade this time. Father recited the blessing in these rooms for the last time: "Praise be to thee, the Eternal One, our God, King of the World."

When darkness fell, Mother put out the candles and switched on the electric light. Julius pointed to the candlesticks and the plate. "What are you going to do with those? You can't take them. The plate will just get broken, and the candlesticks are valuable, we were supposed to hand them in."

Erich picked up the Sabbath plate and looked at it. He remembered how he had seen it when he was a child, and those strange signs around the rim had looked like the eyes of God. But it was just a gray-blue plate, not particularly valuable and not particularly attractive. But suddenly he understood himself as a child again and saw the symbols and letters with a child's eyes. It was something special, it belonged to them, was a part of their religion, their tradition, which bound them more than he had wanted to admit. It was a part of himself.

Meanwhile Mother had put on a knitted jacket. "I'm going to hide the candlesticks in my handbag," she told Father firmly. "I want to take something that was ours. And the plate . . ." She carefully wiped the crumbs off the glaze, wrapped it in a piece of paper, and then slipped out the door. "I'll be back in a minute."

She soon returned. Julius asked where she had been. Melanie answered evasively, "Something that was ours has to stay here. I've disposed of the plate."

"Something that was ours *does* stay here," growled Julius. "The furniture, the silver . . ."

Mother shook her head. "I don't mean that. Something that was really important to us has to stay. Something to remind people that a Jewish family once lived here. The plate is in good hands."

The next morning the small truck that Julius had hired arrived. A young man was going to drive them to Stuttgart, where they were taking the train to Bremen. He and Erich heaved the heavy suitcase into the truck. There were few people out and about on Hindenburgstrasse. It was Sunday, and anyway, it was wiser not to be seen when the Levi family said good-bye. They never knew who was watching them and might report it.

The Fräulein Pfisterers were standing at the front of the building, Marie with a handkerchief pressed to her lips. Martha Bieg was standing on the corner with little Lore, waving. Old Schuster had stationed himself on the other side of the street, and was visibly smirking. Aunt Lea and Uncle Sigmund had come, and hugged them as they said good-bye. They would follow in September. "See you in New York," Lea whispered, waving her handkerchief as the truck jolted and started off. Helmut came running from the marketplace, and stood still as the truck drove past him.

Erich sat in the back with the suitcase. He saw Helmut once more, thought of all the things they'd done together, the memories they shared, and nodded good-bye to his friend. The Fräulein Pfisterers waved. Then the truck turned the corner, and he closed his eyes.

It was over. But he carried all the images that were important to him in his mind. He didn't need to take a last look. And he'd be back again, sometime, to ask a single question. Why?

Epilogue

ELLWANGEN, GERMANY, 2002

THE OLD GENTLEMAN is carrying a thick package wrapped in brown paper, clutching it close. My students have pointed him out, saying that he very much wanted to speak to me, but was even more anxious to have a word with the guest we're all waiting for with such excitement. It's a cold January day, and our big school hall is crowded.

Twenty-one high school students have been working on our exhibition for almost eighteen months, and this evening it opens.

We've called it "On the Trail." Not a very original title, I'm afraid, but it explains just what we decided to do. We have been on the trail of the last Jewish community in Ellwangen, in particular the last Jewish students at Ellwangen High School, a venerable institution dating back 345 years.

And since one name, the name of Erich Levi, kept

coming up again and again, we subtitled our project: "Who Was Erich Levi?"

The old gentleman has seen me now and is making his way through the crowd. At first I don't understand what he wants, but then he takes something out of the thick layers of wrapping paper, carefully, almost tenderly, and proudly shows it to me. It is a plate with a gray-blue glaze. Three objects are painted in the middle of it: two braided loaves of bread and an ornately decorated goblet with Hebrew letters in a semicircle around its base. The rim of the plate has a pattern of strange, triangular symbols. It obviously has something to do with the Jewish Sabbath, for the loaves are probably the traditional challah bread, and the goblet is a Kiddush goblet.

The old gentleman looks at me expectantly. "My mother used to keep a whole range of plates like that for her Jewish customers," he says. "She ran a little china shop. She remembered the Levi family very well. Frau Melanie Levi, Erich's mother, had a plate like that—my mother often used to tell me about it."

"So how did you come by the plate?" I ask, and the old gentleman goes on to tell me that he found it with his mother's things after she died, very carefully stored away.

"Somehow that plate seemed special," he says thoughtfully. "So I'd like to give it to Erich's son, Herr Levi. He's coming, isn't he? I'm sure my mother would have wanted that, too. The plate ought to belong to a Jewish family again."

The Herr Levi he mentions is Professor Michael Levi, a grandson of Melanie Levi. After a long search, we finally tracked him down in New York a few days ago, and although he sounded greatly surprised and a little distrustful when he took phone calls from a town so far away in Germany—a place he knew hardly anything about—he quickly agreed to come over to Ellwangen and open the exhibition. He would be setting eyes on his father's hometown for the first time in his life.

We have probably aroused his curiosity, and we're curious ourselves to meet this American professor and hear the stories we hope he can tell us about his family and his father. For when we first called New York, we discovered that Erich Levi was no longer alive.

"Show him the plate and tell him about it," I suggest, as the old gentleman goes on looking expectantly at me. So we both look forward to seeing our guest, glad to think we can show him that there is still something in this town to remind people of his family, even if it's little enough: just a plate and a few memories. . . .

The old gentleman is disappointed. Erich's son, the professor from America, didn't take the plate with him. He expressed his grateful thanks but said he thought it would be better to leave it here. That way, there would still be a memento of the last Jews in Ellwangen, a town where no Jews have lived since 1938.

I try to console the old gentleman as he carefully wraps the plate up again.

"Take good care of it," I tell him, looking at the boy beside Michael Levi. He's Michael's son, Jacob, Erich's grandson, and his father has brought him along to learn something of the history of his family. It's a story of which father and son knew only fragments until this evening. I feel rather strange, for the boy is looking at us with Erich's eyes. I unobtrusively glance in young Jacob Levi's direction and tell the old gentleman, who is turning to go, "Perhaps someone will come along one day who'd like to have it back. And then it will stand on a Jewish family's table again, with freshly baked challah loaves on it, and a father will say the ancient blessing over it."

What matters is that at least something stay: memories that have grown and will go on growing, and a plate with the eyes of God on it.

Since 2002 there has been another commemoration too, a monument made of bronze and steel: a sculpture placed outside the entrance to the Peutinger High School in Ellwangen and designed by local artist Josef Kieninger. It is in memory of the last Jewish students at the school, and also the earlier Jewish students, over seventy-six of them, who attended the high school and left with their diplomas from the year 1823 onward.

At the wish of the Levi family, the following verse from Proverbs III, 13, is engraved on the monument in German and Hebrew:

"Happy is the man that findeth wisdom, and the man that getteth understanding."

These words are reminiscent of the quotation from Horace given as the text for his speech by the headmaster of the high school (real name, Dr. Josef Fürst), on his retirement in 1935.

It is a remarkable and moving coincidence that his legacy can be felt again in this way.

A NOTE ON THE
GERMAN SCHOOL SYSTEM

The school system in Germany at the time of this story was not the same as it is today. Erich and his friends go to a high school (*Gymnasium*), which they would have left, after their final examinations at the age of eighteen or nineteen, with a certificate of academic achievement. Graduates holding this certificate expected to go on to university studies. Erich's younger brother, Max, is not as good at schoolwork as his brother, and goes to a *Realschule*, which we call a "vocational high school." He would expect to leave school at an earlier age than Erich, with a certificate showing that he had completed a less academic course of study. Also at that time, the new school year began in the spring, just after Easter, and not in the fall, as it commonly does today.

AUTHOR'S NOTE

This novel is a mixture of fiction and historical fact. We have researched the major national events of the time, and those of local and school history, as carefully as possible. What happened in school classrooms and the private lives of the characters, of course, follows a fictional scenario, but one that has been influenced by outside events, eyewitness reports, and the experiences of other Jewish children and young people from the period of the story.

Most of the non-Jewish names have been changed, to allow for the fact that the town where these things happened was much the same as any other German town of its time. And for obvious reasons, it was impossible for the author to describe real people and their lives with historical accuracy.

The names of the Jewish families, particularly those of the main characters, have been kept, in honor of their memory.

Erich Levi returned to Ellwangen in 1945 as a soldier in the U.S.

Army, fighting with the 399th Infantry Division. His local and linguistic knowledge was extremely useful, particularly his mastery of the Swabian dialect. He knew all the leading Nazi figures in Ellwangen very well.

He ordered the reconstruction of the vandalized Jewish cemetery, which had been desecrated in 1944 on the orders of the Nazi mayor of that time.

There are still people in and around the town who remember his arrival in April 1945, or who have heard eyewitness accounts of it. Some are sure it was mainly his doing that Ellwangen was not bombed, as his superior officers obviously planned it should be, since the SS was putting up fierce resistance in the town. In one case, the descendants of a well-known family from a nearby municipality distinctly remember that when the troops marched through it, the young U.S. soldier kept their house from being destroyed.

After the war, Erich Levi started an import-export business in the United States, trading chiefly with South American countries. He became a prosperous man, and the photographs of those days show him with all the rewards of economic success.

He died in a car accident in Venezuela in April 1966, leaving a wife, Inge, who is now elderly and lives in New York; a daughter, Barbara, born in 1950; and a son, Michael, born in 1952.

Erich Levi never talked to his family about his youth in Ellwangen and the trauma of his family's expulsion from the country. He did, however, often mention his education at the high school with mingled pride and melancholy. His son considered him withdrawn and uncommunicative. He had been an unhappy man at heart, Michael thought, a distant father who was always a stranger in his new country. Only the "spaetzle machine" for making noodles in the Levis' American kitchen was there to remind anyone of their Swabian origins.

Max Levi moved from England to Australia, and he too fought in the Second World War, with an Australian unit. With Erich's help, he found a position in New York after the war as a manager in an iron and steel firm. He died of a heart attack in February 1977.

Melanie Levi died of a stroke in 1950. After emigrating, she had worked as a maid in a New York hotel.

Julius Levi found a job as a kind of errand boy in a large apartment building in New York. His family says that after he emigrated he was a broken man. A few letters from him to the two ladies given the surname of Pfisterer in this book have been preserved. They are moving attempts to hide his homesickness and grief by describing the prosperity of his new country— prosperity in which his sons Erich and Max shared.

Sigmund Levi and his wife, Lea, were also able to emigrate before the Holocaust, with their son, Erwin.

Babette Levi, the boys' grandmother, died in 1950 at the great old age of 95. To the last, she lived in New York with her daughter Mina Straus and her son-in-law Louis. When they emigrated, she was the oldest passenger on board the *Queen Mary*. In her death announcement, and that of her daughter-in-law Melanie, their last place of residence is given as Ellwangen on the Jagst.

The other members of the Levi and Süssel families also succeeded in emigrating.

The two ladies called Pfisterer in this novel saw their apartment building and shop burn down only two hours before the town surrendered to American troops in 1945.

Erich would have liked to accommodate them in the former Nazi mayor's home, but they did not want that, and instead moved into the apartment above the cattle sheds on the Jagst that had once belonged to Julius. Several times after 1945, he confirmed their rightful title to the purchase of the property. In a letter to the Levi family, dated 1947, the ladies bemoan the fact that the rebuilding of the shop is delayed because they cannot get the materials. They also thank the Levis for the food parcel sent from the States. At the end of this letter of 1947 they add that everyone in Ellwangen is now able "to go on living as peacefully as before the war."

The boy who, to some extent, was the model for Helmut in this book, bled to death during the war in the wide expanses of Russia.

ACKNOWLEDGMENTS

In writing this book I owe much to the collaboration of many other people.

Thanks go first to the contemporary witnesses, all of whom, in their own way, shared with me memories that were often painful.

Thanks also to my colleagues and the students at the Peutinger High School who took part in the seminar course "On the Trail" and helped with the exhibition. Our work was the basis for the novel. In this connection, I would like to thank Peter Maile, whose research into local history provided many important clues.

Thanks, too, to Sonja Zink, who made the first telephone contact with the Levi family.

Heartfelt thanks, as well, to the archivists of Ellwangen, Pirmasens, Speyer, and Ulm for their interest and the help they gave us.

I would also like to thank Herr Eberhard Frick of the firm

of Kicherer in Ellwangen for access to its correspondence.

I would like to thank the Jewish community of Stuttgart for their help.

Special thanks to my publisher, Klaus Willberg; my editor, Stefan Wendel; and Kristin Weigand, who encouraged this project from the start.

It is difficult for me to find the words to express my gratitude to those who, from the moment when this novel was first conceived, have shown particular interest and extraordinary sympathy, and whom I also have to thank for valuable information— I mean the family of Dr. Michael Levi of New York. I am especially grateful to Gail Hochman, who was instrumental in bringing this book to an American audience.

Since our first meeting in the school, a deep and very special friendship between us has developed. It sometimes seems to me a miracle that we have found a way to come together across the rift of such a dreadful, painful story.

And my most heartfelt thanks of all go to my family and my husband, Hans-Ulrich Grözinger, my tireless supporter and comrade in arms.

GLOSSARY

BROWNSHIRTS (p. 8): the uniforms of the SA (*Sturmabteilung,* storm troopers), originally founded to engage in street fighting; later a feared and notorious instrument of threat and intimidation as used by the National Socialist Party. The black uniforms referred to later in the book belonged to the SS, the *Schutzstaffel,* defense unit, which became a kind of elite army separate from the regular Wehrmacht German army, and was much feared for its power and brutality.

CENTER PARTY (p. 19): a democratic political party founded in 1870 in Germany, with close connections to the Roman Catholic Church.

NATIONAL COMMUNITY (p. 22): a concept in Nazi ideology. The "ideal" was to merge all social opposites by eliminating the opponents of National Socialism, primarily those whom the Nazis saw as "inferior races," such as Jews.

"RAISE HIGH THE FLAGS . . ." (p. 24): the "Horst Wessel Song," the SA war song. It commemorated an SA man who was killed fighting communists, and became a kind of second national anthem in Nazi Germany.

HITLER YOUTH (p. 35): the National Socialist youth organization. It educated boys to reject the precepts of their parents and the church, and gave them premilitary training. The Hitler Youth was declared a state youth organization in 1936.

JUNGVOLK (p. 46): the junior section of the Hitler Youth for boys aged ten to fourteen, who then moved up into the Hitler Youth.

NEWSPAPER (p. 59): the newspaper alluded to *Der Stürmer* ("The Striker"), a virulently anti-Semitic smear-sheet.

HAGGADAH (p. 62): the tale of the exodus of the children of Israel from Egypt, led by Moses.

MINYAN (p. 81): the count of ten men who must be present for a religious service in the Jewish community.

A PEOPLE WITHOUT ROOM (p. 134): a dramatization of the novel of the same name by Hans Grimm (1875–1959). It was extremely popular with the Nazis because it advocated German colonialism.

"THE BETRAYAL OF VERSAILLES" (p. 148): a reference to the Treaty of Versailles that ended the First World War. It required Germany to accept that it was responsible for the war. That fact and the reparations demanded by France caused great, simmering resentment in Germany between the wars, and the Nazi Party was able to draw support from that feeling. Many Jewish German citizens had fought bravely at the front in the First World War, like two of Erich's uncles in this story, often earning decorations. They were all the more bewildered by the Nazi policy of racial persecution.

JANUARY 1933 (p. 161): the month Hitler was appointed Chancellor.

BIMA (p. 180): the lectern in a synagogue.

REICHSFÜHRER-SS (p. 210): "Reich Leader," the title of Heinrich Himmler as head of the SS. He was one of the Nazis chiefly responsible for implementing the infamous "Final Solution" of what they called the "Jewish problem," that is, the murder of all Jews.

BUND DEUTSCHER MÄDCHEN (BDM) (p. 225): the "League of German Girls," the girls' organization within the Hitler Youth. The girls were supposed to aim for physical fitness and a future as mothers, bearing as many children as possible.

STRENGTH THROUGH JOY (p. 246): the name of a Nazi organization in the "German Working Front," which was responsible for a good citizen's leisure time and vacation activities. The German Working Front was the organization uniting employers and employees, as a kind of substitute for the banned trades unions.

HAVDALAH (p. 246): the ceremony for the end of the Jewish Sabbath.

PUTSCH AGAINST HITLER (p. 263): this was the "Röhm putsch," named after Ernst Röhm (1887–1934), the SA chief of staff. At a point when he wanted to weaken the SA as a political force, Hitler claimed that his old companion in arms had been conspiring against him.

PLEBISCITE (p. 291): a vote by which the people of an entire country determine their choice of government or leader.

BENJAMIN FRANKLIN'S SPEECH (p. 297): it has been shown by historians that these alleged remarks by Benjamin Franklin are a forgery, supposedly from a journal that does not exist. This "prophecy" heaping abuse on the Jews was more than likely produced in the 1930s, during the heyday of the Nazis, who naturally enough used it for their own purposes.

ROSH HASHANAH (p. 308): the Jewish New Year.

YOM KIPPUR (p. 308): the Day of Atonement and the most holy day of the Jewish year. It is a day on which people fast, reflect on the past year, and pray.

SHANA TOVA (p. 312): "Happy Year," the traditional Jewish New Year's greeting.

SHOFAR (p. 314): ram's horn blown in the synagogue at services on festival days, particularly Rosh Hashanah and Yom Kippur.